PRAISE FOR LARRY BOND and JIM DeFELICE

"[Bond] displays an encyclopedic knowledge of modern weapons systems and tactics, and he knows how to use his knowledge to full advantage. . . . Bond and DeFelice conjure a chillingly all-too-believable near-future global conflict." —*Kirkus Reviews* on *Larry Bond's Red Dragon Rising: Blood of War*

"A thriller that reads like an account of true events. Fans of military thrillers, especially Clancy's, are the built-in audience for this one." —*Booklist* on *Larry Bond's Red Dragon Rising: Shadows of War*

"No writer living can produce the depth of political intrigue like Larry Bond." —Clive Cussler

"An adrenaline-fueled, multilayered thriller that cuts right to the chase . . . Constant action makes this a must-read for military adventure fans."
—*Publishers Weekly* on *Larry Bond's Red Dragon Rising: Shadows of War*

"Action on every page. Maybe in every paragraph." —*Kirkus Reviews* on *Larry Bond's First Team*

"[A] fast-paced, complex thriller."
—*Publishers Weekly* on *Larry Bond's First Team: Angels of Wrath*

"Techno-thriller fans, rejoice! Larry Bond is good— very, very good." —Stephen Coonts, *New York Times* bestselling author of *The Disciple*

LARRY BOND'S
Red Dragon Rising

BLOOD
OF
WAR

LARRY BOND AND
JIM DeFELICE

FORGE®

A TOM DOHERTY ASSOCIATES BOOK • NEW YORK

LARRY BOND'S RED DRAGON RISING: BLOOD OF WAR

Copyright © 2012 by Larry Bond and Jim DeFelice

All rights reserved.

A Forge Book
Published by Tom Doherty Associates, LLC
175 Fifth Avenue
New York, NY 10010

www.tor-forge.com

Forge® is a registered trademark of Tom Doherty Associates, LLC.

ISBN 978-0-7653-6101-1

Forge books may be purchased for educational, business, or promotional use. For information on bulk purchases, please contact Macmillan Corporate and Premium Sales Department at 1-800-221-7945, extension 5442, or write specialmarkets@macmillan.com.

First Edition: January 2013
First Mass Market Edition: December 2013

Printed in the United States of America

0 9 8 7 6 5 4 3 2 1

To future generations:
May they never have to fight this war.

The term "global warming" is as misleading as it is inaccurate. True, the overall temperature of the earth as measured by annual average readings will rise. But averages tell us next to nothing. A shortening of a rainy season by two weeks in a given area might be reflected by an increase in the average annual temperature of only a third of a degree. But the impact on the water supply—and thus the growing season—would be considerably higher.

Paradoxically, rapid climate change may bring much lower temperatures in many places. It should also be noted that some changes may well benefit people in the affected areas, at least temporarily, by extending growing seasons, negating weather extremes, or having some other unpredictable effect.

Unfortunately, the sensationalistic term, combined with the slow evolution of the effects prior to the crisis point, will make it hard to convince the general population of the true danger.

—**International Society of Environmental Scientists report**

Major Characters

United States

Josh MacArthur, scientist
Mara Duncan, CIA officer
Peter Lucas, CIA chief of station, Bangkok/Southeast Asia
Major Zeus Murphy, former SF captain, advisor to
   Vietnam People's Army
Lieutenant Ric Kerfer, SEAL Team platoon commander
Roth Setco, CIA covert paramilitary officer
General Harland Perry, U.S. military advisor to Vietnam
President George Chester Greene
CIA Director Peter Frost
National Security Advisor Walter Jackson
Commander Dirk Silas, captain of USS McCampbell

China

Lieutenant Jing Yo, commander, First Commando
   Detachment
General Li Sun, commander, Attack Force
Premier Cho Lai

Vietnam

General Minh Trung, head of the Vietnam People's Army

March 2014

Commodity Prices — Chicago Board of Trade

COMMODITY	PRICE	1 YEAR AGO	5 YEARS AGO (2009)
Crude Oil	$765.87	$700.13	$74.86
Corn	$1,875	$1,234	$723
Wheat	$3,902	$1,534	$812
Rough Rice	$967	$310	$20.20

March Temperatures — Major World Cities

	(Celsius)			
CITY	HIGH	LOW	2009 (average high)	2009 (average low)
Washington, D.C.	20	2	13.8	0.1
Beijing	30.2	5.0	12.8	-0.3
Tokyo	15	3.0	13.7	5.9
Rome	16.5	8.7	16.1	6.4
Johannesburg	17	9.2	24.6	12.9

PERSONAL CHRONICLE:
LOOKING BACK TO 2014 . . .

Markus:

Uncle Josh had returned to the United States and given the United Nations evidence about the Chinese atrocities in Vietnam, but the reaction was not what he or the President had hoped for. Even in the U.S., many people were so opposed to war that they wanted to ignore the danger of Chinese aggression. They didn't think that danger could reach our shores.

They were wrong about that.

What none of us knew at the time was that the president had already sent advisors to help the Vietnamese. And he had ordered a U.S. warship to stand by in the region.

Many think he was trying to provoke war.

Blood Sacrifice

1

Hanoi

The war juxtaposed life and death, jabbing each against
each: a baby carriage next to the bomb crater, a shiny
white Mercedes abandoned without a scratch next to
the hull of the mobile antiaircraft gun. Nightmare vied
with banality: the severed leg of a policeman rotted in
the gutter, half covered by a girlie magazine, blood-
speckled pages fluttering in the evening breeze.

Just hours before, downtown Hanoi had been hit by
four dozen bombs and missiles launched from a wave
of Chinese aircraft. The daytime attack had pockmarked
the already battered city, starting fires and destroying
several buildings. The fires burned largely unabated.
The relief forces were drained, and much of their equipment was exhausted as well. A number of fire trucks
and ambulances had been damaged by the bombings;
a few sat crushed by debris from the buildings they had
tried to save. Others sat abandoned where they had run
out of fuel. Fire trucks and ambulances still operating
no longer used their sirens, as if they were too weak
even to sound an alarm.

The center of town had been hit hard. The former
French-dot-com bank, once a landmark, was now a

burned-out hulk. A residential high-rise not far away had lost about a third of its tower; in the dimming light the jagged edges of bricks looked like an arm rising from the earth, about to rake its claws on the city.

And yet, despite the destruction, the city continued to struggle on, its breath labored yet real. Elements of the bizarre mixed with the defiant and practical. In the same street where citizens had cowered in basements and behind whatever thin shelter they could find an hour before, a parade of black Korean limousines now delivered elegant matrons and twenty-something *fashionistas* to the Ambasario Hotel for an annual benefit for Hanoi orphans. The women wore brilliantly colored dresses, their hot pink and fuchsia silks a militant stance against the Chinese onslaught.

Zeus Murphy stopped on the street to let a pair of women pass. The soldier felt like a misplaced voyeur, an uninvited guest at a private carnival. He was certainly an outsider—a U.S. Army major dropped into the middle of an exotic land—though he was also more of a participant in the war than any of the dozens of people walking past him in the street.

Zeus watched the women pick up the skirts of their dresses and step over the dried splatters of blood as they walked across the concrete apron to the hotel's front door. A path had been swept clear for them; a small pile of glass lay a few feet from Zeus's boots, the fragments glittering with the hint of light from the hotel's interior.

Most of the women were ex-pats, the spouses and, in a few cases, daughters of men working in Hanoi or nearby. Zeus wondered if they had come out in defiance or to seek some sort of solidarity in misery. There was no longer a reliable route of escape for civilians from the city or the country. Air transport was close to impossible; commercial flights had ended the day before, not only out of Hanoi but also Saigon much farther south. (Saigon was what everyone except foreigners called Ho Chi Minh City.) Even the American embassy had difficulty arranging for helicopters, although it had two flights scheduled for later that day.

The highways south and the sea ports were still open, though how long that would last was anyone's guess.

Realizing he was late, Zeus started forward, only to bump into a woman who'd been trying to squeeze past him on the pavement. The woman jerked her head around and put up her hands. He reached to grab her, thinking she was going to fall.

She staggered back, regaining her balance. The look on her face was one of dread, as if she had been touched by a ghoul.

Zeus put up his hands, motioning that he meant no harm.

"It's OK," he told her in English. He searched for the Vietnamese words for *sorry* amid his scant vocabulary. *"Xin lỗi,"* he told her. "I'm sorry. Excuse me."

She took another step, then turned and walked quickly toward the hotel, her pace just under a trot.

Zeus waited until she reached the door before starting again. He, too, was going to the hotel, though not for the show. He had to meet someone in the bar.

Two women dressed in plain gray pantsuits, neither much younger than fifty, stood at the doorway to the lobby. They had AK-47s in their hands. Zeus nodded as he approached. His white face made it clear that he was a foreigner—and not Chinese—and that was all the pass he needed to get in.

At the very start of the war, the Vietnamese had posted soldiers at the large hotels used by foreigners, more as a gesture of reassurance than security. The soldiers had long since been shifted to more important tasks. Some of the hotels had replaced them with their own security forces, though in most cases these men, too, had left, answering the call for citizens to report to local defense units, a kind of home guard that was organized around different residential areas in the city. Though trained in name only, some of these units had been transported farther north and west, to supplement regular army units facing the Chinese.

The units included women as well as men of all ages. Posters emblazoned with slogans like COURAGE and FIGHT ON were just now appearing on the walls of the city; the state television channel had broadcast interviews with women who had fought in the home guard during the last conflict with China. Some were now close to eighty; all said they were ready to fight again.

Zeus lowered his head as he passed a foreign camera crew standing at the end of the hallway. They had obviously come to record the charity event, but were being harangued by a hotel manager, who kept waving his hands in front of the cameraman's face. The journalist looked exasperated; he clearly had no idea why the man was objecting.

The hallway was dimly lit, with three of every four lightbulbs removed. People clustered along the sides. Many cupped cigarettes in their hands. Smoke hung heavy in the passage, adding to the shadows. It looked like a scene from a 1930s noir film: gangsters hiding at the far end of the hall, an undercover detective weaving through the unfamiliar darkness toward his fate.

Even in the mixed crowd of Westerners and Asians, Zeus looked out of place. His civilian jeans and casual collared T-shirt did little to disguise his military bearing. People glanced in his direction and made way.

The etched-glass door to the bar was blocked by a crowd of people on the other side. He pushed against it gently, gradually increasing pressure when they failed to move.

"Excuse me," he said, in gruff English, pushing a little harder. He eased up and then jerked his hand so that the door banged against the bodies. Finally they got the message and began to part.

The opening door caught the eye of Ric Kerfer, who was sitting at the bar across the room, angled so he could see the doors without seeming to pay too much attention to them. His eyes sorted through the crowd, waiting to see if whoever was coming through was worth his interest.

Kerfer wasn't surprised that the bar was packed—bars were always popular when the world was going to hell—but it was interesting that there were so many foreigners still left in Hanoi. When he'd left the week before, it seemed like everyone was angling for a way out. Now it looked like everyone wanted to stay and find out what the Chinese were really like.

Maybe it was this way on the *Titanic* as well.

Kerfer had been here for more than a half hour, nursing a single Jack Daniel's straight up. Ordinarily in that time he'd have had four or five or six. But he'd decided Vietnam was no longer a good place to get even mildly drunk. There was too much desperation in the air, too many people with little to lose.

That was when you had to keep your wits about you. The man pushed inexplicably past his breaking point by an accidental event was infinitely more dangerous than a soldier doing his duty.

Kerfer had felt the same sensation in Baghdad, in Yemen, in Syria. In Tripoli, he'd sensed things were past the breaking point, and yet he'd stayed on an extra day, wanting to make sure his job was truly done. It was a foolish bit of overzealousness that had almost cost him his life.

You had to do your duty. But your duty rarely called for you to die. Or rather, it called for you to die only under the most leveraged circumstances. Circumstances that Lieutenant Ric Kerfer, a United States Navy SEAL, could no longer imagine.

Kerfer leaned back on his barstool, recognizing Zeus. Right away he noticed that the Army major had changed. Part of it was physical—Zeus was banged up. Kerfer could tell from the way he moved, shuffling the way an injured man did to divert attention from his injuries.

SEALs were always covering for some ligament strain or muscle tear, pretending they didn't need surgery that would end their time on the firing line. They might hold their shoulders in or be selective in how they leaned their weight, subtly trying to lessen the potential for more injury.

It had nothing to with pain, per se—you got used to pain, unfortunately. It was more that you tried to keep whatever defect you'd acquired from being seen.

But there was more than that. There was something now in Zeus's frown, something in the way he glared people out of his way.

Zeus Murphy was now an extremely dangerous man, Kerfer realized. More dangerous than the enemy.

He finished his drink, then pushed the glass toward the bartender.

"Fill it," he told the man, a Vietnamese who spoke English well, though with a French accent. "And draw a beer. I have a friend coming."

Zeus spotted Kerfer at the other end of the bar. He'd grown to like the SEAL officer, even though like most SEALs Kerfer barely pretended to tolerate him. Kerfer's rank as a lieutenant was the equivalent of a captain in the Army, which meant that Zeus outranked him, but it was clear that rank had exactly zero meaning to Kerfer.

"Hey," said Zeus when he finally reached Kerfer.

"Hey yourself, Major."

Zeus frowned at him. Kerfer smirked.

"Ain't nobody in this place who can't figure out what the two of us are and who we work for," said Kerfer. "And not a one of them could give a shit. Here's a beer."

Zeus was surprised to find that not only the contents but the glass was cold. He took a drink; it was heady and seductive.

"I heard you had some fun north of Haiphong," said Kerfer. "You're becoming a legend."

"Yeah."

"Perry's kinda pissed off I hear."

"Screw him." Zeus ran his fingers along the outside of the glass; the cold felt almost exotic against the tips.

"You're coming over to the dark side, Major. Glad to have you."

"Let's just say my eyes are open. You talked to Perry?"

"He talked to me."

"You told him we were meeting?"

"Why would I do that?" asked Kerfer.

Zeus suddenly felt wary. "I'm surprised you're back in Hanoi. I hear you're a wanted man."

"They don't know they want me," said Kerfer. His men had killed a squad of Vietnamese soldiers who had strayed into their path while they were rescuing an American scientist from the Chinese—at least that was Kerfer's version. The Vietnamese had protested vehemently to the ambassador and to Perry, both of whom had denied they had any knowledge of what had happened.

"They wanted what I brought more than they wanted revenge," added Kerfer. "Revenge isn't going to help them. Never helps anyone. Remember that, Major."

Kerfer was about the last person Zeus needed a lecture from. He changed the subject. "You finished the shipments?"

"All done. I suspect they've used them already."

"So why are you still here?"

"I was told to sit and wait, in case I might be more useful in the future."

"Perry said that?"

"Perry's not my boss," said Kerfer. "He wants me out. He wants you out, too."

"Yeah." Zeus set down his glass. He glanced at it, and was surprised to see it was more than half gone. "He told you that?"

"He was in a talkative mood."

"I have something I wanted to ask you about," Zeus told Kerfer.

"Go ahead."

"This isn't a good place."

"As good as any. Nobody's listening to us, Major. Look around."

Zeus shook his head.

"All right," said Kerfer. "Lead the way."

"I thought you'd have scouted out a place."

Kerfer laughed. "Follow me."

The SEAL was a powerfully built man, with broad shoulders and legs that worked like piston rods. He exuded a certain don't-mess-with-me energy, and the crowd parted as he got up from his seat and led Zeus into a supply room at the back end of the bar. He didn't bother flipping on a light, and there was barely enough to see around the tall shelves of supplies as he walked to the back of the room. There he paused in front of a steel door; he fiddled with the knob for a moment, then pulled the door open, having picked the lock. Zeus hadn't even seen him take the lock-picking tools from his pocket.

"Out here," Kerfer told him.

Zeus followed up a short flight of steps to a long, narrow corridor. A glass door, all but one of its panes missing, stood at the end. There was no doorknob on the inside; Kerfer reached through and took hold of the small handle to unlatch it. They emerged on a wide patio.

A man stood against the far rail, smoking a cigar.

"Take a walk," Kerfer said to him in English. Then he added another few words in Vietnamese. "*Bỏ?.*"

The man frowned, but stuck the cigar in his mouth and left, going through the way they had just come. Kerfer, meanwhile, walked over to the edge of the patio, which was bounded by a short, thick wall. The space overlooked a yard paved with small stones that was part of the hotel restaurant's outdoor dining area; it was closed to patrons.

"I don't think *Bỏ?* really means *go,*" said Kerfer. "More like 'abandon all hope ye who enter here.' "

"Your Vietnamese is getting better."

"It gets the job done."

Zeus looked around. They were alone.

"I need to get somebody out of the country," said Zeus.

"Your girlfriend?"

Zeus felt his cheeks warm.

"Relax, Major, I'm not your chaperone," said Kerfer. "I don't give a crap about where you dip your wick."

"Listen—"

"Why don't you throw her on a military transport? There's a helo coming into the embassy in a few hours."

"Perry won't go for it."

"I'm just a gofer. I bring things in, not take them out. When we left with the scientist, we had a destroyer."

"You think I can bribe some of the people you're working with?"

"The nonmilitary people? Sure, you can bribe 'em." The SEAL rubbed his face. "Whether they can help you or not is another question."

"How much will they want?"

"The question is how much you can trust them," answered Kerfer. "You're not paying attention. I'd say the way things are going, nobody's going to be able to help you pretty soon. Where is she?"

"I don't know for sure," said Zeus. "A military prison. I'm working on it."

"Why is she in jail?"

"It's a long story . . . She saved the life of a POW that the Vietnamese wanted to kill. So she was arrested—"

"Save it," said Kerfer. "Your best bet is to get her out on an embassy flight."

"That ain't gonna work."

Kerfer shrugged. He pushed off from the wall.

"I have something else I need to talk about," said Zeus.

Kerfer stopped.

"Yeah?"

"I need to get in touch with your command. I have something I want to talk to them about. I want to work something out with Trung. But I can't go through Perry."

General Minh Trung commanded the Vietnamese army. Kerfer scratched his ear, then the side of his cheek.

"You want to tell me what the hell it is you're planning?" he asked Zeus.

"No."

"You know, I'll give you this, Major. You're nobody's fool." Kerfer laughed. It was a short laugh, the sort of thing a man does when he finds the world's insanity amusing. "I thought you were kind of a desk jockey pussy when I first met you, like that partner of yours, but I was wrong."

"Christian is dead. He died in the line of duty."

"Oh."

Zeus suddenly felt an obligation to stand up for Christian, even though he had spent a good deal of his time despising the man when they were together.

"Win Christian jumped on the back of a Chinese tank," said Zeus. "He tried to blow it up. He got a bunch of them before he died. He was right in the middle of things. He risked his life. He was a brave man."

Kerfer said nothing. Zeus wondered if he thought Christian was foolish—and if, by extension, he was, too. But SEALs were always doing ridiculous things, always risking their lives on the battlefield.

"I have a plan to help the Vietnamese," said Zeus. "I think it'll stop the Chinese cold."

"How high up at my command do you want to talk?" said Kerfer after what seemed like an eternity.

"High enough to get people into China."

"You should talk to the agency," said Kerfer. "They're the people running the show."

"I want to be involved."

"So tell them that." Kerfer gave him another of his cynical laughs. "You think if you got the go-ahead from WARCOM, they would let you be in charge? You don't know them very well."

WARCOM was the SEAL command.

"You need agency approval anyway," said Kerfer. "Talk to them first."

"Who?"

"Lucas. Peter Lucas. Or the woman he had here, if you can track her down. Mara Duncan."

"Yeah, you're right. I should talk to Mara."

"I can give you a lift back to the embassy."

"I can't go there. Perry wants to put me on a helicopter."

"Well, that's a bit of a problem for you, Major, isn't it? Because you need a secure phone line to talk to anybody important, don't you?"

"You have an encrypted sat phone."

Kerfer shook his head.

"I know you do, Ric," insisted Zeus. "Come on."

I n the end, Kerfer let Zeus borrow the phone, but only with him there. First he led him to a second, windowless courtyard, which he swept with a small electronic device to make sure they weren't being bugged. It was paranoid overkill, but necessary just the same.

Kerfer had to call one of his own people to get cleared up to the CIA contact; that cost him a promise to fill the man in later. He got the number for the Vietnamese situation desk at Langley, made the call, then handed the phone over to Zeus.

Zeus talked for a bit, but mostly spent the call frowning. He looked as if he'd been punched in the stomach when he handed back the phone.

"Problem?" Kerfer asked.

"I have to talk to Perry."

Harland Perry was so famous in the military that even Kerfer had known who he was before coming to Vietnam. The general was a powerful presence in the Army, and not only because he was friends with the president. Even before George Chester Greene had been elected, Perry was on the short list of future candidates for Army chief of staff. Few people would want to cross him, even in the CIA.

"Come on, Major, I'll buy you a drink," said Kerfer loudly. "Or should I just put you to bed?"

"I'm wide awake."

"You're zoning on your feet. Did you even hear what I just said?"

"When?"

"Come on. Another beer. Or maybe some coffee."

Zeus followed Kerfer into the hotel. It was clear the SEAL officer had thoroughly checked the place out; he moved smoothly through the dimly lit corridor and then the back rooms. Finally they reached the metal door that went into the storeroom behind the bar and pulled it open. He led the way around the now-empty shelving where food supplies had once been kept. Just before Kerfer reached the door to the bar, they heard loud sirens from outside.

There was commotion on the other side of the door. Kerfer stopped, listened, then put his hand out, keeping Zeus from opening the door.

"What's going on?" Zeus asked.

"Probably a bomb raid. Hang back a minute. They're probably all heading for the bomb shelter."

"Shouldn't we?"

"Sure, if you want to be buried with a couple hundred strangers when a bomb hits."

"You think the building will collapse?"

"Nah." Kerfer shrugged as if the odds were a million to one. Zeus thought about it, and decided that if the building was hit by any bomb big enough to do serious damage, it would most likely collapse. It would be days, maybe weeks before they would be dug out, if they were dug out.

Better to go out in the blast.

When the commotion inside had died down, Kerfer opened the door. The barroom was completely empty. The lights were still on, and drinks arrayed around the tables, as if the inhabitants had simply disintegrated.

They walked to the bar. The SEAL went over to the liquor well and took a fresh bottle of Jack Daniel's from the shelf. He fished around for two fresh glasses, then set them out.

"I'll just have a beer," said Zeus.

"Suit yourself." Kerfer pointed to the tap. "They're still serving Tsingtao. So your choices are watered-down Chinese beer, or watered-down lite Chinese beer."

"I'll try the lite."

Kerfer tilted a glass beneath the tap.

"You know, if you get too tied up in a place, you end up with problems," he said, watching the liquid run slowly into the glass. "Sooner or later, you get to the point where you can't separate things out into the proper categories."

He dragged the word *categories* out, almost like a word in a song. Zeus knew he was supposed to interpret it as a warning—he'd have been brain-dead not to—but he ignored it. Instead, he glanced around the room. It seemed smaller without the people here.

The red drapes that hung along the walls looked like the cushioned sides of a coffin. The black tiebacks added to the funereal feel.

"So you're having trouble with Perry?" Kerfer slid the beer over to him.

"I really can't get into it."

"Right." Kerfer filled his cocktail glass about a tenth of the way with the Tennessee whiskey. Then he scooped up some ice from a tray below the bar. "He's listening to the people who think China'll flatten the Viets inside a week."

He pronounced "Viets" like "Veets."

"You think that's gonna happen?" Zeus asked.

"I don't go around making predictions. That's the job of assholes and generals."

"If it's so foolish to stay, why are you here?" said Zeus. He felt his cheeks and the skin under his ears starting to buzz.

"Who says I think it's foolish?"

"Why are you helping them? I mean."

"I'm following orders," said Kerfer. "Even SEALs have to do that, now and again."

He smiled and took a long sip from his glass. His eyes had narrowed; it seemed to Zeus that he was looking off into the distance—to the future, maybe, or perhaps the past. Kerfer remained a mystery to him.

There was pain as well as cynicism in his face. Maybe he had lost someone he loved. Or maybe he had killed more people than Zeus had, and they were weighing on him.

Funny. Not one of the Chinese soldiers he'd killed haunted him. It didn't bother him in the least—it was kill or be killed.

Zeus put his drink down. The thought had taken him by surprise—he'd killed many people.

Soldiers, not people. But of course they were people. Until that very moment he had separated the two categories. They were separate—soldiers were not people. The enemy was not people.

He glanced up at Kerfer, thinking that he might ask him about this—ask him, one killer to another, if he kept separate tallies. But Kerfer had turned his attention to the doorway.

A man stood there. He was Vietnamese, short and thin. He wore a stained white apron as if he'd come from the kitchen. He had an AK-47 in his hand.

The man stared at the room, puzzled. Suddenly he seemed to notice Zeus and Kerfer. When he did, he jerked his shoulders up, raising the gun in the same motion.

He shouted words in Vietnamese that Zeus couldn't understand.

"Cái gì thế?" said Kerfer matter-of-factly, as if the man were ranting about the weather. "What's the matter?"

The man pointed the rifle at him and shouted again.

Zeus had his service pistol in a holster under his outer clothes, but it would take precious seconds before he could reach it. By then, he'd be dead. There was no cover between him and the man. He thought of retreating behind the bend in the bar, but that would take as long as pulling his gun.

Kerfer spread his hands, gesturing to the man.

"Tôi không hiểu ý anh," said Kerfer. "I don't understand. I don't understand Vietnamese. Can you speak English?"

This elicited another long rant. The man seemed to calm slightly as he spoke, though his head bobbed emphatically as he made his points.

Zeus noticed that Kerfer was moving almost imperceptibly forward.

That was the strategy—get close to him and rush him. Zeus took a step. Immediately the man turned the gun toward him.

Zeus put out his hands.

"I don't understand Vietnamese," he said. "What do you need us to do?"

The man frowned. Zeus struggled to understand. It was impossible.

"Anh có cần sự giúp đỡ không?" he asked finally. "Do you need help?"

The man lowered his rifle so that it was even with Zeus's chest. He pushed out with it, almost as if he was thrusting an imaginary bayonet in the American's direction. Fortunately, they were still separated by a dozen feet.

Kerfer started to talk, once more in his very calm voice. The man frowned but then turned toward him, answering.

"He thinks we're spies," said Kerfer, talking to Zeus while keeping his eyes fixed on the man. "From what I can make out."

"Spies?"

"Yeah, for China."

"Shit."

"Irony is a wonderful thing, isn't it? What the hell happened to your minder?"

"What minder?"

"You were followed on the way in. I figured Trung or somebody put a guard on you. Really, Major, you didn't notice him? We lost him in the halls. Looks like he took off. And he ain't comin' back."

Kerfer held out his hands as the man began yelling again. He picked up a can of soda from the back of the bar.

"Đồ uống nhẹ?" Kerfer held the can up, twisting it in his hand. "Soft drinks? A soda—would you like?"

It seemed an odd way to placate a crazy man. It didn't work—the man's voice turned angrier. Zeus couldn't understand the exact words, but the meaning seemed clear enough: *I'm going to kill you bastards.*

Zeus angled his left foot forward, getting ready to plunge ahead. The strategy seemed clear now. Kerfer was getting the man's attention. Zeus would work himself close enough, then jump him.

Kerfer could use the bar for cover. The way it was angled, he could duck down.

Or not. The man with the gun had a clear sight down if he took a half step to the right.

He couldn't get both of them.

"Maybe a chair," said Zeus, taking a half step forward. He gestured toward the chair. "Maybe you should sit."

The man's rants turned even more emphatic.

"All right, all right," said Zeus. "I was just trying to make you comfortable."

"*Ô!*" shouted Kerfer. "Hey!"

As he yelled, Kerfer pulled the top on the cola can and tossed it at the man as if it were a grenade. Soda spurt in the air. Zeus took two steps toward the man, preparing to dive at him. Something barked at his ear—twice, three times.

The man spun backward, almost pirouetting, a dancer in a play. He fell back, beyond Zeus's reach, the AK falling to the ground. Zeus stopped, his hands out. He felt for a moment as if he had been plunged into the middle of a dream.

"I almost shot you," snarled Kerfer. He'd drawn a pistol and fired in the split second that the man was distracted, though Zeus couldn't imagine how it had happened; the time seemed too short.

"What the hell?" asked Zeus.

"Some fuckin' crazy," said Kerfer. "He thought we were spying for the fuckin' Chinese. God. How insane is that?"

He touched the barrel of his gun, sliding his hand down it as if to wipe it off, or maybe to see if it was warm. Then he slipped the gun back into the front of his belt below his loose shirt.

"You're pretty fast," Zeus told him.

"Lucky he doesn't like Coke. Let's get the hell out of here."

2

Washington, D.C.

George Chester Greene folded his arms in front of his chest as his aide fiddled with the setting for the iPad, attempting to fix whatever bug was preventing it from receiving the transmission. The morning was warm for early March, and though dressed only in his suit, Greene could feel the sweat rolling down his cheek and neck. Fortunately, there was enough scenery in the Rose Garden that no one would notice.

"I'm sorry, Mr. President," said the flustered aide. "I just had it. I'm not sure what's messing me up here."

"Don't bother," said the president finally. He was annoyed—more than annoyed, really—but didn't want the kid to think he was angry with him. So he added lightly, "They're only going to say what a jackass I am."

The aide, Jason Hanson, looked at him with an ashen face. He grimaced; Greene could have hit him in the stomach and gotten much less of a response.

"It's OK, Jason," said Greene, amused. "That is what my friends in Congress think. They may not use those exact words."

"Th-they're not your friends, sir. They're . . . ass-holes."

Greene laughed. It was the first laugh of the day—his first laugh in probably twenty-four hours.

"I seem to be corrupting the young," he said lightly to his national security advisor, Walter Jackson, who was standing a short distance away. Then he turned back to Jason. "It's all right, son—I'll tell you what. Go tell Mark that I'm ready for the Red Cross people."

"Yes, sir."

The young man stepped back into the small crowd of aides and bodyguards clustered at one side of the Rose Garden. Aside from the pool photographer, no press had been admitted for the simple ceremony Greene had completed just a few minutes before. The pool reporters and a videographer would be admitted with the Red Cross chairman and two volunteers who were here to commemorate volunteerism during the recent hurricane.

"Were we ever that young?" said Greene as his aide disappeared.

"You were," said Jackson.

"Mr. President?"

Greene looked over at his press secretary, Ray Melfi. Melfi came from Greene's old hometown; Greene's mother had babysat for him when he was small. Melfi had been on his staff since he ran for Senate, and was one of the president's only long-term advisors who occasionally called him Chet, though generally not when others were around.

"Do you really want the press in this morning?" said Melfi.

"Too late to bar the press corps now, Ray," Greene told his aide cheerfully.

"Well, if you're going to bring a few in, you might just as well have everybody here. The pool people all hate you."

"And the others don't?"

"Not all of them."

"Give them time."

Melfi had been arguing against having any media present today at all. Greene instinctually knew that was a mistake—even though the last thing he felt like doing today was appearing before some goddamn cameras.

"How long will it take to get them down here?" asked the president, rubbing some of the sweat away from his collar.

"Just a few minutes. They'll run here, believe me."

"All right, why not? It'll give me a second to talk to Brian." Greene spotted the Red Cross director, Brian Gear, coming out of the building. Gear, a former congressman, had played poker with him occasionally some years before.

Not very well, which certainly endeared him to Greene.

"Just to finish my thought," said Jackson, clearing his throat. "General Perry is a problem. If he goes public—"

"He's not going to do that," said Greene. "Do you agree with him? Should we give Vietnam to the Chinese?"

"No."

"Then no matter what Harland does, he won't be a problem."

"Politically—"

"Screw the politics, Walter. And since when do you worry about them? Worry about China. We have to cut that bastard Cho Lai off at the knees."

Greene gave his national security advisor a phony smile, winked, then turned to Gear and began his hail-fellow-well-met routine. The former congressman smiled, then suddenly turned serious.

"Sorry to hear about the, uh, the—"

"Impeachment," said Greene cheerfully. "What a crock, huh?"

"Well—"

"Ah, don't worry about that. All political maneuvering. Here, introduce me to the honorees. I'd like to meet some real heroes."

Gear introduced him to a Red Cross volunteer who had personally saved two young men in the swollen Pohick Creek a few weeks back after a tropical storm had dumped upward of ten inches in the area drained by the river-sized creek.

The storm was far out of season for anywhere, let alone Virginia. Meteorologists were divided about whether it was a completely freak occurrence or one more result of rapid climate change—and therefore a harbinger of things to come.

While ordinarily he would have avoided it, Greene was glad to talk about the weather today. He nodded as the volunteer described how the rain had come down in what seemed like buckets as she was on her way to set up a shelter for the Red Cross. The life-saving skills she'd learned as a teenager during classes run by the Red Cross had certainly paid off.

A volunteer, and a Red Cross beneficiary. Gear really had his public relations machine running on all engines, thought Greene. Had he been this adept in Congress, he never would have lost his seat.

The press filtered around the Rose Garden. Melfi's assistants attempted in vain to provide some sort of rudimentary traffic control. It was a lost cause; the White House gardener was going to have a fit.

How wonderful it would be, Greene thought, if there was a sudden cloudburst and they were all soaked.

The thought carried him through the ceremony, secretly poking up the corners of his mouth as he listened to Gear praise "the unsung volunteers" across the country. Then Greene said a few words, smiling and looking presidential for the mandatory photos—images that would only be posted on the Web pages of the volunteers' hometown newspapers.

"Well now, I know most of you are actually interested in asking me a few questions about things that have nothing to do with the Red Cross," said Greene when the photo op was done. "So why don't we take a few minutes and get that out of the way, and then we can talk about the Red Cross and the excellent job it's doing. The excellent job my friend Brian Gear is doing."

Greene swung his hand over toward Gear and the volunteers. There was a smattering of applause from the family members who had come to observe the ceremony.

The reporters were chomping at the bit. The oldest—Gar Daniels, a septuagenarian who had worked for the *Washington Post* but now had a regular blog on *Politico*—was by custom the first one to ask a question.

He could also always be counted on to say something that would irk Greene.

"Mr. President," he started in his slow, overly studied Georgian drawl, "the unprecedented vote to investigate you—"

"Gar, I'm not sure it's unprecedented," said Greene. "I'm reminded a bit of the attacks by Congress on Lincoln's successor, Andrew Johnson."

Melfi was undoubtedly wincing—he had *strongly* advised Greene not to mention anything that would suggest impeachment, including, and especially, previous impeachment cases. But the hell with that—Greene thought Johnson had been railroaded, and he was being, too.

"Of course, that was a little before our time," added

Greene. He tilted his head slightly, as if speaking directly to the reporter. "Though I suspect most of the rest of the press corps believes you and I were there in the flesh."

That got a laugh, but it didn't do much to disarm either Daniels or the rest of the journalists. Greene let them shout for a few seconds, nodding a bit, relaxing—the truth was, he enjoyed seeing them act like jackals before waving his hand to silence them.

"The congressman from New Jersey is wrong. Yes, let there be no mistake, I'm talking about Congressman Goodwell. I haven't violated the law," Greene added, paraphrasing one of the questions in his answer. He smiled, and paused to let the flashes on the cameras trickle off. There was a certain irony in Goodwell's name—he'd have to find a way to play with that. "And let me make one thing clear to China—we are *not* going to stand by idly while they push around their neighbors."

A skinny female reporter who had pushed her way to the front row shouted a question. "Mr. President, are you threatening to use force against China?"

"I didn't say that at all." Greene smiled at her. He blanked on her name, but he was sure she was with the Indianapolis paper. Or was it Dallas? She didn't sound Texan. "We will deal strongly with acts of aggression. That's how I'd put it."

"Are you prepared to defend Vietnam?" she asked.

"We've already introduced several resolutions in the UN General Assembly," said Greene.

"Are you willing to commit U.S. ground forces?" asked a voice from the back.

Who was that? Kevin Deere from Chicago? He couldn't quite see in the crush.

"I'm not ruling anything in or out," said Greene. "All options are on the table."

"But Congress has specifically prohibited the use of U.S. forces," said the mousy young woman, whose name and affiliation he couldn't remember.

"Congress does not supersede the Constitution," said Greene. "I am the commander in chief."

"They claim you're trying to supersede the Constitution."

"Well, the opposing party can make a lot of claims," said Greene. "They can even claim I'm breaking the law. A lot of good it will do them."

Greene glanced at Melfi. The aide's face was as white as he'd ever seen it—whiter than the Sicilian beaches his ancestors had once escaped from.

Poor man. He'd have to find a way to get him a raise.

Greene took another question. There was a bit more back and forth before Melfi finally stepped in and called a halt to the questioning, citing the president's pressing schedule. Greene glanced around for Gear, but the Red Cross director had wisely faded into the background. The event was over.

Greene thought he had done comparatively well, taking a bit of the edge off the press. But Melfi's face afterward told him something else again.

"They're gunning for you," he whispered as they walked inside. Greene was heading for a lunch meeting with the Army chief of staff.

"When have they not?" asked Greene. "Don't worry. The impeachment vote was bullshit. The Senate will never vote to impeach."

"What if Perry goes public with his opposition—and what we've done?"

"We haven't done much of anything yet."

Melfi didn't comment. Even Greene understood that was the sort of lie he'd never get away with, and must not repeat in public. Not only had the U.S. supplied weapons to Vietnam illegally—shades of the Iran-Contra affair that had nearly brought down the Reagan presidency—but Greene had also authorized advisors and covert action to help the Vietnamese.

Since giving aid to the Vietnamese was specifically prohibited by law, it could be considered a "crime" as specified by the Constitution under the article covering impeachment. But putting U.S. troops in harm's way—which wasn't technically covered by a law—would certainly resonate more with the public. And that made it much more dangerous.

Even after having been presented evidence that the Chinese had provoked the war, public sentiment was running very high against the intervention. Most people didn't understand how much of a threat China actually represented. Nor did the American public feel particularly close to Vietnam.

"All right, Ray, just keep up your good work," said Greene, patting him on the back as they approached the stairs. "I'll try not to make it any harder than necessary for you."

"Yes, sir, Mr. President," said the press secretary weakly. "I'll do my best."

3

Aboard USS *McCampbell*, off the coast of Vietnam, southwest of Beibu Wan

Commander Dirk "Hurricane" Silas steadied himself against the rail of his destroyer, taking a deep breath of the night air. *McCampbell* rolled lightly on the sea, the gentle waves belying the ferocious storm she had so recently weathered.

Silas himself was at peace, content if tired after several days of confrontations not only with the weather but with the Chinese. He had been playing cat and mouse with a Chinese cruiser and a smaller ship, finally succeeding in driving them away. In doing so, he had driven off a small flotilla of disguised merchant ships, which had hoped to land Chinese troops in the Vietnamese port of Haiphong. All without firing a shot.

Much to his chagrin. Silas would have liked nothing better than to have sunk the lot of them.

He could have, too. His *Arleigh Burke* class destroyer was equipped with a variety of weapons which would have taken the cruiser and her escort down in seconds. From the five-inch gun at the bow to his Tomahawks, all of his arrows were superior to what the Chinese mounted. If attacked from the air, he could send a dozen SM6 ERAMs—extended range RIM-174 antiair missiles—against the enemy. These were true silver bullets, as effective as any weapon in the world against cruise missiles. Just behind them were SM2s and SM3s—Standard Missiles—which could handle anything from a fighter to, in the SM3's case, a ballistic missile. His Phalanx CIWS would mop up any "leakers" that made it past the other defenses. (CIWS stood for Close-in Weapons System—the Navy loved abbreviations, even prosaic ones.) Meanwhile, his SM2s and Evolved Sea Sparrows could sink a surface ship whether in sight or over the horizon, while his torpedo tubes could launch a barrage of Mk 54 torpedoes against any submarine no matter how deep or shallow the water.

In short, Silas commanded a ship that had the capabilities of an entire World War II task force. And he was aching to use it.

He paced along the deck. By all rights he should be sleeping; the ship was squared away, and he hadn't had more than a catnap in several days. But he loved to walk his ship at such hours; loved the feel of it beneath his feet, the touch of metal or, better, rope against his hands.

This was the time of day when he felt most like a throwback, most like a captain at sea two hundred years before, his own man, his own law and force.

Today's captain was anything but. A thousand masters tethered him: his destroyer squadron, COMNAV-SURFPAC, CINCPAC, PACCOM, the Pentagon; the White House—Silas suspected even the post office had some part in overseeing his actions.

Fortune favors the brave was his ship's motto. They were words to live by, no matter what strings were wound around you.

The commander moved down the deck toward the

ladder. The Chinese warships were now some ten miles away, no doubt trying to come up with a plan to unbruise their egos.

Sooner or later they would try something else. Silas and his ship would rise to the occasion once again.

He'd even sink the bastards, if Washington would let him.

Hell, maybe if they didn't.

4

Jersey City

Jing Yo floated in the water, oblivious to the present, unaware of the past. He moved only with the tide, unbreathing, unfeeling.

His lover was with him. Hyuen Bo lay entangled against his side, drifting as he drifted. Their past was a blank, their future nonexistent. The soft curve of her breast against his chest, the fold of her hip against his stomach—these were the only things he could feel. These were the only things that were real as he floated, his brain dancing in the glowing infinite.

And then the infinite was no more. The milky white above him began to crack, becoming jagged. The blue below him no longer supported him. As it gave way, Jing Yo found himself floundering, desperate to save himself. He reached his hands up, trying to pull against the waves that were suddenly surrounding him.

As he struggled, he realized Hyuen Bo was gone. He reached for her, desperate to save her, but his fingers failed to find her. He let himself fall below the water, thinking she was there, but the water, angry and black, was empty. He kicked and flailed his arms. He shouted. Jing Yo groped but couldn't find her.

"You have been away for a very long time," said a voice above him. "For very long."

He opened his eyes. Jing Yo found himself in a small room, the walls close. The place smelled of vegetables cooking.

"Do you remember?"

It took a moment to focus. A short man, Chinese, was standing next to him. He was familiar, though Jing Yo couldn't place him at first.

One of the monks who had trained him? One of his military commanders?

Neither. He wore Western-style clothes and stood stoop-shouldered. He smelled of cigarettes.

"You were taken from the water," said the man. "Do you remember the attack on the bridge?"

"With the grenade," said Jing Yo.

He remembered holding the launcher. He was trying to assassinate the American scientist. Jing Yo had followed him all the way from Vietnam, assigned to prevent the scientist from testifying at the United Nations.

His name?

Jing Yo couldn't remember.

"Where is Hyuen Bo?" he asked.

"Who?"

"Hyuen Bo? The girl."

Jing Yo's memory came back in a rush. Hyuen Bo was dead, killed in Vietnam, murdered by the Americans as they escaped with the scientist.

Murdered.

He saw it again, saw it happening. She was an accidental victim of war—her death was as much his fault as theirs.

Anguish overpowered him. Jing Yo closed his eyes and let his head fall back on the bed, overwhelmed. He tried to cry but could not.

The man left him alone, for how long he couldn't

tell. It could have been days, it could have been bare minutes. Finally, Jing Yo opened his eyes and the room smelled of perfumed sweet tea.

The man was back.

"For your wounds," he told Jing Yo, holding a small cup out to him.

Jing Yo pushed himself up in bed. He was covered in bandages. He didn't remember any of the blows that had caused these.

"You have a remarkable body," said the man. "Much energy."

When he said energy, he used a Chinese word that could be interpreted to mean "way" or "direction"—an expression peculiar to the monks Jing Yo had studied with as he learned the Shaolin path.

"You are the tailor," Jing Yo told the man. "You helped me before."

The man's eyes danced for a moment. Then he handed Jing Yo the tea.

"Drink."

Later that day, Jing Yo felt strong enough to get out of bed and explore his surroundings. His body was quite stiff—his calves felt almost as if they had been broken in half, and his hip ached with every step—and just to move felt like an accomplishment.

Outside the room, Jing Yo discovered a short hallway. The door to the room next to his was very similar. There was little furniture, only a simple bed roll on the floor and a dresser. A small shrine was atop the dresser, studded with objects that had meaning only to the person who had arranged it.

Jing Yo studied the arrangement of rocks and bits of plants, then turned his attention to the broken butterfly wing at the right side of the ensemble. It looked as if it were randomly placed, a remnant haphazardly tossed on smooth granite pebble. But nothing here was random.

The broken butterfly. Distraught beauty.

Lost love.

Jing Yo left the room and found the bathroom. He decided to take a shower. When he was finished, he sat on the edge of the tub for a while, breathing in the fading mist of the hot steam. Then he got dressed, and went back into the house.

The tailor was waiting for him in the kitchen, sitting at a brown table made of tin. It was old and battered, but its simple lines filled the space perfectly.

"You are hungry," said the tailor. "Would you like eggs?"

"Is it breakfast time?"

"It is breakfast for you."

Jing Yo spent the afternoon doing exercises and meditating. That evening, the tailor told him he was going out.

"It is not safe for you to be on the street," the tailor warned. "You must stay in."

Jing Yo agreed. Still, as soon as the tailor left, he was tempted to go and take a walk on his own.

He stayed away from the windows, but from what he saw and heard he could tell that he was in a city. He wondered what was on the streets outside, but he stayed put, not because he was worried, but because he assumed this was some manner of test.

Until he was feeling better, it made no sense to invite difficulty. Patience was the rule and the way.

When the tailor returned a few hours later, he found Jing Yo sitting cross-legged on the floor of the living room.

"You have watched television?" asked the tailor.

"No."

"I have a package for you."

He disappeared into the back room. When he returned, he had a thick manila envelope in his hand. He gave it to Jing Yo, then went back to the kitchen so Jing Yo could examine it in privacy.

Inside was twenty thousand dollars in hundred-dollar bills. There were six credit cards, all with different names. Two of the names matched driver's licenses. There was a passport that matched another.

There was also a single piece of paper with an address printed neatly at the top. It was on a county highway in Forthright, Ohio.

Jing Yo returned the contents to the envelope. He was folding it over when the tailor returned, carrying a bottle of Oban Scotch. He had two glasses. He put them on the marble coffee table, and poured two fingers' worth into each glass.

Jing Yo stared at him. The tailor took one of the glasses, waited for a few seconds to see if Jing Yo would join him, then held the glass up and took the smallest of sips.

"When one lives in the world, one must sometimes adopt its customs," said the tailor as he sat on the couch.

It was his way of explaining why he drank the alcohol, Jing Yo realized. Alcohol, though not specifically forbidden, was frowned on by the adepts.

The tailor looked at him, perhaps expecting Jing Yo to speak. When he didn't, he reached again for the glass and took another sip, this one slightly larger.

"I expected to be called back," said Jing Yo. "Or punished. My mission failed."

The punishment for failure was forfeiture of his life, though Jing Yo saw no need to mention this.

"I am not a judge. I have no say. I do not know anything about your future," added the tailor. "Do you require further aid?"

"No." said Jing Yo. "I will leave in the morning."

The tailor nodded. He took another sip, and now the glass was almost empty. Jing Yo took a deep breath, and went back to meditating.

5

Hanoi

The incident in the hotel had changed Zeus's view of Hanoi. Until now he had seen it as a city pulling together under attack, the citizens responding to the government's call for order and sacrifice. Now he saw it not just under siege, but on the point of descent into darkness and insanity.

Outside, the scent of burning metal seemed to have been replaced by the scent of desperation—a thin, powdery ash that stung the nose and settled on lips and teeth, inescapable. A buzz rose from the streets, a hum just audible to his ears—a million whispers together, words of fear and desperation, questions of how to survive, how to escape.

There would be no escape for Hanoi. The Chinese divisions to the southwest were massing to ford the swollen wetlands in Hoa Binh. They would get through, just as Zeus knew they would when he had mapped the successful plan to stall them.

Then they would sweep down to the south. Once they gathered momentum, there was little the Vietnamese could do to stop them. The Chinese would march on Hue, aiming to confront the two divisions the

Vietnamese had moved there in the past few days. The Chinese would meet them with at least three divisions of armor, and twice as many infantrymen. The geography would limit their attack, but the Chinese numbers and air support would inevitably force the issue in their favor.

Or maybe they would take a more difficult route, swinging to the west, bypassing Hue and the Vietnamese forces temporarily in favor of a strong, quick rush to Ho Chi Minh City. Zeus had once favored that approach himself, during the Red Dragon war games that had prepared him for this.

Or he'd *thought* prepared him. Simulations could only teach you certain things about strategy and how to place forces. They couldn't teach you what you really needed to know about war, how it stung your eyes, how it soured the taste in your mouth.

How it threatened to hollow out your head.

Zeus suppressed his shock as he drove up to the gate at the Vietnamese army command complex and saw that there was only a single guard. The army had a severe manpower shortage, but leaving security light here was suicidal—a lightning strike by a SpecOp unit against the top generals would hasten the country's collapse.

Granted, the Chinese had neither demonstrated any bold thinking in their attacks to this point, nor had they made much use of special operations units. Their attacks so far had been utterly pedestrian, an outgrowth of the decades' long concentration on the military as a defensive force. This approach, and the hard fetters of tradition, were all that kept the ragtag Vietnamese forces alive, in Zeus's opinion.

He took out his military ID and the pass signed by General Trung as he approached the lone sentry. The soldier came over to the car—Zeus had borrowed it from the embassy the day before—then with a glance waved him on. By now, he was well known in the complex.

Zeus drove the small Nissan down the long road toward the concrete building that housed the entrance to the complex. He parked near a pair of old troop trucks—Russian equivalents of the famous American deuce and a half—got out, and went to the door of the small structure housing the entrance.

It wasn't until he had descended to the first basement that he saw a guard. The man eyed him for a moment, then gave the slightest bow in recognition.

G eneral Trung stared at the large map spread out on the table of the conference room. The map was new, its surface bare—no markings to show either the forces arrayed against him or the units he had to oppose them.

He had ordered his aide to take the satellite photos and other data the Americans were providing and hold it off to the side. He was thankful for their help, but the reams of information they supplied could be distracting.

Trung wanted simply to look, not at the map, but at the terrain it represented. He used the paper and its shades only to remind him of the physical facts—the way the jungles ran to the highlands, the way the delta flooded.

His predecessors had fought over these same roads and paths, along the same rivers. Their enemies had been, if anything, mightier than the Chinese arrayed against him. France, the United States itself—these were world powers. The Chinese were a regional force, unable to project power much beyond their own borders.

But they were here now, and far more dangerous than the Americans or French. Their proximity made it easy to add supplies and reinforcements. And the Chinese leader saw Vietnam as a place that could solve many of his problems. Its rice and wheat would be welcome, its oil a boon. And the war offered a diversion from his country's growing problems.

Once self-sufficient as the world's largest producer of wheat, China now barely made enough to feed half its population. It couldn't buy enough from other countries to make up the difference. The story was the same with rice and corn. Ironically, the climate changes that had brought sustained droughts to China had showered good fortune on Vietnam, extending its growing seasons and making more land arable. Thanks partly to new hybrids and improved farming methods, the Vietnamese had been able to capitalize on climate change. Their economy, small as it was, had boomed before the Chinese attacked.

Three weeks before, Trung lit incense at an altar in honor of his ancestors, thanking them for helping him see this prosperity. Now he felt as if they had turned their back on him.

Pham, one of his intelligence aides, appeared at the door.

"General, the American hero, Major Murphy, has returned."

Trung nodded. The words were not an exaggeration, Murphy was in fact a hero—he had helped deter two major Chinese attacks. The people owed him a great deal, even more so because he was an American.

Trung owed him as well. The young man had a supple mind for battle. And his presence meant that the Americans would continue to take an interest in Vietnam. Trung's spies had confided that General Perry had lost faith in the Vietnamese; Zeus Murphy was their last hope.

It was a shame. He liked the young American. In many ways, he reminded Trung of the son he had lost many years before. And he would not wish the road ahead on anyone, let alone someone he was fond of.

"**G**eneral Trung, thank you for seeing me," said Zeus, striding into the room.

"It is always a pleasure," said Trung softly.

"I'm ready to review the plans."

"You are here at General Perry's request?"

"I'm here on my own."

Trung nodded.

Zeus leaned over and looked at the map. It was a simple rendering of the terrain. There were no legends on the maps, not even the names of the cities. But then most likely they would have been in Vietnamese anyway.

"Your images and the intelligence from the embassy are there," said Trung, pointing to a pile of folders and papers at the side the room.

Zeus picked them up and started thumbing through them. Nothing important had changed. The opportunity was still there.

"I think we can do it," he told Trung finally.

"I will bring in my lieutenants."

A half hour later, Zeus walked fourteen Vietnamese commanders and their aides through a plan to attack north along the road to Malipo, China. He had first conceived of the idea a few days before. It had evolved considerably since then, but the core idea remained the same: strike the Chinese where they didn't expect to be hit, and use this action to undermine their confidence. If the Chinese acted the way they had acted before, they would halt their offensive, reinforce their lines, and then attempt to regain their territory. It was a stalling action, but it would gain the Vietnamese at least another week.

American satellite images showed that the Chinese had left only a token force in the mountains in the sector below Malipo, concentrating their attack to the east and west. There were good reasons for this. First, the Vietnamese had themselves committed the bulk of their forces to face the two-pronged Chinese attack. Aside from a home guard unit scattered in the hills at the border, there was nothing here to threaten the Chinese.

The Chinese had about a battalion's worth of troops—they were actually drawn from two different units, according to the signals intelligence—near the border below Malipo, spread out in the mines around Huashan. That force controlled the main road north. Given that the surrounding area was mountainous, any commander preparing defenses would not think he had much to fear.

But examining the satellite photos, Zeus had realized that it would be possible to bypass those strongholds by moving west in Vietnam, crossing through a shallow stream in a mountain pass, and then cutting across to the highway via a narrow but passable pair of roads north of Chuantou. (The city was on the border between the two countries and held by a regiment-sized infantry force. What the unit there lacked in equipment—there were only a few artillery pieces and no visible armor—it made up for in troops. If there was one thing the Chinese had, it was people.)

The stream was dry nearly ten months out of the year. There was only water in it now because of the recent typhoon. The satellite images showed it could be easily forded. The roads were rough but even easier to travel. The trick would be to do all of this unseen. Zeus figured that it would take several hours to get a large force through the mountain passes and onto the highway.

Once they were on the highway, they would be around the main defense in that area. They could take Malipo with only a token fight.

Hubris—that was the Chinese problem. They didn't think the Vietnamese were capable of striking them. It was the age-old mistake.

Controlling Malipo would give the Vietnamese access to the valleys beyond. In fact, it would expose all of Hunan province, and all of southern China, to attack. There were no sizeable Chinese units or defenses between Malipo and Wenshaw, some thirty-five miles away, though admittedly over very rough terrain. Once an army reached Wenshaw, it could dissect the country at will.

It wasn't hard for Zeus to imagine a five-hundred-mile romp through the river valleys, hopscotching across the towns and driving deep into Chinese territory. He could have drawn up plans for just such a drive if he was commanding an American force: he would have helicopters and all manner of vehicles at his disposal, control of the skies, almost limitless real-time intelligence. He would own southern China inside a week, maybe even less.

True, the terrain was perfect for guerilla warfare—it reminded him very much of Afghanistan, especially in the areas hardhit by drought. But that sort of resistance would take weeks if not months to materialize in the absence of a strong underground network, and by then the army that had passed through would be on to bigger and better things.

But Zeus wasn't making a plan for an American force. On the contrary, the assault he mapped out would be executed by a force barely two regiments in size, with a handful of armor and no air support. Even the artillery was limited.

Organized around the Vietnamese 15th Regiment, the force had been supplemented with smaller units from several other divisions and pieces of an armored battalion. A total of thirty-eight tanks and about twice as many armored personnel carriers had been cobbled together as a strike force. The tanks were a motley collection mostly of T-54 and T-55s, Russian Cold War models with some upgrades. The same could not be said for the armored personnel carriers, which were BTR-50s and BMP-1s, tanklike vehicles that would have been thoroughly familiar to soldiers fighting during the war with America.

There was one advantage to having such a small force—sneaking through the mountains would be considerably easier than getting, say, a full armored brigade, let alone a division, past Chinese eyes. The key would be timing the crossing to the passage of a Chinese satellite that surveyed the region; fortunately its orbit was well known. Zeus also had data on the Chinese aircraft flights, which showed that there were only two reconnaissance aircraft operating in the area; they tended to fly on a predictable schedule, which he had taken into account.

There was one other key to keeping the force's existence secret, but Zeus couldn't share this with the Vietnamese. The Chinese were using a pair of drones for electronic intelligence gathering all along the border. The aircraft picked up signals and transmitted them back to a processing center in Kunming via a satellite system.

Zeus needed information on when the aircraft were operating. There were several ways the aircraft and their operations could be tracked. The exact method likely depended on how resources were being allocated in the theater, something Zeus wasn't entirely aware of. In any event, the information hadn't been shared with the Vietnamese for some reason, and Zeus knew better than to tell them about it.

Even better would be the means of disabling the drones, which could be done if the U.S. would wipe out the Chinese satellites. But that was absolutely something he couldn't mention to the Vietnamese.

Zeus spent a few minutes going over the plan, elements of which had already been shared with most of the men in the room. As usual, it was impossible to tell how he was being received. To a man, the Vietnamese officers stared intently and without emotion, their eyes fixed on the maps he pointed to. Once in a while, a gaze would stray toward Trung. No matter how much he tried, Zeus never once caught any of the men looking at him.

Trung watched his men as Zeus wrapped up. He could tell they were doubtful, and there was no reason that they shouldn't be. The plan was more than a long shot.

His strategy during the first stages of the war had been to delay, to make the Chinese stagnate. That had served them very well during the wars in 1979 and 1984. Once the risk-adverse Chinese commanders met resistance, they stopped and dug in. At that point, the Vietnamese had the advantage—they could attack from the surrounding hills, use their artillery to pound the

Chinese, and occasionally strike with small forces at weak points.

But the war this time was different. The Chinese had massed many more men, and come much farther into Vietnam. The Vietnamese had done very well to hold them this long.

He could see the end now. He would take this last chance, and join his ancestors in the process.

The room fell silent. Trung's aides would not ask Zeus questions. When he had first come to Hanoi, they wouldn't speak out of a deep prejudice that he was the country's enemy. Now they wouldn't talk because he was its hero.

But there was considerable doubt in their eyes.

Trung rose.

"It is a bold but difficult plan," he told them.

Each word came from his mouth slowly, as if he had formed each sound individually, contemplated its correctness, then sent it into the world.

"It will require our best efforts to implement it," Trung continued. "I will lead the attack myself from the field."

Zeus glanced at his interpreter, waiting for him to translate Trung's words. But he could tell from the reaction of the men what the general was saying.

He was going to lead the attack himself.

This surprised them, just as it had surprised Zeus earlier. Trung had other responsibilities; to give them up to lead this mission personally was in some ways a tacit admission that there was no hope of winning elsewhere.

Or anywhere, perhaps.

The Vietnamese leader bowed his head slightly, then began walking from the room. Zeus followed, catching up to him in the hall. All of the others, including his translator, had stayed back; they were alone.

"The woman," Zeus said. "You said she would be released to me."

"Yes." A pained expression came to Trung's face. "I have not been as successful as I hoped."

"What do you mean?"

"Come with me to my office. We can discuss it there."

Trung turned and walked down the hall. By now, Zeus had grown used to the slightly fetid smell of the deep bunker, which mixed with a static scent of ozone and sweat. The bare concrete walls gave a feeling not of imperviousness to attack but dangerous isolation. He felt blind rather than invulnerable.

Trung sat at his desk, a simple table at the end of the room. Zeus felt that the room had changed somehow from the first time they had met; in fact, he thought it was a different room. But he had no exact memory of the first meeting, let alone the office.

"She is somewhere in the capital area," said Trung. "But we are not sure where."

"I see."

"My aide, Major Chaü, has been making inquiries. He will find her." Trung stared at Zeus's face. "Major, what will you do when you find her?"

"I don't know. Get her someplace safe, I guess."

Trung smiled ever so slightly. Zeus realized that he had just admitted that he thought the Vietnamese would soon be defeated.

"We are very grateful for your government's help," said Trung. "This plan—it is a bold attempt."

"It's not enough," said Zeus.

Trung blinked, but said nothing.

"I'm working on something else," added Zeus. "I may need aircraft."

"We have little."

"Pilots."

"General Gui is the one to speak to. Why?"

"I have to put it together." He returned to his main concern. "I want Anna Anway. She has to be released."

Trung studied him. "A young man as yourself, surely you can find many women."

"Not like her."

"She is Vietnamese."

"So?"

The two men stared at each other. Finally, Trung broke the silence. "Major Chaū will help you find her. I will do what I can to have her released. But I have no guarantees."

"If you give your word to help, that will be enough."

6

Beijing

The Chinese premier watched the television screen intently, staring at the video footage of the American aircraft carrier USS *John C. Stennis*. Cho Lai had always admired the large American ships, even as he contemplated ways of sinking them.

The footage was old, shot last year according to Cho Lai's intelligence chief, but the news report that accompanied the images was accurate enough; the reporter claimed that the carrier was west of Taiwan, sailing with a host of other American ships from the American Pacific 7th Fleet. Meanwhile, another aircraft carrier, *George Washington*, was making its way north from the Philippines to join it.

Two American carrier groups—a very powerful force. Also a tempting target.

For years, the Chinese military had been working on an antiship ballistic missile, the DF-21D. The missile was commonly referred to in the Western press as a "carrier killer." That was not without justification—the Dōngfēng or East Wind missile was loaded with a conventional warhead over several hundred kilograms.

A direct hit would cripple the largest ship; four or five strikes would sink it.

The DF-21D was a critical weapon for China; if properly used, it would neutralize America's ability to project its power into the region. It was fast, had a long range—reported at 2,700 kilometers in the West though in fact somewhat less—and best of all, it was extremely difficult to defend against. But like all weapons, its use presented complexities.

The missile had only recently finished its preliminary experiments. There was one base and exactly twelve missiles—enough, the experts believed, to sink two carriers and perhaps one or more of the American escorts.

But then what?

Cho Lai had contempt for the Americans, but he was not so big a fool as to think them completely impotent. They were cowards, to be sure, but even a coward sufficiently provoked might deal a deadly blow.

Thus far, the American president had been careful not to confront China directly. Arms shipments had been arranged with Russia's help, Cho Lai knew, but these were relatively small and involved only small arms like antitank and shoulder-launched antiaircraft missiles.

Spies had told Cho Lai that there were American advisors in Vietnam, and there had been reports of American commandos in Hainan and southern China. He discounted the reports; the Americans were a very convenient excuse, he knew, for his own army's failings.

But what would the American president do if China sank two aircraft carriers? He had been cautious because the American public was against war with China. But a direct attack like that, against important symbols of American power, might change that. Cho Lai might find that he had stepped on the tail of a tiger.

Cho Lai flipped off the television.

"They are wise," said Tan Jin Mu, the premier's naval advisor. "They're keeping their carriers just far enough away to prevent our firing the missiles at them."

Cho Lai said nothing. Tan Jin Mu wanted the missiles to be used—he was far too confident of success, and too scornful of the Americans.

"Meanwhile, this destroyer continues to flaunt itself in the South China Sea." Tan Jin Mu placed a satellite image on Cho Lai's desk. It showed an American *Arleigh Burke* class destroyer off the coast of Vietnam, with two Chinese warships nearby.

"This is *McCain*?"

"*McCampbell*," said Tan Jin Mu. "It sails in our waters with impunity."

The Americans did not recognize the Chinese claims to the South China Sea, which Cho Lai—and every premier before him—had said was rightfully Chinese waters. Even the Vietnamese had recognized these claims.

"I don't wish any American ship that close to Vietnam," said the premier.

"Then I suggest we sink it," said Tan Jin Mu. "The cruiser *Wen Jiabao* is a capable ship. And her commander is one of our best. With an order to be more aggressive—"

"We have to be cautious here." Cho Lai rose and went over to the window of his study. He pulled back the curtain. He was too far from the mob that was gathered on the street near Tiananmen Square to see the people there, but if he raised his window he knew he could hear the din. For two days now, people had gathered there, ostensibly to protest the Vietnamese for warmongering. But Cho Lai knew that the real reason most had come was the fact that they had little to eat and less to do. After years of growing prosperity, the bubble had burst and the country was at the precipice of disaster.

Cho Lai had not moved against the crowd because they were ostensibly on the government's side. But he also realized that force would not end their uneasiness; only rice would.

Tan Jin Mu guessed what he was thinking.

"If we do not take Vietnam quickly," said the older man, "the crowd will grow even more restless. And hungry."

"They're already hungry."

"In a battle with our ships, the American will lose," said Tan Jin Mu. "If we were to pick a fight, this would be the one. Cruiser and frigate, against a destroyer. If you're worried about taking the carriers—"

"We are fighting a political war, admiral. One ship, one battle—winning and losing is not measured in hardware alone."

Tan Jin Mu said nothing.

"Tell the commander of the cruiser to be aggressive," said Cho Lai.

"If there is a battle?"

"It would be better if it was possible to tell its story in a way that the American was the aggressor," said Cho Lai.

"Very good," said the older man.

"But above all else, we cannot afford to lose such a fight."

"That goes without saying, Your Excellency."

7

Hanoi

Ric Kerfer leaned back in the thickly padded chair, waiting for a signal that the secure line was ready.

In theory, the secure communications room of the American embassy was isolated from all manner of eavesdropping, but Kerfer had his doubts. In his experience, the least secure places were those with the most security precautions. Construct an elaborate mousetrap, and every mouse in the world wanted to test it.

Not to mention the fact that he'd heard rumors that the embassy was a spies' nest. Added to his general distrust of State Department bureaucrats, this made for an impassioned paranoia.

But Kerfer's boss at WARCOM insisted that he use the SCIF, and so here he was.

The light at the bottom of the video panel began to blink yellow, indicating that the secure connection was being established. Kerfer glanced behind him, making sure the room was still empty.

The camera took a few seconds to focus; when it did, Admiral Chris Kelly's face filled the screen. It was pale, his cheeks falling toward the floor, his eyes ringed by folds so thick they looked like targets.

"Lieutenant, good evening."

"Actually, it's morning here, Chris."

Kelly nodded hesitantly, as if confused by the time change. The encryption gear introduced a very slight but noticeable delay in the transmission, and the admiral's lips moved a quarter-second before his words arrived through the headset Kerfer wore.

"How goes it?" asked the admiral. The two men's careers tracked in almost lockstep. He had been Kerfer's superior in a succession of commands practically since Kerfer had been assigned to the SEAL teams.

"I made all the deliveries," Kerfer told him.

"Prognosis?"

"As bad as twelve hours ago. Maybe a little worse. Starting to see some panic in the cities."

Kerfer leaned forward in the chair, feeling the weight of his pistol against his belly. Hopefully he wouldn't have to shoot too many more crazoids before he got the hell out of Dodge.

"Would you suggest sending more gear in?" asked Kelly.

"I don't know." Kerfer rubbed his forehead. "Might slow them down a little. In the end, there's so many of them."

"Mmmm."

The admiral seemed disappointed. Kerfer guessed he was looking for some way of convincing the Pentagon that China should be opposed as harshly as possible—which required an assessment that the Chinese would lose.

Kelly shifted gears. That was one thing he was excellent at: cutting his losses. "What was the agency call about?"

"Murphy has some sort of plan but I don't know what the hell it is. He doesn't like to share."

"What sort of plan?"

Kerfer shook his head. "Behind the lines, I'm guessing."

"Can we do it?"

"Maybe." He hadn't expected the admiral's interest. "I don't know what the outlines are."

"Where is Murphy?"

"He had to go talk to the Viet general."

The admiral stepped back from the camera. The software was supposed to follow his face as he moved around the room, but for some reason it didn't, focusing instead on the admiral's not exactly svelte midsection. Kerfer found this amusing.

"There won't be any WARCOM involvement, I'll tell you that," said Kelly. "But it might be something we'd be interested in backing."

"When you say WARCOM—"

"No teams."

"Why not?"

"There's a shit storm brewing, Ric. Bunch of congressmen want Chester Greene's ass. They may get it, too. They're going to impeach him."

Kerfer snorted in contempt. Nothing zooy politicians did surprised him. But Kelly's disclaimer was not necessarily absolute—it didn't rule out ancillary involvement—say a SEAL or two or three being "loaned" to the CIA. Kerfer felt his adrenaline starting to build. While he'd dismissed Murphy's plan earlier as a nonstarter, now he was angry with himself for not pressing harder to find out what it was.

"General Perry sent his own grenade into the hornet's nest," added the admiral. "Wants us to pull out."

"Yeah. I heard."

"He claims the situation's hopeless. You sounded like you agreed."

"I don't know."

Kerfer didn't see much sense in helping the Vietnamese, who were contemptible as far as actual soldiering went. But he also saw the Chinese as a serious threat to the U.S. If they were allowed to get away with this invasion, then they'd roll into Cambodia and Thailand next.

As for Taiwan, most likely they'd just let it sit out isolated in a Chinese sea, an errant province that was sure to come back home eventually. The only reason to attack it, frankly, would be to provoke the U.S. If that was their goal, they'd probably just as soon go after Japan.

The premier was crazy enough. Which was why he had to be stopped now.

That was all geopolitics. On his own, Kerfer didn't care, except that he liked to be in the middle of things. He liked war, was addicted to it, and this was the war at hand.

"Ultimately, the Viets are going to lose," said Kerfer, deciding it was the geopolitical that the admiral wanted to hear, not the personal. "In the meantime, kicking the Chinese in the teeth as much as possible makes sense."

"And Murphy's plan would do it?"

"No idea," said Kerfer. "He didn't get a good reception from the agency. He didn't get much reception at all."

"I want to talk to him."

"All right." Kerfer wasn't entirely sure where Zeus was, but he figured eventually he would turn up.

"But don't give him much hope. Be straight with him."

"Always am. That's why people love me so much."

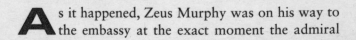 s it happened, Zeus Murphy was on his way to the embassy at the exact moment the admiral

was asking about him. He pulled up to the gate and stopped abruptly, warned by a Marine guard with an M16 in his hands.

Zeus tensed. He wasn't worried about the Marines; it was waiting outside the gate he didn't like. There was a small crowd of people trying to get in, undoubtedly hoping to arrange some passage out of the country. More ominously, Zeus had seen three different groups of young men and women with guns as he drove here; at least one had waved the weapon at him, as if getting ready to fire.

Even though he clearly recognized him, the Marine ordered him to get out of the car so it could be searched. Zeus did so, walking just inside the gate where the gunnery sergeant who was in charge of the detail was watching.

"I've heard some gunfire in the last hour or so," said the gunny.

"It's getting nuttier out there," said Zeus. "Any trouble here?"

"Not yet." The gunny shook his head solemnly. "I thought the Vietnamese were supposed to be pretty self-controlled."

"Looks like somebody took a potshot at you," said the corporal who was looking over his car. He pointed to the rear quarter panel. There were three bullet holes there.

"I didn't even feel it," said Zeus.

"Park on the side," said the gunny, pointing in the direction of a small lot next to the building. "If you need to get gas, there's still a pump working at the back."

"Right."

The Nissan's shifter stuck as Zeus tried to put the car into gear. He rocked the handle back and forth while pressing the clutch, then nearly stalled the little car before getting it through the gate. His hands started to shake; by the time he parked his legs were wobbly and he felt light-headed.

God, he thought. Is this nerves?

Zeus sat in the car for a moment, breathing slowly, trying to recapture his poise. A light mist began to fall. Drops appeared on the windshield, gathering in clumps, occasionally streaking down the glass.

A sharp rap on the window took him by surprise. Zeus started to jerk away but the seatbelt held him in place.

It was one of the Marine sentries. Zeus reached to the window and rolled it down.

"Major Murphy?" asked the Marine.

"Yeah, I'm OK. Can I park here?"

"Yes, sir. Was your car shot at?"

"I don't know. I guess." Zeus smiled weakly, then rolled the window back up and got out. He walked over to the entrance to the building. The guard there asked if he had his personal weapon with him; Zeus tapped the front of his shirt.

"They want, uh, well, you should keep your weapon with you, sir," said the Marine. "Inside."

"Right."

Inside, the hallway was empty. All nonessential personnel had been sent out days before, and Vietnamese nationals working there had been told they needn't report to work. Many of the other embassies in the city had already closed.

In theory, the U.S. had nothing to fear from the Chinese. In theory, they were not enemies.

In theory.

"Major Murphy, I was under the impression that you were on your way back to the States."

Zeus turned and saw Melanie Behrens, the American ambassador to Vietnam, just coming out of a room behind him. She was a petite woman, wearing a polo shirt and khaki pants; in the dimly lit hall she could easily have been mistaken for a teenager.

Until she spoke. Her throaty voice gave an assured snap to her words.

"I'm still here," said Zeus.

"I see."

Behrens was an old friend of Perry's, and so Zeus was on his guard. "Where is General Perry?" he asked.

"As far as I know, he's still sleeping. We gave him a couch upstairs."

Perry had been working nearly nonstop, and though he had quarters in the same hotel where Zeus was staying, he'd spent more than a few nights here.

"I wonder if you could spare a few minutes," said Behrens. "In my office?"

"Sure."

He followed her up the stairs. There was no one else in the halls.

"I understand you were making inquiries about a Vietnamese national," said Behrens as she pulled out her desk chair and sat down. "Why was that?"

"I was concerned about her welfare."

"You know she's been accused of being a traitor?"

"That's ridiculous. She's a doctor. She was saving the life of a wounded man. I think you met her," Zeus added. "When you visited me in the hospital."

"I know of whom we're speaking, yes. And perhaps you're right—for the sake of discussion," Behrens told him. "For the sake of discussion, let's say that I agree that she was innocent. If—"

"I was there the whole time." Zeus tightened his hands into fists, remembering not what he saw in the room when the supervisor argued, but the emotion he felt, the urge to protect Anna from the injustice.

"The difficult part here is that . . ." The ambassador stopped speaking, obviously trying to find the right words. "The U.S. can't be seen as interfering in Vietnamese affairs."

"Sure," said Zeus.

Behrens took this as a surrender, which it wasn't. She was surprised, but moved on.

"Juliet had to mention it to me," she told Zeus. "It was her job."

Juliet was Juliet Greig, the acting consul general. She'd tried to help get Anna freed.

"I don't blame her," answered Zeus.

Behrens pursed her lips, then thought better of saying whatever she had contemplated. Though dressed casually and clearly tired, she maintained a certain dignified composure, the quiet beauty of a self-confident middle-aged woman. Zeus guessed that she had been pretty as a girl, but not stunning; she seemed the rare kind of woman who grew more beautiful as she aged.

"General Perry wants to withdraw all aid to the Vietnamese," she said. "I suppose he told you that."

"He made that pretty clear."

Behrens looked at him a moment. Zeus felt his legs starting to loosen again. What was that? Fatigue? A delayed reaction to everything he'd been through?

Or simply an injury. His body had been battered so badly over the past few days that it was amazing he was still able to stand. By rights he should be in a hospital bed.

Or Anna's bed.

"Do you agree with the general?" asked Behrens.

"What I think . . ." Zeus cleared his throat. "What I think is irrelevant."

"We're speaking off the record, Major."

Zeus didn't answer.

"I think they should be helped," said Behrens flatly. "I think the Chinese have to be stopped."

"You should tell Washington that."

"I already have."

They looked at each other for a moment. Sensing that she might be a good ally, Zeus was tempted to tell her what he was thinking, but he was too worried about the downside if his impressions were wrong.

"How long do you think the Vietnamese can last?" she asked.

"If they can do something to stop the Chinese advance, get them to reassess, then maybe they can hold out," said Zeus. "Once the Chinese armies stop, they have trouble getting their momentum back. Their commanders are extremely cautious. But at this point, doing that would probably take a miracle."

"And if there's no miracle?"

"Another week or two. At best, the Chinese will cut Hanoi off and starve it out. The people are already getting crazy."

Harland Perry rolled over onto his side, his body stiff and cramped. Though in good shape for his age, he had lost a considerable amount of flexibility in his joints and the tissue that connected them. His muscles no longer had the lithe energy they'd had in Ramadi or Baghdad, where he had spent many nights curled up literally on the floor.

The cot they'd set up for him in the small room was barely much better. The crossbar dug into his neck. His neck and spine vibrated gently the way a shocked funny bone would; he felt like a tuning fork that had been accidentally dropped.

"All right," said Perry aloud. He pushed his legs off

the cot and got up unsteadily. He was still wearing his jeans and T-shirt; he and the rest of his small delegation had been ordered to wear civilian clothes during their stay.

He walked over and picked up his service Beretta and holster from the top of the desk. Belatedly he realized it had been foolish to keep it there—too far away to be of use while he was sleeping.

Perry held the gun in his hand a moment. He'd had it a long while. It was a plain weapon, standard-issue: he wasn't a pearl-handle general like Patton.

Then again, no one was like Patton. Patton wasn't even like Patton, at least according to his biographers.

Perry stretched his arms behind his back, trying to loosen his muscles. He sat down on the edge of the cot and pulled on his Merrells, snugging the laces tight before tying them. He picked up his sweatshirt, adjusted his gun belt, then went out into the hall.

He was still getting his bearings when he saw Zeus Murphy in the hall.

"Zeus . . . Major. What are you doing?"

"Coming to see you," said Murphy.

Perry frowned at him. "We have nothing to discuss, Major. A helicopter will pick you up this afternoon at thirteen hundred. That's our flight out."

"You're going to be on that?"

"That's up to the president."

"I have a plan. Sir, I'd like you to at least hear me out."

"I'm in no mood, Zeus," snapped Perry. "I've been damn patient with you until now. Damn patient."

Perry saw Zeus biting the corner of his lip, and immediately felt bad. He'd chosen the officer because he had a head on his shoulders, which to Perry meant that he wasn't afraid to speak his mind—to go against not just what was popular or accepted, but to stand up to a general officer and give his unvarnished opinion.

That was a critical quality, an important trait in a subordinate, or so Perry had always believed. Yet here he was barking at him for doing just that.

Hubris. The occupational hazard of being a general.

"All right, look, I'll listen," Perry told him. "One more time. After I get some coffee. You look like you could use some, too."

"Yes, sir."

They went first to the kitchen, then to the ambassador's office, which she had said Perry could use. They sat in the chairs in front of her desk, Perry upright, sipping his coffee, Zeus pressed forward, his cup on the floor.

Zeus summarized his plan as simply as possible:

Strike the Chinese army group headquarters at Kunming.

It was a DA, or direct action. They'd hit the headquarters, kill the officers, and leave. The Chinese would react with alarm—and not just because they had lost some of their top generals. The entire offensive would grind to a halt while they reevaluated.

"But their headquarters will be well guarded," said Perry.

"You would think so," said Zeus. Unlike the regimental or even divisional headquarters, the army group posts were still staffed as they had been before the start of the war. Security there had always been minimal—which made sense, given their locations.

Zeus knew from the Red Dragon exercises that DAs on group headquarters had been practiced. Even if they hadn't, they were the sort of operation SEALs did all the time. The company that had rescued the American scientist would be Zeus's first choice, but if they weren't available, then he might be able to cobble together a team from the Special Forces unit he had worked with.

Or from Delta. Or a number of other groups, including the CIA.

Zeus stopped speaking. The general brought his coffee slowly to his mouth. The sips he took were quick and small, like a bird nipping at a fountain, thinking any moment it would have to fly off to avoid being swarmed by others higher on the pecking order.

"You don't believe the Vietnamese can pull this off on their own?" asked Perry.

"No," said Zeus. "The Marines who went with me against Hainan weren't disciplined enough to pull it off. They're brave," added Zeus, feeling he should say something positive. "But in this—for this—it would require a lot of skill. And frankly, if we're providing the transport, then it makes sense—"

"You have intel on the location?" asked Perry.

"There's plenty. Kunming's been well mapped. From what I've seen, there's absolutely nothing out of the ordinary there."

"I can't endorse this," said Perry. "I just can't. There's too much . . ."

He stopped speaking and rose from the chair, the coffee cup still in his hand.

"There's too much history here, Zeus. Bad history." Perry paced slowly across the room, looking down at the floor. "And the Chinese are going to win. It's inevitable. They haven't lost; they've only stopped moving. They're way too cautious, but in the end, that doesn't translate into a victory for the other side."

"The Chinese have to be stopped before they go beyond Vietnam."

"Don't you think I know that?" Perry raised his voice almost to a shout. Zeus was surprised—he hadn't realized how angry the general was. "This isn't the place or the time to make a stand. Not with the Vietnamese as our allies. It's . . . it's futile, damn it. And I'm not going to be known as the idiot who told the president anything to the contrary. Damn, it's so obvious . . . Take a step back, Zeus. Take a step back."

Perry lowered his voice. The knuckles on his fingers gripping his coffee cup were white. He put the cup in the other hand, then stared at the fingers, flexing them slowly.

"I'm not going to get into an argument with you, Major," said Perry, still looking at his hand. "I realize you've been through a lot. And that you may have personal complications. I have to do my job. And so do you. I expect you on that helicopter."

It took every ounce of will power for Zeus to walk from the room without saying anything else.

He wasn't sure what he was going to do when he got downstairs. He took a step toward the front entrance, then remembered where he had parked and realized it would be easier to get there from the side door. He turned in that direction.

"Zeus," said Kerfer, stepping out from under the stairwell. "We need to talk."

"All right."

"Not here," added the SEAL officer. "You got a car?"

8

Forthright, Ohio

Josh MacArthur slumped into the big chair in his cousin's living room. He had a beer in his hand but he didn't feel much like drinking. Nor did he want to watch television, though his cousin's wife had left it on for him when she went off to bed—"scooted" was her word.

He was alone in the room. Free not only from his relatives but his bodyguard.

Not for long, however. He heard the toilet flush down the hall and waited for Tex to appear.

Tex was a U.S. marshal who had been assigned to watch Josh after his return from Vietnam with evidence of Chinese atrocities there. At the time, the news was considered explosive, even world changing—more than enough to provide the motive for an assassination.

Tex had stayed on even after Josh appeared before the UN general assembly with his taped evidence. It seemed beside the point now—there were so many different reports coming out of the region, all of them contradictory. And though the UN had condemned China in an initial vote, nothing tangible had come from it. The U.S. was slowly building support for sanctions, but Josh was not needed for that; no one had objected when he bolted for home.

His cousin's home, actually. He himself had no real home; he'd led the life of a nomadic scientist for several years before stumbling into notoriety in northern Vietnam.

"Hey, what are we watchin'?" asked Tex. He had a very un-Texan-like first name—Terrence—but otherwise the nickname fit him as well as his custom-made boots.

"Anything you want," said Josh. "You want a beer?"

"Can't while I'm working."

"It's after nine."

"Yup."

Tex picked up the remote control and fiddled with the channels. He stopped on the Weather Channel, watching the summary for the next day: clear skies, highs in the fifties.

"Warm, right?" said Tex. "Global warming, huh?"

Not long before, Josh would have grimaced. As a scientist who had devoted himself to studying the effects of climate change, he felt personally insulted, even assailed, when people spoke so cavalierly about it. The phenomenon was extremely complex, and not one event, let alone temperature or precipitation pattern, could be ascribed to it.

Now it didn't bother him. He wasn't even sure if he was going to continue in the field—any scientific field. Maybe he'd work the farm. With the recent bump-up in commodity prices, it might actually provide a good living.

Tex continued to channel surf. He settled for a few moments on a rerun of an old '60s era black-and-white sitcom.

"You ever see this?" he asked Josh. *"Andy Griffith Show."* Tex laughed. "Andy Griffith is this small-town sheriff and he's got a little kid. Screwball deputy named Barney. Pretty funny."

"I don't think I've ever seen it."

"Kinda funny."

Tex settled back in the chair. On the screen, the sheriff was trying to find a way to rehabilitate a local ne'er-do-well, who was more misunderstood than evil.

Did sheriffs do that sort of thing anymore?

Did they do it *ever*?

"Ya know, they're thinking I should go back," said Tex.

"I'm sorry, what?"

"My bosses. They're wondering if it would be all right to pull me back. They want to leave it up to y'all."

"It's OK with me."

"They think the guy in New York—they figure that was an isolated incident. I mean like the end of it. After he went off the bridge, no one else was assigned to get you. It'd be besides the point. See, there's been so much publicity and everything—"

"It's not a problem," said Josh. "Really, it's fine."

He looked at the beer bottle.

"You're kind of down about Mara, right?" said Tex.

"What are you, my shrink?"

Tex laughed. "We're a full-service shop."

But the marshal let the matter drop. Mara was Mara Duncan, the CIA officer who had rescued Josh from the jungles of Vietnam after he'd been caught behind the lines. They'd fallen in love during the ordeal.

He had fallen in love. She seemed to have forgotten him, not answering his texts, or picking up the phone when he called.

Maybe he should try harder.

"Well, maybe I'll turn in." Tex rose. "I'll make arrangements. Probably leave around noon." He was quiet for a moment. "But if ya'll want me to stay, that's not a problem at all."

"I like you, Tex, but they're right. I'm kind of irrelevant now."

"You're not irrelevant, Doc. You did an important thing."

"Past tense. Time to move on."

Tex curled his lower lip around the upper, then nodded.

"See ya in the morning," he told Josh.

"Have a good sleep."

Josh angled himself against the corner of the chair, watching Andy Griffith instruct a miscreant on how to improve his life and become a worthy member of society. The man nodded thoughtfully, and promised to try.

Did they ever do that anywhere other than television, Josh wondered. If so, what had happened to that world?

9

Hanoi

Kerfer had Zeus drive over to Da Dinh Square, the center of the large area honoring Ho Chi Minh and the soldiers who had fought to liberate the country. Always a shrine to "Uncle Ho," as the patriarch was known, the area had become an open-air camp for refugees and pilgrims. People whose houses had been destroyed crowded next to others who saw Ho Chi Minh's spirit as their only hope.

Thousands of Vietnamese sat on the grass squares in front of the large mausoleum where Ho's body was interred. Many more thronged around the entrance to the mausoleum itself, waiting to get in, either not knowing or not caring that the leader's body had been removed for safekeeping. They had come to seek solace or guidance from the dead leader's spirit; they hoped somehow that it could be impressed to save them from the destruction their enemy to the north had unleashed. The crowd was so large that the procession of supplicants seemed barcly to move from the distance.

Here and there, tents and cloth shelters had been erected, but most of the people who'd spent the night here had done so in the open air and were wet from the morning drizzle. Though the rain had stopped, the gray sky added to the sense of doom that Zeus felt as they left the car at the side of the road and walked up along the police barriers, edging along the crowd.

Candles and makeshift altars had been left under the barriers, remnants from the very start of the war, when the area had been temporarily closed off by the police and army. Those forces had been moved to more important tasks, and there were now no guards visible anywhere.

Unlike the streets Zeus had passed through earlier, there were no teenage thugs here, no disorder at all. Here, the traditional spirit of Vietnam and the calm stoicism of the people prevailed. Perhaps it was because of the age of most of those in the square—they were mostly old, too old to join actively in the fight except as a very last gesture of desperation.

Many were women. A few had young children with them, so that as Zeus walked he had the sense that an entire generation of Vietnam had gone missing; anyone from fifteen to their early fifties was manning the defenses somewhere.

"Why are we walking here?" Zeus asked Kerfer. They had barely spoken since leaving the embassy.

"Only place I'm sure we can be alone."

"In a crowd?"

"Damn straight. You never heard of that?"

"But the car?"

"It'll be OK."

"You think it's bugged," said Zeus, belatedly deciphering Kerfer's paranoia.

The SEAL just smiled.

A Chinese bomb had made a crater at one side of the square earlier in the war. The space had been trampled down by the feet of the supplicants, the jagged edges of the blast area smoothed away like ancient stones in a riverbed. It was now simply a dirt-lined depression, a feature of the landscape barely noticed by the people sitting and in some cases lying there.

Kerfer threaded through the crowd, moving around so he could survey the area behind them and see if they were being followed. Zeus was too absorbed in looking at the crowd to see anything but the faces of the people near them. He expected maybe despair or blank hopelessness, but that wasn't there. The expressions were more purposeful, eyes set and mouths taut at the edges, the way people on their way to work might face a hill or some other physical obstacle—not an impassible barrier, just something they knew they had to get past to get where they were going. The expressions surprised him; he wanted a neat package of emotions, one way or the other: triumph or despair.

There were a few puddles on the concrete portions of the square. The grass between the paths had been flattened into dirt and red mud; the few bits not covered by people were streaked with ash and soot.

The two Americans drew a few stares as they passed among the crowd, but most of the people were indifferent to them, glancing and then turning back to whatever it was they'd been doing. A number had small hibachi-like stoves and were making breakfast. The charcoal smoke stung Zeus's nose.

"All right, tell me exactly what you're thinking," said Kerfer, stopping. "What's your plan?"

They were almost in the exact middle of a large group of Vietnamese gathered around a half-dozen barrels being used to cook fish and a few vegetables. Steam rose from the makeshift grills, the moisture-laden air sizzling.

Zeus glanced around.

"They're not going to worry about what we're saying." Kerfer frowned, then turned and squinted in the distance, surveying the area. "Not one in a hundred speak English."

"They're going to strike north," he told Kerfer. "Beyond the border. Trung."

"Uh-huh."

"We could use it as a diversion," he told him.

"I'm not following you." Kerfer folded his arms across his chest, then turned around, gazing in the direction of Ho Chi Minh's Mausoleum. "Damn food's making me hungry."

"I want to chop the head off at Kunming," said Zeus, trusting Kerfer would figure out what he meant. "A quick action. Direct."

Kerfer didn't respond. A little girl nearby started to sob. A woman who looked old enough to be her great-grandmother came and folded her against her legs, stooping over to comfort her. She shot Zeus a nasty look, and suddenly he felt as if everyone was watching him. He turned his head left and right, trying to reassure himself that he was still anonymous here—or at least ignored.

"Grab the brass," Zeus told Kerfer. "That's what I mean."

"I know what you mean, Major," said the SEAL, his voice tired. "You don't think I guessed? You don't think the Chinks will? They'll be ready."

The slur bothered Zeus for some reason he couldn't express, or even fathom—after all, he wanted to kill them all.

"They don't think they can be attacked," he told Kerfer. "Their security's not the best."

Kerfer didn't answer.

"You don't think it can be done?" asked Zeus.

"Anything can be done, Major. Shit, let's go get some food. I'm starving."

R ic Kerfer liked to think of his brain as having two very distinct parts. One half he thought of as a doctor—a surgeon, actually, the man he might have been had his interests taken him in a different direction. Kerfer in fact came from a family of doctors, something no one would guess and Kerfer would never admit, not willingly anyway.

The surgeon half was analytic, careful, intelligent. It stood above the world, or at least the patient, analyzing and dissecting, planning coldly what should and must be done. It weighed the odds mathematically, and rendered decisions with cold precision. It did not gamble.

The other half was all impulse and rage. That half loved war and fighting. Action and adrenaline were like oxygen, necessary, craved when missing for only a few moments.

The two halves were at war now, the sensible side saying the plan was outrageous and ridiculous, too far a long shot; the adrenaline side said it was brilliant, genius in its daring, and the only hope for Vietnam.

It was all these things at once, idiotic and beautiful. And Kerfer wanted to be the one to pull it off.

Was that just the crazy, feeling half talking, the side that had managed to get him through BUD/S and then let him survive and thrive in the Teams? Or was the surgeon there, too, thinking, debating, weighing: there was glory in brilliance, and triumph. As smart as the surgeon was, he, too, wanted to show off and be celebrated.

Kerfer had never seen the Chinese headquarters buildings at Kunming, but he knew well how the security would be arranged—he'd practiced a mock take-down against an army corps command post three months before with the Japanese. In fact, Zeus's idea could have been lifted from the doctrine that they had been practicing: guillotine the leaders, and the Chinese would stop dead in their tracks.

It might not even take a successful mission to do it. The Chinese were *so* risk adverse. Kerfer could see it in the way they had stopped almost immediately when Zeus had blown up a few of their tanks near the coast.

They drove to the Discovery Best Hotel, a Western-style luxury building not far from the square. Its restaurant was packed with journalists and probably more than a few spies, but Kerfer knew he could trust the food.

Zeus said no more than a few words as they ate. Kerfer, letting his two sides battle unconsciously, waved for the waiter to take the egg-stained plate from the table.

"Get me a beer," he told the man.

The waiter gave him a slightly disapproving look; it was still well before noon. Kerfer laughed.

"War rules," he said.

The man disappeared into the kitchen.

"I'm assuming you don't want one," he told Zeus.

"No."

"Probably help whatever hangover you got from last night."

"I don't have a hangover."

"You look like you do. You sleep lately?"

"Not really."

"Figures."

Kerfer looked up as the bartender approached. He carried a Tsingtao, but seemed oblivious to the irony. Kerfer thanked him, then gave him a twenty to pay for their bill. It was American, the only currency now being accepted despite the strict laws against doing so.

"Let's go for a walk," said Kerfer, taking the bottle. He rose and led Zeus out into a courtyard at the side. They were alone in the Buddhist-style garden, but as Kerfer sat down on one of the stone benches, a jet screamed overhead, reminding them of the war, the ultimate intruder.

Kerfer took out his small bug detecting device and set it between them. He spoke a few words, making sure it didn't pick up anything, then put it away. The device only detected transmissions, but this was an unlikely place for a bug in any event. Still, Kerfer was cautious, and spoke cryptically.

"Tell you right off, you're not going to get the Teams to do it," said Kerfer. He studied Zeus's face to make sure he understood what he meant—*Teams* being a slang stand-in for SEALs.

"I've pretty much come to that conclusion," said Zeus.

"But that doesn't mean it can't work."

Zeus's eyes, which had been drifting back and forth in the direction of the building and the boarded windows facing them, shot back toward Kerfer's.

Until that moment, Kerfer hadn't been exactly sure what he was going to do, hadn't known which half of him would win out. But now it was clear: he was in, all the way in, because this was too beautiful, too perfect, to miss. His caution melted. He was gung-ho.

"I know a group run by a guy who works for the agency," said Kerfer. "Nasty guy. Very dark."

"Worse than you?"

Kerfer laughed. "I'm Miss Mary Fuckin' Sunshine compared to him. I am fuckin' Gandhi. This guy could do it. His people. I worked with him before."

"How do I talk to him?"

"You don't. I do."

"When?"

"As soon as I can. I may have to go back to the embassy and use the SCIF. I have to talk to a middleman."

"I'm supposed to leave here by one. Helicopter's supposed to pick me up."

"Miss it."

"Go AWOL?"

"Just be late." Kerfer took a long pull from the beer. He didn't like Tsingtao all that much, he decided. Too watery. "Get stuck in traffic."

"Yeah. OK."

"Or you can leave if you want. I can do this on my own."

"You're going to need help from the Vietnamese. I can arrange that."

"I don't want them helping."

"You have to coordinate it with their attack. They're going up to Malipo."

"China?"

"Yeah. You could leave from there. This way, you could use Vietnamese equipment. They'd never trace it to the U.S."

"OK. Yeah. You should hang around then." Kerfer eyed the beer. "Why are you helping them? Not the girl?"

Clearly it was. Zeus didn't answer.

"Where is she?" Kerfer asked.

"I don't know. Can you help me find her?"

"Probably not. The only prison I know of is north of the city. It's a place called Nam Hong. Pretty nasty."

"How do I get up there?"

Kerfer didn't know, and wasn't sure he'd tell him if he had.

"Maybe I'll check it out."

Zeus glanced at his watch. Kerfer lifted the bottle and took another swig. "Sure you don't want some?"

"No."

"Wise." He let the bottle fall from his hand. It bounced rather than broke, the remaining contents swirling on the ground. "Give me a lift back. If you drop me off around the block, no one'll see."

10

Langley CIA headquarters

Mara Duncan ran her fingers through her hair, then reached across the desk for her cola. The can was warm. She'd gotten it hours ago but had forgotten about it.

She'd also lost track of time. That wasn't particularly hard to do in the windowless room Group 86 had taken over. The unit was an ad hoc collection of Vietnam and Southeast Asia experts and others assigned by the CIA to "monitor and affect" the situation in Vietnam and China. It was a subgroup of two larger units, established to study Chinese methods and look for opportunities to sabotage the Chinese advance.

"I'm going to go get something to drink," Mara told Jon Harmuth, who was the only other officer in the room at the moment. "Want anything?"

"No. Thanks."

There was a soda machine at the far end of the hall near the stairwell. Mara got a Coke—she needed the caffeine—then decided to stretch her legs a bit. Not wanting to get too far away, she walked back in the direction of the subgroup's room, passing it and then turning back around. One of the agency's monitoring rooms used to keep track of various news reports around the world was located at the far end. Mara walked down past the doors, turned around and started back. An analyst nearly knocked her over as he came out the door; he fell back apologetically, a bashful smile on his face.

The smile made her think of Josh. She wanted to see him.

Wanted to make love to him, more accurately.

Stop thinking of him, she told herself. She needed to focus on her job. She took a sip of the soda, then started walking again, feeling a little awkward about following the man who'd just bumped into her. He stopped at the soda machine, getting himself a Coke.

"Busy night?" he said as she approached.

"Moderately."

He gave her a smile so tight it could have been a grimace, then bent down to get the soda. Mara sipped hers pensively. This wasn't a place for small talk, but she felt trapped, not wanting to be rude. The man glanced at her as he straightened, perhaps expecting her to flirt. He was about her height; ten years older, heavier. He was wearing a button-down shirt tucked into jeans, and the pants were baggy just below the hips, in her mind the sign of a once-athletic man who'd let himself go to pot. He smelled slightly of sweat.

"Interesting times," he said.

"Oh yes."

His eyes left hers and swept downward, clumsily checking her out.

"See ya," he said, turning and leaving.

The tacit rejection was such a relief that she didn't mind it, rolling her eyes mentally as she watched his sagging rump walk down the hallway. She fished in her pocket for more change; when she couldn't find it she resorted to a five-dollar bill and got another soda for later.

Even with her creds programmed to allow entry, she had to be buzzed back into the task group room—a bit of oversensitive security added since her last return to the States, or maybe just a procedure she'd never been lucky enough to encounter. As she was waiting for Harmuth to go over and look at the monitor, Peter Lucas came out of the elevator and down the hall.

"You're up early," said Lucas.

"Never went to bed."

"Didn't think so."

Lucas was chief of station for Southeast Asia, and until the crisis had been operating out of Bangkok, Thailand. He'd come back to the States to deliver a personal briefing to the president. Given everything that was going on, it was easier to monitor the situation from the States than Thailand, and so he had stayed.

"So—where are we, Mara?" he asked once they were all inside the room. "Do they have a dirty bomb or not?"

"It looks that way, but I still don't have proof. I have the missile shipments, the material—"

"It's not like you're going to find a blueprint," said Harmuth. "It's always going to be circumstantial."

"If they have a weapon there, don't you think they'd be preparing to use it?"

"If they have missile launchers in the mines, they can be ready inside an hour," said Mara. "The roads between Hanoi and the Yen Tu Mountain are open. The area is still a no-fly zone."

"So which mine is it in?" asked Lucas.

Harmuth folded his arms. They didn't know.

"I'd like to go up there and find out," said Mara.

"Take too long. If we're going to have somebody go in there, Mara, it'll be somebody closer."

The area was thick with mines, and they were too widespread to simply destroy each one.

"When are you talking to the president?" asked Mara.

"Soon." He rubbed his chin. Mara noticed for the first time that he hadn't shaved that morning. "How long before they collapse?"

"Any day," said Harmuth. "If not sooner."

"We have to push that off," said Lucas.

"It'll take a miracle."

Lucas pushed his chair over to one of the empty terminals and began scanning the latest updates. Mara went back to hers, and saw that there was a message from Ric Kerfer. He was at the embassy and wanted to talk to her on a secure line.

"OK," she typed on the message system, unhooking her headset from the lamp arm next to the computer.

11

Outside Hanoi

When he left Kerfer, Zeus found himself in a contemplative mood, unsure and unfocused. He wanted to find Anna, but he doubted he had enough time. If he missed the helicopter out, Perry would think he had disobeyed him.

He'd think that because he had. On the other hand, if Kerfer could help him put together the plan to hit the Chinese army group headquarters, that was worth staying for.

So was Anna. More so.

The weight of what he was contemplating—going against Perry's orders—had suddenly become real to him.

He hadn't disobeyed his commander *yet*. He'd gone pretty far, helping the Vietnamese when he was expected to be getting ready to leave. But once he missed that helicopter, he'd be on dangerous ground. What would happen next depended completely on Perry.

Zeus's mind rolled around and around. He drove over to his hotel. He started to go up to his room, then instead went to the desk and asked how he would find Nam Hong.

The clerk wanted to know why. Zeus told him he needed to see a soldier there.

The instructions were easy, once he was out of the city. Zeus thought he might have enough time to get there and get back before the helicopter left. If he could find Anna, they could leave together. He'd insist.

Zeus was a dozen blocks from the hotel when the traffic suddenly thickened and then stalled. He waited for a little while, then saw an opening to his left. He turned down the street, took another left and headed south, trying to remember the way to the road that ran along the west side of West Lake; he knew he could use it to get on the highway north.

But he quickly became lost. To his surprise he found himself at the circle near the Cầu Giấy bridge, a major crossroad in the southwestern part of the city. He managed to get onto the main road heading north, but he hadn't gone more than a hundred yards or so down the divided highway before he came to a blockade.

It was manned by two soldiers, who were blocking off the two lanes north with a troop truck. Neither man seemed particularly alarmed as he came to a stop. They left their AK-47s slung over their shoulders and looked at him quizzically, more like a visitor to a zoo might examine a species he'd never seen than soldiers wary of a saboteur or spy.

Zeus tried to explain that he had to get to the U.S. embassy—he thought mentioning the prison might be problematic—but neither man spoke English. He showed them the passes the Vietnamese had given him; one of the soldiers took the papers and laminated card, frowned deeply, then started to walk back to the truck.

"Wait," said Zeus. He opened the door and got out of the car. He had been told several times not to get separated from his paperwork—the passes might be very valuable to anyone seeking to escape over the border.

The man ignored him. Zeus followed him to the truck; the other soldier stayed behind and began examining the car.

There was a portable radio unit in the cab of the truck. The soldier pulled it out and held it up, apparently radioing for instructions. He continued to ignore Zeus, not even glancing in his direction.

The soldier fell silent, listening. Then finally he put the radio back down in the truck. Whatever the man on the other side of the conversation said didn't seem to settle the matter, for not only did he keep the papers but he continued to ignore Zeus, walking toward his companion.

"All right, so are we going to move this thing?" asked Zeus.

Neither man acknowledged him as they exchanged a few words. Apparently Zeus's car had passed muster, since the man who'd looked it over had closed the driver's door and made no move to stop Zeus as he approached.

"Đ" said Zeus. "Go?" He motioned with his hands. "If you move the truck—"

Zeus pantomimed driving away, then pointed at the truck. Nothing seemed to work; both men stared at him blankly.

"All right—give me my papers," he told them. He was still speaking English, of course, but his gestures made what he wanted obvious. When the soldier didn't hand them over, Zeus reached and took them, his anger starting to grow. The man resisted only slightly— even if he had no idea who Zeus was, the fact that the American had a pass from the man's commander in chief surely had some weight.

There was a deep ditch on one side of the road and

a curb on the other; the truck was situated in a way that there was no getting around it. Zeus started the car and turned to back up. The soldiers finally came alive, yelling at him. Now it was his turn to ignore them. He stepped on the gas, backing up quickly to get away. He glanced up to make sure they weren't aiming their guns at him—the weapons remained slung over their shoulders—and then started to back into a U-turn.

He'd just completed it and started to straighten out the wheel when a pickup truck turned into the intersec·‧ ‧low. Zeus edged toward the far side of the right lane as the truck approached, horn blaring and lights flashing. Suddenly the truck veered across his path. Zeus hit the brakes.

"Shit," he cursed, reaching for his pistol. The other driver jumped from the truck, waving his hands.

It was Major Chaū, the translator Trung had assigned to help him.

"Major Zeus!" shouted Chaū. "Finally! I have been looking around the city since this morning."

"Chaū? Where's Anna? I need to find her . . . General Trung—"

"I will take you. Come now; we need to go to Van Tri."

"Van Tri? The golf club?"

"Yes, yes—I believe that is where she is."

V an Tri was a private golf club, the only private golf club in the country, in fact. Being held at a country club, even one in Vietnam, had to be worlds better than being held in a military prison, where Zeus had been led to believe Anna was.

But he quickly realized there was little reason to be optimistic as soon as they arrived. The army was here in force, and the gate was guarded by an officious cap-

tain who seemed to care little that Chaū outranked
him. It took Major Chaū a good five minutes to get
the man to call his superior, and even then he had to
raise his voice and invoke Trung's name several times
before they were admitted.

Bad signs, not just for retrieving Anna, but for the
war effort.

A sergeant met them in front of the clubhouse, an
elaborate set of interconnected buildings and pavilions
surrounding a pool. The man greeted them with a silent salute, spun on his heel and led them into the two-
story building at the front of the cluster. They walked
straight through to a cement portico and turned right,
heading around the pool to a second building.

Zeus thought for a moment that he might see Anna.
He imagined himself holding her—he lost himself for
a moment in the anticipation, heart racing as the sergeant pulled open the door.

The sergeant stayed behind as they entered a room
set up as an office, with a row of two-draw high vertical files on the left and a large desk in the middle.

"Should we go in?" Zeus asked, pointing to the
open doorway in the partition at the back of the room.

Chaū hesitated; by the time he answered, "I don't
know," Zeus had already reached the doorway. But it
was clear even before he stepped through that no one
was there; the space was completely empty.

"Are they coming to us?" Zeus asked Chaū.

"I'm not sure," said Chaū. "I don't know anyone
here."

The door at the front of the small building opened.
A captain entered, then stepped aside, making way for
an officer so tall that his head was in danger of hitting
the top of the doorway. The man, a colonel, would
have been tall even in the U.S., but in Vietnam he rated
as a giant.

The captain began speaking in rapid Vietnamese. Chaū answered directly to the colonel.

"What's going on?" Zeus asked Chaū.

Chaū held him off with a gesture of his hand while he continued to press his point with the colonel. Zeus's anger began to rise. He could shoot the son of a bitch, him and his punk-faced captain, take over these idiots' prison, and free Anna himself.

"Anna isn't here," said Chaū finally.

"Where is she?"

"He doesn't know."

Something in Chaū's voice warned Zeus not to ask any more questions—Zeus guessed it was because one or both of the other officers spoke English and he was afraid that Zeus would say something that might anger them.

But Zeus was angry himself.

"I'm not leaving here without Anna," he told the colonel. "General Trung himself said she would be released to me. You're not going to disobey him, are you?"

The colonel frowned but didn't respond. Zeus turned to Chaū.

"Tell him. Tell him to comply."

"We do not have the girl," said the captain in thickly accented English.

"Well, where is she?" demanded Zeus.

The captain said something Vietnamese to Chaū.

"He's insisting she was sent to Hanoi," explained Chaū. "That can't be . . . I'd have known."

"We should look over their prisoners. Maybe the identity is mistaken," Zeus added.

"Yes."

The possibility of a mistake gave them a face-saving way to produce Anna, but it didn't work. The captain continued to insist that they had sent her to Hanoi.

Zeus continued to insist that they show him the

other prisoners. Finally, the colonel frowned, raised his hand, and left.

"All right," said the captain. "Come then."

Zeus and Chaū followed him out of the building and across the patio to the last building in the small complex. Zeus was surprised when they continued past the building in the direction of a pair of troop trucks parked in the rough of the nearby golf course. At first, he thought that the captain was going to use the truck to take them to the actual prison. It wasn't until the captain pulled aside the tarp at the back of one of the trucks that Zeus realized the vehicles themselves were the holding cells. Two dozen people, all bound hand and foot and chained together, sat in the truck. A few stared at him; the others dozed or gazed aimlessly at the canvas at the top of the truck. The captain barked orders, apparently telling them to rise. A few struggled to do so, but it was hopeless; they were either too tired or too closely bound to make more than a token effort.

"Anna?" said Zeus, "Anna, are you there?"

He craned his neck, then pulled himself up onto the bar that formed the rear bumper and looked the prisoners over. She wasn't there.

Zeus jumped back down. He followed silently to the second truck. How many of these people, he wondered, were guilty of what Anna had done—their jobs? Prosecuting a doctor for trying to save a life was surely not the way to win a war.

There were more inmates in the second truck, and if anything they were in an even more pathetic state. The stench of human waste nearly knocked Zeus over. But he climbed up onto the back of the truck, glanced around, and called Anna's name several times before giving up. The people seemed in such a bad way, he was tempted to claim one was her.

"So you see, we do not harbor her," said the captain.

As Chaū and the captain talked, Zeus tried to focus his thoughts on what to do next. If he was going to catch the helicopter, he had to get back soon. It might already be too late.

Love or duty? How did a man choose?

Duty first. Always. Yet in his heart, she was what he wanted.

"Major?"

Zeus snapped out of his thoughts. He was surprised to see that the captain had left them.

"I'm not sure what to do," said Chaū. "We can go back to Hanoi and I can make calls."

"What about Nam Hong prison?" said Zeus.

Chaū got a funny look on his face. "Nam Hong?"

"Someone told me I should look there."

"I doubt she's there. I don't think so, no."

"Let's see for ourselves anyway."

"Major, we can, but it's probably a waste of time."

"Let's go there anyway," said Zeus.

"If you wish."

12

Hanoi

Kerfer plopped down in the chair.

"About fuckin' time you got back to me," he said as he pulled on the headset. "What the hell do you people in Washington do?"

"We're having an orgy in the office, Ric," said Mara Duncan. "What the hell do you think?"

"I think I'm in the middle of a fuckin' war and I expect some backup," said Kerfer. He knew he was being over-the-top cranky, but in his experience that was the only way to deal with the agency. If you didn't go balls-to-the-wall with them and hit them hard, they never paid attention to you.

Besides, she should have gotten *right* back to him, not made him sit in the stinking embassy basement jerking off. What if his life had been on the line?

The video on the screen showed nothing beyond Mara's face. The program blanked out the back of the room behind her. If she moved too quickly back, her features blurred, as if it were some sort of funhouse mirror effect.

Fortunately, she tended to sit in one place and stare

at the small camera he imagined was at the top of her monitor.

Not the prettiest girl he'd ever seen, but she'd do. She was a tough one in a clinch.

"I need to talk to a guy I worked with," Kerfer told Mara. "I know he's with the agency."

"Who?"

"Roth Setco."

"Roth?" She threw her head straight back; her eyes merged with her chest. "Why?"

"Murph has an idea."

"Major Murphy?"

"Yeah."

"I thought he was in the hospital."

"He's out. The Vietnamese are planning to attack north. He wants to set up something to go further. It's actually a pretty good idea. Setco and I did something similar in Malaysia."

"You were in Malaysia?"

"You don't have my résumé?"

"It's not in there."

As Kerfer explained Murphy's plan, Mara reached over to the keyboard of her computer and began punching up files. Kerfer's assessment of the typical security arrangements seemed overly optimistic, even to Mara, who had dealt with the Chinese in Malaysia up close and personally. She keyed in the access codes to the briefing data on Chinese army headquarters from memory, even though she hadn't looked at the files since coming to the States, and began paging through.

When she found Kunming, she tapped in the most recent satellite images and then the running blog data of intel assessments connected to the headquarters.

There were way too many entries to even scan easily, and so she had to add different filters to make the list more manageable.

In the meantime, Kerfer outlined a mission that would last no more than two hours, in and out. The core was breathtakingly simple; once past the outer ring of guards, security was light—typically two men at or near the door, then a single one in the hall beyond.

Mara saw a reference in an agency document to an exercise that had been conducted to test the contingencies of hitting a Chinese corps-level headquarters. It had been undertaken by a Japanese special operations team and a platoon of SEALs; the report author's initials were R. K.

Not a coincidence, she guessed.

"All right?" said Kerfer. "You gonna hook me up with Setco or what?"

"I don't understand. This is a SEAL operation?"

"I don't think we can get it approved," said Kerfer. "WARCOM's gonna balk. You guys can help run it. I know Setco's got people."

"He's in Thailand."

"A half hour away by plane."

Mara shook her head, the edges fuzzing. "I can do it."

Kerfer didn't answer right away—naturally, because he didn't think that a woman could run a black op. Asshole.

Mara started working details in her head—she had already had some of her best contacts lost during the conflict. But there were plenty of people available. A dozen Korean mercenaries were sitting around getting wasted in Myanmar at the moment, smoking white tiger weed and having hallucinations.

Dependable enough if you sobered them up, willing enough if you promised them enough money.

"No offense, but I've never worked with you," said Kerfer. "I have worked with Setco."

"Where? On training missions?"

"Screw you."

"And why do you think an army corps command is going to be as easy to hit as a Chinese army command?" added Mara. "I know you studied the corps—"

"First of all, the way the Chinese are organized, their idea of a regional army *is* a corps command," said Kerfer. "In our terms. The equivalent. You don't fuckin' know that? Shit."

Mara felt herself flush. She was out of her depth when it came to talking about army organization—to be honest, she had only the barest textbook understanding of what a corps actually was—two or more divisions working together in an army command. Kerfer had found her weakness, one of them anyway.

"I can get intel," she said defensively.

Why was she back on her heels? Why was she feeling embarrassed? The hell with Kerfer—she'd seen more shit in Malaysia than he had in his entire career, she was sure of it. Goddamn SEAL blowhard.

"If we're going to pull this off, it's gotta come together fast," said Kerfer. "The Viets are ready to move. So either get me in touch with Setco or get over here yourself."

"What's your command going to say when we ask permission to use you?"

"Why the hell would you ask anyone permission?" demanded Kerfer indignantly. "Get me fucking Setco's contact info, would you?"

"Calm down, Ric," snapped Mara. "Take a deep fucking breath, and let's see what we can come up with."

13

Kunming, China

Li Sun, freshly promoted to two-star general from the rank of colonel, looked around the staff room. Yesterday, every one of the dozen men staring at him with barely disguised contempt outranked him. Now he was their superior.

And yet, being their boss did not make him their leader. It took nothing to guess that they did not respect him. He was sure that, to a man, they believed his promotion was due entirely to the fact that he was the premier's nephew.

Certainly, there was truth in that. But the greater truth was the fact that the offensive had stalled. It had stalled because these men were mice. They were timid holdovers from the antique times—remnants of the age when America had ruled the world.

Now it was China's turn. The new generation—Li Sun's generation—would push the old West out of the way.

The commander of Army Group South Two, General Cài Ming, had been recalled to Beijing, where the premier would present him with a choice: resignation from the army in shame, or quiet suicide with a guaranteed pension for his family.

Li Sun believed the old general was such a coward that he would resign. That probably would not save him: The premier did not particularly like to have old generals available for the opposition to rally around.

But that was not Li Sun's concern. He had to deal with these men, the division commanders and top staff for what had now been designated as the Eighth Chinese Expeditionary Army Group—a title chosen by Li Sun for its appropriateness: bā (Pinyin for eight) signified prosperity and had long been associated with good luck and the empire. Thus in one fell swoop the unit was linked with the past and the future. It made considerably more sense than the dull association with the region that had been used in the past.

Li Sun turned to a map of Southeast Asia, encompassing a good portion of southern China as well as Laos, Thailand, and Vietnam south to Hue. Large red pins marked the location of the Chinese troops in western and eastern Vietnam. The markers that showed the goals of the advance by this date of the battle— considerably farther south—had been removed before Li Sun's arrival. He had ordered them restored, a reminder of the generals' collective failure.

Army Group South 2 had taken a purely defensive posture, spreading its forces along the border. From the beginning of the war, the group's three divisions had been profoundly unaggressive. A few units had moved a few hundred meters over the border. The rest had simply dug in.

Li Sun had spent the last twenty-four hours studying the situation. While admittedly the group had been given a small role in the overall attack, it had wasted even that. To Li Sun's disappointment, he had reached the conclusion that the divisions closest to the front could not be moved quickly. So he had devised an elaborate plan to take three different divisions, which had been reserves, and put them on the offensive. As the drive proceeded, he would move units piecemeal from those on the border, feeding them in to fuel his attack on Hanoi.

The situation here was a microcosm of the war in general. Overall, China had a numerical superiority to the Vietnamese that should be overwhelming. But its forces were poorly arrayed. In any given sector, the greatest part of the Chinese troops was in the rear, held as reserves. Even in the western area, where there had been great gains, two entire divisions were still in China, more than eight hundred kilometers from the front.

Why?

Why indeed. Things were even more absurd in the east along the coast, where the Chinese had been stalled by a much smaller force of Vietnamese. But Li Sun's concerns were here, in the central front, which had yet to be exploited.

"Our most important task is to meet the enemy and crush him," said Li Sun. He went to the map and tapped at a blotch just to the right of dead center. "The enemy has concentrated a force at Tuyên Quang," he said. "It is the equivalent of a tank brigade, though they call it a division. It is their finest unit, and the only one capable of meeting us on the road to Hanoi. We will attack and demolish it, then we will go on to Hanoi."

Li Sun looked at each general in turn. Each wore the same emotionless, pasty face, the same clueless expression. Finally, one of them—the youngest as it happened, a brigadier named Chan—ventured to ask what Li Sun's plan was.

"We will take the Twelfth Armored Division and use

it to spearhead the attack south," said Li Sun. "With the infantry catching up as the battle progresses."

Currently one of the units held in reserve, the Twelfth Armor was not "native" to the local army group. It had been detached from the 21st Army Group in the Lanzhou military district for the Vietnamese operations. That in itself was part of the problem, Li Sun thought—"foreign" units were not favored by the "local" generals.

"The unit will move as quickly as possible," added Li Sun. "They should expect only light resistance at the border—it is doubtful that the Vietnamese can even mount that."

Li Sun began speaking of the mountain passes near Viet Quang, where he expected the Vietnamese would try to use their artillery to stop the tanks. There were roads to the east that could be used to bypass the most problematic area; as the tanks moved south on these roads, the infantry could sweep behind it and eliminate bypassed strongpoints. The key would be speed.

"The Vietnamese do not have much supplies," said Li Sun. "Our intelligence estimates show that they have exhausted their anti-tank weapons, and even their artillery is low on ammunition."

"Pardon me, general," said Chan. "How do our units get to the border. Won't that be a problem? We, too, are traveling through narrow confines, and our own units hold the choke points."

Li Sun stared at Chan, trying to judge if he was asking the questions because he was trying to bait him or to curry favor. Either seemed possible. There were no hints from the other generals, who remained as quiet as the walls and floor.

Li Sun decided to treat the question as if it was meant legitimately. Passing divisions through each other could actually be a very delicate act, difficult even for an accomplished army like the Americans to pull off quickly.

"I have thought about this," Li Sun said. He went back to the map. "There are only a few places where we have sufficient highway access without a large troop presence to slow us down. We can use Route 210, muster south of Malipo, and then proceed along that route. We will draw up a plan and attack within twenty-four hours."

Now the other generals began making sounds—*hmmmmm, hmmmm*—and exchanging glances.

"There are questions? Difficulties?" asked Li Sun. "Name them."

One by one, the generals began mentioning problems that Li Sun had already considered. The terrain was difficult—true, but these roads were paved. The force had a long way to travel—absolutely, but there were no other divisions to take its place. The Vietnamese had troops along the border—barely two companies' worth stretched out over a hundred miles, according to the latest aerial reconnaissance, they could be easily defeated if they attempted to resist.

Li Sun had anticipated all of these questions, and had no difficulty turning them back. The plan would naturally have to be filled out quite a bit with staff work, but the outline was there.

All that was needed now was to convince his new army that he was in charge. He could tell from the way the generals asked their questions that they would resist him; not in the manly way of speaking directly to him, but going behind his back like the mice they were.

He needed a chief of staff, a second in command whom he could trust. His goal at the meeting was to see if any of the generals might be suitable.

The only one who seemed a remote possibility was Chan. The general had been in command of an armored regiment in the Beijing area. The unit itself had stayed near the capital; Chan had come down to help advise on armored aspects of the campaign. As such, he seemed somewhat more flexible and certainly less beholden than the others.

"Tell me, General Chan, what do you think of the plan?" Li sun asked.

"Tackling the enemy head-on has advantages and disadvantages," said Chan.

It was a mealy-mouthed beginning. Li Sun frowned.

"If we had an overwhelming force, the decision would be easy," continued the general. He walked to the map. "One looking at the map might think we do not. But if we come down these roads, admittedly in the mountains and difficult, we can surprise the enemy at Phuong Tien. There is nothing there beyond a few troops of old age guards. A few tanks down this road here, and then the forces at the Vietnamese border will be surrounded as the main attack begins. They will flee or be killed. Once that is accomplished, the path is clear. The Vietnamese are exhausted. As we move down from Phuong Tien we have many options. The force that has been harassing our western army will fall back, and then we can choose where to move them. From the images I have seen, Hanoi should be taken within a week."

The general continued. The strategy was not much more than an elaboration of what Li Sun had already said, but Li Sun was impressed by the confidence in Chan's voice. He started to test him by asking how he would deal with a Vietnamese counterattack. One of the other generals began to answer but Li Sun cut him off.

"General Chan has the floor," said Li Sun.

The answers were assured. Li Sun took a different

tact, playing devil's advocate. He pressed General Chan, wanting to see if he would fold.

"What if I told you this was a charade?" asked Li Sun finally. "That this was just to test your loyalty to the premier. The original plan was his and it must be followed. You are a traitor."

"I am soldier and will do as ordered," answered Chan. He bowed his head slightly, but his voice stayed strong. "I, however, believe the course I have outlined is a sound one. I would wager my life on it."

"Your life?" thundered Li Sun. Suddenly he was caught in the drama of the moment. Without thinking, he unsnapped the cover on his holster and drew his pistol. "You are a traitor! You will pay with your life."

"I serve my country," said Chan, looking up though his head was still bent. He held Li Sun's eyes for a moment, then lowered them.

Li Sun raised the pistol and aimed it at his skull.

Brave, at least.

Li Sun's emotion nearly overwhelmed his control—he had the ultimate power here, he could kill this man and no one would lift a finger against him.

Of course, if he failed to crush the Vietnamese, then he would be the one dead. The wheel of fortune spun endlessly, and its decisions were without mercy.

He lowered his pistol slowly.

"You are a brave man, General Chan. You believe in what you say, and will stand behind your words with your life," said Li Sun. "That is an admirable quality. And because of that, you will be my chief of staff. Come."

"What about the rest of us?" asked one of the other generals.

Li Sun looked at him with disgust.

"Study the map," he said.

Chan followed him out of the room. Li Sun stopped in the hallway and gestured to his two personal bodyguards, whom he'd brought with him from his old command.

"Go ahead," he told them. "Be quick about it."

The two men entered the room. Chan started to say something.

"Come, we have much work," said Li Sun, starting down the hallway.

The sound of automatic weapons fire began echoing from the room. A new slate, Li Sun thought to himself. There would be no one to blame if he failed.

14

Walter Jackson, the president's national security advisor, waved his hands adamantly.

"The missiles are an immense threat," insisted Jackson. "It's not just the carriers. Any ship."

"That tells me we should eliminate them," said President Greene. "Sooner rather than later. Then we could put our damn carriers anywhere the hell we want."

He glanced around the room. There were over three dozen people packed into the national security situation center. Not one of them spoke, or even looked like they wanted to speak. The screen at the far end of the room played a live video feed from the Pentagon, where the Joint Chiefs of Staff and their aides were gathered in a similar room. Not one of them looked ready to comment either.

"You're all afraid of China?" asked Greene angrily. "We can kick their ass back to the Stone Age."

That was too far—way too far—and even Greene realized it. It was late, he was tired, but that didn't justify his acting like an out-of-control teenager. He took a deep breath, reining himself in.

"What I think the president means is that we don't

really have to fear the Chinese," said Jackson. "Though we don't—"

"That's exactly what I mean," said Greene. "We don't have to fear them *now*. We *will* have to fear them in five years if we do nothing. I want to deal with this now so that someone else doesn't have to deal with it then."

Technically, it could be Greene dealing with it—this was only his first term. But the way he felt now, there was no way he'd re-up for four more years. Assuming that he didn't get impeached.

"We can make a strike," said the chief of the Air Force. "We have B-2s on Guam. I can have them in the air inside thirty minutes. The Chinese will never know what hit them."

"That would be a clear act of war," said the secretary of state, Theodore "Tad" Knox. "We just can't do that, Mr. President."

"If they hit us first," said Greene, "we will do that."

"Even in that case—"

"What the hell?" Greene's anger stoked up again. He felt as if his head was exploding. "Are you telling me that we have to sit here and watch our people die and do nothing? I'm sorry, Mr. Secretary, no way. That is not going to happen. Not while I'm president. No, Tad, no."

Greene struggled to get hold of his anger. He realized he was playing straight into his political opponents' hands; even though this was a top secret meeting, surely one or two of the participants would be leaking to friendly media about his outburst within minutes of its ending. But he just couldn't let this go—he just could not believe that a good portion of his cabinet and his military advisors were willing to let China proceed unchecked.

Damn them!

"I think it's pretty clear that we have to stand up to China," said Jackson, still trying to play the conciliator. "The question is how to ratchet that."

"Yes, ratchet," said Greene sarcastically.

Greene tried to keep his focus as the meeting continued. He struggled to temper himself, aware that the others were now far more interested in his behavior and demeanor than the matter at hand. The session ended quietly, without any grand pronouncements or decisions. The Seventh Fleet was gathering, the Air Force was ready to strike, a Marine Expeditionary Unit was steaming toward the area—but what everyone really wanted to know was whether the president going to lose his composure entirely.

Not today, thought Greene to himself as he rose to leave the room. Not today.

"Mr. President, I need two minutes," said Peter Frost, the head of the CIA. Peter Lucas, the point man on Vietnam, was behind him, along with two other aides.

"Of course." Greene glanced at Jackson as he sat back down. Jackson nodded, remaining in his seat.

"You have confirmation of the Vietnamese weapon?" asked Greene. Frost had mentioned the possibility of a dirty bomb the day before, but the report seemed too vague to be believed, let alone acted on.

"Nothing beyond what we've told you, Mr. President," admitted Frost. "But . . . we have a new idea, something that might keep the Chinese from continuing their advance. That would give us more time to look at the dirty bomb issue. As well as, possibly, making the Chinese completely reconsider."

That was definitely worth being late for, Greene thought.

"You remember Mara Duncan?" asked Frost, introducing her.

"Naturally."

Greene smiled. In actual fact, he had completely forgotten who she was until Frost reintroduced her. She'd been at the UN—she was the CIA officer who got Josh McArthur out of Vietnam, and rescued the little girl. How could he forget her?

Pressure? Senility? He was old, tired . . .

"Ms. Duncan, how are you?" Greene turned on the charm, trying to chase his own doubts away.

"Good, sir. Yourself?"

"Tired. And you should be, too." Greene tried to make a joke of it. "You'll be pleased to know the little girl Mạ is doing very well."

"That's good, Mr. President."

"What do you have for me?"

"A strike on the Chinese army headquarters. It would blunt their offensive entirely. Stop them in the tracks."

"Stop the advance?" Greene turned to Jackson, who said nothing. He looked back at Frost. "We hit one headquarters and this would stop the advance?"

"The army is very top-down," said Frost. "They're also very conservative. An attack like this would make the entire army rethink its security."

Greene decided Frost was being far too optimistic, undoubtedly under the influence of his analysts and the others who were selling the plan. Still, the idea of doing something to slow the Chinese had a great deal of appeal. And the way Mara described it made it seem even better: a behind-the-scenes commando strike that would decapitate the leadership of China's third largest army group.

Admittedly the one least effective so far.

Greene tried to check his enthusiasm as he listened to Mara's plan. The security arrangements at the headquarters site seemed too lax to be true; she made it sound as if the force would simply walk past the gate.

"We have a SEAL platoon that has practiced attacking a Chinese command installation," said Frost. "They could be in place within forty-eight hours. It would be high risk though—they won't have trained on this specific mission."

"We can't put American troops on the ground in China," said Jackson. "Even Vietnam is a risk."

"What about DevGru or Delta?" asked Greene. DevGru was the covert-action SEAL unit often called SEAL Team 6; Delta was Delta Force, the Army equivalent.

"No, that's what I'm saying." Jackson shook his head violently. "American troops on the ground."

"Actually, the platoon we're thinking about has had experience in Vietnam as well," said Mara. "And one of the Team officers is in country. The only problem would be getting them there quickly. This—"

"The group that helped you get out of the country," said Greene, putting it together.

"Yes, sir."

"You're talking about forty-eight hours. Most of them are in the States, though, aren't they?" asked Greene.

He could feel himself coming out of his funk. His brain was working harder—this was what he needed, a problem to work out. He could tell he impressed the others as well.

Why hadn't he been able to do this twenty minutes before, with the NSC honchos? Damn. He had to stay on his game.

"So it would take longer than just forty-eight hours, because they'd have to gear up," continued Greene. "So we're talking at least seventy-two, maybe a full week."

"Possibly," said Frost.

"The war may be over by then," said Greene. He felt a little disappointed.

"And there would be American ground troops in China," said Jackson.

"I'm not so worried about that," said Greene. "Not with these guys."

"We could put together a strike with mercenaries," said Frost. "Our own people. People we've worked with before. We've been moving some of them into Thailand, in case the Chinese come into the east."

Greene suspected that this presentation might have been rehearsed—try the idea in a risky, unacceptable form, get his interest, then present it in a way that made it seem far less risky.

Very Machiavellian. Yet Greene couldn't deny he liked the idea. A lot.

"What do the Vietnamese think?" he asked Frost.

"We haven't told them. Major Murphy hasn't shared the idea with them."

"General Perry is behind this?" said Jackson.

"Not Perry," said Lucas quickly.

"The only person in-country we've spoken to was the SEAL who's been coordinating weapons deliveries," said Mara. "He and Major Murphy worked the plan out. We think that General Perry would probably be . . . opposed. And telling the Vietnamese would be very problematic. At least until the strike is underway."

Perry was another problem.

Delaying the Chinese, even by a few days, might give Greene more time to rally more support in the UN. Ultimately, it looked like they were going to fail—no one really wanted to stand up to China and its aggressive premier. But still, he had to do something.

Like striking the DF-21D missile bases. He had B-2s ready to hit them. But striking unilaterally was sure to raise a fuss.

Now if the Chinese used them first . . .

Maybe if he delayed the advance, he'd get the chance.

"Should we take it through the NSC?" Frost asked.

"Hell no," said Greene. "That will take days. Move ahead."

Jackson, clearly uneasy, started to ask Greene if he might reconsider. He got only the words "Mr. President" out of his mouth before Greene recognized the tone and cut him off.

"Put it in motion," insisted Greene.

Frost glanced at Jackson.

"Do it," insisted Greene. "Now excuse me, but I have a few more things to do before I turn in tonight."

15

Nam Hong, north of Hanoi

Nam Hong had been the home of a small Vietnamese command, described officially as a division but in fact only a battalion strong, if that. There were three buildings, all a hundred years old, maybe more. They were stone, and empty. Two of the three had been used most recently as barracks. The units housed there had left at the start of the war, and already dust lay thick on the floors. The third was a small administrative building, staffed by a skeleton team of clerks, all older women.

Major Chaū led Zeus through the barracks and then to the administrative building, showing him how bare the place was. He stopped at a large steel door at the end of the hall.

"That's the jail?" asked Zeus.

"There are cells there, but they're empty," Major Chaū told Zeus. "She's not here."

"I want to see for myself."

Chaū reluctantly agreed. He went back inside and spoke to one of the women. Within a few minutes he returned with a key.

When he opened the door, the stink of a hundred

years of agony stung Zeus's nose. The light was dim; Major Chaū supplemented it with a tiny LED flashlight, lighting a pencil-thin path down the rickety wooden steps.

By the time he reached the base of the steps, Zeus's stomach was starting to turn. He forced himself to go on, clamping his teeth, and then put his arm over his face, filtering his nose in the crook of his elbow.

Bars lined the wall on the right, dividing the area into small cells. The left was green and black, thick mold covering what Zeus presumed were stones, though he couldn't see them.

"Anna," he said. The words came out of his mouth, a pathetic croak. He tried again, but could muster nothing louder than a whisper, his voice cracking.

At the worst moments of the battles he had just come through, Zeus had never felt nearly as afraid as he felt now, walking down the prison aisle. It wasn't that he worried something would leap out at him. He worried instead that he would see her, chained to the links in the wall, head slumped down. A thousand nightmares clung to him as he stepped down the corridor, taunting from the black rim of the light, dodging as he swung his hand back and forth.

Anna, where are you? Have I lost you forever? Anna?

Thirty paces from the stairs, the beam of Major Chaū's flashlight caught something white. Zeus stopped, closed his eyes, then reopened them.

There was a leg, a body.

Zeus took another step, his brain not quite comprehending. Then he realized he was looking at a skeleton, bare of flesh, long dead.

He forced himself on. Several cells later he found another set of bones, these on the floor, corroded manacles loosely around the arms and legs.

Otherwise the place was empty. Zeus returned upstairs.

Zeus noticed that Chaū was walking slower and slower as they came out of the prison. He seemed to have been affected even more deeply than Zeus by what he had seen.

"I have a confession," said Chaū as they reached the car. "I feel I must tell you the truth."

Zeus forced himself to keep walking. His fingers clenched.

She's dead. She's dead, and they were afraid to tell me.

His shirt stuck at the back of his neck. His pants chafed at his thighs. Every movement felt awkward, his knees creaking, his elbows stiff. Zeus kept moving, unsure how to react or what to say.

I'll kill the person who killed her.

"General Trung is worried that you would leave. As long as you are here, your country will support us. They will listen to—"

"It has nothing to do with me," snapped Zeus. "I'm just a soldier. I'm nothing. The decision is not mine, and they don't care about me."

He saw his body stop. He saw himself turning and facing Chaū. He saw his face red. He saw his mouth open to say more.

Nothing came out. He could not find the words.

"I believe I know where she is," said Chaū. "My orders were to keep you here and make it seem . . . If I take you—will you still help us?"

"Take me," insisted Zeus. "Now."

It wasn't until Zeus walked into the large room in the hospital building in Hu'ng Yên that he was sure

Anna was alive. Even then, he hesitated to let himself believe this.

The room was large by Vietnamese standards, thirty feet by thirty feet, completely empty, walls painted white, with thin-framed metal sash windows that filled about two-thirds of the west side. The air was musty; though the room was clean, it smelled as if it hadn't been used or aired out for months.

Chaū stood next to him, almost motionless.

"How long will it be?" Zeus asked him, more to break the silence than to ask for information.

"Not very long."

Zeus nodded. He thought of breaking her out—there were guards around the building, and two men in the lobby, but the security wasn't particularly formidable.

And then do what?

Escape back to the States? What sort of legal entanglements would ensue?

They could go somewhere else, the Philippines, Africa—did it matter if she was with him?

Certainly it would. He was thinking irrationally. He needed to keep himself under control, keep his emotions pushed away. He was and had always been a rational man, thinking before doing. Falling under her spell had changed him dramatically.

It was war that had changed him, the hot emotion of war. But he wouldn't be in war forever. He wouldn't always have that excuse.

The door opened. A short, thin man with a neatly trimmed gray beard entered. A nurse followed, then a soldier, broad-shouldered and tall. Few Vietnamese were as large as this man; he could have played linebacker for a professional football team.

"Where's Anna?" said Zeus.

"I am Dr. Lin," said the man with the beard. He held out his hand.

"Where's Anna?" insisted Zeus, refusing to shake.

"Your wife is in good health."

"I want to see her." Zeus wasn't sure whether the marriage status was a mistake or some sort of subterfuge, but he decided to let it pass.

"She is on her way. Technically, she is a prisoner."

"She was framed."

The doctor grimaced, but said nothing. They stood awkwardly for a moment.

"You speak English very well," offered Zeus finally.

"I attended UCLA and did my internship in Los Angeles."

Zeus nodded.

The door opened. A Vietnamese soldier armed with an M16 entered. The M16 was an old model, and well worn; it looked as if it had been inherited from the South Vietnamese army.

The man looked around, then tapped on the doorjamb. A woman dressed in nurse's scrubs entered, followed by Anna. Two more soldiers brought up the rear, but Zeus barely noticed them; he was too focused on Anna.

She was as beautiful as he remembered, her face like porcelain, her body lithe and full of life. She was a prisoner, yet she had more energy than anyone else in the room. Her eyes widened—apparently they hadn't told her he was there—and she took a step toward him. The nurse put her hand out, but Zeus was already striding across the room. He folded Anna into his chest and in that instant all of his doubts melted away.

He loved her, and he would do anything to get her back.

The large soldier and the one with the M16 started to push them apart.

"Back off," shot Zeus.

The doctor said something to them in Vietnamese.

The men stopped pulling them apart but continued to hold him.

"I am sorry I have caused you trouble," said Anna softly.

"It's not trouble. I'm going to get you out."

She looked at him. "I'm helping here."

"You're a prisoner."

"I know. But I am also a doctor. There are many wounded."

"I'm going to get you out."

"Major Murphy." Dr. Lin put his arm on Zeus's. "Your wife is right—there is much for her to do today."

Zeus closed his eyes. Tightening his grip for a moment, he pressed her close, felt her, then let go.

"I'm going to get you out," he said. She stared at him for a moment, then the nurse steered her gently back to the door.

"General Trung will release her," said Chaū as they drove away. "He is a man of his word."

"How can I believe his word when he's lied?" asked Zeus.

"He hasn't lied. He—"

"He told you to keep me from finding her."

"He meant no harm. He wanted to delay your leaving. General Perry said you were leaving on the helicopter flight. He asked that you be allowed to stay but the general was against it."

"Perry will just send me on another aircraft."

Chaū had no answer for that.

Zeus wasn't sure how much Trung could really do for him. According to Chaū, the man who had ordered Anna's arrest was connected to the highest political levels in the country, and if it were not for Trung's intervention, she would be in a prison worse than what he had seen at Nam Hong.

"I promise she will be released," said Chaū. "If you can continue to help us—I do promise that."

"Take me back to the embassy," said Zeus. "I have to talk to General Perry."

Both men remained silent the rest of the drive.

16

Aboard USS *McCampbell*, off the coast of Vietnam, southwest of Beibu Wan

Silas grit his teeth as the admiral repeated his orders.

"No, Commander, let me be very, very clear about this: you are not, not, repeat not, to engage the Chinese vessels. Do you understand?"

"If they begin firing on the Vietnamese—"

"You are not to engage the Chinese."

"What if they go after a civilian ship?"

"I will relieve you this instant if you say another word."

Silas closed his eyes. Nearly a minute passed before the admiral spoke again.

"I'm glad we understand each other. Out."

The com screen went blank. Silas rose from the desk chair in his small cabin, stifled a curse, then went out to check on his crew.

17

Washington, D.C.

"You're not going to Vietnam under any circumstances, Mara," Lucas said as they walked toward the door of the West Wing of the White House. "Your cover is blown."

"This isn't a mission that needs a cover."

"For Christ's sake, what the hell do you think the Chinese would do if they caught you? They've spent the last few days spreading your face around the Internet, claiming you invented the massacre. How long do you think it would take them to get you to confess to that? Huh? For crapsake."

Lucas quickened his pace as they went through the door. The sudden rush of outside air felt good. It had been late afternoon when Mara and Lucas reported to the White House to attend the national security briefing; now it was well past midnight, with a full moon so bright it seemed almost day.

"Then send me to check out the caves," Mara said as Lucas aimed toward the car. "Let me find out what's on the ground there."

Lucas stopped short suddenly, turning and holding

his arm out as if to catch her from falling down a hole.

"You don't really get it, do you?" he said.

"Don't get what?"

"Damn it, Mara." Lucas glanced around, making sure no one was nearby. "Look—it's over. Do you understand? I feel bad—terrible. But you're going to have to move on to something else."

"Are you saying I should leave the agency?"

"No."

"Because I'm not going to work as an analyst. I'm not going to . . ."

Mara let her voice trail off. Lucas waved his hand at her and started in motion again. She watched him for a moment, then ran to catch up.

"Peter. Peter . . . wait." She caught him and tugged him around. "Look, I'm sorry—"

"You're on leave," he told her.

"What?"

"You're on leave. Medical leave."

Her eyes started to well with tears. It was inappropriate, it was weak, she hated it, she despised it—but she couldn't stop it. They began to spill from the corner of her eyes.

"I have to finish . . . I have to find out where the weapon is. And what exactly—"

"Harmuth can take over on his own."

"No way. Come on, Peter."

Lucas didn't answer, and remained silent as he drove back over to Langley. Mara absolutely needed a break: She wasn't herself.

"I'll finish pulling the information together on the site," she said finally as they turned onto Dolley

Madison Boulevard, a few miles from the headquarters campus. "I'll talk to Ric—"

"I'll handle that myself."

"OK," she said in a soft, nearly inaudible voice.

Lucas felt bad for her. It was a difficult thing to realize that your career was, if not over exactly, certainly taking a turn you hadn't wanted. And he liked her. Mara's enthusiasm reminded him of the people he had worked with when he first started at the agency.

He tried to think of ways to soften the blow, but there weren't many.

"You want to get some coffee?" he asked as they neared Langley.

"No. I'm good. I want to get back to work."

"OK, great. Good," said Lucas, turning onto the long driveway that led to the security checkpoint.

"**Y**ou realize the odds on this are long," Ric Kerfer told Lucas when they spoke over the secure connection in the embassy basement. "If I'm not using SEALs, I'm not giving guarantees."

"Who said you were going?" said Lucas.

"Give me a break, Pete," responded Kerfer. "Who's gonna run this?"

"Setco."

"I'll work with him, but I'm here."

"This is an agency op, Ric. Ours."

"You can own it," said Kerfer. "But you need me."

"Not really," said Lucas.

Kerfer laughed. "Listen, I'm going to need some help on this end arranging things. I need somebody the Viets trust."

Lucas cringed, expecting Kerfer to ask for Mara.

He didn't.

"I want Zeus Murphy," said Kerfer. "He's on Perry's staff but Perry told him to come home. He hasn't left yet. I want him."

"Done."

"All right. Give me Setco's contact information so I can start getting this set up."

18

Hanoi

Whatever body chemistry had kept Zeus from feeling the pain of the battering he had taken over the past two weeks had left him by the time they pulled in front of the embassy gate. His legs hurt so badly when he got out of the car that he could barely lift them properly.

"I will watch after her," Major Chaū told him. "I promise."

"Right."

"Are you leaving? Or are you staying?"

"I don't know . . . I'm not sure what I'm going to have to do."

"Major—"

Zeus looked back. "Thank you. For all you have done."

"Right."

Zeus shut the car door. The line of people waiting outside the embassy had grown, even though signs in English and Vietnamese said visas were no longer being issued. The people seemed unwilling to abandon whatever slim hope they had of escaping. They stood patiently, eying Zeus with a mixture of envy and plaintiveness; he expected any moment that they might ask his help if he stopped, so he stared straight ahead and kept to a deliberate pace.

The guards knew him, of course, and waved him in.

Zeus still wasn't sure what to do. He was going to stay . . . he was going to leave. He was going to urge Perry to change his mind and push his plan. He was going to get Kerfer to free Anna from the hospital jail.

"You look like you've seen a ghost."

Zeus looked up. General Perry was standing near the guard shack, practically in front of him. He'd been talking to the gunnery sergeant in charge of the gate.

"General, I—"

"Not out here," snapped Perry.

They walked into the building in silence. Rather than going up the stairs to the ambassador's office he'd been using earlier, he went down the hall to one of the clerks' rooms. Ric Kerfer was sitting on the edge of one of the desks inside, a big Kerfer grin on his face.

"General, I'm sorry I missed the helicopter," said Zeus. Seeing the SEAL suddenly made him want to be entirely honest—he wasn't going to hide behind a fib. "I—"

"Stow it," said Perry. "Excuse us, Mr. Kerfer."

"Not a problem." Kerfer got up. "I'll be in the hall."

Perry exploded as soon as the door closed.

"Who the hell do you think you are, going over my head?" said the general, face red. "Do you forget who you work for? You're a member of the U.S. Army, Major."

"I don't—"

"Why is the CIA telling me—*ordering*—to assign you to some bullshit deal with Kerfer. This is your plan, that cocked-up Rambo plan to get the Chinese brass."

"I really don't know what's going on here," said Zeus.

"You're being detailed to work with Lieutenant Kerfer. They won't tell me why, but I can guess."

"Sir—"

"Get the hell out of my sight," said Perry. "Go."

"General."

"It's not whether the idea was a good or bad one, though you know what I think about it," said Perry, only slightly calmer. "It's going around me that I can't abide."

"I didn't."

Perry frowned and shook his head. "Good-bye, Major."

Shell-shocked, Zeus walked out of the room. Kerfer was waiting at the end of the hall.

"General's pissed?" said the SEAL.

"He thinks I went around him."

"Screw him. He'll get over it."

"I didn't—"

"You gonna worry about that, or are you going to focus on our real problems?"

"I just don't want to piss him off."

"You start worrying about who you piss off, and you'll never get anything done. Let's take a walk."

In Ric Kerfer's experience, ops were of one of two types: carefully planned for months, with preparations that bordered on the pathologically anal, or completely winged, thrown together not only at the last minute but with the wildest and most outlandish expectations.

This was definitely the latter.

"I been thinking about how to run this," he told

Zeus as he led him out of the embassy. "Easiest way is to fly in and out on a Chinese military plane."

"Yeah, sure. That's gonna happen."

Kerfer reached into his pocket and pulled out a piece of paper, unfolding it as he handed it to Zeus. It was a satellite image of a scratch airfield, bulldozed in the nook of a valley. The ground around it seemed to have been stripped as well.

"It's an air base at Malipo. We fly into there, refuel, then go from there into Kunming. Assuming your man Trung can take the city."

"He should be able to."

"Should be isn't going to be good enough. He has to get the city. The airfield's only a couple of miles away."

"Why can't you fly straight in?"

"I don't think I can get an aircraft that will get far enough and still have fuel to return," said Kerfer. "And I know I can't get a helicopter that far. Whatever I use is going to have to be able to take off from a pretty broken up runway down here. That limits the options to a small plane. Or a helo. This base helps a lot."

"Looks like a little dinky terminal and a couple of hangars."

"As long as there's gas there, it's fine. You helping or you're not?"

"I'm in."

"Good. Let's go pick up some gear, then we both got a lot to do."

19

Washington, D.C.

"You."

Greene looked up from the floor of his cell. The guard stood just outside the door, inserting a key into the lock.

There was no sense in resisting; it would simply add a beating to what was to follow. Still, Greene never moved quickly off the deck. It was his way of preserving a scrap of dignity.

Like all of the others, he had held out as long as he could before breaking. He had weathered multiple beatings, several water dunkings, and two sessions with a cattle prod. They had taken off his fingernails. He had passed out countless times, and not told them more than he was required to—his name, his rank, his serial number. He added a few useless details, but didn't give them what they so dearly wanted: a "confession" that he had killed innocent Vietnamese without provocation.

A lie, of course. He resisted it with all his might.

And then one day he simply could resist no longer. It was toward the middle of the second week, or maybe the beginning of the third; he'd lost track of time. They pulled him from the cell, and on the way to the room, he heard someone scream. He thought he recognized the scream; he thought it was the man who had been in the cell next to him. They'd only communicated by taps to that point, but he was sure somehow it was him.

When he heard that scream, his legs gave way. Greene was dragged into the interrogation room. The session started with a punch to the head—that was the way it often started with this interrogator, a sadist they called Igor. Greene closed his eyes and started talking about his assignment to bomb a military base just north of the Demilitarized Zone between the two Vietnams.

He'd been wrong about who screamed—it was actually a new prisoner he hadn't met—but by then it didn't matter.

"You will write about this," said the interrogator.

"Yes," answered Greene, giving in for the first time.

From then on, he had cooperated reluctantly, sometimes hesitantly, but always in the end giving in to avoid the worst punishments. It was what they all did.

The guards took him, one on each side, and marched him down the hall.

Why?

To write a letter claiming he was being well treated.

No, to write his "confession" that he had killed innocent women and children.

No, no, he was going to be released . . .

G reene woke with a start. He'd been dreaming—or rather, reliving the nightmare of his captivity. He'd nodded off reading in his chair.

It was very late. By rights, he should go to bed. But there was much to be done. He retrieved his book from the floor where it had dropped, placed it on the nearby desk, then went to find himself some coffee in the White House kitchen.

20

Hanoi

Kerfer took Zeus to a safe house that he'd established on the north side of Hanoi. There he gave him a Teton hiker's pack, a civilian model that was roomy enough for two laptops, a pair of secure satellite radios, and a short-barreled AR15. The gun looked *almost* like a toy, with only a seven-inch barrel and sliding stock. It was, however, an extremely potent weapon, with a red-dot laser sight and half a dozen 30-round mags for 5.56×45 ammo.

"Call me when everything's set," Kerfer told Zeus, dropping him off at his hotel.

Zeus went upstairs to shave and shower before going back out. He had more than two days of stubble on his chin, and his disposable razor was now well past its prime. It snagged against his nascent beard, tearing and pulling.

A shower was impossible; so little water trickled from the faucet that it wasn't worth the effort. He changed to fresh clothes instead, putting on his last pair of clean underwear, pulling on a pair of black jeans and a thick, plain gray T-shirt. He tucked his Beretta into its holster, leaving it under his untucked shirt but making sure the bottom was visible. Making it clear you were armed was now a good thing in Hanoi.

Dressed, he went downstairs. Even as late as yesterday, there had been drivers milling in or near the lobby offering to take visitors by taxi or bicycle to various spots in the city. But this evening the lobby was deserted, and Zeus had to walk a few blocks before he found a ride.

His storm of indecision had passed; he knew what he was going to do: He was going to help the Vietnamese, and they were going to release Anna.

He called Major Chaū from the cab, telling him only that they had to talk. Chaū gave him an address; Zeus changed the number, directing the driver several blocks away.

There were few people on the street. There were no streetlights. A few, very dim lights shone from inside storefronts, but the night itself was bright. The earlier clouds had cleared and the moon hung large over the city. It was one of those moons that conjured the image of a face, and though Zeus was hardly in a mind to fantasize, he felt as if it were a person watching him walk.

He circled the block, turned around in an alley, then went into the backyard of what looked like an old office building but which turned out to be a tenement: dozens of eyes peered out at him as he climbed onto the back railing of a fire escape and clambered to the roof, past several families camped out on the gratings. Most turned their heads as he climbed; the rest stared.

It was a surreal moment: trying to escape notice he'd blundered into a crowd.

The roof, at least, was empty; he went across to the front and looked down, making sure he wasn't being followed, then did the same on each side. He jumped to the next roof, only a foot or so away and nearly at the same level; he ran across two more until he reached an alley, and went down from there, once again sheepishly skirting the living quarters of a few families.

Major Chaū was waiting on the street when he arrived, leaning nervously against the fender of a Hyundai Sonata.

"Where'd you get the car?" asked Zeus. The Sonata was a large car in Vietnam, and a comparatively expensive one as well.

"Government," said Chaū quickly. "Come."

Zeus slid his pack off his shoulders and slid it into the car. Then he followed.

"General Trung has moved with the army north," said Chaū. "He would welcome information on the disposition of the enemy."

"Of course."

"Do you need time or—"

"I have everything I need. How long to reach Trung?"

"Two hours. Three at most."

"OK." Zeus unzipped the backpack, took out the rifle, then removed one of the laptops. Propping the rifle next to his leg, he booted up the laptop, and waited for the password screen. He'd memorized the passwords, which would only be good for twenty-four hours; if he needed the computers after that he'd have to obtain new codes.

The laptop took a while to work through its startup routines. When it finally finished, he opened a program that looked like a Web browser, typed two more passwords, then waited as the machine made a connection through the stubby satellite antenna plugged into the port at the side.

Kerfer had arranged for a direct link to CIA resources, which meant that he could get real-time images from one of several UAVs being used to cover the

Vietnamese area. While he'd had access to the imagery earlier, he had been working through army intel specialists and received them with notations indicating what he was seeing and its significance. The CIA imagery was raw, with no attempts at interpretation. On the other hand it was also instantaneous: he could see things exactly as they were happening. There was typically a few hours lag with the Army data, as the intel people had to agree on what it meant before passing it to him.

Zeus saw the forward edge of the Vietnamese forces heading toward the border—a few vehicles driving at the very side of the road, trying to take advantage of the vegetation to stay sheltered from the Chinese reconnaissance aircraft and drones.

The Chinese might see them as well. Would they tip them off?

No. A force this small would not be seen as a threat. And a Chinese commander—any commander—would logically think that it was heading to reinforce the border.

Zeus scanned northward, moving the screen up to check on the Chinese positions. Even with the encryption, the feed was quick—two or three times faster than a normal 4G connection—but there was so much data in the image that it seemed to come in one line at a time, nearly overwhelming the video card in the laptop.

The largest Chinese formation close to the target area was holding the highways north of Lao Cai on the Chinese border some one hundred kilometers to the west. The force, roughly a division's worth (it had some attached units and armor), was scattered through the area in defensive positions—the tanks were in bulldozed redoubts; the troops in foxholes, trenches, and the like.

Lao Cai was not far away and would have been an easy place to assault, but aside from a few scouting missions and random shelling, had so far been left alone. The Vietnamese believed this was because Chinese businessmen owned so much of the city, which before the war had been a popular "rest area" for Chinese in the region, a kind of Asian version of Las Vegas, only with a bit more vice—what happened there, stayed there.

Zeus slid the map farther north, tracking the Chinese supply lines through a series of depots and truck stops. If America was involved in the war, that line would be broken within a half hour—between Tomahawk strikes and a few fighter sorties, the supplies would be destroyed and the roads blocked. But this wasn't a war with America, not officially anyway. The Vietnamese had no way of striking that deep behind the lines. And so the Chinese operated with impunity, and a lax attitude that would be criminal under any other circumstances.

All of which would help at Malipo and again at Kunming—the Chinese would be secure in their complacency.

The two attacks had to come relatively close together. Otherwise they might be ready for the second.

Even two hundred miles away.

Zeus slid the map west, looking at Malipo. Clinging to the top of a ridge, it formed a sloppy *L* surrounded by strip mines and vast stretches of forest. The tiny Chinese force was spread out. The largest portion—a half-dozen armored personnel carriers—were parked together east of the city, down the hill from it. There were tents and temporary buildings nearby, but according to the signals intelligence, the division headquarters was in a building about a kilometer away at the southern end of town. There were two military trucks, similar to Humvees, in front of the building, with an armored car about twenty meters away at the edge of the road.

The rest of the force—far less than a battalion, though called a battalion in the American intelligence briefings—was scattered in the mines and along the roads.

Zeus started to doubt his plan. Would an attack on such a small force really worry the Chinese? Wasn't it likely that they had sent one of their most inconsequential units here? Why would they care if it was pushed aside?

How much easier this would be if he were planning an American assault. Rather than sneaking across mountain roads and mounting what was essentially a large commando raid, Zeus could lead a lightning assault right through several Chinese divisions, ripping them to pieces as he went. Blow out the command and control, flatten the armored and mechanized units, just keep moving—Patton would have been proud.

He moved the map around, then back over toward Malipo. His finger slipped, and the map shot up two quadrants, along Highway S210.

A dark blur filled the road. At first glance, he thought it was a malfunction, a shadowy artifact induced by his moving the screen too quickly.

Then he touched the zoom and realized what he was seeing.

"How long will it take us to get to General Trung?" Zeus asked Chaū.

"Two hours, at least—"

"We need to go faster," said Zeus. "As fast as you possibly can."

21

"All right. Everyone leaves. Even you, Mr. Kittle." President Greene smiled at the Secret Service agent who had accompanied him into the secure communications room in the White House bunker.

"Mr. President—"

"Really, Jack, do you think the equipment is going to assassinate me?"

"Well, no sir, but—"

Greene cocked his head. The Secret Service agent nodded, then after the rest of Greene's aides and the technical people had left, followed them out and closed the door.

Alone for the first time that day, Greene took off his jacket and then his tie. He slid into the office chair behind the com station.

"All right, General," he told Perry. "Just you and me now. What is it you want to say, Harland?"

"Chet, this is the biggest mistake you've ever made in your life. We can't start a war with China."

"I'm trying to avoid war."

Perry, grim faced, shook his head solemnly. He

seemed to have aged ten years since Greene sent him to Vietnam. That country did it to you.

"You're not fooling anyone," said Perry. "Taking the Vietnamese side? It's insane."

"Letting China run over Southeast Asia is insane. What happened, Harland? I thought you agreed with me when I sent you?"

"I had an open mind," said Perry. "I told you I would come to look at the facts, and I have. I don't think the Vietnamese are worth the effort, frankly. There's nothing here to convince me that they would be worth spilling American blood over."

"The question is, how to avoid it being shed in the future. More of it, that is."

Perry's face darkened. The lighting in the embassy secure room wasn't that good, but Greene guessed that he was flushed. He had lost one of his aides in the fighting, and Perry was not the sort of commander to take that lightly.

"You sent me to give you my opinion," said the general. "That's what I'm doing."

"You were to help the Vietnamese as well," said Greene. "And obviously you're no longer in a position to do that."

"I—"

"Harland, I appreciate the work you've done. I put you in a difficult position. I know that. I'm not going to keep you there. I want you out on the next available flight."

"Yes, Mr. President."

"Oh, don't give me that 'yes, Mr. President' shit." Greene folded his arms. For the first time since they'd started speaking, he was genuinely annoyed. "What kind of jackass would I be to keep you in Vietnam when you don't believe in what you're doing?

And I understand you've ordered all your aides to leave."

"I told Zeus Murphy to go home because he's been through enough," said Perry. "And now that you bring that up, I resent his going over my head."

"As I understand it, the CIA asked for him," said Greene. "The Vietnamese did as well. And State."

"That may be. But he deserved to leave if he wanted."

"Did he want to?"

Perry said nothing. Greene rose. He couldn't sit when he was agitated; it was too difficult.

"Chet?"

"Hold on. My legs are getting cramped. Damn it." Greene pulled the chair back and sat down again. "Have you heard what's going on back here?"

"Congress wants to impeach you."

"That's right. I expect they'll subpoena you."

Perry stared at the screen.

"The subpoena will be quashed. But I am wondering who told them that you were in Hanoi," added Greene.

"It wasn't me."

"Congress isn't reaching out to you?" said Greene, putting a sarcastic twist on his words.

"You know I wouldn't speak to those assholes. I told Kelly at Asia Command, and Jamie at the Pentagon what I thought. They asked. Obviously it spread. But I'm not talking to Congress. Either party. Why would I do that?"

Jamie Ramada—the undersecretary of defense and a holdover from the last administration. Clearly the source of the leak, thought Greene.

Damn.

"Harland, I respect your opinion," said Greene. "You know I do. I don't have a replacement yet, so I'd like you to stay in contact with the area, but at the same time not subject yourself to danger. So I'd like you to move yourself temporarily to the Philippines, and prepare a report for me. The rest of your staff can stay—you're too valuable to lose."

"Now listen—"

"Excuse me, General?"

Greene put a little snap in his voice. Perry reacted with a touch more humility—but only a touch.

"Mr. President, I don't want to be in a position where I'm being used as a political football."

"You're not," snapped Greene. "I want you out of Vietnam, and I want to read your report. I fully expect that I will disagree with it—but that's all the more reason for me to have it. After that, if Congress subpoenas you, we'll play it by ear."

"But the agency operation. Or operations—"

"Those aren't your concern," said Greene. He was still calculating how best to handle this. He might even let Perry talk to Congress. Having the general state frankly that he was opposed to the president's policies was not necessarily a bad thing; it was all in the spin.

And the timing. He needed a little more time—to take care of the missiles, and the Vietnamese weapon, whatever it was.

Greene considered telling Perry about it, but he didn't want to tip off the Vietnamese—not until he destroyed the damn thing.

Which he had to do. Let them use it, and the Chinese would never stop the war. And who could blame them?

"I don't think further operations are a good idea," said Perry.

"Noted. How long before you're safely in the Philippines?"

"Well—"

"The ambassador is scheduled to leave in two hours," said Greene, glancing at the clock on the wall that showed Hanoi time. "She's leaving her consul and a handful of Marines. Get on the plane with her."

"Yes, sir, Mr. President."

Greene reached to snap off the communications, then thought of something else he wanted to say.

"Harland?"

"Yes, Mr. President?"

"I realize this has been difficult for you. I'm sorry."

"So am I, Chet."

22

Da Nang, Vietnam

Ric Kerfer paced along the concrete pier, one eye cast over his shoulder at the hulking luxury liner to his right. The ship had been attacked on the first and second days of the war, and was now a blackened wreck. Water lay a foot over its deck, the result of several holes in its hull. But for all the damage, the large windows in the solarium overlooking the stern remained intact; moonlight glinted off them, a curious sparkle in a night otherwise filled with ghosts and foreboding.

Kerfer caught the sound of a motorboat and walked down to the end of the pier, lowering himself to his haunches. He held his MP4 over his knee, ready. The gun was a private label version assembled for him by a retired SEAL; the trigger pull was extremely light, just under a pound—if he put his finger through the ring he meant to fire.

A small runabout cut through the black shadows beyond the stern of the wrecked liner. Kerfer breathed slowly, catching a whiff of exhaust on the breeze. The small craft cut its engine and coasted toward the end of the pier. It never really stopped—a figure leapt from the side onto the cement and it circled away.

"Hey," said Kerfer.

"What the fuck are you doing? Praying?"

"Screw you." Kerfer rose. "I almost shot your ass. What if it wasn't me?"

"I knew it was you."

Roth Setco walked toward Kerfer. Barely average height, he was wearing a bulky black sweatshirt over pair of dark green fatigues. He had no visible weapon, though Kerfer knew from experience Setco would be packing at least two pistols and a combat knife. The moon caught his face—it seemed gaunt, more a collection of bones than flesh.

"How you doin'?" Kerfer asked.

"Shitty. You?"

"Can't complain, really."

"I had to take three frickin' boats up from Thailand. Fast, but pieces of crap. You got a helicopter?"

"There's a Huey waiting for us at the airport."

"Huey?"

"All I could get."

"Fuckin' Vietnamese deserve to be run over."

Well, this is a great start, Kerfer thought to himself.

The helicopter smelled of fuel and hydraulic fluid, but it flew well enough, and within fifteen minutes they were hovering over the forward deck of a small cargo carrier.

A landing pad had been hastily erected on the bow of the ship. A pair of chem lights had been placed cattycorner on the platform; they were the pilot's only guides, aside from his landing beacon. Kerfer, standing in the rear of the small aircraft, saw the target and decided he'd do better not watching.

The pilot circled twice, then shifted the helo nervously back and forth before putting it down with a rather hard bang.

"He ain't doin' shit for us, that's number one," said Setco, pulling open the door.

Kerfer followed Setco onto the deck. The CIA paramilitary officer walked aft toward the superstructure, clearly familiar with the ship. They passed two deckhands who had pistols strapped to their legs in drop holsters; the barrel of a machine gun poked out beneath a tarpaulin not far from the ladder leading up to the bridge.

Inside, Setco took a quick right and descended the sharply angled steps so fast that Kerfer nearly lost sight of him in the dim light. Though a Navy officer, Kerfer had spent precious little time on a ship, especially over the last few years, and he had trouble adjusting to the slight but very real roll of the boat as he went down. He felt his feet going out from under him and caught himself just in time, pushing hard on his right hand.

"Son of a bitch," he growled to himself. "Damn good thing I made it through BUD/S. This would be my freakin' life."

Setco had entered a compartment just to the right of the ladder. Kerfer followed inside and found himself on a catwalk above some machinery. It took a moment but then he realized he was supposed to follow along the suspended walkway to a portal that led into a passage so narrow his shoulders nearly touched both sides. He went down two steps and turned right into a large room that looked like a cross between an airplane hangar and an electronics lab.

Three long black benches were set up in the middle of the space, each stocked with computers, video screens, and other electronics gear. The bulkhead on his right as he came in was covered with maps. On the other side, a pair of old couches with their legs sawed off sat on the deck. There were two coolers near them, and some cubbies for gear.

Three men stood near the maps, congratulating Setco on his safe arrival. It was the most animated Kerfer had ever seen Setco, or anyone around him, for that matter.

Two of the men were Asian; the other looked vaguely Spanish—Filipino, Kerfer guessed. He stood and waited, watching Setco as he pulled the hood of his sweatshirt back.

They'd spent most of the time in the dark, and Kerfer hadn't had much of a look at the CIA officer. Now he was shocked at what he saw. Not only was Setco thin and pale, his lips were quivering. He couldn't be more than forty—Kerfer guessed he was actually somewhat younger—yet he looked like an old man ready for a nursing home.

Or the grave.

Kerfer had first met Setco two years before, after a mission the CIA officer was running in Myanmar—Burma to most of the West—had cratered. Kerfer and half a company of SEALs had been choppered into the jungle to get him out. The planned rendezvous turned into a search, with Kerfer personally deciding to disobey orders to return; he found Setco some twenty-four hours later, walking on a trail in the direction of the meeting place. The para smiled and waved, as if he'd known the SEALs would be there all the time.

Kerfer had never been given details of Setco's operation—it was strictly need-to-know. The scuttlebutt was that he had been involved in a plan to assassinate a terrorist who was in Bago for a meeting with a Chinese military attaché. Given the complications that followed the rendezvous—they had been chased through the jungle for several days by troops armed with Chinese weapons—it seemed apparent that the Chinese had somehow gotten wind of the op and reacted.

They had worked together twice more since, and trained on another mission as well. Each time Setco seemed to have grown darker and quieter, as if he were dissolving into the evil wraith of a science fiction horror tale.

"This is Tony, Zig, Squirt," said Setco, pointing. The names seemed randomly chosen, as if Setco said whatever popped into his head.

The mood instantly changed. Kerfer stuck out his hand to shake. Instead, each man locked eyes with him a moment in turn, nodded ever so subtly, then glanced back at Setco.

A wave of anxiety pressed up from Kerfer's belly, a physical thing—he always had reservations about running a mission without SEALs, but now he was getting absolutely bad feelings. The men looked more like drug runners than spec warfare operators, even to Kerfer, who wasn't exactly a poster specimen himself.

The one thing about being a SEAL—you always knew you could trust the other people on your team. Granted, even SEALs had their limits, but at least if you were working with fellow SEALs you knew they had gone through a pretty rigorous vetting process.

These guys . . .

Setco started talking in Korean. The others nodded. Kerfer waited a few moments, expecting him to explain what he was saying. Setco pointed at the map and continued to speak, ignoring him. Finally, Kerfer asked what he was saying.

Setco put up his hand. Kerfer barely managed to stifle his anger at being so casually brushed off. Finally he reached over and took hold of Setco's upper arm.

Or would have, had Setco not jerked away, spinning

into a ready position as if he were going to be attacked.

"I don't speak Korean," said Kerfer.

"Don't touch me."

"Don't ignore me."

"I'm explaining what we're doing."

Kerfer raised his hands, trying to signal that he meant no harm. Setco lowered his arms.

"How do you know what we're doing?" Kerfer asked. "I haven't told you."

"I have the target. I have all the data. We can take it easy. We've done this dozens of times."

"Excuse me—you've landed halfway into China? Blown up an army group headquarters?"

Setco frowned, then resumed talking to the others.

Kerfer watched the other men. They looked at the CIA officer like angels at the rapture.

I've stepped into an insane asylum, Kerfer thought to himself.

Finally, Setco turned to Kerfer. "So how do we get there?" he asked.

"I'm working on that," said Kerfer. "I have an airplane. I need a base in China. Once we're sure of that, we're good to go."

"Why do we need another base?"

"Plane can't carry enough fuel to get to Kunming and get back."

"We don't need the round trip."

"I do." Kerfer guessed that Setco meant they could refuel there, but he wanted a margin of error in case that didn't work out.

"You have a pilot?" Setco asked.

"Yes," said Kerfer. "We need to be ready by tomorrow night. I want to hit the place as soon as it's dark."

"We'll be ready."

"Five guys aren't going to be enough." Kerfer was counting both himself and Setco.

"I have more coming."

Setco went over to the nearby bench and woke up the computer. The others sifted over behind him as he brought up satellite imagery to show Kunming. There was an aircraft on the runway. The detail was so good that Kerfer could see scratches in the paint around the cowling.

"I've been here," said Setco.

"To Kunming?"

"Couple of times. There's a military academy there."

Kerfer waited for him to explain, but Setco didn't. Instead he examined the roads around the airport, then the highway south. He knew exactly where the base was, finding it without Kerfer's help.

"They have a missile complex on the same base," said Setco.

"Problem?"

"Nah. Makes it easier. If they get worried, they'll think the attack's heading there. You remember Malaysia, Ric?"

"I remember it very well."

Setco smiled at him, and went back to looking at the map.

23

Ohio

The address belonged to a farm. It was small by local standards, just over two hundred acres, but to Jin Yo it seemed immense. He drove by it twice after finding the address, the second time turning the rental car around in the driveway that led to the barn. The house was set back on a hill, out of sight. There was a tractor, green and shiny, sitting at the edge of the field near the barn as if it were waiting to be used. A few dozen cows bumped up against each other in a penned corral area on the other side of the barn.

Jing Yo drove back to the motel. Now that he had located the farm where the scientist lived, there were a number of items he needed to purchase.

One was a rifle. From what he had seen of the farm, the easiest way to deal with the scientist was to stalk him on the property. There were woods, wide open fields, and a clear yard in the back. If he got the right equipment, he could do it easily.

Jing Yo didn't know that much about American stores, and it took him a few tries before he found a place that sold any. It was a large department store not far from the interstate. Though he had been practicing his English he still felt unsure of it, and so remained silent as he looked at the guns from behind the counter. All he needed was a decent hunting rifle, but there were so many choices, it was impossible to tell which to buy.

"Can I help ya, young fella?"

Jing Yo looked up at the clerk, an older man with a large belly and a bald head.

"I need, want . . ."

"Hunting rifle?" asked the man.

"Yes."

"What are you hunting?"

A man, thought Jing Yo, though he was careful not to say that. But he wasn't really sure what they would hunt here. Cows?

"Deer hunting?" said the clerk.

"Deer, yes."

"You're a deer hunter?"

"No," said Jing Yo, sensing that would be the wrong answer—he clearly wasn't a hunter, and it was no use pretending that he was. "For a good friend. He helped me. I was a resident of China. Now this country."

"Ah."

"He likes to hunt deer."

"So it's a present?"

"To thank him. His wife said he does not have one. They sold."

The man nodded knowingly. "Thirty-odd-six? Three-oh-eight?"

Jing Yo recognized the American calibers. The .308 Win was essentially the same as a 7.62 NATO round, very similar in size to the cartridge used in an AK-47.

"Three-oh-eight," said Jing Yo.

"And how much did you want to spend?" asked the clerk.

Jing Yo had no idea what to say. He had plenty of

money—he could use cash or the credit card—but he wasn't sure what the price range was for a good weapon.

"He is a good friend," he told the clerk. "So. A good gun. For fair price."

The clerk took down a Kimber. It felt light in Jing Yo's hands, not insubstantial, but slightly off. He asked to try another. The clerk gave him a few different weapons, then handed him a Remington. While only a little heavier than the Kimber, it immediately felt more substantial.

The clerk, meanwhile, had been watching the way he handled the gun and inspected the action.

"You hunt yourself?" asked the clerk.

"No."

"You know guns."

"Oh. I was in the army. When I came to America. To gain my citizenship."

The man nodded. "You'll need a scope."

"Of course."

"Listen, friend." The clerk leaned across the counter and spoke in a whisper. "I'm going to do you and your buddy a favor. There's a gun shop down the highway a bit. If you bought a Remington Seven there, he'll set it up for you real nice. Make sure everything was in proper working order. He'd give you a good deal, too. Prices are about the same, but you'll know exactly what you're getting. He can fix it up real nice for you—give it a custom trigger, take care of any little thing."

"Where would I find this place?"

"Here's the address," said the man, pulling over a pad. "Just hand him this piece of paper and he'll take good care of you. I'd suggest a Nightforce scope or something in that league. We don't sell that here, but he'll give you a good deal."

Jing Yo took the paper and thanked the man. America was certainly an incredible place.

24

Gulf of Tonkin, South China Sea

Commander Silas raised the binoculars and trained them on the silhouette at the edge of the horizon. It was a bare bump in the distance, visible mostly because its sharp lines contrasted with the round curves of the sea around it.

The ship was the *Wen Jiabao*, a Chinese cruiser refurbished from the Russian hulk once known as the missile cruiser *Moskva*. *Wen Jiabo* was not quite the pride of the Chinese navy—that honor would undoubtedly go to one of the two aircraft carriers up near the coast—but she was one of the country's top warships, both in sheer size and armament.

Silas had just received an update on *Wen Jiabao*'s most dangerous weapons, her 3M-54E1 "Klub" missiles, which according to the briefing had replaced earlier (and still deadly) Moskit 3M80Es. The Klubs, sea-launched versions of the Sizzler, were antiship weapons that used inertial guidance and then radar to find their targets. Though subsonic at launch, the low-flying missiles increased their speed in terminal phase, making them harder to shoot down. They could reach out several hundred kilometers.

Silas believed that Fleet's intelligence brief on the cruiser and its missiles had been meant as a subtle caution. Ever since he had sailed into the region, his superiors had been hectoring him like anxious nannies, worried lest their charge return home with a little dust on his pant leg. Silas had already had words with one of his superiors, and while he hadn't been insubordinate, he was sure it had earned him some personal time with the admiral once he returned to shore.

During which he would be sure to mention the SEAL team members he had rescued, the Chinese ships he had bluffed away from the coast, and the civilian craft he had protected.

Throw a typhoon into the mix, and all in all it hadn't been a bad little cruise around Southeast Asia's hot little tourist spot.

But what would *really* cap it off would be sinking *Wen Jiabo*, something he was expressly prohibited from doing.

Unless they fired on him.

"Captain, that frigate is changing course," said his executive officer Lieutenant Commander Dorothy Li, who was in the ship's combat center. "Looks like she's moving to engage the Vietnamese coastal patrol."

"Hmmph."

The frigate was some twelve miles to the north, heading west in the direction of Vietnam. The Vietnamese coastal patrol was *HQ-372*, a Russian-built Tarantul I missile boat that carried four P-15M surface-to-surface missiles. Known in the West as the SS-N-2C Styx, the missiles were technically obsolete but not inconsequential weapons. The frigate's own missiles were much more modern.

"He's going to fire," predicted Silas. "Is the Vietnamese doing anything?"

"Negative. Not sure he even knows he's there."

"He knows," said Silas. The Vietnamese vessel's radar was powerful enough to spot the Chinese ship on its own, and its sensors could also detect the Chinese radar transmissions. The Chinese were not being subtle. But even if the Vietnamese boat hadn't seen the Chinese ships on its own, the U.S. was supplying Vietnam with intelligence regarding the disposition of Chinese forces. That was why the Vietnamese craft was there: to shadow the Chinese warships.

Silas put his binoculars down and walked over to the bridge's combat display. The display plotted the positions not only of the Chinese and Vietnamese ships, but everything else within several hundred miles. The information was gleaned from the Navy's satellite surveillance system as well as *McCampbell*'s own sensors.

The Chinese were testing him, Silas realized. The Chinese commander wanted to know what Silas was going to do.

Interesting.

The frigate continued to separate from the cruiser. It was roughly thirty miles from the Vietnamese craft, well within the range of its missiles.

"No reaction from the Vietnamese yet," said Li. "His radar is active," she added.

Silas considered whether he might make a feint toward the frigate, just to see what the Chinese commander would do. But his orders from Fleet specifically precluded any interference if the two navies fought, so what was the sense? If he moved in and the Chinese vessel fired, it would look as if he had shied from a fight.

And what did it look like now?

The frigate soon made the matter moot. Now at twenty-five nautical miles from *HQ-372*, the Chinese Type 54A turned so that it had the Vietnamese ship forty-five degrees off its bow. If Silas had had any doubt whatsoever what was going on, the maneuver would have vanquished it.

McCampbell's crew was poised at battle stations and prepared in case the frigate—or the cruiser for that matter—decided to turn its weapons on them. The sensors aboard the destroyer could tell when it was being specifically targeted by the Chinese, and while there was always some slight possibility of error, at this point it was clear that they were not the intended victim.

Silas warned his crew to be ready anyway.

"Commander Li—reaction from the Vietnamese?" asked Silas.

"Negative. Does he think it's a bluff?"

Silas considered the possibility that the Vietnamese skipper couldn't see the maneuvers, or didn't know how to interpret them. But it was more likely he was under orders to avoid an engagement if at all possible, and was hoping that the frigate was simply trying to egg him on.

Silas was more curious about the Chinese. The cruiser was maintaining its position, moving northward roughly in parallel with *McCambell*.

We're two boxers, watching each other from the corners of the ring, thought Silas.

"Watch them," said Silas.

"Affirmative."

The frigate had boosted its speed to about fifteen knots. Extrapolating from what he had seen the Chinese do earlier, Silas predicted that they would slow almost to a stop to fire. He mentally imagined what was going on aboard the frigate—he saw himself standing on the cramped bridge, plotting his position and then ordering the engine room to cut back power.

"He's launching!" said Li. "The Chinese frigate has

launched two Ying Ji eighty-threes. Target is the Vietnamese missile boat."

Silas looked up at the sea in the direction of the frigate, even though they were too far for him to see it or even its missile. He imagined everything that would be happening aboard the ship.

"Not heading for us," repeated Li.

"Steady."

The two Chinese missiles climbed from their launchers, rising above the waves. With delta-shaped wings fore and aft, they were relatively small missiles—not necessarily a disadvantage in a naval engagement, where agility and accuracy could more than compensate for a few hundred pounds of explosives. As the rocket booster fell off, their small turbojet engines would kick on and the missiles would drop suddenly, skimming across the wavetops at some 594 knots. If they performed well, they would stay within five to ten meters of the surface, and strike home within two and a half minutes.

Silas went back to the plot to see what was going on. Both the cruiser and the frigate remained on their course.

"Missiles," said Li. "The Vietnamese are launching."

Roughly thirty seconds had passed since the Chinese launch—a long, long time, Silas thought to himself.

They saw the launch with their eyes. They were ready but they had to process it mentally.

The Vietnamese antiship missiles climbed skyward. Unlike the cruise missiles the Chinese fired, the Styx trudged up to three hundred meters altitude and stayed there, arcing in the direction of their target.

The higher you are, the easier it is to see and shoot you, Silas thought.

And now things got interesting. The Chinese frigate, seeing it had been fired on—a quicker reaction than the Vietnamese, Silas noted—began dishing HQ-16s into the air. Directed by a Type 354 radar (called Front Dome by NATO), the HQ-16s were antiair weapons, able to strike a wide range of antiship missiles and cruise missiles in flight.

"Five, six missiles launched," said Li. The frigate's forty-five degree angle to the incoming weapons allowed it to bring three of its four directors into action, putting two HQ-16s on each incoming Styx.

So the Chinese commander had seen two steps ahead. Could he see further?

"Be alert!" said Silas, as much to himself as to the others on the bridge.

By now, the Vietnamese ship had turned sharply to put the incoming missiles on its quarter. Her engines up full, she threw chaff into the air, a countermeasure designed to fool the radar guiding the Chinese missiles.

The sky between the two enemy ships lit with balls of lightning as HQ-16s reached the Styx. A necklace of flash and fire strung out above the ocean, bits of detonated missile and burnt metal raining down.

"Two Styx down," reported Li. "Two missiles inbound to frigate."

Only a fifty percent kill rate, noted Silas. Far less than he would prepare for.

The Chinese frigate's 76 mm gun began firing. It had about as much chance of hitting the incoming Styx as a sailor with a revolver, but there was no shame in trying. Chaff bloomed from the frigate as well.

But the real defense was its missile system. Six more HQ-16s launched in rapid succession. The sheer number of missiles was impressive, even if the results were not. One set of missiles struck home, destroying one of the Vietnamese weapons. The last Styx flew on.

Meanwhile, the Vietnamese ship maneuvered desperately, employing all of its countermeasures against the two YJ-83s, which were now furrowing in. The AK-630 30 mm guns aft fired furiously at the enemy, spewing two bright lines at the missiles' flight path.

It was useless. The first Chinese missile struck the Tarantul on her starboard side just below the super-structure. One hundred and sixty-five kilograms of high explosive ripped a large hole in the craft. There were immediate secondary explosions, 76 mm and 30 mm ammo prickling into fire.

Then the second missile hit. The Vietnamese patrol craft disintegrated into a debris field, its outlines high-lighted by a slick of burning oil.

For a moment, Silas thought the Vietnamese ship might get some measure of revenge, as its last missile remained in the air, streaking past the furling missile trails and flailing close-in gunfire. But it had been thoroughly confused by the Jiangkai's jammers and chaff—it passed nearly a mile astern, cratering into the ocean in a last gesture of futility.

Silas expected the frigate to make another attack—there were small vessels nearby the ship he had just sunk. But the Chinese captain seemed content with what he had already done; perhaps he was listening to the radio calls as *McCampbell* was.

Silas pondered the next problem: if the Vietnamese put out an SOS, should he respond?

He was duty-bound as a mariner to do so. Yet that might be considered an act of war by the Chinese, and therefore contrary to his own orders.

An interesting dilemma. But one he didn't have to face: the two small Vietnamese craft responding to the sinking spoke only to themselves.

"Frigate is heading back toward the cruiser," re-ported Li.

Probably gloating the whole way, thought Silas.

25

Near the border of Vietnam and China

"That's absolutely a spearhead of an armored division," said Zeus. He tapped his finger on the laptop screen. "That's how they move."

Trung stood next to him in the truck he used as a mobile office, staring at the laptop. The vehicle was an old deuce and half, with the canvas back replaced by wood; from the outside it looked like something a town might use to collect leaves or other debris.

Zeus's feelings about the Vietnamese general were jumbled. He was angry that Trung had tried to keep him from Anna. Yet he wanted to help him and his country. Partly because he wanted to free Anna, and partly because having fought the Chinese he wanted to defeat them utterly. There was rage and revenge and anger, the professionalism of a soldier—a dozen emotions, all tied in a knot.

Could Trung have had Anna released if he wanted? If he had, would Zeus have stayed?

He looked at the laptop, trying to focus.

"If we block this road here, they have to come through this highway," said Zeus. "The entire column will be restricted. We have a landslide right on this stretch of road. They have to form a column, and the way their infantry is situated, the armor will be in the lead. Then we split the armor down here with an ambush. We isolate the lead element, making it easier to attack. It's exactly what I did to the east. The Chinese will stop and regroup."

Trung put his hands on the desk that filled nearly half of the rear of the truck. He gazed at the map on the wall opposite him; it was a map made from satellite images of the topography, blown up several times and taped painstakingly together to show the area where they were attacking.

Zeus followed his gaze, then looked around the interior of the truck. Even for the Vietnamese, the setting was austere. A pair of old ammo boxes held some supplies. A rifle and a pistol in webbing sat beneath the desk—the general's personal weapons. There was an extra magazine taped to the one loaded in the rifle, and a grenade was clipped onto the belt.

Zeus had more data on the Chinese push that he couldn't share. He was sure the unit was a full armored division not just because of the way it was traveling, but because of "SIGINT"—signal intelligence gathered by snooping spy satellites. The satellite picked off pieces of routine communication between the units. Decrypted and analyzed, these provided a picture of what was happening that was even more comprehensive than the satellite images.

The Chinese had taken one of their reserve tank divisions, the 12th Armored, and sent it down the road in what looked like the start of the boldest advance into Vietnamese territory yet. The Chinese commander had identified a weak spot between the Vietnamese formations and was clearly aiming to shoot through the gap. Two infantry divisions were following, though as usual for the Chinese, they were making relatively slow progress.

On paper, a full armored division contained as many as 240 tanks divided among three regiments. Like many Chinese units, the division heading south was considerably smaller than it should have been, with only about a hundred and eighty tanks. These were about equally divided between Type 96 main battle tanks and older Type 85s, with a handful of brand new Type 98s thrown into the mix. The unit also traveled with mechanized infantry and a support unit of antiaircraft missiles. It was the mechanized infantry that Zeus's plan aimed to separate from the tank; the armor would be much more vulnerable without the foot soldiers around it.

Still, the vanguard might contain as many as forty Type 96s. The lead regiment was strung out in about a two-mile long convoy, hurtling directly for Malipo.

"Your plan is of course good," said Trung. "But to get my men in place to block the road—it would be very difficult."

"I'll take care of that," said Zeus.

"What do you mean? Another guerilla raid?"

"No," said Zeus.

"How?"

"I can't go into it at the moment." He was thinking of a Tomahawk strike similar to the one that had been launched against the dams early in the war. He'd have to arrange it with Washington.

Trung looked at the map. He pointed to the spot where the ambush was to take place. It was a sharp switchback in the hills, a difficult place for the Chinese to defend. The image blurred as he pressed his finger against the plastic screen, flashing as if the computer itself were calculating the odds for or against success.

"To get to this point . . ." The general's voice trailed off, but what he meant was clear—it was impossible.

"It's only six kilometers beyond where you were going to stage your troops," said Zeus.

"But a half day ahead of that schedule. And the terrain is very difficult—to get that far, that fast. I do not know that it can be done."

Trung took his finger away from the screen. He looked up at the large map, staring intently.

"You can do it," said Zeus. "You have to. Because there's no way what you have here can deal with that size of a force. And you have to keep them out of Malipo. We need the airport."

"Why?" asked Trung.

"To hit Kunming," said Zeus. "We're going to take out the Chinese group commander."

"You are?"

"Yes. It'll stop their advance."

"It is two hundred and sixty kilometers away."

"A little more," acknowledged Zeus. "Closer to three hundred."

"So this was your plan all along."

"No. I only thought of it later."

A slight smile curled at the edges of Trung's lips, the sort of smile a parent might have when catching a child's white lie. Except that Zeus hadn't lied.

"The idea came up after the plan to take Malipo had been mapped," said Zeus. "The U.S.—we're not making an attack officially. It's a long shot. Just a very long shot."

Trung looked at the map. Zeus thought again of Anna, this time not as a prisoner, but as she had been in the first night they were together.

It was a spell, the sort of thing he had never experienced, never thought possible. Such an attraction.

"They'll expect an ambush there," said Trung finally.

"It would be the most logical place. Better to break them in two here, as they pass near this mine. We would attack first from the low ground here. They would naturally retreat toward this end, the high ground, and then we could surprise them."

Zeus went over to the map, where the topography was easier to see. The mine Trung was talking about was a strip mine nearly three-quarters of a kilometer long, another quarter wide. An ambush there would have some advantages—the Vietnamese could use the high ground better, and they could swing their tanks in from the north. But it was also closer to the city, and because the mine itself was relatively flat, the individual tanks would have more room to maneuver once they got past the road.

"These are bridges, are they not?" asked Trung, pointing to the road. "We eliminate them as the battle starts. The armor is isolated because of your diversion.

"Our tanks attack from the side and hold the attention of the Chinese," continued Trung. "As the Chinese maneuver, they are struck from this point. Our anti-tank units attack them."

"The problem is the number of Chinese tanks," said Zeus. "After the initial skirmish, a strong second wave will wipe you out."

"We will take the city at the same time, and withdraw to it," said Trung, speaking as if he hadn't heard Zeus's objections. "The Chinese will then have a choice—retreat and go back to the west, attacking in that direction south, or battling us in their city. Malipo will be destroyed—they will pay a heavy price."

Zeus saw how Trung was fitting things together, thinking beyond the ambush. He wanted the Chinese to commit to an attack along the highway at Malipo. The idea wasn't that he thought the Chinese would be more vulnerable to the Vietnamese there; it was that it would take them longer to go down into Vietnamese territory, especially once their noses were bloodied in the city.

Would that work?

Perhaps in conjunction with the attack at Kunming. With the army group commander out of the picture, it would be more difficult for the divisions to coordinate. They would have Malipo as a goal—take back the Chinese city—and then the tendency would be to stop.

A truly smart commander would bypass the city entirely after the ambush, simply plunging south in the direction the Vietnamese had come. But Trung had the Chinese gauged fairly well—certainly they would want to take back their territory.

"So Major, this is what we will do then," said Trung. "I need to speak with my staff officers."

"OK," said Zeus. Trung's voice seemed less tired, as if making the decision had given him a burst of energy.

"You will arrange the strike."

"I'll do that now."

Zeus picked up his backpack but lingered. He wanted to ask Trung about Anna.

It was Trung who brought it up.

"Did you find the woman?" asked the general.

"Yes, as a matter of fact I did," said Zeus sharply.

He'd expected Trung to be surprised, but on the contrary, the general nodded slightly, as if he had planned for them to meet all along. Zeus wondered if Major Chaū had told him.

"She is in good health?" asked Trung.

"Why didn't you order her released?" asked Zeus.

"Is that what you wish?"

"Absolutely," said Zeus, suddenly angry.

"I do not have omniscient powers. I will do my best."

"Why did you keep her from me?"

Trung studied him for a moment, looking into his eyes. Zeus almost believed that Major Chaū had lied. But Chaū had no reason to.

"You found her," said Trung finally. "If I had wanted to keep you from her, would that have been possible?"

Zeus had no answer for that. Yet he was sure that Trung had delayed him, sure that he had meant to keep him.

"Will you arrange the strike?" asked the general.

"I'll arrange it," said Zeus. "Keep your word about the girl."

Outside the truck, Zeus walked across the clearing to the administrative tents. Two were being used as mess areas; the sharp, pungent smell of food bit at Zeus's nose. Trung had planned to rest the troops for a few more hours, but already there was activity indicating that they would be leaving soon—troops were being pushed through the food line, and some of the cooking gear was already being packed away.

The first order of business was to arrange for the Tomahawk strike. Zeus circled around the tent area and walked to the small creek beyond, crossing over to find a place where he could be alone. A knot of soldiers sat hunched near the water, smoking cigarettes—smoking was rare in the U.S., but widespread in Vietnam. Zeus walked about twenty meters downstream, then swung the ruck off his back. He took out one of the sat phones, and after glancing around several times, called Lucas.

"There's no way that's going to be authorized," Lucas told him when he heard about the Tomahawk plan. "Just no way. Haven't you been paying attention,

Major? The U.S. cannot be openly involved. How does this fit into Kunming?"

"If we don't take Malipo, we can't get to Kunming. "There's an armored force that's coming down the highway ahead of mechanized infantry. If they get through to Malipo, the Vietnamese will be slaughtered."

They might be slaughtered anyway, he thought.

"Yes, I've seen the data, but I don't get the connection with Malipo."

"We need the airport there."

"You're going to have to find another way. The president is not going to allow us to use Tomahawks." He started to hang up.

"Wait—there's something else I need," said Zeus, practically shouting.

"What is it?"

"Javelin missiles. They're antitank weapons—"

"I know what they are." Lucas's voice gave Zeus the impression that he was sorry he'd ever answered the phone. "Again, any indication that the U.S. is involved in anyway—"

"They could come from our allies. Like the Russian missiles did. We need to get more antitank weapons up here and the Javelins are better. We need them right away."

"Major—"

"And I know how to fire these," added Zeus, not wanting to get into a weapons debate. "I can show them how to use them. It's what we need to stop the tanks."

The Russian weapons would work as well, but Zeus trusted the Javelins much more. And, they were closer.

"We've sold them to the Indians," said Zeus. "General Perry and I discussed this just the other day. There were plenty of shipments just recently. If you phony up the serial numbers, the Chinese can't trace them. You can get them over from India in a few hours—if you get Russian equipment it will take days, like before."

Lucas didn't answer.

"I'll get back to you," he said finally.

26

Kunming

The scent of bleach still hung in the staff room, a faint reminder of Li Sun's decision to purge the old wood that had held back the army. Otherwise, there was no trace of the tired mice, nothing to remind him of the men who had stood in China's way.

He paced the room, alone with the map that had just been updated to reflect the army group's latest movements. The advance teams of the division leading the spearhead would arrive in Malipo by mid-morning tomorrow, well ahead of schedule.

He considered whether he should hold them there. The armored unit's speed had brought other problems. It was now roughly two days ahead of the two infantry divisions and support units that were supposed to accompany it on the drive through Vietnam. Even worse, he could tell from the latest reconnaissance photos that it was getting too spread out, its subunits at times out of communication with each other.

The mountains ate radio signals. Most of the troops under Li Sun's commands were still communicating with older TBR-134 20W radios, state of the art when they had been introduced some ten or fifteen years before, but little better than tube radios in the rugged conditions where they were now operating. Even the newest versions, which operated with more power but on the same standard frequencies, could not always be relied on to navigate the interference of the choppy terrain, let alone any active jamming.

Satellite radios were severely limited in the Chinese army for several reasons, not the least of which was the fear that their features preventing eavesdropping would allow them to foment a revolt. There was only one encrypted satellite phone in the tank division, and that belonged to the command's political officer, not the division commander.

Something Li Sun would eventually have to fix. He added it to the long list he kept in his head.

There were thousands of details to see to. Working with Chan's help, he had promoted a number of underlings to positions of responsibility, but there were still many gaps in his organization. He had sent for several old friends to fill key positions, but they had yet to arrive. He was doing much of the work himself.

He could handle it. He was only facing the Vietnamese, after all.

Li Sun bent over the map. His enemy was huddled in the area of Lao Cai, which was to the west of his attack route. Lately, they seemed to be trying to reinforce the general area, but their effort was so puny it was hardly worth notice.

During the border wars of the last century, the two countries had had several fierce battles in the mountain valleys around Lao Cai. Much had changed in the two decades since—China was now a superpower, and Vietnam an even more inferior bug.

Li Sun straightened. There was a folder of images from the reconnaissance aircraft's latest runs at the far edge of the table that he had not yet reviewed.

This was another thing that annoyed him—the intelligence system was not fully automated. The images had been taken with a digital system by the aircraft, downloaded to a computer at the air base, then copied *by hand* to a memory device. This was walked to an intelligence area in another building where they were interpreted. This alone took two hours.

Finally, a report was presented to his headquarters, sent by a secure communication system. But there was only one computer terminal dedicated to that system at headquarters, and information sent there could not be shared directly to any other computer. The report and the images had to be printed out, if they were to be shared. His division commanders did not have any other access to it.

Absurd.

This, too, would have to be fixed.

As he worked through the images, one caught Li Sun's eye. Two tanks and an armored personnel carrier had been seen on a road north of Ha Giang, Vietnam.

Curiously far north, he thought.

Or at least it looked to him like two tanks. The image was very blurred. The intel notation indicated only armor.

It was a pathetic force, but Li Sun wondered—hadn't the earlier reports declared that all of the Vietnamese armored units were accounted for elsewhere? There was a small force to the east, engaged in action. Were these just strays?

Two tanks alone? In China, that was next to impossible. But Vietnam, with its skimpy resources and disjointed command structure . . .

If they were tanks, they would date from the 1960s or perhaps the '70s, relics of the country's war with the Americans.

Two tanks.

Had they missed something? Surely there must be an entire unit to go with these. Where was it?

"Chan!" Li Sun bellowed. "Come in here now! I need you."

27

Peter Lucas had lost track of time, and not just the hours. He honestly could not have told whether it was day or night without looking at the clock on the paneled wall of the conference room.

But that was the least of his worries.

Zeus Murphy had been absolutely correct, no doubt due to the staff work that had been done several days earlier. There were plenty of Javelin missiles available in India. Not only had Lucas found them, but he had managed to find an MC-17 to deliver them. The problem was getting an OK to use the plane, which was a military asset, and outside his immediate reach.

No one else gathered in the top-floor conference room could offer much of a solution either, starting with their boss, CIA director Peter Frost.

"Forget the Air Force," said Frost. He ran his hand through his hair, then leaned down toward the table, as if the thoughts in his head had made it so heavy it needed another support. "Send them by boat the way you sent Setco over."

"I don't have any more speedboats in Thailand," said Lucas. "I had to use a chain of them. If I use a regular ship—it'll take days. We need them there in hours."

The door buzzer sounded. Frost turned to Sally Nolan, an analyst who'd become essentially his administrative assistant on the Vietnam matter, and signaled for her to open the door.

It was Mara Duncan. She passed a tight smile around the room, then slipped down the side, squeezing past the empty chairs and circling around toward Lucas while he resumed his argument.

"If we're not going to get them over in time for this battle, we might just as well forget about giving them to the Vietnamese in the first place," Lucas said. "If we're going to have any impact on the Chinese at all—"

"It's a losing proposition," said James Smith. Smith, a retired Army colonel, was a specialist in Asian warfare. His opinions tended to carry a lot of weight, not so much because they were generally right, but because he had published two well-reviewed books on World War II.

They were so dull that Lucas hadn't made it past the first chapter in either one.

"The Chinese are going to steamroll them now. It's just a matter of time," added Smith. "This latest move—it's not the best strategic or tactical use of their forces, but frankly they don't have to be geniuses to beat the Vietnamese. Hell, if this were World War II, the Italians could have."

"I thought you said the attack down the western valley was pretty smart," said Roni Yellis, another analyst. She hated Smith, as her body language made clear.

"It was, but they didn't exploit it."

Mara leaned next to Frost and whispered in his ear.

"I ID'd the launch vehicles," she said. "Scud-ERs.

That narrows down the possible sites to about a dozen."

Lucas was temporarily distracted, and missed some of the give-and-take between the others.

"Peter? Did you want to respond?" asked Frost.

"I'm sorry," said Lucas. "I missed the question."

"How much of a difference will it make if we get these missiles to them?" asked Yellis.

"It will make a big difference," said Frost. "It lets them take Malipo, and it sets up our operation in Kunming. We need to refuel up at Malipo to make the distance safely. I confirmed it with Ric."

It was significant that he'd talked to the SEAL rather than his own man, but no one else picked it up. Setco had bouts of recklessness. He trusted him to get the job done if it was possible, but not to assess whether it could be accomplished or not.

"Even if they take the city, they can't hold it," said Smith. "How long will they be there? Twenty-four hours? Two days?"

"Just the fact that they're there will unnerve the Chinese," said Yellis.

"I'll need permission directly from the president," said Frost, ending the argument. He looked over at Lucas. "I'll ask if it's worth it."

"I think it is," said Lucas.

"Good." The director looked at Smith, in effect ordering him to be quiet. The decision had been made.

"Mara has information for us on the Vietnamese weapon," said Lucas, eager to move on.

"I found their delivery system," said Mara. She was still catching her breath—Lucas thought she must have run all the way from the information center to the meeting. "Missiles. They're Rodong 1s—extended range Scuds. The technology was obtained from North

Korea. I have a presentation." Mara held up a thumb drive.

"Possibly Rodong 1s," said Smith. "Or Scud Cs. Or Scud ERs. E-R is a Western designation," he added, putting on his most professorial voice. "It simply means extended range. If these really are those missiles, then Hong Kong is within their reach."

"Yes," said Mara as she placed the drive into the computer slot in front of her. "I think we have the entire picture now."

Mara did her best to control her excitement as she went through the slides she'd hastily put together after getting the missile data. She'd never been much of a PowerPoint jockey, but the presentation program was ubiquitous inside the agency and in government at large. Most people were so conditioned to seeing pictures and bullet points that if you didn't use it you were generally not taken seriously.

"Bottom line—material for at least two dozen radiological bombs. Dirty bombs," she said, clicking into her last slide. "And these kits that the North Koreans supplied—two dozen at least."

Mara left the slide on and looked around the table.

"There may not be as many missiles. But the mines in the area could contain at least that many. There could be as many as six or eight with TEL launchers in each shaft. We don't have an asset with ground-penetrating radar deep enough to locate them. Not in the area."

"Why not?" asked Frost.

"There are only two satellites, and frankly, everyone thought the Vietnamese were already well mapped. It will take at least another forty-eight hours for anything with close to the ability we need to get into range. And by then—"

"What about this interpretation of the technology sale from RNK," said Smith, using the abbreviation for North Korea. "You buy it?"

"I know it's open to interpretation," said Mara. "They're concluding that these were kits based on where they were originally shipped from—the manifests that are recorded were machine parts coming from Kimchaek. Now that port is near Musudan-ri, the North Korean assembly and launch facility on their east coast. As I said earlier, there's a bit of guess work here, but it does follow a logical progression."

"Interesting," said Frost.

"I'm convinced," said Smith suddenly.

Mara looked at him, surprised. It was the first time she'd heard the analyst agree with anyone, let alone her.

"If they did make these alterations," continued Smith, "then these missiles are potentially a big problem."

"There are twelve possible shafts, clustered in threes and twos," said Mara.

"We should hit all of them," said Smith.

"That's too many missiles," said Mara. "We have to send someone there first; if we get someone on the ground, he or she can check it out."

Frost shifted in his chair beside her. She knew he was interpreting it as another play on her part to get over to Vietnam. But in truth, she realized that would take too long.

"Who?" asked Frost.

"Someone already in country," she said. "Roth Setco would make sense."

"Not Setco," said Lucas. "We need him for Kunming."

"How about Zeus Murphy?"

"Maybe. I don't know."

"Let's work on that," said Frost, picking up the phone. "In the meantime, I'll update the president. We'll meet again in two hours."

28

Forthright, Ohio

It was a beautiful day, bright and just a touch on the crisp side, a perfect day for farm work. Or, if you didn't have to do farm work, for just walking through a field.

After breakfast, Josh borrowed a light jacket from his cousin and went out in the back for a walk. He took off the jacket by the time he reached the old well pump about ten feet from the old section of the house. He draped it carefully over the handle—the pump still worked, though it was generally used only by the kids looking for a drink without having to go inside.

As soon as he started thinking of Mara he tried to mentally focus on something else, jump-starting his thoughts by reminiscing about his days visiting the farm as a young boy. The place had been in the family for several generations, and the family had ties to the area that went back before the Civil War. Tales of hardships and bad weather and triumph against the odds had fueled many a daydream in his youth.

None of those memories would stick today, not even the wild flights of fantasy concerning relatives who might have ridden out their horses or gone hunting in the woods when Indians were still a possibility. Josh wandered as aimlessly in his thoughts as he did on the ground, heading eventually into the woods. Tex had left at dawn to catch his plane, and he felt oddly alone, even with his family nearby.

The woods were thinner than he remembered, with big gaps on the field side. They ran about fifty yards deep, but nearly a mile wide, extending into two neighboring properties.

This would be a great place to take Mara, thought Josh.

He turned his attention to the trees, then to the base of the trees. He saw a mushroom—Exidia glandulosa, a black, jelly fungus—clinging to some downed branches and bits of bark at the base of the tree. Though common in North America, he couldn't remember seeing examples here. The fungus family thrived on warmer, wet temperatures.

You might make an argument that this instance of Exidia glandulosa was a product of the rapid climate change over the past few years. Then again, the mushroom was common elsewhere, and the fact that Josh couldn't remember seeing it here wouldn't be taken as scientific evidence of anything—except a possibly faulty memory.

You had to be careful with science. Especially something as tricky as climate change. People always wanted to blame the weather. They always looked for the simple argument, the equation built only from prime numbers. Yet complexity was much more often the reality.

Something cracked to his right. Josh spun in the direction, tense. For a moment he was back in Vietnam, trying to escape—alone with Mạ, the little girl, desperate to keep her safe.

Thank God for her. Taking care of her had kept him

from panicking. Caring for someone else was the key to his own survival.

But he wasn't in Vietnam; he was in Ohio. A squirrel shot out to his left, ducking into some crinkled leaves.

God, I miss Mara, Josh thought to himself. *Maybe I'll try calling her again from the house.*

Jing Yo watched the scientist walk past him. He considered leaping out—it would be nothing to grab his neck and snap it.

But assassination was not something accomplished by impulse. It required patience and planning. The only thing he had aimed at doing today was scouting the area—he'd left the rifle back at the motel.

He had his hands and his knife. It would be easy.

Snatch the opportunity.

Was his way to escape clear? He had left the car where it could be easily seen, and had not yet had a chance to check the local roads, or thought of where he would go after he killed.

Jing Yo hesitated, and with that hesitation, whatever chance he had slipped away—someone near the house called to the scientist, and stood watching him as he emerged from the woods.

Patience was the key. There was no rush to take him. Jing Yo would plan the operation correctly, then wait.

29

President Greene was alone in the Oval Office, waiting to receive a delegation of businessmen from Missouri, when Frost called with an update on the Vietnam situation.

"I have exactly sixty seconds for you," the president told him. "Go."

"We pinned down the information on the dirty bombs. The Vietnamese have a delivery system—Scud missiles with extended range. From North Korea. They could hit Hong Kong."

"That far?"

"Absolutely. I have no information on the actual targeting data, but they could have as many as twelve weapons. The Chinese would be defenseless against them."

"Hold on," Greene told Frost. He pushed the hold button on his phone, then slapped the button to connect to his appointments secretary. "Joyce—"

"They're on their way, sir."

"Damn."

"Should I call them back?"

"No, no," said Greene. He slapped the phone button

and reconnected with Frost. "You're one hundred percent sure?"

"Nothing is one hundred percent."

"Do you have specific locations on the missiles?"

"No, sir—I have a dozen possibilities."

"You need to narrow that down."

"I'm working on it."

"Prepare a report for the NSC. We'll talk—"

There was a knock on the door.

"Mr. President, there was one other thing—the Chinese are launching a tank attack on a new front. They need antitank weapons."

"Didn't we just give them a shipment?"

"They've used those. We have Javelins that we can get from India, so it won't be clear that we helped get them there. But the problem is—"

"Will this buy us time?" asked Greene. As Frost hesitated, he put the question more succinctly. "Will this make the Vietnamese less likely to use their dirty bombs?"

"It's likely to slow if not stop the advance. But it would, yes, give us more time to get the exact locations of their weapons. As I said—"

"What exactly do you need? Bottom line?"

"Help from the Air Force. They have an MC-17 and could fly into Vietnam. If—"

"What are the odds of the Chinese stopping the plane?"

"Well, the MC-17 is designed for this sort of thing, but if you're looking for a guarantee then—"

"Get the Javelins there as soon as possible," said Greene, starting to hang up.

"One last thing."

"Peter, the next time you tell me you have only one thing you want to mention, please mean it."

"The cyber project has stalled. The technical people

say they need a physical node to get into the Chinese system. Until they have that, there's no guarantee we can stop anything they do. We can only react."

"In English?"

"They need one of their workstations. I was thinking that we could solve the problem."

Greene listened as Frost outlined the plan.

"The payoff is immense. And even if that element fails—"

"Put it in play," said Greene. He hung up the phone just as his aide stuck his head in the door, the businessmen crowding behind him.

30

Near the Chinese-Vietnam border

Zeus hunched over the laptop, calculating the progress of the armored group approaching Malipo. They were moving quickly. Too fast—they were going to get to the Y in the highway before he could turn around to block the road.

If he couldn't send the tanks down the other road, they'd miss the highway where Trung was arranging the ambush. Trung's entire plan would be worthless.

No Tomahawks. He'd calculated earlier that it would take three, though he'd want six to play it safe. It was an easier strike than the dams, but the location was more important.

A thousand pounds of explosive, times three.

Actually, you didn't need anywhere near that much—the goal was just to start an avalanche, and the Tomahawks were the weapon he'd thought of. They were overkill, really. If you placed the explosive perfectly, you could use less, a lot less. More than a hand grenade, but less than a five-hundred-pound bomb.

All you needed was enough to start an avalanche.

He could do it with explosives, as Trung had suggested.

* * *

"I need to find Major Chaū," Zeus told the orderly. "I need his help arranging something."

"Major Chaū has returned to Hanoi."

"What? Why?"

The orderly's command of English quickly disappeared. Frustrated, Zeus walked a few yards away, then took one of his sat phones out and tried calling Chaū, but there was no answer.

Zeus was just putting away the phone when a thin infantry officer approached. Speaking with an Australian-English accent, he introduced himself as Colonel Dai.

"General Trung asked that I assist you," said Dai. "The orderly said that you were looking for Major Chaū."

"Where is he?"

"He has gone back to Hanoi on assignment. Do you require a transport there?"

"No." Zeus wasn't sure what to make of his translator's disappearance. Certainly, Chaū might have many things to do. But he couldn't help wonder if he was being punished for helping Zeus find Anna.

Or was that just paranoia? How much could he trust the Vietnamese? Or Trung—it was Trung, really, whom he had to trust. He had no way of knowing. He had to just guess, just move ahead blindly.

"I need a lot of explosives," Zeus told the colonel. "For General Trung's plans—I can't get the missiles I wanted, so I'm going to have to substitute explosives. I'm going to need them, and a way of getting them up there."

"Up to where?"

"Above Malipo in China."

* * *

Colonel Dai was as good as his word, finding him explosives, a truck, and two men to help. The men were explosives experts drawn from civilian life rather than professional soldiers, but this was an asset—one had worked on highways, clearing passes, and seemed confident of the solution when Zeus showed him the problem. The other had worked in mines, and recommended a much smaller amount of explosives than Zeus had requested.

Though heartened by the estimate, Zeus stuck with his request.

Both of them called themselves Joe, which was somewhat confusing. More seriously, neither man spoke English, and Dai couldn't find anyone else in his unit who did. The driver knew a few words, but they had mostly to do with curses and drinks.

"I am Liu," he told Zeus, shaking his hand profusely. "We go now?"

"Where's your vehicle?"

The man pointed to a Chinese-made BJ-212, essentially a Jeep knockoff with an extended rear cargo area. There were small gun mounts on the side, but no guns.

Fortunately, there were plenty of explosives, along with electronic blast detonators, wires, and a pair of control boxes. They packed them quickly—Zeus gingerly, the others with the practiced indifference of men long inured to the trade—and set off.

31

Hanoi

Harland Perry glanced at his wristwatch, mentally calculating the time difference between Hanoi and California. He didn't want to wake James.

That wasn't true at all. James wouldn't mind being woken for this. No reporter would—it was the biggest story of the year, perhaps decade:

The United States was supplying material aid to the Vietnamese. Not just intelligence, but weapons and advisors. It had already lost one soldier, and come damn close to losing another. And its men had killed Chinese.

He toyed with the phone. He'd known James for a long time—he'd gone to college with his son, and the three had gone hunting together at least once a year for the past decade. He could trust him to keep his identity secret—"a Deep Throat source."

But . . .

Was he simply mad because Zeus had gone over his head? Was he somehow trying to make up for Win Christian, whom he had sent to his death?

Or was he trying to do the right thing? What was he out to accomplish?

Save the lives of countless Americans. Avoid a costly, impossible-to-win war with China.

Or was he really out to screw the president, his friend?

The scandal would undoubtedly bring Greene down. Congress was already trying to impeach him; this would be the last nail in the coffin.

Where was his responsibility?

To his oath as an officer, surely. And from that oath, to his country. He owed the country his opinion—the Constitution was being dangerously skirted. Even if the actions Zeus Murphy had undertaken fell short of the legal definition of war, Perry was convinced that Greene would soon go over the line.

Where was the line? A dozen troops, two dozen—a division? Greene might be on the right side of the line at the moment, but his actions could easily provoke China into a foolish act, which would then bring the U.S. into the war, one that surely couldn't be won.

But Perry's oath also meant that he answered to his superiors, and ultimately to the president—directly in this case. Was it right to pit his judgment against Greene's?

He certainly had a responsibility to tell Greene what he thought of remaining in Vietnam. He had discharged that responsibility. It was the larger question that remained.

What if one of Kennedy's advisors, or Johnson's, had gone public early during that war? Would sixty years of excruciating American history have been altered? Would half a million men still be whole?

God.

There was a knock on the door. It was one of the Marines, come to take his bags.

"Helicopter's two minutes out, General," said the private.

"Take my clothes," said Perry, pointing to the large bag. "I'll be right there."

"Yes, sir."

Perry glanced back at his phone. His duty was to inform the president, not to make the decision for him. And just because he disagreed with the decision, deep in his heart, didn't mean it was necessarily the wrong decision.

And the question of whose right it was to declare war? Of whether the president was above the law?

No one was above the law. And his ultimate duty was not to the president, but to the country.

Perry punched the numbers for James's phone.

32

The border of China and Vietnam

The driver Colonel Dai had given Zeus drove like a maniac, pushing up and down the hilly roads without using his lights. The BJ's springs seemed theoretical only, and Zeus felt every bump and pothole. Even though he knew the explosives in the back were safe—he'd seen a demonstration once where someone had struck a block of C4 with a hammer without it going off—he couldn't help but be nervous about it. He kept thinking some sort of freak accident might somehow crush the bricks together in a way that beat the one in a million odds against them igniting.

They were just approaching the border when he got an encrypted message on the satellite phone's text system.

The missile drop had been approved. He had contact information for the aircraft.

Zeus checked his watch, then looked at the GPS. It was two a.m.; his last estimate had the Chinese arriving no later than six. The plane would be over northern Vietnam roughly at five.

The spot where he wanted to set up the demolition was almost exactly thirty-four kilometers away by air.

But it was nearly four times as far by road, or at least by the roads they would have to take. There was no way he could get there, then get back across the border in time to get a drop from the aircraft, let alone travel back north with the missiles.

He could give the recognition codes to one of Trung's men, but that wouldn't leave enough time to get the missiles north.

They needed to arrange the drop in China. It was the only way it would work.

Here was a problem the programmers who designed the Red Dragon war game had never thought of—scheduling conflicts.

Zeus had enough experience with covert missions to realize that the last thing he was going to do was call Lucas or anyone else in Washington to ask for a change in the drop site. No, the only way to guarantee that he could get the missiles to the place he needed them was to talk to the pilot himself.

It wasn't exactly standard protocol, but the ad hoc nature of the mission made it easy. He had the pilot's radio frequency; he was supposed to confirm the drop point when the plane was fifteen minutes out. All he had to do was give him a new set of coordinates over the border.

A few klicks one way or the other weren't going to make much difference to whoever was flying the plane.

Assuming he got the right pilot. He'd have to take that gamble.

They made good time, reaching the spot where the road had to be blocked a little after 3:30 a.m. Zeus, watching their position on the GPS unit, tapped the driver as they approached the spot. They stopped in the middle of the road, brakes squealing.

Zeus got out, signaling to the driver to stay where he was. The Joes followed, walking along silently, examining the terrain like a pair of detectives looking over the scene of a crime.

It didn't look anywhere near as promising in person as it had in the photos. Zeus walked up the road to the curve, trying to orient what he had seen on the satellite image earlier with what he was seeing now. The road curved to his left about twenty yards ahead, tucking around a ledge of rocks. His idea was to hike up the side and start a landslide, but now as he looked at the road he realized that the area on both sides of the pavement was quite wide; he wasn't sure the boulders would completely block the road.

The Joe who'd worked on highways definitely agreed. He made a long explanation in Vietnamese, the vast bulk of which was lost to Zeus. But the word "no" was pretty clear. The expert pointed with his hand that they should look farther north along the road. He had brought a paper map, and pointed to a spot marked as a small bridge.

That was a hundred yards up the road. They went there, but Zeus decided the banks of the streambed it forded weren't deep enough to stop a determined commander—and the speed of the armored units indicated they were being led by one.

They checked their maps. Zeus found a bridge two miles away. The Vietnamese expert agreed it was worth trying.

"We have to go on," he told the driver. "There's a bridge, about two miles—three kilometers."

The driver stared at him.

"*Ba,*" said Zeus, using the number for three and pointing. Finally, the engineer in the back leaned forward and told the man where to go. He must have warned him that they were running out of time, for the man sped recklessly. Even with the wide roadway and apron, they barely avoided sliding into a set of boulders at the far end of the turn.

Zeus gripped the GPS unit in his left hand, holding on to the BJ with his right. His pack was wedged between his feet, the rifle stock visible and easily reached through the unzipped top.

"Here," said Zeus. "Stop."

The BJ nose-dived to a halt. Zeus got out again. Worried that the Chinese would be getting closer, this time he took his weapon as well as the GPS.

The bridge was a simple structure with trusses below, and nothing above. While he was confident that he had enough explosives to blow it, he was worried that it would be an obvious sign of sabotage.

Would that tip the Chinese off that something was up?

It absolutely would.

He looked around at the nearby landscape. The waning moonlight cut it into a succession of shadows and angles, small trees and jagged hills.

Zeus walked across the bridge, debating. The road narrowed just ahead—could he set charges in the rocks and tumble enough down to block the bridge?

He trotted up to take a look. The problem was that he didn't have enough experience with explosives to know exactly what to do. Unlike the other area, where the rocks were loose, here the wall seemed solid.

Zeus suddenly felt defeated, as if the Chinese had already swept past. He fought against it, looking around. There were trees on the other side of the road. He could set charges there.

He could blow up the bridge and make small potholes—he could make it look like artillery shells hit somehow.

He ran back to the truck. The Joe who was the mining expert pointed down at the bridge. They had worked out how to blow it up.

"I need it to look like an accident," Zeus tried to explain. The soldier listened, then shaking his head, he waved—was he saying it wasn't important? Or it couldn't be done?

Then the man pointed at the trees.

They had the same idea he did—to make it look like an artillery attack or a bombing run gone bad. Zeus nodded.

"Good," he told the men. "Let's go."

They began setting the charges. After making sure the others had enough explosives, Zeus took several bricks of explosives and ran across the bridge to a spot where the slope started. He climbed up to a thick, knotted trunk leaning down toward the bridge and taped a charge to the trunk. Then he inserted the long, thin cap that would detonate the plastic explosive. He strung some of the wire, using both his combat knife and his teeth in lieu of the wire cutters, which he'd forgotten to fish from the box in his haste.

There is a science and an art to blowing things up, and while Zeus had taken two classes on using explosives, he was not anywhere near expert enough to be able to gauge either the absolute best place to put the charges or how much to use. All he could do was use a lot of explosives. He sensed that he was putting in too much, but at this point he knew it was more important to simply get it laid out. He finished the first set and looked for another tree.

About five yards farther up he found another with a curved trunk leaning downward, and went to work. He connected the wires, made sure his connections were good, then slid down and put a few charges in the rocks.

He'd wired in four charges with caps and was

starting back for more explosives when he heard a noise in the distance. It was faint, barely audible above the steady grunt of the nearby BJ, and it took Zeus a moment before he was sure what it was—the lead vehicles in the approaching column.

How far away? It was impossible to tell in the hills.

"They're coming!" he yelled, starting down.

The others shouted to him. He guessed from their gestures that they wanted him to fix the wires. He started grabbing them, pulling them together and working his way back toward the truck.

Sweat poured from his hands. As soon as he had sorted the wires at the detonator box, he realized he didn't hear the vehicles any longer. He set the wires, made sure they were ready to be connected, then took some more caps and bricks of explosive to finish the job on the other side.

He went out under the bridge and helped the man who'd worked in the mine. Together they taped a pair of bricks onto a beam. Joe tucked a little slot in the bottom charge, then slipped a slim detonator inside.

Sweat poured down the side of the man's face. They were both nervous, working quickly and trying not to show their fear.

As soon as he was on the embankment Zeus heard the vehicles again, much louder.

"Damn. They're coming. Come on!"

Zeus pulled the wires together and worked his way back with the reel, trying not to trip in his haste.

It was like a case of déjà vu—he'd done almost the same thing a few days before, destroying a bridge as the Chinese attacked. But this time everything was a little off—it was darker and more desperate somehow. Yet how could that be? He'd been fired at the last time, and blown it up with . . .

With what? He couldn't even remember what he

had done. He couldn't remember anything. It was like a scrambled dream, or nightmare.

Stay together!

Keep your head on. It's panic, and it's messing you up.

He gave them a pep talk, even though they couldn't understand what he was saying. It was more for him anyway—something to keep his mind moving in the right direction.

"We have to get it done before they're close enough to see. We have to get this going."

The sound was loud. Was it enough to cover the explosion?

It was immaterial now.

"Pack up! Get the boxes back in the truck. Go! Go!"

Zeus wired the detonator switch box, a small, battery-powered device with a pair of switches—a charging button that needed to be pressed and held down for a few seconds to activate the device, and then the actual detonating switch, a simple rocker.

With the Chinese vehicles this close, he was tempted to wait until they were on the bridge to detonate the charges. But the last image he had seen showed that the lead vehicles were light Humvee-like trucks; to do real damage he'd have to wait until the tanks were on the bridge. That would mean he'd get into a firefight with the soldiers in the Humvees who came over first. That simply wasn't worth the risk.

As he checked his connections, his secure sat radio began buzzing. He had a direct communication—the MC-17 with the antitank weapons was trying to contact him.

Perfect timing, Zeus thought.

He pulled the radio from his pocket. It looked like a standard stat phone with a five-line screen on the face below the earpiece and an extended number pad just below that. He had to tap a code in to unlock it, but momentarily blanked on what it was.

The vehicles were getting closer. Finally Zeus got the combination right and was connected to the copilot of the aircraft, who was handling the communications.

"Looking for Zeus," said the air force captain. There was only the slightest bit of tension in his voice.

"I'm going to need to give you new coordinates," Zeus told him, without even bothering to identify himself. "But I need five minutes. Maybe ten."

"Ah, yeah, all right. Roger that. We have a rough location and—"

"It's gonna be north of that."

"North?"

"Just hold on and I'll get back to you." Zeus cut the communication.

He glanced behind him, made sure that the others were behind the truck, then pushed down on the charge button, arming the detonator switch.

I'm too close, he thought, even as he flicked the switch to blow the charges.

A long second followed. Nothing happened. Zeus thought he had screwed up the wiring somehow. He glanced down at the connections.

Then the world in front of him exploded.

Most of the force of the blast was contained by the embankment and the metal and concrete of the bridge. Even so, it threw him back. The side of the hill crumbled—trees, rocks, and dirt falling in an avalanche. A thick cloud of pulverized rock and wood filled the air.

Warmth swelled over him. Zeus felt Anna, lying next to him, her arm draped over his chest. "Anna," he whispered.

She nuzzled next to him. He smelled the light scent of her perfume mixing with the faint sweetness of his own sweat. They were together and he would never have to leave her again.

Zeus began to choke. His lungs felt as if they were filled with rocks.

Something scraped his back. It was like a knife, dragging down from his shoulder blades to his rump to his leg. It kept cutting, the pain extending itself somehow.

He was being dragged.

Where am I going?

Zeus finally regained consciousness as he was pulled up into the cab of the BJ.

"The box, the box, we need the box of explosives," he said, half stumbling into his seat. "The box."

The two men pulling him shouted at him. Zeus realized he couldn't hear.

"The box." He gestured, trying to get them to understand. They lifted him up and shoved him into the truck.

"The explosives," said Zeus. "The boxes?"

"We go now!" shouted the driver. The ground was vibrating with the sound of the heavy armor approaching.

"Go," said Zeus. "Go, yes, go. OK. Before it's too late. Get us back east—take us to the road east."

They backed around and sped off. Zeus turned and tried to look back, but couldn't see anything.

"My radio," he said aloud, reaching into his pocket. "I have to talk to the pilot."

33

Kunming

General Li Sun sat down in the well-padded office chair in front of the long table in his command post's communications center, waiting while the aide made the connection with the 12th Armor Division. The unit had just stalled above Malipo, due to a damaged bridge.

Undoubtedly destroyed erroneously by Chinese bombers earlier in the war, thought Li Sun, then covered up by the area commanders. Such incidents had been rife, enabled by the informal networks among the different generals, who covered for each other.

While he waited for the connection to be made, Li Sun opened his briefing folder and looked at an area map. The highway snaked through the hills and mines around Malipo; there was only one real alternate south, a mining road that had been installed in the bed of an older passage. The surface was rough, but the bed had been reinforced for mining vehicles and it could easily bear the weight of the Chinese main battle tanks.

"General, the connection with General Fan Shen has been made." The aide held out the handset.

"General Fan, explain your situation," snapped Li Sun, his voice brisk. "What is going on?"

"There was a rock slide on the road below Piaopiao Dazhai," replied the general. "It demolished the bridge. We will have to go back and proceed on the highway to the east. I believe—"

"A rock slide, General?"

"It may have been a guerilla strike. We've seen some damage that looks—"

"Guerillas? Vietnamese? That far into China? That's not possible."

"I . . . didn't mean—"

"It's impossible. The Vietnamese can't even protect their own border."

"I realize it is unlikely, General. As I said, it appeared to be a rock slide. But there may have been explosives."

"It's more likely to have been one of our own bomb strikes," said Li Sun. "Or our missiles."

Fan didn't answer. That confirmed it for Li Sun—the general must be protecting whatever unit had been involved.

"Is this delaying your offensive?"

"We are taking an alternate route. It won't delay us."

The general told Li Sun that the division would now take the highway directly into the town, swinging east through a hamlet known as Moshan Xiazhai. While the surrounding area had once been lush high jungle, it was now mostly barren because of the changing weather patterns and strip mines. Many of the poor farmers who had lived there had gone north or east, seeking factory jobs; the region had about a twentieth of the population it had had some ten years before.

"If you take that road near the mines, your unit will bunch up in the hills," said Li Sun, consulting his map.

"You can avoid the problems by going straight through the open mines near Songshanpo. You then come back west through the valley and rest below the town. By daybreak, we will have a better idea how much progress the infantry will make. That will determine the timing of our next move."

"Yes, General."

"I would prefer to put you directly into action," added Li Sun. "I would prefer to have you attack across the border as soon as you can organize your tanks."

"General, we will group ourselves to strike as soon as we reach Malipo. This will not slow us down."

Li Sun handed the handset back to his aide and rose from the console. He was surprised to find General Shaun, his chief of staff, standing behind him.

"Do you feel that the Vietnamese could possibly have blocked the road?" General Shaun asked.

"This far north of the border?"

"There have been incidents to the east," said Shaun.

"You don't feel he's covering up for someone?" asked Li Sun. "Such as the five hundredth and third? Their incompetence was passed off as a Vietnamese artillery assault, when we all know the Vietnamese don't have artillery in that sector."

"That incident, yes," admitted Shaun. "I can check with some of the units."

"That will only antagonize them." Li Sun considered the politics. He had little use for the missile forces, but some contacts among the air force he needed to preserve—in fact, he would have to call on them soon. There was no sense making trouble.

Shaun's eyes rebuked him. He shouldn't put politics above expediency—and wouldn't have, just a few days ago. But he was learning the limits of idealism. Word of his decision to "replace" the moribund leadership of the army group had apparently reached some of the dead men's cronies, and they were starting rumors that Li Sun couldn't achieve his objectives. He knew from his own sources that questions were being raised about his leadership.

Li Sun wasn't surprised that the older generation would see him as a threat, or that they would work behind his back to undercut him. He had to be careful in dealing with them—and make friends or at least placate enemies, something he wouldn't have thought necessary just a few weeks before.

"Most likely it was an errant missile," Li Sun told Shaun. "But you are right—Fan should be more suspicious. Call me when he reaches Malipo. Who is our commander there?"

"A pensioner," said Shaun with some derision. "A major named Shang. I would not count on him for much."

The fact that the command was held by a major, and an older one at that, indicated how small the force was. Clearly, the landslide or whatever it was that had blocked the road was the result of their own attack: if the Vietnamese wanted to attack somewhere, surely they would have struck the city, blowing up the police station or some other symbol of authority.

"We won't count on him then," said Li Sun. "But have Fan talk to me when he is in the city. I want him to move south as quickly as possible. And you might remind him that speed is of the essence, if you have cause to talk to him before I do."

"Yes, General."

"All of our people need a little push," Li Sun said. "Give it to them."

34

The aircraft's copilot had been trying to reach Zeus for several minutes when Zeus finally made the connection and acknowledged.

"There you are, Major," said the man. "We're only zero-two to the drop point."

"No, I have new coordinates," said Zeus. "I need you to come northwest. Stand by."

"Northwest how far?" answered the copilot.

"Stand by."

"Major, northwest is pretty damn close to Chinese territory. If not over it."

"I need you to go over it. I'm working on it."

The copilot was silent.

Zeus studied the paper map. The only good spot for a drop was in the large strip mine where he planned the ambush. Anywhere else would either take too long to get to or run the risk of losing the gear to a bad drop.

Zeus checked himself with the GPS, then looked at the MC-17's likely course. The aircraft was cutting north through a valley at very low altitude, about a hundred miles south of Zeus and roughly sixty miles from the border. The Chinese defenses weren't sophisticated enough to detect it, as long as it stayed in the carefully calculated flight path and didn't go too much farther north.

He read the coordinates for the strip mine to the copilot.

"Major, our orders are to stay in Vietnamese air space," said the copilot.

"You copy those numbers?"

"Oh yeah, roger, I copy them all right. That isn't the problem, sir."

"That's where I need those crates."

There was another pause, then a new voice came on the line. It was a woman's.

"Major Murphy, this is Lt. Colonel Baum. I'm the flight commander and pilot."

"Listen, I need you to come north. The situation is desperate. Beyond desperate."

"I know what you need. Do you realize what you're asking us to do?"

"Affirmative. Listen, I'm not going to tell anyone about it. I'm just asking because—"

"Is there a marker?" she asked, cutting him off.

"Excuse me?"

"Have you set up navigational aids?"

"Negative. I don't have time. I just need you to drop it on that spot."

"We're flying over a jungle. In the mountains. My gear is good, Major, but—"

"The coordinates are in a strip mine. It'll be at the northwestern end. There's a mining road there. If you miss there's plenty of leeway."

"I'm *not* going to miss."

"My intelligence is there's no radar up here and no antiair to speak of, so—"

"Stand by."

Did he have a backup plan? If she decided not to go across the border, what could he do?

Go back, break Anna out. Shoot everyone in the damn prison where she was being held.

That was about as realistic as anything else.

"All right, Major," said Baum, coming back on the line. "We are ten minutes from your target. We are going to make this very quick. Very, very quick."

"Yes, ma'am. Thank you. Thanks."

Zeus felt a wave of relief and gratitude. It passed quickly—the jeep veered sharply right, nearly running off the road. Zeus reached up and grabbed the side of the door, barely holding as the driver overcorrected. There was an animal or something in the road dead ahead—an ox or a cow, Zeus thought. Then suddenly they were weaving through four, five, six of them. A small figure ran toward them on Zeus's side.

One of the men in the back began to fire.

"Shit!" yelled Zeus. "Stop! Stop!"

The loud report of the gun once again took away Zeus's hearing, this time painfully. Wincing, Zeus saw the figure spinning to the right as they passed. He couldn't tell if it had been hit, if it were a man or a woman—it disappeared into the shadows. They were past the animals as well—two houses appeared to the right, then several more beyond them, dark and huddled against the backdrop of the hills.

"No more shooting," said Zeus. His voice buzzed against the bones in his skull, the sound foreign and extremely muffled. "We have to get past—we have to be quiet and fast."

Whether the driver understood or even heard what he was saying, he kept the vehicle moving and stayed on the road, rushing past the small settlement. In the back, the two Joes eyed the shadows nervously, fingers on the triggers of their guns. Zeus turned around and motioned to them with his hands, trying to get them to calm down. He had heard the Vietnamese expression for calm or taking things easy, but he couldn't quite remember it.

"*Bình tĩnh,*" he tried. "*Bình tĩnh.*"

It had no effect. The soldiers continued to look out the windows, clearly on edge. He worried their fingers would hit the triggers with every pothole.

35

Beijing

Cho Lai sat in his car, waiting for the security team to make sure the road ahead was clear. Lately there had been overnight protests in various areas around the capital, protests of a bizarre nature: desperate peasants would run out onto the highways and throw themselves down to be run over.

Which, in most cases, they were.

The first few had seemed like accidents, or simple suicides, if such desperate acts could really be called simple. Yet they had developed into something of a movement, with regular press coverage and copycats across the nation.

Cho Lai's first reaction was contempt, and he still felt that way for the most part. But he also realized the depth of the people's despair—China was suddenly sinking back toward chaos, and the people needed relief.

That was what the war with Vietnam was all about.

"How much longer?" he asked his driver.

"Security says ten minutes, Your Excellency."

"They said that ten minutes ago."

"Yes, Your Excellency." There was a resigned note in his voice.

"How is your family?" asked Cho Lai, trying in a small way to show the man that he was not blaming him for the delay.

"Well, Your Excellency."

"Very good. Very good."

Cho Lai leaned back in his seat and picked up his phone. He might just as well get some work done. He took the notes his aide had prepared—because he preferred traveling alone, his aides were two cars back, behind the security detail—and began dialing.

Qingyun Pu, the general in charge of the air force, was his first call.

As usual, the general's report was very upbeat and aggressive. Cho Lai appreciated this; talking to Qingyun Pu always put him in a good mood. He also had a nice way of painting the Vietnamese as inferior baboons.

He was in rare form tonight, despite the late hour.

"The savage enemy is being beaten into the ground," said the general. He gave Cho Lai a mind-numbing list of statistics regarding bombs dropped and enemy installations destroyed.

"I have been hearing rumors of bombing missions that have struck the wrong targets," said Cho Lai finally.

"Oh no, not at all. Rumors and innuendo—never worry about that, Your Excellency. There is so much infighting among the army—it's a terrible rat's nest."

Cho Lai had no doubt about that. "What about their weapon," he asked. "Has it been destroyed?"

"Not yet. The intelligence is incomplete."

"I am told the data is incontrovertible."

"Perhaps. But the sites have been inspected by our

flights," said Qingyun Pu. "We would think such a weapon would be visible. I must confess that given our searches and their results, I don't believe it exists."

That was not what Cho wanted to hear; it sounded too much like an excuse for incompetence. His intelligence people believed that the Vietnamese had obtained long-range missiles from North Korea and were planning on using them shortly.

North Korea. There was another problem that should be stamped out in a quick blow.

"Whether it is a rumor or not, any weapon that harms our people will be a blow to more than our prestige," said Cho Lai sharply. "There will be consequences."

"We have searched the area thoroughly," said the air force leader. "There is nothing there. I have even ordered a bombing run or two. But, Premier, if you wish—"

"I wish more surveillance," said Cho Lai. "And results."

If the Vietnamese really did have missiles—and something deadly to put on them—Cho Lai wanted them destroyed before they could be used.

If they did launch the missiles, that could be used as part of the propaganda war, Cho Lai thought. It might in fact be very useful. On the other hand, there would be no practical way to retaliate—they were already doing as much to Vietnam as he dared. He needed the country to maintain its ability to farm and produce oil, otherwise there was no point to the invasion at all.

His intelligence people had made ridiculous predictions about poison gases and biological weapons, none of which Vietnam had—surely they would have been used by now. There was some word from sources in Hanoi, or supposedly in Hanoi, that the Vietnamese had managed to purchase a nuclear warhead. But Cho Lai dismissed that outright.

Most likely, the missiles had conventional warheads and would be fired indiscriminately at urban targets. But even so, those would kill many of his people.

The car lurched forward.

"General, I have other business," Cho Lai said. "Keep me informed. Remember—results are most important."

"It will be my pleasure to keep you updated, Your Excellency."

Cho Lai hung up, wondering why all of his commanders couldn't be so positive.

36

Above Malipo, China

Zeus checked his watch. They were making good time—the driver was going even faster than he had on the way here; Zeus had the bruises on his rump to prove it. Even so, they were never going to get there before the plane made its drop.

In fact, the MC-17 was somewhere just ahead, on the other side of a hill—how far, exactly, he couldn't tell. According to the GPS, he was still nearly ten miles from the strip mine.

The driver suddenly veered to the left, turning so hard that Zeus almost flew out of his seat. The BJ's wheels slipped, spitting gravel as they struggled to find their footing on a dirt path. A wall loomed on the driver's side; Zeus saw it and involuntarily flinched, sure they were going to ram it. Somehow the truck veered off at the last moment, careening to the right and then once more straightening out.

"You're going the wrong way," Zeus told the driver.

The driver said something in Vietnamese. The road they'd been on had given way to an open space; they were on the rim of an open mine built on the edge of the hamlet. The terrain to the right dipped sharply; the ground to the left was almost nearly as steep.

"You better flip on the lights," said Zeus. "Lights."

He searched for the word in his memory but it wouldn't come. The jeep continued on, the driver hunched over the wheel, refusing to slow down. They started down a hill, then took a sharp turn right, charging through loose dirt.

"Damn it," yelled Zeus. "Where the hell are you going? Crap!"

The driver paid no attention. A few seconds later, he found a hard packed road and they started to climb. Zeus reached over for the paper map, held tight against the steering wheel by the driver. He refused to let go.

"Do you know where you're going?" asked Zeus.

A torrent of words, all unintelligible, followed. In the middle of them, the driver veered hard to the left, and they were once again on a black-topped road. They accelerated, then suddenly took a hard turn right. Zeus flew forward, barely managing to get his hand out on the dash. He looked up and saw that they were on a road skirting a valley; they'd just barely missed going over the edge.

Something dark passed to their right.

The MC-17?

Zeus pulled up the sat radio.

"Bear, this is Greek," he said, using the coded contact names. "Are we looking good?"

"Package delivered," said the copilot. "Godspeed, Major—we're silent coms from here."

"Roger that."

The rest of the trip was a succession of bumps and hairpin turns, the driver negotiating the narrow country roads and dusty mining lanes as fast he could.

By the time they finally reached the strip mine, every muscle in Zeus's body had double-knotted itself around a bone. His fingers were tight claws, and when he got out of the BJ to get his bearings he had trouble moving his legs.

Some Chinese strip mines were massive. Vast hills and mountainsides were lowered by an army of large machines on a scale that dwarfed even America's. The mines in this area, however, were on a smaller scale. This wasn't out of concern for the small population scattered around the hills, much less the environment; it was a result of different feuds among the local and national leaders who had dibs on the land and the mineral rights, and therefore divvied up the plots in smallish parcels.

The mine where Zeus stood was relatively flat, the dirt and rocks stripped out for tantalum, used for capacitors and other electronic components. The yield had not been particularly significant, and friction between the Chinese government and Australia had led to the cancellation of the contract with the Australian mining company two years before; the Chinese had yet to restart the operation.

The center of the mine looked like a large, lumpy plate in the gray night. There were some ledges to the east, and another roughed out section at the south. Zeus dug into the backpack and took out the infrared monocle, one more goodie courtesy of Kerfer. He didn't need the light to see; its sensors would make it easy to pick up the beacon from the dropped crates.

The on-off switch had jammed off, possibly because of the bumping he'd just experienced. Zeus had to pry the device on with the help of his combat knife.

Zeus scanned the site slowly, going left to right, looking for the skids. When he didn't spot anything, he took another look at the GPS and began walking forward. Ten paces later he stopped and scanned again, and this time caught a red flash to his right.

The pallets had come down at the southwestern end of the site, resting on their sides against a low, uncut mound of earth about sixty-five yards from the GPS target. There were three of them, two leaning against each other on the side of the hillock, and the third upside down a short distance way. Each was stacked with large green boxes containing the weapons.

Zeus went to the farthest skid. It had apparently hit the hill as it landed, tearing some of the netting, though the boxes inside were still intact. He went to work with his knife, peeling back enough of the mesh to get one of the boxes out.

It was heavier than he thought it would be. The end thumped down as he pulled it out.

The two Joes ran over to help. They were excited, but carefully taking hold of one of the boxes, they flipped it over gently, dropping to their knees to open it. Zeus was amused; demolition experts always seemed to like to get their hands on new weapons.

The box contained the launching tube and the targeting assembly (technically, the Command Launch Unit or CLU), but not any missiles. It also included an instruction manual . . . in Hindi.

Fortunately, there were diagrams, and between those and Zeus's familiarity training a few years before, he was able to get the weapon together and ready. He let the Vietnamese soldiers examine it while he went back to the skids.

Six missiles, each in its own crate, were netted to the skid. The other skids were a little larger, with eight missiles and two launch units apiece.

The three crates represented roughly a million dollars' worth of aid to the Vietnamese. The launch units alone cost a total of just under half a million dollars.

Take out one tank, and the investment would have paid for itself. But if they hit just one, the mission would be a failure.

It could very well fail even if every missile hit. There were no reliable statistics on shoulder-launched Javelin strikes in combat—it was briefly used in combat in Iraq, but never in a large scale tank battle. A ratio of two shots per kill would be a reasonable expectation for a well-trained unit in the heat of battle; neophytes would do well to get close to that.

But even if they got one shot with every kill it might not be enough. There were upward of sixty tanks coming for them.

Zeus walked up the rise and waved in the direction of the jeep, which he could just barely see. They'd have to take at least two trips to get the missiles down the road to meet Trung's advance unit. It might even take three.

The driver waved and started toward him. Zeus looked back to the north. Once again, seeing terrain in person made a world of difference—the road to the west was even narrower than he had thought. Trung could definitely hang up the tanks with a small force.

They'd try to come in the other end, sweep through the wide open area of the mine. If Trung was daring, he could mousetrap them—let them start across, then attack at their rear.

The Chinese tanks would be on the low ground, their support troops vulnerable from gunfire on the hills. The Vietnamese tank force—tiny as it was—would have a slight tactical advantage operating from the eastern flank if they joined the battle once it had begun. They'd never win a sustained exchange, but firing at the rear of the Type 96s would make thing a little less lopsided.

They didn't really have to win. Just slow the Chinese

down long enough for Kerfer and his crew to land and refuel.

And Zeus?

He'd leave before it started. Make Trung live up to his promise.

Could he resist the battle? He'd want to see how it went.

The truck came up. Zeus and the others began loading the missiles into the back of the jeep

They were nearly finished with the first load when they heard the sound of vehicles approaching.

They sounded as if they were coming from the east, which meant they were Trung's. Zeus went to the cab of the BJ and picked up the handset to contact them, glad that they were moving quicker than he'd expected.

The hail went unanswered. That was to be expected, unfortunately: unlike the American satellite equipment, this was just a simple radio, easily affected by the terrain.

Zeus put the radio handset down, listening. The hills threw the sound around. The vehicles were coming from the east, but farther north than he expected.

That made no sense. Trung's forces had to come through the mining area to get to that side for the ambush; he'd worked it out himself.

Unless . . .

"Get everything you can into the truck!" Zeus shouted, starting down the hill for the launcher. "Load it up! The Chinese are coming—they skipped around the roads and went farther east through the other mines. Come on! Hurry. Hurry!"

37

Da Nang

It was easy to find a pilot in Vietnam—the entire Vietnamese air force had been shut down by the Chinese attacks. They were eager to volunteer, or so the liaison air force officer at the Hanoi air force headquarters told Kerfer when he called him from the CIA operations ship.

The officer told him he had two who could fly two-engined transports.

"American aircraft, Russian?" asked Kerfer.

"American, Russian, yes. Anything they fly."

"Good enough for me," said Kerfer. "You wouldn't happen to have a plane I could rent, would you?"

The officer didn't, but he knew of an air freight company grounded since the start of the war. A few more phone calls, and Kerfer had his plane and his pilots—and Uncle Sugar, as he called his CIA paymasters, was considerably poorer.

Setco, meanwhile, continued to shepherd his motley group of mercenaries. Besides the men on the ship, he had six Koreans in Ho Chi Minh City. Another three men—two Australians and a South African—were coming in from Thailand. He told them all to meet him in Da Nang, where the airport would pick them up around mid-afternoon.

"You have any Americans in your crew?" asked Kerfer.

"I don't trust Americans, as a general rule," said Setco. "Too idealistic."

Kerfer decided he would ignore the remark.

"I'd like to run through the takedown before we get there," he told Setco. "Make sure we all know what we're doing."

"We know what we're doing."

"Yeah, well, just to be sure."

Setco frowned at him. It was the kind of frown that always tempted Kerfer for some reason; he wanted to knock it off Setco's face with a solid punch. It wasn't exactly a rational desire, and he stifled it.

"The chopper's going to be here in ten minutes," Kerfer told Setco. "I'll meet you in Da Nang. I have to see how my friend Major Murphy is doing. I'll pick up weapons and other gear while I'm in town. I should be able to find a warehouse while I'm there."

"We don't need to rehearse," answered Setco. "We've done this sort of thing before."

"Right. We'll rehearse it anyway."

Topside, Kerfer waited against the railing, watching the sky above the low shadow of land off the starboard side. The helicopter was behind schedule—not good, he thought.

Setco had always been somewhat difficult to deal with before a mission. Once things got rolling, though, he was completely professional. Sometimes he was even pleasant.

Something about his mood bothered Kerfer, though. Kerfer was considered by some of his peers to be rather dark and cynical, but compared to Setco he felt he was Mister Optimism. And tonight, Setco had the look of a man who'd decided he was going to die.

Not the kind of person Kerfer wanted to trust with an op, let alone his own life.

The sound of the helo rose above the cranky churning of the ship's engines. Kerfer strained to see it in the distance, finally spotting it just above the waves a few hundred yards out.

His sat phone rang as the helicopter angled for the temporary landing pad on the deck. He took out the phone and held it to his ear, cupping his hand against the roar of the chopper.

"Kerfer."

"Ric, it's Peter Lucas. I have something important I need done."

"Like?"

"Where are you? I'm having a hard time hearing you."

"I'm on Setco's yacht."

"What?"

"Hold on a second," Kerfer yelled. "Just hold on."

He ducked his head—it was reflex—and ran across the narrow decking to the ladder down to the deck where the helo landed. Pushing his head forward against the wind of the chopper blades, he made his way to the rear door, then realized the pilot was alone in the cockpit. He changed direction and climbed in the front. The helo began to rise as soon as he was in the seat. He looped the seat belt on and continued his conversation.

"Yeah, so I'm good," Kerfer told Lucas. "Can you hear me now?"

"It's a little better. We need you to check some material out east of Hanoi."

"What do you mean, check some material out?"

"I'm going to have Mara explain."

"Listen, I'm pretty damn busy with this trip north, if you get my drift."

"This is more important. Forget the trip north. Roth can handle that."

Thinking Lucas was just trying to make the mission an entirely agency affair, Kerfer started to object. Lucas cut him off.

"I don't have time, Ric," snapped Lucas. "This is more important, believe me. You'll understand when Mara explains it. Stand by."

38

North of Malipo, China

Zeus sat with his legs curled against a rock to keep himself steady. He had his head in the control unit—it seemed almost to swallow it, the screen extending around the sides of his face.

The Chinese Type 96 tank appeared, climbing up the road a half mile away.

It was easy—he didn't hesitate, he didn't agonize, he simply zeroed the cursor and fired.

The missile popped from the launcher, almost stumbling into the air. Then the main stage caught and it was gone in a rush.

Zeus was back to himself, back to fighting—it was so clear and simple now, just fight. Kill the enemy. He didn't have to worry about people lying to him or trying to use him; didn't think about love or even hate, for that matter: he just fought.

And he was good at it.

"Missile! Missile!" he called, as if he were back at Fort Benning, in the last exercise, pounding away at pretend targets instead of the real thing here.

One of the Vietnamese soldiers stepped over—Zeus

helped him load the launcher as the ground rumbled with a secondary explosion.

He'd hit the second tank in the column, reasoning that it was the one that would cause a bottleneck—it was close to a rock formation, making it hard to squeeze around. Now he aimed at the first tank, which seemed completely oblivious to the attack. He continued on his viewscreen as if it were part of a training exercise—no, an asset in an arcade game, stumbling forward.

"Firing," said Zeus as the missile popped from its tube. Again, a slight hesitation was followed by a rush of exhaust. The rocket shot upward, a blur vanishing into the darkness. Then the night flashed, a white circle of heat and melting metal appeared on the far side of the mine as the warhead pummeled its way into the top of the Chinese main battle tank, striking between the two open hatchways and instantly killing the crew.

A third tank appeared on the far right, coming up from the side of the road. Zeus got the launcher loaded as the tank stopped, either confused about what was going on or trying to help its companions. He lifted the viewer, steadied and fired. The tank began to move as the missile left the tube, but it was too late; the Javelin had no trouble adjusting, tucking downward directly behind the 125 mm gun.

A machine gun began firing. Two more tanks appeared, rounding up the hill and drawing parallel to the last one Zeus had destroyed.

"Missile, give me another," said Zeus. The two soldiers were crouched next to him, each with a Javelin in his hand. As Zeus turned to get one loaded, one of the tanks fired its main gun. The shell flew overhead, well into the distance, landing somewhere in the rocks and jungle so far off that Zeus couldn't even feel the ground shake with its thud. The tank's muzzle and turret glowed hot in his screen as he pulled the weapon back onto his shoulder. He locked and fired.

The ground shook as his missile hit home, the Javelin igniting a violent secondary explosion. Zeus turned to get another missile, then felt himself sliding down the side of the hillock where he'd been sitting. He felt rain falling, thick drops pummeling him. Then he was tumbling.

Another of the tanks had fired, this time at the rise. Two shells had struck the ground directly in front of the hill, pounding into the dirt and sending geysers of stone into the air. Zeus flew backward through the air, landing on his stomach and losing the launch tube. He was lucky that the shells had hit the ground in front of him, but his head was scrambled and he couldn't find his bearings.

"Up, up," he told himself, pulling his arm under his chest and then pushing up. There was so much dust in the air he started to choke.

Heavy machine-gun rounds were flying overhead. Zeus found the launcher but he didn't have any missiles.

"Joe!" he yelled. "Load me! Missiles!"

He looked around for his escorts but couldn't see them. He couldn't see the BJ, either.

Damn.

Zeus turned back toward the hill, thinking he would retrieve one of the missiles there. As he did, another shell hit the ground, farther away than the others, but still close enough for the shock to knock him backward. He hit the ground so hard his head rebounded upward.

Damn.

Another round flew by. Zeus felt himself moving—one of the Vietnamese soldiers had grabbed him under the armpits and was dragging him backward.

"Shit," Zeus told him. "We have to get the tanks. I need the radio—I need to call General Trung."

The explosions and gunfire drowned out his voice. Another set of hands grabbed him by the legs and Zeus was shoved into the backseat of the BJ. They were moving—both soldiers were firing their AKs, the world reverberating with the loud, hard reports and the ground bashing shells exploding somewhere to Zeus's left.

He struggled to get his bearings. He had to call Trung and warn him. He had to stop the Chinese tanks.

Zeus grabbed onto the back of the seat in front of him. He pulled himself up between the driver and one of his escorts.

"Swing around to the west," he yelled. "We have to get to the west."

The driver yelled to him, then motioned with his hand. Zeus couldn't understand.

They'd piled the rest of the missiles into the backseat and onto the floor of the front. The two demolitions experts were clinging to the sides of the truck for dear life as the driver drove in reverse toward a copse of trees at the edge of the cleared field.

He needed to find Trung.

The BJ pulled into a U-turn, then bounced along the road away from the strip mine, winding down the hill. Zeus reached down between the crates for his pack, trying to get his GPS. When he looked up, he saw something coming toward them.

A vehicle.

The BJ jerked to a stop. Zeus threw himself forward, grabbing for his gun in the well in front of the seat. He was going out shooting—not because he wanted to be a hero, but because the shame of having given the Chinese a dozen or more antitank missiles would be too humiliating to bear.

Just as his fingers touched the gun, someone pulled him back. Zeus swung his elbow back, trying to break free.

"Major! Major! Stop! Stop!"

Zeus jerked around. Colonel Dai, the officer who had given him the jeep and the men, was leaning into the vehicle over him.

"The Chinese are coming from the northwestern end of the mine," Zeus told him.

"Yes, my scouts saw them." The colonel extended his hand. "Hurry, we haven't much time."

39

Da Nang

Ric Kerfer didn't like being talked down to by anyone. But it really torqued him to be talked down to by a supervisor in the CIA. While there were exceptions, the agency bosses were a collection of pansy-assed pretty boys and the occasional tomboy out to prove they were smarter than anyone else. They drove their best field people crazy or out of the profession.

Usually both.

So he wasn't in the best mood to take Mara's call, especially when she missed the appointed time. He had half a mind to just turn his sat phone completely off and ignore her and her boss. Instead, he went to a bar on the waterfront in Da Nang's tourist center, commandeered a table in the corner, and ordered a beer. He'd already finished his chores, arranged for the airplane and turned everything over to Setco. The CIA para wasn't exactly broken up by the change in plans.

"Fine," was the entirety of his response.

The war had thinned what would have been a healthy late-night crowd in the hotel bar, a fancy penthouse affair overlooking the ocean. Only three other tables were occupied in the room, one by an older woman who seemed to be British, and the others by pairs of middle-aged Asian men who cast occasional nervous glances in Kerfer's direction but otherwise kept to themselves.

Kerfer had spent more than his share of time in countries at war. They all shared certain qualities, most especially a hollowness that came from staving off despair. Unlike in the movies, visible panic was rare, certainly in the absence of actual gunfire or bombs. But fear was nonetheless a permanent condition in such places, barely kept hidden by the usual conventions of booze and drugs. Cynical sneers and nervous laughter were mostly Western devices; in Asia, feigned stoicism and forced indifference were the general shields.

Thus the waiter with the very stiff gait stood at precise attention when Kerfer asked if he could have a Guinness, which was advertised by a small plate on the tap at the bar. The waiter nodded and left without a word, only to return a short time later to tell him there was no more.

It was a fact he had undoubtedly known, though he played out the charade as if life were normal and all of the taps full.

"What do you have?" asked Kerfer. "Just tell me."

The only beer they had was Chinese beer—the waiter said the words very quickly, without naming the beer.

"Tsingtao?" asked Kerfer.

"Chinese," said the waiter.

It didn't matter what it was, if it was the only choice.

"That'll be fine," Kerfer told the man, who bent his head ever so slightly and left.

Kerfer took his phone from his pocket and put it on the table. He gazed out the window. It was late. He should try to sleep.

As if that were possible. He laughed at himself, a

little too loudly—everyone else in the room glanced at him, then looked away as he turned in their direction.

Kerfer smiled. Anyone seeing him would surely think he was a spy. There was no way to alter their impressions—after all, why would a foreigner stay in a country about to be overrun?

And who were they? Probably spies themselves. Desperados of some sort or another.

He thought of checking in with Zeus and telling him what had happened, but that was Setco's job now. It was always best to divorce yourself from the mission if you were pulled off it; he'd learned that long ago. This was true even if you had planned it, even if you were the one who'd sweated all the details out and plotted every step.

In that case, you were in a truly suckful position. You were likely to be blamed for everything that went wrong, and receive exactly zero credit if it went well. Keeping tabs on it was only a way of torturing yourself. Taking a knife and stabbing your thigh until you passed out was easier, quicker, and had about the same effect.

He envied Zeus in one respect:

Kerfer could never imagine loving a woman enough to risk his life for her.

He'd saved several women in the course of his career as a SEAL, and his life had certainly been in the balance each time. But those situations were different—he was acting on impulse, moving quickly to take a civilian out of the line of fire. Once he had rushed into a building literally as it fell to the ground, pummeled by a rebel mortar attack. Another time he'd dashed across a street being laced by gunfire so close, the rock splinters tore up his pants—a fact he didn't realize until he got her out to safety.

But none of those times had anything to do with love. Those were things you did as a SEAL. Those were things you did reflexively. You were selected and trained to be like that. People thought of it as being a hero, but to Kerfer it was no more a heroic act than shooting a gun was. It was a warrior reflex, and while the people who didn't have it didn't understand, the people who *did* have it rarely cared to think about it, let alone analyze it.

But *loving* a woman, and letting your emotions guide your actions—letting *that* emotion guide your actions?

It was something Kerfer found foreign. Worthy, but foreign.

He'd been with plenty of women. Sex remained his favorite pastime, outside of war. But it was *sex*.

Fun. Pleasant. But no more than that.

He was on his second beer when Mara finally called back.

"What took you?" he asked, without saying hello.

"There's a mountain area east of Hanoi. It's a place called Yen Tu. There are a number of old shrines there, and some mining. Are you familiar with it?"

"Not really. I assume I can find it."

"Can you get there?"

"Eventually."

"Soon enough to inspect and possibly laze a site twenty-four hours from now? Maybe sooner?"

As soon as he heard the word "laze"—slang for shining a laser designator at a bombing target—Kerfer's entire mental state changed. It was as if he had been struck by lightning. He was charged with energy, primed for action.

He tried not to show it outwardly; he reached over for his beer and nonchalantly leaned back in his seat. But he was charged.

You didn't laze insignificant targets. You went and had a look at something important, then you shone the light on them while all hell broke loose above.

"I'm arranging for a designator," Mara continued. "Are you familiar with the SOFLAM?"

"That's an old unit," said Kerfer. The SOFLAM–Special Operations Force Laser Marking Unit—had been issued in the 1990s. It looked like a very blocky set of binoculars. "I may have used one in training, but come on. I need a newer unit."

"Ric, you're in Vietnam, remember? We need you to move right away. This is going to be the best I can do on short notice," said Mara. "The alternative will be a commercial laser pointer. So this is by far the better choice. Either way, I'll have it available for you at the embassy."

"Where am I taking it?"

"I told you."

"That sounds like a pretty wide area."

"It is. That's why you're going. I'll give you approximate coordinates when you're in the vicinity," added Mara. "But you're going to have to eyeball the place. We need you to find the actual target."

"Which is what?"

"A missile in a hidden bunker. With a dirty warhead. Probably as many as a dozen of them."

And you want me to laze the motherfuckers?

"You better leave now," added Mara. "The Chinese are massing for a fresh attack. We think if the Vietnamese feel Hanoi is threatened, they'll launch."

"Where's the downside in that?" said Kerfer, softening his voice to a hoarse whisper. "We don't like the Chinese."

"Ric, I'm sure you understand the implications. They'll retaliate. And all Indochina will be a waste dump for the next thirty years."

"It already is," said Kerfer, hitting the End button to kill the conversation.

40

Gulf of Tonkin, South China Sea

As soon as it was clear the Chinese ships would not take any further action, Silas went to school on the engagement. Ever since *McCampbell* had spotted the two warships, he had imagined how they might act in battle. He had theorized how they would fight, how they would move. Now he had something tangible to work with.

His crew had already drilled for a series of engagements over a range of distances. With Li and the department heads, Silas set up new drills, honing his own strategy in light of what he had seen. In theory, there was little to fault the Chinese frigate captain for. He and his crew had won the engagement handily. His tactics were by the book, taking advantage of his ship's strengths against a much weaker opponent.

But Silas saw flaws. The antiship missiles had not performed well, even compared to the admittedly scant known data involving Russian-handled weapons a decade before. Against *McCampbell*'s missiles they would be hard-pressed to provide an adequate defense.

But more revealing to Silas was the prejudice he perceived on the Chinese captain's part. He was extremely cautious, and really didn't understand how to use cruise missiles. He'd only launched two weapons at an alert opponent. He'd gotten away with it, but what if the dice hadn't rolled his way? One shot down, the other misses, and now he has to fire another two. Will they be enough this time, or will the same thing happen again? This was a subtle point, but it told Silas what kind of man he faced.

There were other ways to interpret the frigate captain's actions—launching only two ship-to-ship missiles might be seen as arrogance rather than a sign the captain was keeping one eye on the American to his south. But Silas saw signals of caution. He worried about defending himself, and wanted to save as much of his ammunition for a further fight.

Caution could be useful in some instances, Silas admitted to himself. But if it led to hesitation—even by only a few seconds—a clever opponent might turn it to his advantage.

A s the Vietnamese rescued what was left of *HQ-372's* crew, the Chinese moved farther north at an even pace, cruising to a point some sixty miles north of Hue. The Chinese island of Hainan lay to the east; they were well within air coverage if they decided they needed it.

The Chinese air force had not had much of a presence over the waters near *McCampbell*, and the destroyer's Aegis system had only tracked a handful of planes in the general vicinity over the past few days. All were clearly busy with tasks on the mainland, reconnaissance mostly, though in one case they had watched a wayward bomber stray east before correcting its course back over land.

Around the time the rescue operations for the

Vietnamese ship were completed, a pair of Chinese aircraft made a low, high speed run in the destroyer's direction from the northeast. When *McCampbell*'s radar officer identified them, Silas at first thought he had made a mistake: J-15s, Chinese variants of the ubiquitous Su-27. But it wasn't a mistake at all—the aircraft had come off one of the Chinese carriers sailing to the east of Hainan, below Macau.

The ship's Aegis radar system picked up the aircraft and tracked them from a good distance. Silas waited for the planes to activate their weapons radars—if they had, he would have ordered his own systems to lock and prepared to fire at the slightest sign of aggression. But while the planes roared over him at about a hundred meters, they didn't take any actively aggressive moves, and about all the crew could do was spit in their general direction.

In one sense, the Chinese actions helped the Americans—the intelligence they were gathering from the encounters was worth years of spying and speculation. But Silas still fumed.

Shortly after the aircraft turned north, the Chinese cruiser changed course as well, coming hard to the east and then moving southeast at a fair rate of speed. The frigate quickly followed. Silas didn't react at first—his instructions were merely to monitor Chinese shipping, and he considered if he might interpret that to mean checking out the Chinese aircraft carriers, though these were hundreds of miles away. But when Lt. Commander Li reported that there were two civilian vessels sailing where the Chinese ships were headed, Silas quickly changed his mind. *McCampbell* headed in their direction as well, bending on the knots.

On paper, the two Chinese ships were faster by a knot or two than *McCampbell*, and had the advantage of having started south earlier than she had. But Silas took great pride in his ship and crew's ability to "beat expectations," and while this may have been an empty boast from many masters, it was an understatement from Silas. The destroyer practically flew through the water, and within two hours had drawn ahead of the Chinese frigate, which was leading the cruiser by about two miles.

By then, the civilian ships were on a course two miles to the south, on *McCampbell*'s starboard side. The crew had long since ID'ed them: One was a cargo vessel carrying humanitarian supplies; the other was a UN hospital ship. The cargo vessel flew a Panamanian flag, though it was in fact a South Korean-owned ship with a South Korean crew. Silas suspected that her cargo included items other than medicine and food, a not unreasonable assumption especially given the South Korean government's open support of Vietnam. If it did, and if the ship proceeded to Vietnam, it and its cargo would be in violation of UN resolutions declaring neutrality.

Silas suspected that the Chinese were going to ask to inspect the ship's manifest. By one interpretation of international law, they could not board the ship—the only jurisdiction that applied on the open sea was that of the nation whose flag it flew. On the other hand, if the ship contained contraband, then it *was* subject to boarding; the UN resolution disallowed any shipment of military supplies to either China or Vietnam. Additionally, international conventions allowed navies encountering "suspicious" vessels to inspect their papers to make sure they were in fact registered to the country whose flag they flew.

The location of the ship was another gray area. While by American interpretation this was international waters, China had declared an "interest" in the South China Sea—and Vietnam, a few years before, had acknowledged that interest. Whether that gave China a right to inspect ships there had never been tested.

There was enough of a legal thicket that Silas decided he had to consult with the Pentagon, and so he went up the chain of command to ask what to do. He was told to "observe."

"That's a horse's ass directive," grumbled Silas to himself. He was so disgusted he stepped out from *McCampbell*'s bridge to breathe some fresh air.

He was close enough now to see all four ships, their running lights dancing on the dark water. Silas gazed at each one in turn, then walked across to the other side of the ship. His crew had been on alert now for quite a while; they'd surely be straining soon and he would have to take some measures to lighten their load.

Not that he wanted to get the reputation of being easy on his people. He didn't even want them to think that he was *considerate*, necessarily.

Silas was still considering what he might do when his exec came out on deck to talk to him.

"The Chinese ships have slowed their pace, Captain," said Lt. Commander Li.

Silas nodded.

"I was wondering, Cap, what do you think they're going to do?"

"Probably ask to inspect their papers," said Silas.

"And what are we going to do?"

"You saw the order. For the moment, nothing."

"Why don't *we* inspect the papers?" asked Li. "Shouldn't we be checking their manifests?"

Silas got it immediately.

"You are going to make one hell of a ship's captain one of these days, Commander," he told Li, before charging back onto the bridge.

* * *

The Korean vessel apparently realized what Silas was up to, for within a few moments it sent a message that they were "happy to welcome the esteemed visitors" aboard—or at least that's what the heavy accent of the sailor on the radio seemed to say. Silas dispatched a boat with instructions to stay for as long as possible—until, in fact, he called to inquire what they were up to.

A few minutes after *McCampbell*'s boat pulled up to the cargo ship, the commander of the Chinese cruiser radioed it to say he intended to inspect the ship's papers as well, Silas radioed back that he was currently in the process of making an examination, and would gladly share the results with him.

"And if the captain wishes a share of Scotch whiskey," added Silas, somewhat impishly, "he is welcome to have a taste in my wardroom."

There was no reply, and no further word from the Chinese.

Silas arranged his course so that he was sailing between the warships and the two civilians for a while, in effect shepherding them toward their destination. Finally, the Chinese ships changed their bearing, heading further east.

"Give them about ten minutes," Silas told Li. "Then recover our people. Tell me if they come about. I'm going to take a short nap."

"We beat them, Captain," said Li. She was grinning.

"Yes. It was an excellent idea," said Silas. "But I'm sure we'll need a few more good ideas down the line."

41

North of Malipo, China

Zeus's attack on the spearhead of tanks had confused the Chinese, stopping the company that had been leading the battalion south toward Malipo. Rather than continuing through the strip mine to the highway, they halted at the edge of the open pit area while the officers frantically called for reinforcements.

A half dozen tanks fanned out across the edge of the mining area; several more began climbing the hills to survey and provide cover for the mobilized infantry coming up from the rear. Vehicles were moving frantically on the road behind them, trying to get into a defensive formation in case the unseen enemy renewed its attack. But this wasn't easy—the winding mountain approach made it tough for even two tanks to pass.

The vehicles bunched up, making it difficult for their commanders to organize them. It didn't help that it was still dark. At fifty yards, the larger vehicles faded into shadows, and it was hard to see a man until he was ten or twelve yards away.

Colonel Dai's Vietnamese soldiers, meanwhile, dismounted their trucks and APCs and clambered up the ridge that extended along the western side of the shallow pit. The ridge ran for nearly three kilometers, though because of the geography, not all of it had an unobstructed view of the Chinese armor.

The colonel assured Zeus that his men could handle the antitank missiles on their own. All of the operators, he said, were trained on Russian weapons; with quick instruction from the two Joes, they were ready for action.

Zeus, said the colonel, should stay out of danger as much as possible; if he were captured or killed, the Chinese would use his presence as a propaganda coup.

There was a great deal of truth in that, but Zeus agreed only with the greatest difficulty, shouldering his backpack and staying close to Dai as he established a roving command post.

With the exception of two snipers posted as scouts who picked off tank commanders whenever they had a shot, the Vietnamese stayed below the ridge line out of sight as they organized their attack. Dai split up his battalion, putting about a third of it on top of the hill; he divided the rest in half, sending one group on a long sweep east to keep the Chinese from flanking him there, and holding the last third in reserve, to be used as the battle progressed. Zeus was impressed by how quickly the men moved. Within ten minutes, the force was ready to attack.

The Chinese infantry was just coming up to join the tanks when Colonel Dai launched the first wave of his assault. Besides the Javelins, he had a pair of 9P135M Russian anti-tank launchers. The missiles, code named AT-4 Spigots by NATO, were tripod-mounted, and had a range of about 2,000 meters—just beyond the nearest Chinese tank. Dai used them to open the attack, aiming at the closest vehicles.

The missiles thumped from their tubes. The sound seemed disconcerting to Zeus after the more sure-handed swoosh of the American weapons. But guided by the line-of-sight directors, both of the first missiles reached their targets. The Chinese immediately began returning fire, forcing most of the Vietnamese to duck for cover.

The Javelins began answering the onslaught. Operated by the two Joes and two other teams hand-picked by Dai, the missiles knocked out three more tanks in two salvos. A pair of tanks began moving across the open area of the mine, their smoothbore guns firing as they went.

Such fire was notoriously inaccurate, but it was one thing to know that and quite another to be able to remain calmly at your post as the shells began whizzing overhead. The Javelin shots became less sure; fired in haste, the missiles rocketed over the formation, hunting for targets on their own in the rear.

A few of the Vietnamese soldiers broke, running down the hill. One of Dai's sergeants began yelling at them, screaming and chasing them down.

He tackled one of the men, rolling with him to the road. Zeus watched, transfixed for a moment by the minor drama. The sergeant pulled the man up to his feet and slapped him across the face. Then he reached down to the ground and picked up his rifle, handed it to him, and pushed him up the hill.

The man took a few steps. The sergeant pointed at him and yelled emphatically. The soldier ran back up the hill.

Zeus turned back to the battle as the sergeant went after another of the deserters. One of the Javelin teams was nearby, firing at the Chinese tanks at the far end of the formation.

A Javelin popped out of its launcher nearby, rocketing into the blackness. A moment later a white flash appeared at the far end of the field. It had found its target, and another Chinese tank was destroyed.

Black figures crossed in front of the circle of light. The Chinese infantrymen were charging across the field, running ahead of the tanks now in an attempt to flush the Vietnamese out. Machine guns started firing nearby. The air turned heavy with lead, both sides firing wildly, counting on the sheer volume of gunfire to flatten their enemy.

The Vietnamese were outgunned, but their ferocity slowed down the Chinese assault—men threw themselves down, unsure if they were being aimed at, unwilling to make the enemy's job easier.

The key to the battle, Zeus realized, was to keep the Chinese tanks from coming forward with the infantry and gaining any sort of momentum; they had to be held in place until the second force could launch its attack on their vulnerable flank. But the antitank missiles were running low, even as the inexperienced and rushed troops manning them were distracted by the heavy fire. They took more time between shots. Finally two more launched, followed quickly by violent explosions and white orbs. But the sound of the advancing tanks grew louder. Even without using his night vision monocle, Zeus could tell that the Chinese armor had pushed aside the blown-out hulks at the neck of the approach and were moving to attack the Vietnamese positions.

"We must fall back on the flank," yelled Colonel Dai, running along the ridge after checking on his men. He grabbed Zeus on the shoulder. "We will have to give way on the north."

He pointed to the left.

"They'll reach the road there," said Zeus. "The road is another hundred yards. Once they're there, they'll roll up your position."

"It can't be helped. Come."

Zeus followed up a trail that led to the southern rim

of the property. A small band of trees and brush edged against a bulldozed trail; Dai rushed through the foliage to another trail, this one barely wide enough for a bicycle to pass.

Two of his men were already here with radios, manning a new temporary command post behind some fallen trees. A few wounded had been brought nearby. Zeus nearly stepped on the chest of a man being treated for a leg injury as he climbed up a narrow rill to check out the surroundings.

A flare ignited overhead just as Zeus got to the top. He was on the left side of the Chinese attack, facing due north as the Chinese moved eastward. Three Type 96 tanks rumbled toward one of the berms where the Vietnamese were hunkered down. Chinese soldiers knotted behind each one. Farther back, a pair of armored personnel carriers had maneuvered past the bottleneck of damaged tanks and were trailing the attack.

There were dozens of bodies down on the ground. Zeus could see at least two tanks stuck behind damaged hulks to the rear, trying to get up the angled side of the mine. Either the dirt was too soft for their weight or the drivers simply weren't skilled, as both tanks seemed to be stuck, rocking back and forth but getting nowhere.

Zeus's original idea for the ambush would have had the Vietnamese coming across from that area. He realized now it would have been a mistake because of the soft dirt; they would have gotten hung up and been vulnerable to an ambush from the north.

Luck in war. It was never to be undervalued.

Zeus turned back in time to see a pair of rocket grenades hit the side of a tank about fifty yards away. The explosions didn't stop the tank, but the shock and shrapnel scattered the men behind it. A machine gun began firing from the berm. Then another joined in, and another. The Chinese APCs rushed forward, their own machine guns answering the Vietnamese. Bullets began flying in the direction of the command post, and Zeus had to duck.

By the time he looked again, the battle had swung strongly toward the Chinese. One of the three tanks in the lead had been destroyed by a missile, but the other two had reached the berm. The infantry, though depleted, followed.

The Vietnamese who hadn't been killed were forced to retreat into the jungle. Meanwhile, the bottleneck at the entrance to the mine had been cleared again, and half a dozen tanks and several armored personnel carriers rushed into the pit area, guns blazing.

Despite the Chinese pressure, Dai held to his original plan, counting on the men he had sent north. He hoped their attack to the rear of the Chinese would break the assault, but they had yet to materialize. Hoping they merely needed more time, the commander moved up his reserve to slow the Chinese. Trucks began moving up the road behind the command post, depositing men who swarmed up through the jungle to the lip of the open pit area. Dai's two howitzers— ancient though still potent American M101 models that had once belonged to the South Vietnamese Army— reached the main group and began firing from a road at the rear. The first shells landed well beyond the Chinese assault, but this was soon corrected.

At first, the Chinese hardly noticed the fresh troops. A third and then a fourth tank came up along the berm, then rambled onto the higher ground at the west, flanking the berm. Together this small armored force began pressing down the Vietnamese side. Then, as the howitzer fire became more deadly, the flow of Chinese troops toward the berm abruptly stopped.

The tanks were isolated, their supporting infantry cut down by the Vietnamese who had retreated across a road into the jungle.

A solid artillery barrage at that point might have cut the Chinese attack off completely, stranding the tanks and resealing the bottleneck. But there were only two howitzers, and neither had more than a handful of shells. As soon as these ran out, the Chinese attack regained strength. The Vietnamese were soon outgunned by the tanks, and once more began falling back into the jungle.

With the Chinese starting to gain momentum, the command post itself came under heavy fire. Zeus was knocked off his feet by a succession of rounds exploding nearby.

The Type 96s raised their guns and began firing into the trees, cutting them down so that the Vietnamese had no more cover. Dai tried rallying his men, but his force was overwhelmed. They were out of Javelins and the rest of their antitank weapons. The battlefield was littered with Chinese machinery, but other assets kept squeezing into the fight to replace them.

"You're going to have to retreat!" Zeus yelled, finding Dai shouting instructions into a radio handset. "Move down to the ridge above Malipo. You may be able to string the attack out."

A loud whistle drowned out Colonel Dai's answer. Zeus started to cover his head.

In the next moment he couldn't hear and his upper body felt numb. A shell from one of the tanks had exploded nearby in the trees. The shock threw everyone down and splintered wood in every direction.

One of the Vietnamese staff officers had fallen on top of Zeus. Crawling backward, Zeus freed himself. He reached for the man, then saw that his chest was covered with blood. A large piece of wood had spiked into the man's face, striking through his right eye and impaling itself as if it were a spear.

Zeus looked away.

A group of Chinese were rushing toward the lip of the strip mine, guns up but not firing. Zeus scooped up what he thought was his rifle and pointed it in their direction. Only when he went to fire did he realize he'd grabbed an AK-47. He fumbled with it, then fired, quickly shooting through the magazine.

Another tank round passed overhead. Zeus moved through the wrecked foliage and charred bushes on his left and found his gun and pack. He picked up the rifle and hooked his arm into the backpack loop.

Dai was hunched over nearby. Zeus dropped to a knee next to him, and gingerly touched him—he wasn't sure if he was alive or how badly he had been hit.

The Vietnamese colonel shook his head and said something in Vietnamese.

"You have to fall back," Zeus told him. "You're about to get overrun."

"Yes," repeated Dai, though he didn't move.

Zeus pulled him to his feet. The colonel had been hit by something; his eyes were dazed, as if he might have a concussion.

"Back to the road," Zeus told him. He hooked his shoulder under Dai's arm. A Vietnamese soldier came over and took Dai's other side, and together they started away.

What had been thick jungle just a few minutes before had been laid low by several tank blasts. The trees were scattered like the pins in a bowling alley; they had to pick their way through. There was plenty of light from the flares, at least. Zeus could see not only to the trail but to a road about fifty yards farther down the hill.

Two vehicles were parked there; as Zeus and the

others came down, a pair of soldiers ran up and took the colonel.

"Fall back to the ridge over the highway," Zeus told them, but he had no idea if they understood.

Turning to go back up the hill, he heard fresh automatic-rifle fire above, then a machine gun. If he dropped his pack, it would be much easier to climb the hill, but the gear was too valuable. He swung his rifle up and ran, feet digging into the soft, peat-mossy ground.

Tracers flew violently overhead. Zeus angled to his right, head low. Suddenly the foliage in front of him gave way and he could see the open area of the strip mine before him. Chinese troops were spread out across the plain. Two APCs and a tank were leading them.

One of the tanks that had breached the Vietnamese line on the west had been disabled, leaving only two tanks to fight there. They were moving slowly along the rim of the mine, stopping every few feet. The tops were open; their commanders were deluging the area with machine-gun bullets. More flares had been fired overhead, and the night was now white with light

A body loomed in front of him. Zeus looked toward the man's head. He was wearing a helmet with an ear flap.

Chinese.

He fired, catching the man in the chest. The soldier was wearing armor but they were so close that the bullets pushed him down easily, and may in fact have penetrated the plate they hit. Zeus fired again as the man fell, this time at his head.

This wasn't the place to take chances.

Dropping to his knee, Zeus looked down the slope, but didn't see anyone else coming up. An APC moved to the edge of the clearing. The vehicle was a sleek Type 85, a tracked wedge of steel topped by a turret with twin 14.5 mm heavy machine guns. Its guns weren't firing, and there were no infantrymen on the ground behind the vehicle.

As Zeus watched, an RPG round flew from the jungle and struck the side of the Type 85. The round struck the armor and bounced away, unexploded. A second round hit the tracked assembly and the vehicle stopped, though it wasn't clear if it had been damaged. The turret swiveled, and the guns began firing in the direction of the RPG launch.

Zeus slid back between the trees, hunkering against a trunk as the Chinese machine gun blistered the foliage. As he waited for the bullets to subside, he saw someone moving to his right. Thinking it was another Chinese soldier, Zeus took aim. Just before he pressed the trigger he realized the man was Vietnamese.

The soldier was carrying an RPG. The man glanced in Zeus's direction, then pirouetted down to the ground, hit by a bullet from the side.

Zeus threw himself down as a fresh volley of lead flew through the air. He crawled on his belly to the soldier. As he got close, he saw two helmets bobbing up the hill. He pulled his rifle back and, as the faces and chests of the Chinese infantrymen appeared, fired into their faces. Both men fell.

He waited for others to appear.

Tufts of smoke drifted across the battlefield. Light and dark battled with each other, exchanging positions, casting the plain and then the rim in darkness, illuminating the Vietnamese and then the Chinese, then neither.

Finally confident that no one was following the two men he'd shot, Zeus crawled over to the Vietnamese soldier who'd been carrying the RPG. Thick bullets from a heavy machine gun had practically severed the man's head; it hung off his body at an angle.

Zeus reached for the grenade launcher. He unhooked it gingerly, afraid that if he moved the man too harshly his head would roll off. The weapon had a grenade loaded.

Launcher in hand, Zeus moved back to the edge of the trees. The APC had rolled up to the edge of the remaining woods and was starting to angle down toward the trucks where Zeus had left Dai. Zeus moved in that direction, half-crouched, his heart pounding. He climbed up a rise, moving above the Chinese vehicle.

The Type 85's armor was 24 mm thick; in theory it could be pierced by an RPG, assuming the shell was fired from relatively close range and hit at a good angle. But Zeus had already seen that theory and practice were two different things.

I have to get close, he told himself.

The turret swiveled. Zeus threw himself down, expecting a hail of bullets, but none came. The vehicle continued to move, edging down the side of the hill on a diagonal path that took it to Zeus's left.

As Zeus raised his head, the war seemed to shift away from him. Only he and the APC existed. The bullets and heavy shells that had been exploding only a few seconds before mysteriously disappeared.

The back quarter of the Type 85 moved below him, twenty-five yards away.

Zeus felt his throat constrict. He ignored it, rising with the launcher on his shoulder. His rifle slid on its sling down to his elbow just as he was about to fire. Zeus caught himself, stopped his finger—had he fired at that moment, the grenade would have sailed high.

Calm and fire. Calm and fire.

The APC continued to move. He had a point-blank

shot at the rear compartment just behind the turret, not thirty yards away.

He pulled the trigger.

The rocket struck the hull.

For a split second, Zeus thought the grenade had merely flattened itself against the metal body of the vehicle. Nothing seemed to happen. The vehicle continued to move. Then Zeus felt a low thud, and jerked his arm up to protect himself from the blast shock.

Smoke poured from the vehicle as it continued down the slope, derelict, its crew dead.

Zeus found himself on his knees, unsure exactly how he had gotten there. He dropped the now empty launcher. He pulled his rifle up so he could use it. A squad of Chinese soldiers were charging forward, trying to catch up with the APC. He fired at them. They started falling, caught by surprise.

Out of bullets, Zeus slapped a new magazine into the gun. As he did, he felt a heavy rumble under his knee.

One of the tanks was moving along the ridge in his direction. He started to slide down the hill, but stopped as a fusillade of bullets came up from that direction— some of the Chinese soldiers he'd been firing at had slipped down the hill. He looked right, thinking he would run that way.

He couldn't. An APC was moving in his direction across the field, twin guns winking in his direction.

He was trapped.

Zeus closed his eyes for a moment, gathering himself. He had two more boxes of bullets, then he'd be down to his pistol.

He should trash the gear.

He'd do it with the pistol.

He thought of Anna, then pushed her away—too seductive, too much distraction.

He opened his eyes and started calculating his attack. He would go down the hill, attack the men. He might get one of their weapons.

Hunched against a tree, Zeus did his best to control his breathing, trying to calculate when it was best to charge. The Chinese soldiers had stopped firing in his direction; possibly they thought he was dead.

He couldn't see exactly where they were. He rose slowly behind the tree, then stepped to his left, wedging his foot into the slope. He moved down left.

A dark figure passed in front of him, ten yards away, maybe less. He had a Chinese helmet.

Zeus leveled his gun and fired. Almost immediately, someone started returning fire on his right. He saw a muzzle flash and fired in that direction.

Conserve your bullets.

A shell whizzed overhead. The ground rumbled. The APC was firing again in his direction.

He saw a muzzle flash down the hill from him. He brought his gun up and fired directly into it.

Zeus started to move to his left. He took one step, then tripped and fell, tumbling against a tree trunk. Three, four Chinese ran at him from the side, shouting and firing their guns. But the fall had left him below their aim. They ran past, above him, screaming and yelling.

Up! Up!

He pushed himself around, trying to fire at the backs of the Chinese, but it was too late; they were lost in the trees and shadows. The ground shook fiercely. Zeus turned back around and saw a tank up on the narrow road, pushing aside the brush. It was a Chinese Type 85, slightly older than the others but just as deadly.

The long barrel of its gun poked through the foliage. It blew back—there was a concussion, a hard thud as the gun fired.

This is what death looks like, Zeus thought.

In the next moment, the tank turned white. The earth seemed to implode around it, and Zeus's nose was filled with sulfur and metal oxide.

The tank had been hit by a Javelin fired by the last third of Dai's battalion. The last claw of the trap had finally been sprung.

42

Ohio

American foods intrigued Jing Yo. There was a seemingly endless supply and variety.

On his first day in town, Jing Yo ate at a McDonald's. He was of course familiar with the worldwide franchise, though he had not eaten the food more than once in China, and never in America. Used to meals with a lot more vegetables and centered around rice, he was both intrigued and slightly revolted. The French fries were good; the meat less so.

The next day he decided to try someplace different. He felt a little more comfortable talking now; his accent was thick but not unintelligible, and while his vocabulary was still lacking, pointing to items on a menu was easy. There was a small restaurant diagonally across from the motel where he'd gotten a room. The clerk had pointed it out when he registered, and so he decided to try it.

There were plenty of empty tables. He glanced around, then walked to the side of the room and sat down.

"Didn't ya read the sign?" asked a middle-aged woman walking toward him from the back. She was dressed in a white uniform, and he assumed she was a waitress. "Wait to be seated?"

Jing Yo, surprised by her scolding tone and not really sure what she meant, shook his head.

"Oh, don't worry, honey, I'm only pulling your leg." The woman laughed. "You can sit anywhere you want. Coffee?"

"Tea?" asked Jing Yo.

"Lipton's OK? It's all we got."

Jing Yo nodded. Since it was all they had, why even ask? he wondered.

He watched the woman go to the other two tables where there were customers. She talked to each one, bantering.

"Here's the menu, hon," she told him when she returned, menu and cup in one hand and a pot of water in the other. Under her arm she had a newspaper, which she flipped out as soon as she had put the menu down. "And the paper. Do you like milk or lemon?"

"No milk, no lemon," said Jing Yo, not entirely sure he understood.

"Sugar's on the table. You're Chinese?"

"Chinese-American," said Jing Yo.

"Visitor?"

"I have business in the area," said Jing Yo.

"What sort of business?"

Jing Yo had worked out a cover story, but the woman's inquisitiveness bothered him.

"I am looking for property for a corporation in New York," he told her. "Farm."

"Mmmm, won't find any farms around here." She looked at him seriously for a second, then began laughing. "Well, you came to the right place, hon."

She put her hand on his shoulder and paused, waiting for something.

"Tom is my name," he told her, guessing at what she wanted. It was one of the names on the credit cards.

"And I'm Muriel. Check the menu and I'll be back in a minute."

Jing Yo examined the plastic-coated card. There were small pictures next to most of the dishes. One had pancakes; he ordered them when she returned.

He started scanning the newspaper. There was a story on the front page about Congress wanting to investigate the president. His vocabulary wasn't rich enough to make a lot of sense of the article, but it seemed critical of President Greene's support of Vietnam. Curious, Jing Yo struggled to read it, but couldn't get much out of the first few paragraphs and finally gave up.

The other stories seemed a bit simpler. One was about a fire, another about a youth basketball team. He put the paper aside when his food came and began to eat.

The restaurant began filling up. Another waitress joined Muriel. They seemed to know most of the customers and joked with them all.

The place was not that unlike some of the provincial towns in China where he had been stationed. The people were a little more friendly toward strangers, perhaps—Muriel came back twice to check on his tea and see if he needed more water or a new teabag. But it seemed remarkably similar.

A pair of policemen came into the restaurant as Jing Yo finished his pancakes. He eyed them curiously as they took seats at a table near the counter area. They seemed little different than the police officers he'd observed in China—undisciplined, too friendly with the populace.

The waitress came over and handed him the check. "You pay at the register," she said, gesturing to the front. "How was breakfast?"

"Breakfast was very good."

"Glad you liked it. Try us for lunch and dinner."

Her expression was sincere. Jing Yo was surprised. He had heard and always believed that Americans did not like Chinese people. Maybe it was just part of her job to pretend.

"Thank you," he said.

Jing Yo got up and went over to the register. As he waited, one of the policemen glanced at him, then got up. He braced himself for a confrontation.

He was unarmed, but his skills as a fighter would easily overmatch the man. The only question would be what to do next. His rental car was in the lot behind the motel; it would take him quite a while to reach it.

Escape!

"Excuse me," said the officer.

Jing Yo turned to him.

"The newspaper on the table," said the policeman. "That yours?"

Jing Yo looked over. "Uh . . ."

"Mind if I have a look?"

"You want the paper?"

"Yeah, if you're leaving it. Otherwise—"

"No, no, take it. Please. My gift."

"Thank you." The officer gave him a smile and went over to the table.

Interesting place, America, thought Jing Yo as he left the restaurant.

43

North of Malipo, China

The late arrival of the last group of the Vietnamese attackers caught the Chinese off-guard. The Vietnamese first bottlenecked the armor already in the strip mine by disabling a tank near the entrance. The infantrymen then went to work on the force in the open area, disabling as many as possible with the rest of their missiles and picking off their crews and infantry support.

Two T-54 tanks, which would have been completely outclassed by the Chinese tanks, bypassed the strip mine and ran into a column of Chinese armored personnel carriers rushing to join the fight. These were easy targets for the Vietnamese, and the two T-54s went to town, destroying six of them before the others began to retreat.

The heavier Chinese main battle tanks came up to return fire, destroying one of the T-54s. But it was too late to turn the battle; with the mechanized infantry now cut off from the tanks in the strip mine, the Chinese forces began to panic. Harassed by Vietnamese RPGs and machine guns, they tried to rally together on the ridge. But they were thrown into further chaos when the Chinese up the road began peppering the area with tank shells.

At this point, the only possible option was to attempt to fight their way out. The Chinese tanks tried bulling their way back through the damaged vehicles in a bid to escape. Two T-96s became bogged down and were abandoned; another was blown up by a soldier who braved the gunfire and threw a grenade in a hatch.

A pair of tanks finally succeeded in pushing the damaged tank blocking the road, and the three survivors of the battle sped away, soldiers clinging desperately to their hulls.

The Vietnamese had won a significant battle, surprising and devastating a much larger force. But they had taken serious losses in the process. Colonel Dai had lost nearly a third of his men; most were wounded, but some seventy were dead and another dozen missing.

Dai himself had been hurt, but after being bandaged by a medic, he regained his composure and his command. By the time Zeus reached him on the road below the strip mine, the colonel had started to regroup his forces.

"We have stopped them for tonight," he told Zeus. "Thank you."

Zeus, battered and bruised but otherwise unharmed in the battle, nodded. "What now?"

"We move back to Malipo. General Trung radioed fifteen minutes ago. He has taken the city with little resistance."

"I need a ride to the airport," Zeus told him.

"Your clothes are covered with blood," said the colonel. "We will get you something to change into."

"These are fine for now. I need to make sure the field is secure."

Zeus ended up hitching a ride into Malipo ahead of Dai, riding on the back of a pickup truck headed for the temporary aid station with wounded. The aid station was in the middle of the city, in what had been a clinic, though it had few supplies. The sun was just coming up over the hills, chasing away clouds not of moisture but gunpowder.

The small garrison had been taken almost without resistance. There were only sixteen Chinese; they were locked in the basement of the town police station in a pair of jail cells barely big enough for them to fit. About the same number were believed to have fled as the fighting started.

The building next to the police station had been the local army headquarters; its only occupant when the Vietnamese arrived was a major, who had put a pistol into his mouth and fired when the troops arrived.

A number of city residents had fled into the night, but most remained in their houses. The Vietnamese ordered them to stay in their basements, warning that anyone who came out would be treated as an enemy and shot. There was not much to worry about from them; as a general rule, the Chinese did not allow peasants to own guns, and after a precursory search the Vietnamese left the civilians to tend to more important matters.

Trung's command vehicle was parked near the clinic, but he had taken over the police station as a base, and Zeus found him upstairs in what had been the central office, hunched over a map spread over a pair of desks.

"I have had a report from Colonel Dai," said Trung, looking up as Zeus approached. "We are grateful for your weapons, and for your efforts. Once more, the tiger has shown his stripes."

Trung gave him a wan smile before continuing.

"The Chinese were completely taken by surprise," he told Zeus. "They had barely a platoon guarding the city."

"The tank division will regroup," said Zeus. "We didn't get a third of it."

"We will be ready." Trung extended his hand toward the map. Zeus stared at the side of the general's face. The bottom of his eye lids sagged, running down from the crooked wrinkles that formed a *V* back into his temple. There, dull brown age marks dotted yellowed skin, as if the flesh along his hairline had been stained by tobacco.

Trung turned to look at Zeus. Though tired, his dark eyes were calm and, together with his upright posture, gave the general an air of certainty and confidence.

More than the situation warranted, probably.

"There is only one highway to the town," said Trung. "We will have it mined within the hour. If they move up through the side roads, then we will trap them from above."

"They may come across the way Dai's forces did," said Zeus, pointing to the small trails in the hills to the east of the mine where the ambush had taken place. "Then they will come down the highway to the west and get below you. They'll trap you here."

"If they try that, we will blow up the hillsides and trap them in a landslide," said Trung. He pointed to the map. "And there is a bridge here, and one here."

"Yes." Zeus looked at the map. Trung's solution might delay an attack, but the town would remain vulnerable. And if the Chinese swept in from the west, they could easily cut the Vietnamese off from the south.

"How long do you plan to stay?" Zeus asked.

"How long before your mission to Kunming is launched?"

"The plane should be up here by this afternoon," said Zeus. "I'm on my way to check on it."

"Are you going yourself?"

"Yes," said Zeus.

"You are a man of much ambition, Major. May you do well." He bowed his head slightly in respect.

Zeus had not, in fact, planned to go. But now it seemed impossible to stay back. He wanted to fight the Chinese; he wanted to kill the general.

It was his plan, his idea. He wanted to see it triumph. And Anna?

She was still there, still there. He would see her soon.

Zeus's anger at Trung had completely dissipated, and he thanked him when he gave him a driver and a guard to take him to the airport. The small facility was located to the east of the city, on the other side of a low, lush ridge, one of the few in the area that had not been attacked by mining machines.

There was a bonus waiting at the airport: a Xian Y-7-100. The aircraft was basically a Chinese-built An-24, a two-engine workhorse used for various transportation duties throughout Asia and Europe.

The flight crew had apparently been in the city when the assault began, and had not been located. But the Vietnamese platoon that took over the small administration building had captured a pair of maintainers, and proudly showed them off to Zeus. Both were old, at least sixty, and while neither was frail, Zeus nonetheless felt sorry for them. They wore sullen gazes firmly clamped on the ground.

There was a Chinese interpreter with the platoon. Zeus enlisted his aid as he tried to question the men about the pilots. Both indicated that they didn't know anything, mumbling and gesturing.

The interpreter repeated his questions twice, each time his voice raising another notch in volume. He then took out his pistol and swung at the nearest man, screaming at him.

"It's all right, it's all right," said Zeus, grabbing the interpreter's arm. "Don't bother."

The interpreter said something to Zeus in Vietnamese—a curse or a putdown, from what Zeus could tell of his expression.

For just a moment he thought the man would take a swing at him, which would have been a serious mistake—Zeus stood a good foot over him, and if his anger was unleashed there was no telling what he might do. Probably realizing he was overmatched, the interpreter shook his head and holstered his weapon, stalking off.

The Chinese workers stared at Zeus, their eyes wide. But if they were grateful, they didn't offer any show of cooperation, and in the end Zeus left them and went to look at the rest of the building.

There wasn't much to it: a medium-sized hall with three rows of chairs bolted to the floor, a small office with an empty desk and a folding chair off to the side, and a pair of lavatories. There wasn't even a control tower.

Two hangars sat near the building. Neither was particularly large. One appeared to be used for maintenance, housing a fuel truck and a white Nissan pickup. A single metal cabinet held tools, and the only thing on the long bench that ran nearly the length of the building was a single oil-stained rag.

The second hangar had a small aircraft, an older Cessna 172. The plane's paint was faded and its front tire looked nearly flat. Zeus walked around it quickly, but not being a pilot or an aircraft mechanic he had no idea whether it could fly or not.

Back outside, he took out his satellite phone and called Kerfer to tell him that the airport had been secured.

"You took your damn time about it," said the SEAL.

"Fuck you," Zeus told him.

Kerfer laughed. "I'm glad to hear you're coming over to the dark side, Major. I was just bustin' your ass."

"Bust your own ass. When are you getting up here?"

"I'm not."

"What?"

"I have to do a little something for Uncle. The CIA is going to run this themselves."

"Shit."

"He didn't get a hold of you yet?"

"I haven't talked to anybody."

"His name is Setco. Roth Setco. He's a psych job. But he's pretty good. Don't get in his way. As long as the field is secure, you're good."

"I'm going with him."

"Why?"

"Because it's my mission."

"Talk to Setco, not me," said Kerfer. "He'll be up there no later than eighteen hundred. Can your Viets hold out till then?"

"Probably," said Zeus.

"Oh, that's positive."

"It's the truth. It depends on how long it takes the Chinese to regroup. They got their butts kicked pretty well."

"Setco will need to be refueled," said Kerfer. "Otherwise he's completely self-contained. I gave him your contact information, he should be calling you. He should have done it already."

"I'm going with him."

"Talk to Setco. I have my own problems."

Zeus put his thumb over the end button.

"Hey, Murphy."

"What?"

"I'd hang back and see the girl if I were you. You don't need to go with Roth. You've done enough. Go home."

"Screw you."

Kerfer laughed. He was still laughing when Zeus clicked off the phone.

44

Kunming

General Li Sun stared at the video screen, unable to fathom what the division commander was telling him. It wasn't that he didn't understand the words—the transmission was clear, despite the encryption and mountainous terrain. It was just that their content seemed completely impossible.

The man on the screen, 12th Armor Commander General Fan, seemed equally incredulous. He pursed his lips, then opened his mouth to speak, but no sound came out.

"You are telling me that the Vietnamese are in Chinese territory?" Li Sun tried to tamp down his voice; he knew he was close to screaming. "That they have a force strong enough to defeat an armored division."

"Not defeat, merely—"

"Are you telling me you were ambushed above—*above*—Malipo?"

"General—"

"Get out of my sight."

Li Sun slapped at the console, punching buttons indiscriminately until he found the one to close off the transmission. The communications aide stood at his

side, either fearing to incur Li Sun's wrath or too
shocked by what he had heard to help.

Sun slammed his hand on the desk and rose quickly.
A thousand thoughts came to him, all contradictory—he
would go there himself, he must keep this from his
uncle, he would hurry the infantry . . .

This simply could not be real. The Vietnamese were
beaten. There was no way they could come over the
border and attack.

Attack! A good portion of the 12th Armored had
been laid to waste. General Fan—not the brightest
commander, but still—reported that his men were dis-
illusioned and disorganized. Fan wanted to retreat to
Wenshan and reorganize there. His tanks were spread
out now in the mountain roads and he claimed it
would be days—days!—before he could reorganize.

This was beyond unacceptable. This was insane.

And impossible.

"Niu!" said the general, calling for one of young
captains he had taken as an aide. "Niu—what are you
doing?"

The captain came quickly. "You told me to stay in
the hall, general."

"Get me the latest satellite data."

"It's a day old, General."

"Get it!"

Niu walked over to the computer and sat down.
Typing furiously, he soon retrieved a series of images
from the area that had been taken the previous evening,
before the battle. Even at maximum resolution, Li Sun
could see nothing to indicate the Vietnamese were in
the area, or even near the border.

Certainly, it could not have been a large force to
hide and then move so quickly. And yet only a large
force—a massive force, with weapons that the Vietnamese did not possess—could have defeated two

Chinese tank companies and sent a third scurrying for cover.

It was impossible.

Li Sun looked at the area where General Fan had been surprised. Fan had been foolish to let himself get trapped there.

Li Sun had warned him! Surely he had warned him. And still he was trapped.

The general slid back in his seat, considering the situation. It had to be reversed quickly. Immediately!

"Where is General Chan?" Li Sun asked Niu.

"In his office."

"Have him come here."

Niu left. Li Sun resumed his pacing, his mind feverish. He needed to send reconnaissance flights over the area, but doing so might alert the air force to the disaster. They'd see the tanks littering the field, and who knew what else?

Other generals would hear. His enemies would tell Beijing.

What would his uncle say? He'd been here for only a few days, and already he had disaster.

Where else were the Vietnamese? What would they do? Would they pull back now that they had bloodied his nose? Or would they take territory and hold it?

There were a number of cities and towns nearby. Malipo. Had they gone there?

He needed reconnaissance. It was an absolute necessity.

"General?"

Chan stood at the door. Niu was behind him.

"Come," said Li Sun. "Captain Niu, you may stay as well. We have a grave problem."

"I know, General," said Chan. "Fan allowed his forces to be ambushed. He is a fool."

"Do we have contact with the garrison commander at Malipo?" asked Li Sun.

"No," said Chan. "The telephone lines are down. They have been for a few hours."

"Try them again. Now."

Chan walked to the phone. He pulled over a small directory from the rack beneath the unit and looked up the contact number before dialing.

"There is still a problem with the circuit."

"Does he have a secure video connection?" asked Sun.

"Not there. That is a small outpost, on the edge of the mountains. They'd never be worth the equipment, even if they were trusted."

"Have you tried the radio?"

"It's useless in the mountains."

Slowly, Li Sun told the others about Fan's situation. He had lost about two-thirds of a battalion of tanks, with heavy casualties among the mechanized infantry traveling with him. He still had two more battalions, but they were a good distance away. More critically, the entire division was disorganized and discouraged—they had been surprised on Chinese soil, thrown back by what should by all rights have been an inferior force.

"Our 12th Armor were north of Malipo when it was attacked," said Li Sun. "We must assume the city has fallen as well."

The others stood in stony silence as Li Sun spoke. Explaining the situation somehow calmed his anger. It was the first step toward solving the problem.

Too late, perhaps.

"We will organize a counterattack immediately," said Li Sun. "I will lead it myself."

Niu nodded, but Chan objected. His manner was

extremely submissive—one didn't speak too boldly to commanders, whatever their rank, and Li Sun had already proven that he was not a man to be dealt with lightly. But one of the reasons the general liked Chan was his determination to speak what he believed. It was a trait he saw in himself.

"General, with your permission."

"Speak."

"Your division commanders won't have the intelligence reports you can get here. In the field, we won't be able to download the satellite data or reconnaissance to you. And you won't have communication with the air force—"

"I don't need the air force," snapped Li Sun.

"That would be up to you, sir," said Chan. If he was going to say anything else, the words died stillborn—Li Sun's retort had taken away a bit of his verve.

Which was regrettable, thought Li Sun. And yet he couldn't help himself—he was angry and he had to fix this.

His chief of staff was right. While the army possessed sophisticated communications gear, very real fears that it could be used to organize a coup had restricted its use. And setting up a sophisticated field headquarters with a mobile command center would take several days, even if he could locate all of the necessary equipment.

But deep in his heart, Li Sun knew he should go. Every instinct was telling him—go. *Go!*

A commander lived by his brains, not by instinct. Yes, he needed to make the sweeping command gesture, he needed to play the right odds. But he also needed to direct his troops.

He would have Fan regroup and attack immediately—nightfall if not sooner. And he would get the infantry commanders moving. *Moving!*

And find some way of breaking this to his uncle.

Impossible.

"Your point is well taken, General," he told Chan. "Get the maps of Malipo."

"Right away."

Li Sun turned to Niu. "Send an alert to all posts in our area. Tell them that they are to double the guard, and be alert against saboteurs."

"Even here, General?"

They were some three hundred kilometers by air from Malipo; there was no way the Vietnamese could attack this far north, no matter how audacious their commander.

"Even here," said Sun. "We will set them an example."

Niu bent his head and started to leave.

"Captain." Sun stopped him. "You can always feel free to speak your mind, as General Chan has. Even when the comments are not welcome, they are deeply appreciated."

This time Niu bent his head nearly to his chest before leaving.

45

Dickson Theodore, the president's chief of staff, held up a cell phone as Greene got out of the car behind the restaurant.

"You're running late," Theodore told his boss. "You should have given your speech a half hour ago."

"And you're supposed to be home with that pretty wife of yours," Greene said. He patted his jacket. "Remarks, not a speech. If it were a speech I would need a teleprompter."

"Jablonski needs to talk to you. Very urgent."

"Billy? What's up?"

Theodore shook his head.

Even in the midst of a thousand crises, there was one man President Chester Greene would take a phone call from: William Jablonski. Occasionally rude and often unkempt, Jablonski was also the world's best political operative, a maestro of nuance and infighting. He'd singlehandedly gotten New York to vote for Greene in the presidential race, and could probably take credit for California as well.

Of course, to hear Jablonski tell it, he'd delivered all fifty states and Guam to Greene—an accomplishment that the electoral college, which had only counted thirty-four in Greene's column, had yet to catch up with.

"Billy, give it to me straight," said Greene, taking the phone.

"There's a story coming out tomorrow in the *L.A. Times*," said the political aide. "They're going to contact your press office right at deadline so they get a no comment."

"What are you talking about?"

"They're going to claim you sent U.S. troops into Vietnam and supplied their army. They have some sort of source. I couldn't get the whole thing—the reporter isn't on the national desk, and I don't know him. I tried calling him but he didn't take the call. Maybe he's busy. I'll get him."

"You're sure about this?" asked Greene.

"Damn sure. All this true?"

"True enough," said Greene.

"Mmmmm."

Greene pictured Jablonski rubbing his mouth and making the faces he always did when things weren't lining up the way he wanted.

"Gonna be a shit storm," said Jablonski finally.

"We'll get over it."

"I'll be in Washington tomorrow morning."

"Oh, it's not—"

"Yes it is." Jablonski hung up.

Greene handed the phone back to Theodore. "Big story about our helping Vietnam coming in the *L.A. Times* tomorrow," the president told his chief of staff. "Better get the press people in the loop. We'll meet back at the office as soon as I'm done. Sorry about your dinner."

46

Malipo airport, China

Zeus heard the airplane from a good distance away, a high-pitched whine that grew unevenly as it approached. He folded his arms and stared into the fading blue sky directly beyond the runway, waiting.

A black wedge finally appeared close to the nearby hills, so far to his right it was almost behind him. Zeus wasn't sure it was Setco's airplane at first—the direction seemed wrong, as if it were a Chinese flight that hadn't learned of Malipo's takeover yet. The plane grew larger, and Zeus thought it might be a reconnaissance flight surveying the town. If so, it would pass unharassed; the Vietnamese force had only two anti-aircraft trucks, and both were up in the city with the main force.

The plane banked sharply, legged uneasily toward the runway, wings dipping sharply with the turns. There was definitely something wrong; one of the engines growled and coughed. The plane moved fitfully, dipping toward the hills then rising uneasily before finally coming onto the runway. It hit hard, bounced up, then settled, angling slightly to the side where Zeus stood. By the time it reached him, only one of the props was spinning under power; the control surfaces were extended and the rudder bent to keep it straight.

The aircraft was a Russian version of the plane parked near the terminal, an Antonov An-24. Aside from the markings, the only visible difference was a large cargo-style door located just aft of the cockpit. This swung up slowly; when it was about halfway a short, stocky man in camouflaged BDUs dropped down to the tarmac. His uniform was Chinese, with a red flag on his right shoulder and gray name bars above his chest pockets, but he was Caucasian. Roth Setco.

"You Murphy?" Setco barked.

"That's me."

"I'm Roth Setco. You got fuel for us?"

Zeus reached to shake his hand. Setco looked at him for a second, then belatedly extended his own.

"You had engine trouble?" Zeus asked.

"We'll make it. The pilot sucks."

"The Chinese left a plane," said Zeus. "It's by the terminal building. Maybe you can use that."

Setco turned to look, but couldn't see because his view was blocked off. He walked over to the front of the plane.

"What's wrong with it?" he asked Zeus.

"Couldn't tell you."

"It flies?"

"I have no idea. It was here when I got here."

"Hmmm."

Setco walked over and stood near the nose of the plane that had just landed. He shouted up to the pilot in Vietnamese. The engine of the aircraft immediately began to rev. Zeus stepped back as the plane began taxiing again, this time in the direction of the terminal building.

"I'm taking Kerfer's place," Zeus told Setco.

"Doing what?" Setco started across the dirt infield to the parking area where the Chinese plane was sitting.

"Do you have enough people?" Zeus asked.

"I could use a couple more, actually," said Setco. "If they speak Chinese. I only have two guys who speak it without an accent. Three if you count me, but I'm thinking no one's going to believe I'm Chinese."

"We can get some guys," said Zeus. "I'll talk to Trung."

"Trung?"

"General Trung. The head of the Vietnamese army."

"What the fuck is he doing up here?"

"He's overseeing the assault."

Setco shook his head and continued toward the Chinese aircraft. He puts his hands on his hips and surveyed it. Meanwhile, one of the men in the plane that had just landed jumped from the cargo door as it taxied to a stop and ran up to take a look. He reached up and unlatched the cockpit door, pulling himself up.

"He's a pilot?" asked Zeus.

"Thinks he is. He's a mechanic. Decent one. I don't know how much he really knows, though—you can't trust the damn Koreans." He looked at Zeus. "Where are these translators?"

"In the city."

"Screw that. We're not going into the city. We're running late as it is."

"There's at least one guy here," said Zeus.

"Well get him. I can use a couple more gooks with guns—we're going to have to protect the plane at the airport. They'll need their own weapons."

"Listen—"

"Don't get sensitive on me, Murphy," said Setco. "I'm in a hurry."

"I have maps and a layout of the command post. I've been thinking—"

"Don't waste your time. I have all that stuff. I've done this before."

Zeus figuratively grit his teeth, deciding the best way to deal with Setco was to ignore his insults and manner, at least for now. "I'll be right back."

"There's fuel here someplace?"

"There's a truck in the hangar."

"I need to be in the air in an hour," said Setco.

"Right." Zeus started away.

"Hey, Major."

Zeus stopped.

"What'd Kerfer tell you about me?" Setco asked.

"Nothing. Except that you were a prick. And you knew what you were doing."

"Well, he got one of those right, huh?"

Zeus found the soldier who had questioned the Chinese maintainers, and by hand signals and slow English—more the former than the latter—he was able to get the man to come with him to the officer in charge of the platoon. The commander, a captain, was eating his dinner, a small cup of noodles with some bits of fish; there wasn't much fish but its pungent smell filled the building.

The captain's English was good enough for him to understand what Zeus wanted—three men, plus the translator, for a special mission further behind enemy lines.

"I need permission," said the commander. "I will send someone to city."

"There's no time," said Zeus. "Call General Trung and get his OK by phone or radio. I need them now."

"OK."

It sounded as if the man was agreeing, but his face made it look like a question.

"It's OK. He'll say it's OK," insisted Zeus. "I need them now."

The captain went back to eating his dinner, pulling the noodles out with his chopsticks.

"I need them now," said Zeus. "Now."

"Eh?"

"We need to go." Zeus turned and pretended to run. Communication would be comical if it weren't so critical.

Putting his food down, the commander rose from the desk and walked out of the office. Zeus followed him into the large hall, thinking he was going for the radio. But the captain stopped at a knot of men near the door. Speaking quickly to them, he pointed at two.

"They will be with you. The translator is sleeping. Hangar," added the captain. "You will take him."

"That's three." Zeus held up his fingers, showing he wanted four.

"All I can give," said the captain, shaking his head.

While Zeus had been rounding up the men, Setco determined that the Chinese aircraft was in better shape than the one he had come in. They were in the process of fueling it when Zeus came over with his three Vietnamese soldiers in tow. Setco stood near the wing, watching as one of his men connected the hose.

The men with Zeus jerked up their weapons as soon as they saw the Chinese uniforms.

"It's OK," said Zeus. "They're on our side. Disguises—they're wearing disguises."

"*Chúng ta là bạn*," shouted Setco. "We're friends. American."

Only Setco was American, but they got the idea. The Vietnamese soldiers lowered their guns.

"You trust these guys?" Setco asked.

"You just need somebody to guard the plane, right?" said Zeus. "I trust them for that. Where they'll be there won't be much sense in running away, right? This guy speaks Chinese." Zeus pointed at the translator.

Setco went over to him and started speaking rapid fire. Whatever the translator said, he wasn't impressed.

"He's worse than the Koreans," Setco told Zeus. He frowned, then pointed toward the door at the end of the fuselage. "Get them in the plane. You better go inside and explain we're all on the same side. We have two complete uniforms and a top. Whoever wears the top should just stay in the plane."

"I don't speak Vietnamese."

"What the hell are you doing here then? What good are you?"

"I planned this op."

"No, I planned this op," said Setco.

"I suggested it."

"Big fucking deal. I suggested they build the Golden Gate Bridge. Does that mean anything?"

"I'm going."

"I'm not arguing with you, Major. If you're going, get aboard. You speak Chinese?"

"Not really."

"Fuckin' Army." Setco waved his hand dismissively. "Don't let these jackasses point their guns inside. My boys'll kill them."

A small set of metal steps had been placed below the doorway, making it easier to get into. Zeus climbed inside.

"My name's Murphy," he announced loudly as he went. "I'm the one who set the mission up. How are you guys doing?"

The men sitting in the aircraft didn't seem impressed. Mostly Asian, they were sitting across seats or on the edge of the aisle. A few were talking, a couple smoked cigarettes. A black man took a slug from a Thermos in a way that made Zeus think it wasn't water he was drinking.

The plane was set up like a civilian airliner, with two seats on either side of a central aisle. There were small open areas fore and aft of the dozen rows. The seats were very thin and narrow, almost like padded lawn chairs. They made even the simple units that were put into the holds of American military transports look lush by comparison.

The Vietnamese stayed together at the back. Setco climbed in a minute or so later.

"All right, you degenerates," he said in a voice so loud the metal shook. "We're about ready to go. Move forward and I'll go over the game plan. This is Murph. He and the natives here are going to guard the plane while we have our little fun."

Setco brushed past Zeus and walked up to the front of the aircraft. Zeus had been called Murph before—it was an almost mandatory nickname for someone with his surname—but he didn't particularly like the way it sounded and he hated the way it sounded when Setco said it.

Nor did he intend on staying back with the plane when they landed. He was in this all the way.

He followed Setco up to the front. A pair of black duffel bags sat on the floor in the front. Setco reached into one and pulled out a laptop computer. He opened it and turned it on.

"It's Zeus or Murphy," Zeus told him, putting his own pack near the duffels. "Not Murph."

"Right." Setco didn't even bother looking up from the computer.

"I'm going in with you. I'm not staying with the plane."

"I don't think that's a real good idea."

"I know the layout. I practiced a takedown just like this two years ago."

Zeus was exaggerating slightly—he had certainly practiced plenty of takedowns, but he hadn't been at one exactly like this, nor had he gone through an exercise against a Chinese facility. He was an expert on Chinese tactics and weapons, could probably predict how they would respond, and even had a reasonable idea of what sort of gear they'd have at the army group command post. But he had never run through a building with a submachine gun in his hand, hunting for a Chinese general, real or fake.

Setco looked at him. "No offense, *Murph*, but this ain't a Sunday school exercise. We're not playing here."

"Don't be an asshole. How do you think I got up here? I was on Hainan. I walked back through China. I blew up more fuckin' Chinese tanks than you'll see in a lifetime. I'm not here for my health. I want to kill these bastards."

Setco stared at him. He squinted slightly, then seemed to see something in Zeus's face.

"I'm not trying to give you a hard time, Major," he said gently.

"You could have fooled me."

"Good chance we don't come back from this."

"And?"

Setco turned back to the laptop. He typed in a few words, pulled up a half-dozen screens in quick succession.

I really am angry, Zeus thought to himself. *Why?*

Because of the people the Chinese killed? Because of Win Christian?

I stayed in Vietnam to rescue Anna—I want to get her home. I love her.

I want her. I don't want the war. I should jump out of the plane now.

I'm here for love, not killing.

Ain't I?

"All right, listen up," Setco said, rising and once more raising his voice to megaphone levels. "The security arrangement here is exactly like it was at Sabah. Same fuckin' thing. With a couple of exceptions. Starting with the fact that these guys *are* Chinese, instead of just taking their orders from them. So they're going to be even bigger pussies."

There were a few snorts and chuckles from the others. Sabah was a state in Malaysia that had been taken over by a rebel group receiving aid from the Chinese. Zeus gathered that Setco had led essentially the same men on a raid there, though he had to guess at most of the details.

The Chinese army group headquarters was in a sleek new campus along Highway S102 on the southern side of Kunming, not far from Dai Chi Lake. During ordinary times, there would have been up to a regiment stationed in the camp adjacent to the headquarters complex. Those troops had been sent south during the opening assault, and while a fresh battalion was supposed to be moved here, the Chinese had assigned it to supplement forces at the border. It would certainly have seemed a smart move on paper: the border was a much more dangerous area than a city some three hundred or so kilometers behind the fighting.

There were two gates in and out of the complex. They'd go through the side gate, which Setco expected to be manned by two men. A Korean nicknamed Zig would pose as a colonel coming to check the barracks for the new occupants. The others would be a skeleton team of cleaners, coming in a second van a few minutes later.

"Assuming the vans are there," added Setco. "We should have passes with them."

"And beer," said one of the whites. It was Roo, the Australian. "I was promised plenty of beer. And not the watered down Chinese piss, either."

They all laughed.

"Cover story shouldn't be necessary," Setco added in an aside aimed at Zeus before he continued outlining the plan. "Ordinarily the Chinese see an officer and they just salute and stand back. But we'll be ready."

About fifty yards from the entrance, the road split off, with a spur to the right heading toward the headquarters area. There was a fenced communications area with satellite dishes and an array of antennas on the left; these were guarded by a Type 63 armored personnel carrier equipped with a 12.7 mm heavy machine gun.

The vehicle was old, and presumably too worn to join the front lines. But the machine gun was certainly formidable, and they would have to assume the vehicle was mobile.

Across the way from the communications area was a battery of mobile antiaircraft missiles. Unlike the armored personnel carrier, the missiles were among the latest in the Chinese inventory: HQ-9s, sometimes known in the West at FT-2000As. The battery had eight TELs or transporter erector launchers—truckbeds that raised the missiles to fire. There was also a search radar and a tracking radar, along with a trailer used as a command center. A generator truck and a few smaller trailers for personnel rounded out the battery.

"Tempting target," said the black man. His name was Robbie, and he had an accent from the American south.

"Tempt not, want not," said Roo.

"We'll have to leave it be," said Setco. "We're not getting bonus points this time around."

The missile unit was separate from the surrounding

army base, operating under a different chain of command. As such, it had its own security. While Setco didn't consider it too formidable, it was nonetheless not to be taken lightly—the facility would be heavily mined, and there were typically two dozen soldiers available as guards. He expected at least a third would be on duty, walking the perimeter and manning a light machine gun post near the entrance. They were trained to remain at their posts, a plus for the attackers in this operation.

"Best thing to do as far as they're concerned is ignore them. Shoot right by," said Setco. "No pun intended."

Finally, there was the headquarters building. This would have two men at the front door, along with two men patrolling the corridor inside. He expected there would be no external security because of the fact that they were inside the base. Still, they couldn't count on that entirely.

"They're not in the reconnaissance twenty-four hours ago," said Zeus.

"I'll remember to tell them that if they show up," said Setco. "It's not the past but the future we're dealing with here. The general's office will be in the middle of the building," he said, continuing. "Far end of the building are conference rooms. Bunkers and situation rooms are downstairs. Lay everybody out, no prisoners," added Setco.

"We're not going to take the boss?" said one of the white soldiers. He had an Australian accent. "Big propaganda, no?"

"Can't use it," said Setco.

"Let Zig and Squirt take him," said the Australian. "Blindfold him, knock him out. Won't know there's any Yanks involved."

"Or any 'roos," said Robbie.

They all laughed.

"It's a shame, but he's not worth the hassle." Setco glanced at Zeus. "Right, Major?"

"We'd have to kill him in the end anyway."

"Better to keep it simple," said the Australian. "Dead for one and dead for all."

"Even Roo comes around in the end," said Robbie. "As long as there's killing involved."

There was less laughter this time.

Setco went over more of the layout, then made assignments. If the vans weren't there, they would take three cars at the airport—military vehicles if they could find them. Setco had already identified the locations from the satellite images.

"We should have real time pictures just before we land." Setco checked his watch. "Anything else?"

"What do we do if we're stopped at the airport?" asked Robbie.

"We won't be," said Setco.

"You're guaranteeing that?"

"I'm guaranteeing that."

To Zeus's surprise, no one snickered.

"Play it by ear," said Setco. "If things start going to shit, we shoot our way out, take the headquarters down, then do our best to get back."

"Same ol', same ol'," said Robbie.

If he meant it as a joke, it fell flat. No one laughed, or even grinned.

"All right, let me go check with the pilot." Setco looked at his watch. "Anyone needs to take care of business, you got five minutes. After that, we leave without you."

Zeus went forward with Setco into the cockpit. The two Vietnamese pilots who'd come up with the other plane were going over a checklist. Setco interrogated them in rapid-fire Vietnamese. The pilots seemed

nervous to Zeus—not a good sign. Finally, Setco
pointed to his watch, then left the flight deck.

"What was that about?" Zeus asked.

"I don't like the way they fly. I need them to go
faster. Frickin' Chinese are freaking me out they're
so quiet. They may be expecting us."

"Expecting us?"

"Relax, Murph. They're not. I just want to move.
They'll hit Malipo pretty soon. They're going to want
it back. If they weren't such pussies they would have
attacked already."

Setco took a seat in the first aisle, propping his feet
up on one of the duffel bags. Zeus slid into the seat
next to him. He glanced out the window but it was
pitch black.

"So you're the guy that stopped the tanks going to
Haiphong, huh?" asked Setco.

"We were pretty far north of that."

"I heard you shot up an airport in China."

"Not really. We had a little, uh, misunderstanding
and had to leave."

Setco smirked. He thought Zeus had been down-
playing what they'd done, but in reality he was telling
the truth—it had been an accident. But finally Setco
seemed, if not impressed, at least mollified.

"Do you have a uniform for me?" Zeus asked.

"Nothing that's going to fit."

"I need a jacket or something."

"You'll do fine if you stay down. Your face isn't going to fool anyone, no matter what you wear. You just
stay cool and keep moving. You're sure you're in?"

"I'm in."

Setco stretched in his seat, sliding down slightly.
Zeus looked at his profile and realized the CIA officer
wasn't nearly as old as he'd thought; he very possibly
was younger than he was. But he wore the world and

all that he'd done in it like a blanket made of age. Every year of his life in the agency, Zeus guessed, was like ten or twenty outside of it.

"What do you think of Kerfer?" asked Setco.

"He's OK."

"Fuckin' SEALs are always full of themselves," said Setco. "He *did* save my ass."

"That's good." Zeus didn't know what else to say.

"And I saved his. He didn't tell you that part of the story, right?"

"He didn't tell me any part."

"Hmmph." Setco shifted around in his seat. "What you doing in Vietnam, Major?"

"I was assigned and—"

"You're like a ghost from the past, right? Materializing to help us get it right this time? Except it doesn't really work that way. Because the Vietnamese are on our side now, and we're on theirs. We're the Viet Cong. At least as far as the Chinese are concerned."

"Maybe more like the Russians."

"You know your history."

"Why are you here?"

"Because they won't send me any place where there's too much of a chance I'll come out of it alive."

They took off a few minutes later, the aircraft slipping so smoothly off the runway Zeus wasn't sure it was airborne until he saw shadows below his window. Right up until takeoff, there had been murmured conversations and occasional laughter, but now the talk was gone, the only sound the drone of the engines.

Kunming was roughly two hundred miles from Malipo by air. The An-24, however, had to take a roundabout route so that it would appear that it was a

Chinese aircraft coming from the north. The pilot first flew northward toward the peaks of the Dalou Mountains in the Guizhou region. During this portion of the flight, the plane flew only fifty feet above ground level, hugging the contours of the mountains and valleys. It was tedious yet difficult work, the pilots struggling to anticipate the upcoming terrain without the benefit of advanced radar systems or satellite-generated maps. Several times they had to jerk upward at the last moment, engines straining.

It took nearly two hours to reach the area of Zunyi, a major city on the Xiang River barely three hundred miles north of the airport. At that point, the aircraft banked sharply and began to climb, exploiting a gap in the Chinese civil and military radar coverage. Setco went into the cockpit with Zig, who spoke excellent Chinese with a Beijing accent, to make sure the proper transmissions were made to the controllers.

By this point, the long flight was wearing on Zeus. He wanted to be there already. He wanted it to be over.

He wanted to see Anna.

Setco came out of the cockpit and stood at the front of the aisle. "We're twenty minutes out," he announced. "Everything is set. Get yourselves ready."

The men started shifting around. The three Vietnamese soldiers had donned the Chinese uniforms and shirt. They sat near the rear door with a Taiwanese member of the team nicknamed Longjohn, who drilled the translator on the proper responses if challenged.

Most of the rest of the men double-checked their gear and weapons, getting ready.

Zeus took his gun from the pack.

"What you packing there, Murph?" asked Setco.

Zeus glared at him. Setco smiled—clearly he got a kick out of riling him with the nickname. The para took the rifle, looked it over quickly, then gave it back.

"Nice. You sure you're coming with us, huh?"

"Absolutely."

"Duty? Or adventure?"

For just a moment, Setco's face seemed to soften. It was as if he'd been wearing a mask, and it instantly dissolved. But then he started to frown, and it was back, hard, cold, uncaring.

Is that how I look? Zeus wondered.

"You figure it's your duty to go ahead with this," said Setco, no longer asking a question. "So you want to see it through."

"Something along those lines."

Setco nodded. He looked at his watch. "We're on the tarmac in fifteen. I'll be up front."

47

Kunming

General Li Sun paced the conference room, anxious. He'd spent the entire morning and afternoon fuming, urging his forces to move, and ultimately raging at the vast gap between his men's promises and their performances.

Ordered to mount a counterattack no later than noon, General Fan at 12th Armored had reported that he was still organizing his units. Meanwhile, neither of the infantry battalions Li Sun had ordered to break off and accelerate their march had reached the division.

Malipo itself was silent, a mountain city cut off from the world. Li Sun had persuaded a family friend of his at the 11th Air Surveillance Squadron to fly reconnaissance flights over the area—and more importantly to be quiet about it. The most recent images, a few hours old, showed military vehicles along the main street of Malipo. These could only be Vietnamese.

The force appeared to be small. Word had not yet reached Beijing, a minor miracle, but surely would by the time the next flyover data from the infrared satellite covering the area was processed—not more than two hours from now. And that was if word from the reconnaissance flight didn't filter back through the chain of command.

When it did there would be hell to pay. Malipo might be a distant, insignificant outpost, but it was Chinese territory. Word of this disaster would not only raise his uncle's wrath, but might very well threaten the government's existence—the people would hardly listen to a premier who could not keep a puny enemy like Vietnam in line.

Before it came to that, Li Sun himself would be gone, his body dragged by dogs through the streets of the worst provincial slum.

The city had to be retaken immediately. That was the only possible hope. It had to be secured, and then his army had to march directly into Vietnam—he could not stop until he was in Hanoi.

Only if he was the victor of such a battle could his uncle forgive him.

And the only way he was going to win that battle was if he was there personally. General Fan was not capable of organizing his units quickly enough. And Fan was his most aggressive general—the infantry leaders were undoubtedly far worse.

Li Sun went to the door. "General Chan!" he bellowed. "General!"

His aide ran from his office, his face stricken. The man had not slept in over twenty-four hours.

"Has General Fan attacked?"

"He is planning to move against the city at nightfall."

"He was supposed to strike at noon!"

"General, his forces were in disarray. I'm not making excuses for him," added Chan, "I am just relaying what he told me."

"The sun is down. Has he attacked?"

Chan shook his head.

"I will go to the 12th Armored myself. You will stay here and be in communication with me at all times. I will take Niu with me."

"General, if Beijing—"

"*When* Beijing contacts you, tell them I am in the field and left strict orders for you to refer them to me."

"But—

"We don't have an alternative, General," said Li Sun. "We will tell them that we have been fighting this battle back and forth. I am going to make my way to Hanoi. I will either walk through the streets there as a conqueror, or you will never see me again."

"Sir, let me go."

"It's our only hope." Li Sun shook his head. "I won't fail. Have a helicopter from 23rd Aviation meet me at the airport. Two of them—I'll take some of our guard detail. Maybe they will be useful in the fighting, if only to lend me their weapons."

48

Approaching Kunming airport

Good SpecOp missions always had a touch of the surreal.

An aircraft that not only looked like a Chinese army transport but was an army transport landed at an airport used by civilians and military flights all the time . . .

The aircraft taxied to a spot on the tarmac near the military area but not quite inside it . . .

A group of men in Chinese army uniforms filed down the rear of the aircraft to a pair of civilian vans waiting nearby. Four men took up positions around the plane, QBZ-95 assault rifles ready . . .

It all *looked* extremely ordinary, and yet it was exactly the opposite, a rash gamble that could fall apart at any moment.

Zeus, head lowered to stay as inconspicuous as possible, trotted from the plane toward the vans. Setco had given him a bulletproof vest and a soft black campaign cap; from a distance at least, he looked like he belonged.

There were two vans waiting, as promised. Zeus started toward the second, then realized he'd been assigned to the first. He changed course, hopping in behind one of the Koreans. He squeezed into the middle row of the three bench seats right behind Setco.

There was a driver at the wheel, dressed in the uniform of a Chinese army private.

It took a moment, but then he realized that the private was a woman.

And one he knew: Solt Jan.

"You," said Zeus. "Solt."

"And you," answered the Vietnamese agent. "Major."

"You got out of China?" Zeus asked.

"We are still in China."

Solt had helped Zeus fool the Chinese amphibious force off Hainan into thinking that the Vietnamese were mounting a major attack on them. They had become separated as they escaped through mainland China.

"You never got out?"

"I was more useful here. What happened to your companion?"

Zeus shook his head. "He didn't make it."

"That is too bad."

"You two have met?" said Setco. There was no surprise in his voice.

"We worked together," said Zeus.

"You get around, don't you?" said Setco.

He started speaking to Solt in Vietnamese. Zeus studied her face as she responded. She had a thin, soft face, and looked almost waiflike in the soldier's uniform.

She looked like Anna. Her hair was wrong, close cropped in a men's cut, but her face was definitely feminine. She took her hat from the dashboard in front of her and put the van into gear.

Everyone in the team had a short-range radio, a high-tech discrete burst rig tuned to a shared frequency.

Setco spoke into his, telling Zig in the second van to follow them out. Solt was alone; how she had managed to get both vehicles here was the least of the questions Zeus wanted to ask her.

They circled around the back of the plane and headed for a road that led to the terminal area. The An-24 would wait exactly two and a half hours for them; if they weren't back by then, the pilots and the security team would leave.

"No ifs, ands, or buts," said Setco.

The terminal was well lit; while the airport wasn't extremely busy—there were only four jets at the passenger gates—there was certainly no sign of a blackout or other precautionary steps that might be taken because of the war. There were no extra patrols, and the controller hadn't even questioned the aircraft once it gave its actual Chinese registration. No one at Kunming felt they had anything to fear from the Vietnamese.

In fact they didn't. Only the men at the headquarters south of the city did. And their assailants weren't even Vietnamese.

A pair of Harbin Z-9 helicopters—license-built Chinese versions of the French Dauphin—took off from the base of the runway as the vans came around. The rear wheels of the first helicopter seemed perilously close as it passed.

"Watch it," barked Setco.

Solt responded in sharp Vietnamese.

"Where are you going?" asked Setco as Solt turned to the right. "Go out the front gate."

"They have a security team checking vehicles." Solt was speaking English now, with only a bare accent; she was fluent in several languages.

"What? They're stopping people going out?" asked Setco.

"The local police," said Solt. "They're looking for smugglers. Some Chinese think they're going to set up business in Vietnam once the war is over, and they're bringing down currency and gold. Lots of it."

"Are you kidding?" asked Zeus.

"It's a gold rush," she answered bitterly.

Lights off, Solt sped past a 757 being refueled, then threaded her way through the tank farm area and reached a small cluster of buildings where the emergency vehicles were based. The highway was only a few yards away, separated by a fence. Zeus braced himself, thinking she was going to ram through the chain links. Instead she veered right at the last possible moment, continuing along a ramp used by military aircraft en route to the runway. The fence was to their left, just across a narrow strip of grass about three feet wide. Cars sped by on the highway, a steady stream.

To the right was a row of darkened warehouse buildings. The walls were right up to the concrete surface of the ramp. The ramp was about the width of a road, wide enough for a small aircraft but not a large one.

Setco said something in Vietnamese. Solt responded tersely.

"Shit," muttered Setco in English. "What are the odds?"

Up ahead, a pair of J-11 fighters outfitted with a full load of bombs and missiles were taxiing toward them. The J-11s—Chinese adaptations of the Su-27 Flanker—were staggered one behind the other so that their wings covered practically the entire span of the ramp.

Solt didn't slow down. Zeus stared in disbelief as the jets came at them, their running lights a blur and shadows dancing off the wings and fuselage. He grabbed the back of the seat and tucked his head down, bracing for the impact.

The van swerved hard to the left, the side crashing along the fence as the jets passed. Zeus turned his head sideways and looked up, surprised to see that they were still intact. They had barely missed the fighter.

The second van wasn't as lucky. The pilot of the aircraft saw the vehicle and started to veer to the left. But the driver of the van was trying to escape that way, squeezing next to the warehouses rather than the fence. The wingtip ECM pod smashed into the corner of the windshield, hooking the vehicle and dragging it around. The van rolled on its wheels, catching the rear of the jet, which spun hard to the left and clipped the other aircraft. One or both of the planes caught fire instantly; a few seconds later they both exploded. The van rolled on its side through the flames and also ignited in a massive fireball.

"Keep going," said Setco calmly. "Get us out of here.

49

The South China Sea

Silas jerked up in his bed as the buzzer sounded. He was needed on the bridge.

He pulled on his shoes—all he'd removed to sleep—then went out to the bridge. The officer of the deck met him practically at the door.

"What?" demanded Silas, still half-dazed from sleep.

"The Chinese ships are challenging another merchant vessel," said the lieutenant. "Crew is at general quarters."

The ship being challenged was a small cargo vessel, currently several miles south of the Chinese cruiser. The cruiser was just under twenty-five miles away, at the edge of the horizon; her frigate was nearby. They were making good speed, steaming toward the merchant ship.

"What nationality?" asked Silas.

"She's Korean, but she's not flying a flag. She's not responding."

"Do we know who is she?"

"The *Nam Nam*," said the officer. "Left Seoul two days ago."

The fact that she wasn't responding and wasn't flying a flag were more than enough to make the ship suspicious. The Chinese had every right to stop the ship under international law, and this time Silas was too far away to intervene.

A few moments later, the Chinese ratcheted the confrontation up several notches by putting a shot across the merchant ship's bow.

"Should I notify Fleet, Cap?" asked OD.

"Absolutely. But I'm not waiting for them." Silas tapped the button on the command unit for his headset so he could speak directly to the CIC. "Li?"

"We're ready, Cap—Jesus!"

"Li?"

"They just hit the port side of the freighter's bow," said Li. "That wasn't a warning shot. They're firing again."

"Well I'm goddamned if I'm going to watch this. Korea's an ally of ours."

Li hesitated. "Captain, I should point out that our orders–"

Silas cut her off. "Duly noted." He turned to his helmsman. "Get me between those ships."

"Captain, sir, you want to be in the line of fire?" asked the sailor. It was not an unreasonable question.

"Damn straight, Johnny, get me there."

McCampbell immediately began cutting to the east. But there was too much distance between them—there was no way the destroyer could get there in time to do anything but fish out survivors.

The only way to stop this was to fight.

Which was exactly what he had been ordered not to do.

Before he could ask if Fleet had responded to their call, Li came on Silas's circuit with a new warning.

"Both Chinese ships are locking their gunfire control radars on us."

They were well out of gun range, but the message was clear: *Keep off the grass.*

"Hold our course. Our radars—"

"Aye, aye, Captain. We're locked and ready. Tit for tat."

They had played this game before.

Silas had his comm officer attempt to reach the Chinese commander of the cruiser. He didn't acknowledge.

"Tell him that he is to stop firing immediately," said Silas. "And to cease acting in a hostile manner."

That had exactly the effect that Silas expected it would—none. The Korean ship, meanwhile, had changed course south, by all appearances attempting to run away. Silas had to admit, it didn't exactly look innocent. Still, firing on a civilian ship in international waters was not exactly a peaceful activity. The cruiser sent another round at the vessel; this one fell short.

"They're trying to see what I'm going to do," mumbled Silas.

"Captain?" said the helmsman.

"Steady as you go. Communications?"

"Transmission from the Chinese, Cap."

"Patch me onto that line," said Silas.

"American vessel. We are enforcing a blockade of a war zone. You are in the way and in a danger area. We suggest you sail out of the range of fire."

"Stop firing on a civilian vessel!" said Silas.

The Chinese commander didn't respond. His gun sent another shell toward the Korean. This one narrowly missed the Korean vessel.

"We will not permit you to continue firing on an unarmed vessel," warned Silas.

"Cruiser is ceasing fire," reported Li. "Turning."

For a moment, Silas thought he had won, once more bluffing the Chinese away. Then he saw that the frigate was moving, too.

"Communications, where is Fleet?" demanded Silas. "I need the admiral himself. Now."

His communications officer was just about to respond when Li's voice cut through the slight static in his headset.

"The Chinese are launching missiles!"

50

Kunming

No one spoke as the van sped out the unguarded gate at the north side of the Kunming airport complex. Solt took a left and then a quick right, driving through some local roads before finally reaching a ramp to the highway. This took them to a massive circular interchange, where several regional arteries came together.

"Forgot your lights," said Setco, finally breaking the silence.

Solt flipped them on. It was the first indication that she was nervous, or had been affected in any way by the accident they had just escaped.

There was fortunately little traffic on the circle, making it easier to navigate the complex network as they found their way south. They got on S102, the Kunluo Highway, and started to relax. They were about fifteen miles from the base.

"You might cut your speed," said Setco. "We don't need to be stopped."

"We won't be."

Zeus was just as glad to be moving quickly. The sooner they had something real to do, the better.

About a mile from the base, Setco had Solt pull off

the road so they could arrange their positions in the vehicle and go over assignments. Kam took over the driving; his accent was the best. Setco reviewed what he would say—almost nothing—and even made him practice holding up the counterfeit ID placard the Chinese used as passes.

Once inside, Setco would lead the team into the building, with Longjohn and Gimhae, another of the Koreans, right behind him. Solt and Kam would stay outside. Everyone else would be in the middle.

"Hold off shooting as long as possible," Setco told them.

"We might be able to sneak around the back," said Zeus. "Since there's usually no one there. We could drive—"

"We're going straight in, Major," answered Setco. "No change in the plan now."

"We have less people—"

"We're going straight in."

Zeus pursed his lips but said nothing.

The telephone landline ran through a conduit just around the corner from the entrance. Solt or Kam would cut it, using either a knife or, if that proved impossible, a charge of plastic explosive. The power ran through a conduit next to it. If they blew the line, the power in the building would die as well, but Chinese headquarters buildings always had backup generators. Because of that, Setco believed the lights would stay on in the building during the raid. Night-vision glasses would have been problematic in any event; they were easily defeated by flashes of light from flash-crash grenades, and were heavy and bulky besides.

"I'm the first to fire," added Setco. He said it in Korean and Vietnamese, then looked at Zeus. "I'm the first to fire."

"OK."

Setco turned to the others. "All right? It's only half of us, but we've dealt with this shit before."

The others nodded. It wasn't much of a pep talk, but at this point no one really wanted one. They wanted to get in and get the job done.

There were eight of them now, roughly half of what they had started with, a number that itself Zeus had thought barely enough to pull off the job. But it was too late to change things, too late to turn back.

All the way in. That's where they were now.

Zeus swapped places with one of the Koreans, while the Taiwanese mercenary who'd been sitting next to him went up to the front. Setco took the middle where Zeus had been. It was a tight fit. The vehicle smelled of sweat and farts; someone's stomach was acting up.

Zeus was grateful it wasn't his.

He positioned his rifle barrel down between his legs, set his hand so he could grab it easily, and hunkered down, waiting.

It seemed to take forever to drive the last mile to the base. Zeus breathed slowly, his mind empty. He stared down at the rifle, focusing on the trigger loop barely visible in the dark van. They slowed. His heart pounded inside his chest. He emptied his lungs carefully, feeling the breath move between his teeth.

He thought of Anna. He saw her on the bed, their first night together in Hanoi.

I would die for this woman. I *will* die for this woman.

Setco raised his Glock. "I fire first," he said in English, then in Korean and Vietnamese. He slipped it back down under his jacket.

No one spoke as they came up to the gate. They slowed; the driver rolled down the window and held out the card.

And then they were in.

Just like that, past the guards, who were too busy with whatever gossip they were sharing in the guardhouse to do more than glance at the papers.

They were in.

"Another fifty yards," whispered Setco. "Everyone careful now."

The fifty yards could have been fifty miles as far as Zeus was concerned. He clenched his teeth, waiting. He was afraid to think.

The truck veered right.

"Steady. Steady," hissed Setco.

Solt said something in Vietnamese. Setco answered. Zeus closed his eyes. His fingers started to press against the trigger guard. He jerked them away—an accidental shot now was the last thing they needed.

Kam whispered something to Setco.

Setco repeated it in English for the others. "We're coming up to the armored car."

Another whisper.

"All right. We're past. Here's the door. Kam flashes the ID. Let's move in. Don't fire until we're stopped, or we're all in. Whichever comes first. Look sharp."

The men started to pile out of the van. It was dark. There were no lights in the missile complex to the right, the side that Zeus got out on. Only a single light marked the entrance of the headquarters building.

Zeus looked toward the entrance of the missile battery. He could see black shapes moving around.

A shot rang out behind him. Kam had been challenged, and Setco took no chances.

Two, three—a burst. Zeus pulled his gun up. But the gunfire had already stopped.

Everyone was running into the building. There were shouts from the missile barracks.

Zeus told himself to ignore them and followed the others.

Kam was at the threshold. He dropped a duffel bag to the ground, then bent over it. Thinking he'd been wounded, Zeus slowed to help, then stopped as Kam pulled a small, thick tube from the bag.

It was an RPG 27, a stubby short-range antitank weapon manufactured by the Russians. It was loaded—he had it ready and was kneeling.

"Ha!" he yelled, or something close.

Zeus stepped to the side. The launcher roared.

Almost instantly, the armored car exploded.

I need to be inside, thought Zeus. He turned quickly and followed to the building. There were two bodies by the door.

Bullets flew around him.

The doorway was open. One of the Korean team members, Squirt, was on his knee just inside the door. Zeus ran to him, squatting next to him. Then he pointed inside, and thumbed his chest:

I'll go first.

Squirt nodded.

Zeus took a breath, then lunged inside. He caught the sight of a small green chem light on the floor to his left, in the threshold of room—it meant it had already been cleared. Then he saw something moving on the far side of the long hall. He thought it was another member of the team, but something was wrong—the man was wearing the wrong kind of uniform.

His brain couldn't process what he was seeing. There was gunfire, a pop. Zeus brought his rifle up but unsure what or who the shadow was, held off from firing. He managed to tuck his shoulder down and tried to roll, ducking down in case he was fired on. He landed against the wall, hard, struggling to process what he saw.

A full green uniform.

Not one of theirs—they were wearing camis.

The AR15 jumped in Zeus's hand as he fired. The man went down.

Squirt took a step and bounded in, sliding in next to Zeus. Further down the hall, someone emerged from one of the rooms.

"It's clear, it's clear," he yelled with a decided accent. There was a loud pop and a series of bangs downstairs—a Polish flash-crash grenade going off.

Zeus glanced to his right. There was a dead body behind him. As he rose, Zeus felt something wet on his knee—the man's blood.

"Blue, blue, blue," yelled Setco, emerging from another room. "Move to the stairs. The stairs!"

The stairs were where the man in the green had come from. Just beyond his body was another, this one in Chinese camis.

One of their guys. Park.

"Down, coming down!" Setco shouted.

"Clear," yelled whoever was downstairs.

Zeus was the last man in the small train down the steps. Setco crouched in the hall, listening as the Korean who'd met them explained something.

Setco waved at him, then pushed him forward. There were four of them, tight now as a group, Zeus at the back. Two men took a room, the others stayed outside. They used the grenades, swarming in and hugging the walls, taking no chances.

Zeus told himself not to look back at the man, their man, lying on the floor. It was his job not to look back.

Someone had screwed up or guessed wrong or been incredibly unlucky for him to have been shot. Most likely it was the man himself—he probably had been left to hold the stairs. The soldier in green who came up must have been the one who shot him.

Setco had it under control now. They worked in and out of the rooms, each man taking his role—the door-banger in, another, Setco directing, Zeus tailgun, watching the hall.

"That's a comm room," said Setco, thumbing at the next door. It was closed. "Jooch'll take the door, we'll toss a grenade. Stay down for the shock. Zeus, watch the hall."

Zeus nodded. There were only two more rooms that they hadn't checked. But he could hear gunfire upstairs; there wasn't much time now.

He crouched, waiting. Jooch—the Korean who had been first-in upstairs—rose and fired at the door handle. Even as he pulled his gun back, Zeus had his foot on the door, trying to slam it in.

It didn't go.

He cursed and tried again.

The door remained in place.

"Leave it." Zeus tapped the other Korean on the shoulder. "Stay."

They ran to the next room. This door was locked as well. Setco went to a knee, then removed a small box from his cargo pants pocket. He popped it open; it contained a small amount of C4-like plastic explosive, and some igniter charges. He put the plastic on the door and shoved in the igniter.

"Back!" he hissed.

All four of them retreated to the stairwell. Zeus pressed the back of his arm against the banister. The pressure somehow felt reassuring.

The explosive went off with a sharp bang, amplified by the hallway. Zeus's ears rang as he followed the others back into the hall. The explosive had punched a large hole in the door, nearly obliterating most of the wood; bits hung around the frame on either side like a fringed decoration.

"Back!" yelled Setco again as he tossed a grenade underhand into the room. A few seconds later it exploded, the sound softer than the C-4, muffled not only by the walls but by whatever temporary damage had been done to Zeus's ears.

Zeus caught a whiff of acrid smoke as he stepped through into the room. Two bodies were laying at the far side, behind an overturned table. They were officers.

Jooch stepped over and fired a burst into the nearest man's head. Zeus, scanning right as he went down along the wall, saw the Korean going toward the other officer. He was moving. He had a pistol in his hand.

Zeus pumped three bullets into the body, catching the Chinese officer in the neck and the back of skull. Jooch jerked back, then glanced up at Zeus, confused.

"Come on! Come on!" Zeus yelled.

By the time they left the room, an explosive charge had been set on the door to the other locked office. Once more they retreated to the stairs.

"Why did you shoot?" whispered Jooch, settling in below Zeus.

"He was going to shoot you."

Jooch gave him a strange look.

"He moved," added Zeus. "And he had a gun in his hand."

"Didn't move. I don't think there was a gun."

The charge blew down the hall. It was a smaller blast, scaled back after the earlier one. They filed quickly into the corridor.

Someone was shouting in Chinese from inside the room.

"What's he saying?" asked Zeus.

Setco yelled back at the person in the room. Whoever it was responded with a few words. Zeus saw Setco reach into his vest for a grenade.

"If he surrenders," said Zeus. "Maybe—"

Setco shook his head. But before he could toss the

grenade, there was a gunshot inside the room. He hesitated, then tossed in the weapon. As soon as it exploded, he darted forward, sliding on his haunches as he came even with the doorway.

"Clear," he yelled.

Zeus followed him in. A man lay on his back in front of the communications consoles. At first glance, he seemed eerily calm, his eyes wide open.

Then Zeus saw that his head was surrounded by a pool of blood, soaking into the carpet. He'd shot himself in the mouth; the gun had tumbled off to the side as he fell back, lifeless.

He had a star on his shoulder.

The general.

Zeus bent to get a good look at his face. Something was wrong—this man seemed older than Li Sun, and fatter. Zeus tried to remember the image.

"Take the hall, Murphy," said Setco. "We gotta get ready to move."

"This isn't the guy in the briefing."

"I got it, I got it," said Setco, pulling out his camera. "Watch the door. We don't need any more surprises."

Zeus moved back to the doorway. He checked up and down the corridor, then moved so he could see inside the room.

"Take pictures, check his pockets," Setco told Jooch, giving him the camera. He took a small black device about the size of an iPhone from his hip pocket and went to the computer.

"What are you doing?" asked Zeus.

Setco smirked at him. He pulled at the side of the device, removing a cover and then pulling a wire from the side. Then he bent and plugged it into the USB port. He slid open the top of the device, revealing a touch screen. He tapped it furiously, then set it down. As the screen flashed, he took another device from a different pocket and set it next to it. He plugged this into the second one.

Jooch took some papers from the dead general, then came out of the room. Setco checked something on the devices he'd just hooked up, then came out.

"What were you doing?" Zeus asked. "What did you put on the computer?"

"You don't think they sent me all this way just to kill that asshole, do you?"

51

The South China Sea

Silas's first thought when he heard the missile launch warning was one of triumph: *Now I have the son of a bitch*.

His second thought was more realistic: *Holy shit*.

He spewed orders, but in fact the crew responded so quickly it was difficult to know if his words were even heard.

Sixteen 3M54 Klub missiles sprang from the deck of *Wu Bei*, a virtual forest of weaponry heading for *McCampbell*. It was half the cruiser's allotment of anti-ship missiles, a heavy investment in destruction.

But Silas felt relief when the count stopped at sixteen. He'd drilled the crew to defend against sixty-four—a drill that included a run to the lifeboats.

"ERAMs!" ordered Silas.

The ship's Aegis system was already picking out targets for the missiles, also known as Standard 6s or Extended Range Active Missiles. They were the product of an unholy marriage between an Air Force AM-RAAM antiair missile and a Navy Standard Missile, with the best attributes of both.

But there were only twelve aboard *McCampbell*.

SM2s were launched at the others, guided by *Mc-Campbell*'s three SPG-62 directors. The ERAMs didn't need directors—"Thank Neptune," muttered Silas as the SM2s lofted.

As both vertical launchers spewed missiles, Silas had the ship turn beam-on to the attack. This ensured that he had all his illuminators, mounted on the centerline, bearing on the targets.

A half minute had passed, a lifetime to Silas. His first priority was to protect his ship. But even as the Aegis system selected targets for the launched SM2s, Silas was shifting from defense to offense.

"Now," he said, talking in shorthand as he followed a plan the crew had rehearsed several times. "One director on *Wu Bei*. Then the frigate. SM2 missiles. Six and six. Shift the others to attack the ship when appropriate."

Six SM2s popped up from the launchers and twisted their contrails in the direction of *Wu Bei*. Another half-dozen launched shortly afterward, heading for the frigate.

My boat. *Your boat.*
Silas tightened his hands into fists.
You're done, Wu Bei. *You and your frigate shadow.*

The sixteen Klub missiles skimmed over the ocean only a few meters from the thin tips of the waves. The ERAMs, traveling at Mach 3, roared out to meet them. Though subsonic, the Klub missile presented a small target to the American interceptors; its stealthy radar signature and the low altitude made it a difficult target. But the ERAMs had been designed for this.

The ERAMs began finding the Klubs some four and a half miles from *Wu Bei*. On paper—or rather in computers—the missiles would strike their targets some 75 percent of the time. In real life, they did slightly better—eight Klubs were destroyed, flaring rather undramatically in the dark space between the two ships.

The SM2s, arriving shortly afterwards, thinned the remaining attackers to two.

The battle was only two minutes old. .

Silas listened to his people as they tracked the missiles. Their comments were quick, brief, numbers and a few words. All emotionless.

The crew was a well-practiced machine, as efficient as the weapons they were guiding.

Nice.

"Two missiles in-bound," reported his exec. "Aegis has them."

"The Chinese?"

"Reacting. No second launch."

"Frigate?"

"Negative. Still moving to shield the cruiser."

The Chinese captain had undoubtedly believed sixteen missiles would be enough, Silas knew. Probably he'd been trained to believe that half that was necessary. It was a fatal mistake.

Now he was concentrating on defense, as well he would have to.

Two of the SM2 missiles intended for the Klubs were redirected toward the cruiser. They became the lead element of an eight-missile attack, a barrage heading at Mach 2 toward *Wu Bei*. The size of the missiles made them hard for the Chinese radars to find.

When they finally did, SA-N-6 Fort and SA-N-4B Osa 2M SAM began launching.

One of the American missiles that had been diverted was struck by an SA-N-6 missile, whose 90 kilogram warhead met it far enough away to harmlessly disintegrate the smaller weapon. But the second American missile streaked past the Fort missile aimed at it, and also eluded the SA-N-4B. This left it for the cruiser's 30 mm rotary guns, which threw a furious spray of shells in the missile's path.

Some of the shells hit the missile a thousand yards from the ship. The fusillade was enough to shred the airframe, but it was a pyrrhic victory: turned into a flying ball of burning debris, what was left of the missile struck the main deck of the cruiser, flattening and spreading like a balloon filled with napalm.

Thirty seconds later, the rest of the SM2s arrived. The Fort system managed to destroy two as they came on, and the antiquated Osa system killed one more. But two warheads and another fireball struck the superstructure, shredding it.

Detonating inside the ship, the intact missiles spread shrapnel and fire in every direction. They cut the ship's electricity, and damaged the steering controls leaving her at least temporarily rudderless.

On *McCampbell*, the Phalanx 20 mm cannon took aim at the last incoming missiles, a stream of bullets heading toward the two warheads. One of the Chinese missiles, confused by *McCampbell*'s countermeasures, veered off to the south.

The other continued toward the ship.

At that point, three of the six missiles launched at the frigate struck the escort vessel, as did the remains of a fourth warhead. One ignited directly in the engine room, obliterating equipment and starting an electrical fire that soon did even more damage than the initial explosion. Plumes of toxic smoke poured through the corridors of the ship, choking the crew and hindering damage control efforts. The frigate had already begun taking on water where she had been hit; the fire hindered efforts to cope with the damage and she soon listed heavily to the starboard side.

McCampbell's Phalanx cannon caught the last Chinese missile. Shrapnel from the warhead rained down on the port side of the destroyer's fantail, pockmarking the paint but mercifully sparing the ship and her crew any real damage.

Silas, realizing that his enemy had been crippled, changed course, pointing his bow in the direction of the merchant ship so he could get down to help it.

At this point, he could easily have finished off the Chinese vessels with another salvo of missiles. He wanted to do just that. But he also realized that Fleet, as well as the Pentagon, were watching via their satellite and spy plane connections. With the two enemy ships disabled, he called his command for further instructions.

"What the hell is the situation?" demanded CIN-PAC commander Admiral Meeve, coming on the line with his usual bluster. Meeve hated Silas, and had made those feelings clear on any number of occasions

"I was fired on," said Silas. "I provided a measured response. Both Chinese ships are crippled. Request permission to sink them."

"Denied!"

"Should I have let them sink me?" snapped Silas.

It was out of line and he knew it; as soon as the words left his mouth he wished he could grab them back. Meeve didn't say anything for a moment. Silas started to apologize, but the admiral cut him off.

"You . . . Keep clear. Watch them, but you don't do anything until you hear from me. Do you understand?"

"Admiral, I was fired on."

"*Do nothing.*"

"I'm going to the aid of a stricken civilian vessel," said Silas. But the admiral had already cut the line.

52

Hanoi

It cost Kerfer only a hundred dollars American plus gas to get a car for Hanoi, a bargain price considering the circumstances. The gas was potentially more costly, and much harder to find. Kerfer knew there weren't many stations in the city that still had gas. In fact, the only reliable place that he could think of was the embassy.

But given that was where he was going, Kerfer didn't mind agreeing.

The Marines at the gate were used to him, but even so made both him and the driver get out while they searched the ten-year-old Toyota. Kerfer told them that he needed the vehicle filled with gas, then told the driver to follow the guards and to meet him out front when he was done. The Marines rolled their eyes but in the end agreed to help while the SEAL officer went inside for his gear.

Kerfer found a sleepy Juliet Greig sitting at a secretary's desk in the office wing, waiting with a box.

"Keeping you up?"

"Just from dinner," said Greig, rising from the chair. The acting consul general's hair was rumpled; she was wearing an oversized sweatshirt and khaki pants frayed at the seams. Her face looked washed out, as if she hadn't worn makeup in a month. But she was still damn good-looking to Kerfer, and her handshake was neither too soft nor overtrying hard.

"That for me?" Kerfer asked, pointing to the box on the floor.

"Apparently so."

Kerfer took the box. It was a large, nondescript cardboard box taped with a special tamper-evident tape.

"Top secret stuff, huh?" she said.

"Just my lunch," said Kerfer, wondering if the agency idiots could have made it any more obvious.

"What's this all about?"

He shook his head. "Damned if I know. They just got me running errands. I have to deliver this to Ho Chi Minh City. Or Ho Chi Minh himself, if I see him."

"Some people think he'll come back from the dead," said Greig.

"Hey, you never know."

"Place is falling apart."

She crossed her arms, folding them down below her breasts. Beautiful breasts, even under the sweatshirt. Some women were just too pretty for their own good.

"I'd ask you to have a drink," said Kerfer, fighting off not only the distraction but the urge to be distracted, "but I kind of have a time deadline here. Long drive."

"Sure."

Kerfer cradled the box awkwardly under his arm.

"I'm supposed to call home," he told her.

"SCIF's empty."

Kerfer nodded. "You getting out of Hanoi?"

"I don't know. Probably not. We're not at war with the Chinese, Ric."

"We oughta be."

She gave him a sweet, though slightly sardonic, smile, the sort of grin that in Kerfer's experience smart women gave you when they thought they were just a little wiser than you were. That was one of the downsides of being a SEAL, even for an officer—the macho image carried with it a stereotype of being not quite that sharp. In reality this was almost always the opposite of the truth—just getting through BUD/S, let alone the advanced schools, took a great of intelligence. But stereotypes and clichés were hard to get beyond.

Shame. She was definitely worth the effort.

"See you around," he told her, leaving the office.

"Hopefully."

Kerfer went downstairs to the secure communications room and contacted the agency over the secure video conferencing network for the exact location of the site he was supposed to check. Instead of Mara he got her boss, Peter Lucas. If Greig had been tired, Lucas was exhausted to a point just shy of death. He looked as if he hadn't slept for a week—and very possibly he hadn't.

"You're familiar with Quang Ninh?" asked Lucas.

"We've been all through this," Kerfer told him. "Mara was going to give me some GPS spots."

"All right, I'm sorry. Here's a map."

A satellite image came on the screen. Details began popping in over the terrain, roads and other highlights magically materializing.

"There's a temple called Chùa Cao," said Lucas. "You can see it on your screen."

"You're blowing up a temple?"

"No." Lucas frowned. It was one of those agency frowns, Kerfer thought—the "I can't believe I'm working with this big a dumbshit" frowns. "Where you're going is about a mile west of that. There are a set of mines. They're all pretty deep. We need to know which one to hit."

"And I figure that out how?"

"Inside your package you'll find a radiation detector. What we need you to do is get readings at the places we suspect where they are. If your readings are positive, we blow the places. As many as it takes."

"Why don't you just blow them anyway?" asked Kerfer.

"There are too many. They're deep, so we have to use special bomb combinations. And we're afraid if we start at the wrong end of the complex, the Vietnamese may be able to launch before we can get the right ones."

"All right. So I'm looking for radiation."

"Right."

"Enough to fry me?"

"No. You're pretty far away in any event. It's just traces. You need technical instructions on the instrument?"

"Hold on."

Kerfer took out his pocketknife and slit open the box. A plastic box sat inside, snug against the cardboard. He cut away the sides and took out the box. There was a pair of combo locks on the side, similar to those on a briefcase.

"This is all locked up," he told Lucas.

"We didn't want anyone to know what we're doing."

"You going to give me the combination?" Kerfer asked. He started to fiddle with it, moving the first number around.

"1-2-3," said Lucas.

"You're kidding, right?"

He was. Lucas gave him the right combination and

Kerfer opened the case. There was a new satcom radio/telephone inside, a GPS locator unit, the bulky laser designator, and the radiation screening device.

The radiation detector looked something like a large garage door opener, with a black sensor end atop a soap-shaped control area. A small screen ran across the body just below the sensor. Kerfer couldn't see a way to turn it on.

"You squeeze the sides," said Lucas, watching him on the video.

"OK." The LEDs in the text window came on. It read 0.000. Then it shut off. "That's it? That's how it works?"

"So simple, even a SEAL can use it."

"Ha-ha."

Kerfer took the laser designator out of the box. It looked very much like a slide projector with an eyepiece at the back. It weighed about twelve pounds, and was a little larger than a hardcover book.

Lasing targets for a bomber was a battle-tested procedure, but it had fallen largely by the wayside thanks to newer technology and changes in tactics. Common for high-value sites during the first Gulf War, by the time of Operation Iraqi Freedom it had become almost passé, replaced for the most part by GPS-guided missiles and other smart weapons that didn't put a poor schlep on the ground at risk. But computers and fancy sensors couldn't completely replace people on the ground, and the capability remained, though mostly confined to exercises.

"You can use that?" Lucas asked. "I can get an expert to walk you through the instructions."

"It's all right," said Kerfer, holding it up. "I'm not going senile yet."

He'd used this particular model years before and only once, but the device was designed to be relatively easy to operate in the field, and he was thoroughly familiar with the principles. It could range from approximately two hundred to a thousand yards.

He definitely wanted to be at the far end of that range when the bombers came in.

"All right, it's working," he announced, finished looking it over. "Battery is charged and everything."

"I have some contact frequencies for you, and some backups. You're going to be talking directly to the pilots. They'll start listening for you in an hour."

"Gonna take me longer than that to get there."

"Not too much longer, I hope," said Lucas. "The Chinese are heading toward the border. The Vietnamese are getting pretty desperate."

"So am I," said Kerfer. "Can you get me a map of the area?"

"Use the GPS."

"I want a paper map. Call me old-fashioned. I like to fold things up and put them in my pocket."

"All right. I'm sending it on the secure system. Print it, but eat it if you get caught."

Kerfer stifled a laugh when he saw that Lucas didn't mean it as a joke.

Spooks.

"Good luck," said the CIA officer.

The screen blanked.

53

North of Malipo

General Li Sun knew that the situation was worse than he'd suspected as soon as he saw General Fan standing stiffly next to the back of the command building. Fan held his hands at his sides like a chastened recruit.

Fan's embarrassment pained Li Sun, and not simply because it meant that his own situation was even more perilous than he had supposed. To see any Chinese commander humiliated by a *peasant* army was heart rending.

On the one hand, Li Sun wanted to pummel him with his bare hands. On the other, he felt . . . pity at the man's shame.

"General, we must talk," he told Fan sharply, striding toward his command post.

Fan followed him into the mobile headquarters. It was a large trailer unit, originally designed as a mobile home and converted for military use. Equipped with communications equipment, computers, and other gear necessary for directing a war, the trailer was divided into three areas. The back, closed off, was an office used by Fan. The section in the middle had a conference table for staff meetings. A *U*-shaped ring of consoles sat near the front. Men were working over the consoles when they entered, most wearing headsets and hunched forward, peering at screens.

Everyone rose as the generals entered.

"Empty the room," said Li Sun. His voice was soft, but even the men wearing the headsets instantly complied.

"We were ambushed here," said Fan, unfurling a map on the table. He pointed to the strip mine pit, and led Li Sun through a brief recitation of the battle.

It wasn't pretty or flattering. He had moved his units on secondary roads because of the blocked bridge, which he realized now had been destroyed as part of the Vietnamese plan to trap him. He thought his decision to use the strip mine to move his tanks faster had probably helped him—if the Vietnamese had cornered him on the road, they might have bottlenecked his entire force. Still, he had let his tank regiment move without adequate infantry screening. And allowing himself to then be attacked on the flank and nearly surrounded was a critical mistake. He should have withdrawn earlier.

"You should have protected your flank better," said Li Sun. "You could have turned back the few Vietnamese tanks and still had a victory."

"There were more than a few," said Fan.

"The reconnaissance counted less than a dozen," said Li Sun. "Had you placed a battalion at this spot here, all would have been well."

Not exactly, since he would still have been ambushed deep in Chinese territory, but at least the Vietnamese would have been defeated.

Fan said nothing.

"Where did these troops come from?" Li Sun asked. "How did they get so far north?"

"They must have been planning this for days," said Fan.

It was a reasonable theory, Li Sun thought. Perhaps they had even crossed over the border before the actual declaration of war. The old commander's negligence was now his problem.

"Take me to inspect your troops," said Li Sun.

Fan complied in silence. The main camps were only a few kilometers away. The ride was slow, and painful.

Li Sun wasn't entirely sure what he would do with Fan. He was surprised at the amount of sympathy he felt for him. It was especially inexplicable, since Fan's failures threatened Li Sun himself.

Clearly, the general had to be removed. There was no debating the decision. And yet. . . .

There were many excuses. First and foremost, he had no one to replace him, or at least no one he trusted.

Li Sun was shocked when they reached the regimental headquarters of the unit that had been battered. The officers looked like walking ghosts. Every man he met seemed to be shell-shocked, flinching as he strode among them.

And well they should flinch. Well they should.

But this would not do in battle.

The regiment's commander and his second in command had been killed during the ambush. In his place, Fan had appointed a lieutenant colonel from his third regiment. Lt. Colonel Zhi, a fiery officer about Li Sun's age, had been with his own tanks many kilometers back when the assault began. He had brought up two battalions and gathered the survivors of the first battle, organizing them into a new unit roughly a regiment strong.

"How would you deal with the Vietnamese?" Sun asked him.

"Attack before they have a chance to dig in," said Zhi without hesitation. "I have seen from the battle at the mines that their antitank weapons are slow to fire.

They used them in the beginning, but not at the end. We should have doubled our attack, not retreated."

Fan tightened his lips at the implicit criticism. It would be easy for a man who had not been in combat to say that.

But Li Sun liked the commander's aggressive attitude. He would be useful.

I see what I have to do, he said to himself.

They would rebound. The first step was to rally the men.

"Listen to me, you men!" Li Sun walked to one of the dirt-spattered Type 96 tanks, gripped the wire mask over the headlight, and pulled himself onto the hull. "Listen—you have tasted your first blood of battle. You were surprised, and shocked at the reality of it. I know—I had a first battle myself! I was scared, scared beyond belief!"

Li Sun paused. The admission of fear—an emotion he was sure nearly everyone who listened to him had shared at some point in the battle—got their interest. Now it was time to use it.

"They put us back on our heels—they were tougher fighters than we thought," said Li Sun, his voice starting to rise. "But we fought back. With the right leaders, we fought back. We were able to push the Vietnamese back. Because they were inferior—they were brave when they were winning, but cowards once the battle turned."

The men closest to him shifted uneasily. They were ready to come with him, he saw, but only with the right push.

"We have a plan to strike back at the dogs," he thundered. "The Vietnamese animals who were not content to attack tanks, but killed Chinese women and children in Malipo. Prepare yourselves for a great victory! Prepare yourselves for revenge!"

There was silence for a moment, each man looking

around to see what his comrades thought before committing. Finally, Zhi raised his fist and yelled. The men followed, still tentative, but loud.

Li Sun hopped down from the tank.

"I will meet you in one hour to discuss the plans for the attack," he told Zhi.

Geneial Fan was quiet as they got into the car and drove back toward the command trailer. Perhaps, thought Li Sun, the general had already come to the conclusion he himself had.

Li Sun leaned forward as the driver turned off the road toward the trailer.

"We will walk," Li Sun told him. "You go on ahead."

Li Sun opened the door and got out. Fan slid across to his side and followed. The delay irked Li Sun slightly— the imbecile should have had the sense to move quickly.

The car drove up the road. Li Sun waited until it had gone, then reached to his holster and took out his pistol. He chambered a cartridge, then slid out the magazine, leaving a solitary bullet ready to fire.

He handed the gun to Fan.

"Your family will be provided for," said Li Sun.

Fan stared at the gun a moment, then took it. Li Sun began walking up the trail.

When General Fan did not fire, Li Sun worried for a moment that he would use the bullet on Li Sun. He braced himself, prepared to die.

Then the sound of a gunshot echoed behind him, louder than he expected. He continued up the trail without looking back, already absorbed in the problems he would have to overcome in the attack.

54

Kunming

Zeus trailed Setco back to the end of the hall where Park, their wounded team member, was lying. He'd been hit twice in the front of his vest. The ceramic plate had shattered, bruising and cutting his chest. But the more serious injuries were to his leg, which had been hit in several places. He'd managed to stop some of the bleeding himself by wrapping a tourniquet around the largest wound, but he was going in and out of consciousness.

Zeus checked on the wounds, then adjusted the bandage, moving it to cover the wound better. He tightened it, hoping the blood would clot.

The lights flickered, went off and then went on. The team members outside had cut the phone line.

"About fuckin' time," said Setco. He put his hand to his ear. "Kam, what's going on out there?"

Solt answered, speaking Vietnamese.

"Right," said Setco, responding in English. He turned to Zeus and the others. "There are vehicles coming from the camp area. We have to move."

"I thought the place was empty," said Zeus.

"Perfect like every intelligence briefing since the world began," said Setco in a sneer.

"The general—was that Li Sun?"

"I don't know. It doesn't matter now. He had a star. We got the ID and we got pictures. The place is clear," said Setco. "You want to hang around and look for somebody else?"

There was an explosion outside. That put an end to any discussion. Zeus bent to put the wounded man on his shoulder.

Setco grabbed his arm.

"We have to take him," said Zeus.

"No shit. I got him," added Setco. He bent down and in a smooth motion hoisted Park onto his back.

Zeus was surprised—not only because he thought Setco would leave the man as he'd left the others, but because Setco was smaller than Zeus, and if logic were involved, Zeus should have been the person doing the carrying.

"Let's go, let's go!" barked Setco. If he was straining with the weight, he didn't show it. "Jooch, you're point. Let's go!"

They ran up the stairs, Setco and the wounded man sandwiched between Jooch and Zeus. The other two team members joined them on the main floor, and together they ran outside the building.

Outside, Setco sent Kam back for the dead member of the team.

"I don't want to leave him here if I don't have to," he said.

Kam nodded, then went inside with Squirt to retrieve him.

The gunfire had quieted. Solt was crouched behind the van, eying the interior access road.

"Two trucks came out along the road but stopped,"

said Solt when Zeus ran up to her. "You see them over there."

Zeus could just make them out in the shadows against the other buildings. They were about a hundred yards away, maybe a little more.

"There're troops in there?" he asked.

"I can't tell. I didn't see anything moving. There hasn't been any gunfire."

"What's going on at the missile battery?" he asked. The battery was to their left; if someone started firing from behind its fences, they could be pinned down.

"We took out the two guards at the gate and blew up their machine gun with one of the RPGs. No one inside has peeped since."

"Let's get into the van and go," said Setco.

Zeus and Solt moved up to cover the others as they climbed into the van. Zeus stared at the black hulks of the trucks. They had probably been parked in one of the buildings toward the rear of the complex.

"Come on, come on," shouted Setco.

Zeus backed against the truck, the hopped on the running board as the vehicle started to move. As soon as he did, a wave of gunfire rose from the field in front of the trucks. Suddenly, he was surrounded by a hail of bullets. Lead flew at him so quickly he couldn't even answer the gunfire. There was no time and he had no balance; he could barely hold on.

Something popped him in the back, hard. A bullet smacked into the door. The window burst next to him.

A white light blinked ahead.

More gunfire.

Zeus tucked his gun under his shoulder and rolled off the van, landing on his side on the ground. He jumped to his feet and fired two bursts into the area where he'd seen the muzzle flashes.

The van kept moving. Zeus got to his feet and started running after it. The men in the field near the trucks continued to fire at the vehicle. Someone on the other side of the gate began shooting as well. Zeus lowered his rifle, pointing in that direction, but couldn't see a target and didn't shoot.

The rest of the small team was firing from the van. Someone fell off—Solt, he guessed. He changed direction, running toward her and yelling her name as the gunfire eased down.

The gates were closed. The van barreled into them, veering right, then jerking left and heading toward the highway. A few soldiers from inside the missile battery fired at it. A light machine gun rattled near the guard post, its violent burst long but futile.

Solt was just getting to her knees when Zeus caught up to her.

"Are you OK?" he asked.

"I think. I don't know."

Zeus put his hand to his ear and tried calling Setco on the radio. He couldn't hear a response.

"Is your radio working?" he asked Solt.

"The earpiece came off."

Probably they were out of range by now anyway, Zeus thought.

"We have to get out before they start a search," said Solt, getting to her feet.

"The machine gun," he told her. "Come this way."

He tugged her to the right, away from the main entrance.

"The van!" cried Solt.

"They're out. They won't wait for us. Come on," said Zeus.

They ran together for about thirty yards. In the darkness, Zeus didn't see the wide drainage ditch that ran across the field about fifty yards from the fence. He slipped and fell on his back, skidding down into the muck at the bottom.

"Up, up," yelled Solt. Now it was her turn to tug him to his feet. They climbed out of the ditch and started running for the fence. As they did, someone in the field near the trucks saw them and began firing in their direction.

Zeus nearly collapsed as he reached the fence. He went down to one knee, catching his breath. Solt huddled next to him.

"We need to get out," she told him between gasps of air. "We have to get to the highway. We can steal a car."

"Can you get over?"

She looked up at the fence. It was topped with razor wire. There was a second fence about ten feet beyond it, also topped with wire.

"We'll be easy targets," she told him. "We're better off going through the gate."

"There's a machine gun."

"They can't see us from this side," she told him. "We're behind them. Come on."

Zeus followed her, his right shoulder dragging along the fence. He saw something moving near the guard shack but didn't fire, figuring all that would do was tell them they were coming.

They were still about twenty-five yards from the entrance when Solt reached down to her fatigues and took out a grenade. Running, she thumbed off the tape.

"Let me throw it!" yelled Zeus, but it was too late; she'd already cocked her arm back and let the grenade fly.

"Down!" she yelled, turning back and grabbing hold of him, pulling him to the ground. He crashed on top of her, then cringed, waiting for the explosion. It came a second or two later, a dull crackle nearly lost in the sound of the machine gun starting to fire.

"You got another one of those?" Zeus asked, leaning to the side so she could push out from under him.

"Just one."

"Give me."

Her eyes stared at him from the shadow of the fence line. They were beautiful eyes; they reminded him of Anna's.

"Here." She pressed the grenade into his hand. "You have to undo the tape."

"Yeah, I know."

He took it carefully. The machine gunner was across the entrance road, behind a thick set of sandbags. The gunner's view across was partly blocked by a set of low cement road barriers and the broken fencing, and as long as they stayed low it didn't look as if he could get them.

But of course that worked both ways. As long as Zeus stayed low, he couldn't tell exactly where the gunner was, or how far he had to toss the grenade.

Zeus eased upward against the fence, trying to gauge the distance to the gun. It wasn't much—thirty yards or so—but plopping the grenade between the sandbags and cement barrier in the dark was going to be as much a matter of luck as skill.

He steadied himself, then tossed the grenade. He lurched forward, swinging up his rifle to fire as he burst out into the open.

He barely heard the explosion. Instead of stopping as he planned, a sudden burst of adrenaline took hold of him and he ran to the concrete barrier nearest the entrance road and leapt over it. He leveled his gun at the machine-gun position and fired, squeezing through the rest of the magazine before he reached the sandbags.

The man who'd been there was dead.

A bullet hit into one of the nearby sandbag, sounding like a clod of dirt hitting the ground. Zeus ducked. The gunfire was coming from the missile battery. He started to turn the machine gun in their direction, then stopped as Solt came running up.

"Come on, through the entrance," she yelled. "Run!"

He leapt out of the position, and ran, head down, following her out of the complex. More gunfire followed him out, but it was poorly aimed, fired only in the general direction of the trouble.

They ran until they reached the highway. Cars passed, apparently unaware of them. Solt, a little ahead of him, slowed and began to walk along the shoulder.

"Let's get to the other side," said Zeus.

"I need my breath."

"Come on." He grabbed her hand—it felt small—then pulled her across. They made it just in front of a truck, which showed no sign of slowing, let alone stopping. They hadn't been seen in the dark.

Zeus lay on his back in the grass. Every part of him hurt—his body had been pounded, and not just by bullets hitting the vest. He needed to rest. He wanted to sleep for a few days if not weeks.

"What do we do?" Solt asked.

"Get the hell out of here," he told her.

"To where?"

"Anywhere we can. Do you have contacts?"

"Some. If things are too hot, they won't help."

"If we can get a car, maybe we can get to the airport," Zeus said.

"It's too late for that. I know someone in Yaowancun I trust." Solt's voice became more assured as she spoke. "She can help get us closer to the border. Or to Beijing."

"All right," said Zeus.

"Come on." She started to tug him back in the direction of the camp.

"South?" He held fast.

"Yaowancun is south of here. Come on."

"We'll never make it past the base."

"Yes. Come on. If we hurry. Come on."

Zeus hesitated. But really, what choice did he have? She knew the country far better than he did. Setco was gone. They were completely on their own.

He'd gotten out of China before.

"All right," he said.

They trotted a few yards along the ditch, Solt in the lead. She quickly grew tired and slowed to a fast walk. Zeus caught up and started to walk himself.

The base was quiet. There was some activity back near the buildings, but nothing at the road.

"It took us too long to get to the phone lines," said Solt. "I'm sure they made calls out."

"Don't worry now," said Zeus. "There was someone in the radio room. I'm just surprised there's no one here yet."

"They must be on the way."

A handful of cars passed. The ditch became shallower after they passed the gate; before they'd gone twenty yards they were nearly at the level of the road.

Zeus thought of getting rid of the armored vest he was wearing. Its weight drained his energy. But it had already saved his life; very possibly it might have to do so again.

"Keep moving," Solt urged. "Come on.

A car sped past from the north. Almost as soon as it passed them, the driver hit the brakes and pulled a U-turn.

Solt flattened herself. Zeus dropped to a firing position.

Zeus heard Setco yelling from the car.

"Get the hell in the car," he growled. "Why the fuck didn't you answer our hails?"

Zeus pulled his radio unit from his pocket. It had been hit by two rounds, one of which was still embedded in the unit.

"Not covered by warranty," said Setco.

The van had been so banged up that Setco decided to exchange it for a new vehicle within minutes of breaking out of the base. They had ended up pulling over two cars, the nondescript JAC sedan that had picked up Zeus and Solt, and a small Lifan SUV.

The SUV was waiting for them about a quarter mile up the road. They stopped, then arranged themselves in what Setco thought was the least conspicuous groupings. He had Solt sit in the front of the JAC with him; Zeus went into the back, sitting in the middle.

The three people who'd been pulled from the cars when Setco grabbed them were sitting against the back of the battered van, tied up and blindfolded. Zeus felt a twinge of regret when he saw one was a woman; none of them had been harmed but this wasn't exactly going to be the high point of their lives.

"They didn't see me," said Setco as Zeus stared. "Once they were blindfolded, I spoke Vietnamese, though I doubt they realized that's what it was."

"Yeah."

"The pistol I left at the base was Vietnamese," added Setco. "The black boxes will have blown up by now and taken out the control center. Kam set satchel charges outside that the Vietnamese use, complete with watches made in Saigon. There'll be enough confusion. As long as we make it back. And if we don't who cares?"

"Is the plane there?" asked Zeus.

"Yeah. Longjohn won't leave without us unless a lot of shit really hits the fan."

Zeus couldn't help but wince—more than a little shit had hit the fan by any definition.

"I just talked to him," Setco added. "They're there. They'll tell me if they have to leave. And if he blows up, his radio sets off a distress signal if it stops transmitting."

"I see," said Zeus.

"Hell on the batteries."

Zeus settled back in his seat, trying not to feel the bruises and scratches covering his body. Solt steered their car into the lead, moving steadily but not past the speed limit up the highway. She was quiet, following but not acknowledging Setco's bare instructions as they drove back north toward the airport.

Zeus wondered why her eyes had reminded him of Anna's. How could he be confused about that?

He leaned his head back on the top of the seat, trying to empty his mind. The world rushed by, a confused jangle. The op was back to being surreal, back to moving well, back to succeeding—they were driving through a Chinese city, having just assassinated the general of one of the country's armies. The dead body of one of their teammates was inside the trunk. They smelled of sweat and blood. Yet no one who saw them passing would suspect any of this.

There were almost no cars on the highway as they went into the city proper. Setco fooled with both the car radio and the team scanner, trying to see what if anything was going on at the airport. About two miles from the large circle, cars started bunching up and the traffic thickening.

"We better come on to the property from the north," Setco told Solt. "We can climb the fence. There's no sense taking a chance at the gate."

She didn't acknowledge, but angled the car to the right lane, leaving the highway near Zihuncun district. From there they took a succession of local roads, tracking around the warehouses and the adjoining housing developments to circle toward the airport. Setco used the satellite map on the laptop to guide her through the thicket of warehouses abutting the airport property; they finally made their way to a fenced field where they could see the blinking runway lights a few hundred yards away.

There were also blue emergency lights in the distance.

"We're going to have to cross the runway to get to the plane," Setco said. "Everybody out. Take everything you have. Except the grenades. They're Vietnamese. Leave those."

"All of them?" asked Zeus.

"No, just leave one," said Setco, reconsidering.

He got out and went to the SUV, telling them the same thing. Then he came back and opened the trunk.

"Give me a hand," he yelled.

No one moved.

"He looks Vietnamese," said Kam. "Leave him."

Setco frowned. "Zeus?"

Zeus walked over.

"They might figure out he's Korean somehow," said Setco. "I don't want to take that chance."

Zeus nodded. He knew now the explanation was just a way of covering for his emotions—Setco didn't want to leave his man behind.

The Chinese would figure out from the van that they weren't Vietnamese, at least not all of them—Roo and Robbie were pretty clearly not Asian, and unless their skeletons were completely disintegrated, the Chinese would eventually figure out or at least suspect who had hit them.

Setco was acting partly out of professionalism, just as he had leaving the Vietnamese gear at the base. But it was more, much more, that he felt responsible for his men, and wanted to bring him home.

Zeus respected him for it. He helped lift the man onto Setco's shoulders, checked the trunk for anything that might have been left behind, then joined the others at the fence.

The area on the other side of the complex where the planes had crashed into the van earlier was awash in light from mobile floodlights. The bright, artificial white was polka-dotted with flashes of blue from police and emergency vehicles.

Their AN-24 was parked a good distance from the accident. But there were plenty of vehicles between them and the plane. The runway seemed to have been closed down; there were aircraft over by the terminal building, but none queued for takeoff.

Setco got on the radio and spoke to Longjohn at the airplane. Once again he assured them that the plane was ready to take off, which it would do as soon as they were aboard.

"So far, they're leaving them alone," Setco told the others. "But we can't be too long at this. We gotta get in."

Kam had already started cutting the bottom of the fence, making a hole large enough for them to pass through one at a time. Kam went first; the wounded Park, who was huffing but claimed he was feeling better, went next.

One by one, the others followed until only the dead man and Setco remained. As they pulled their dead companion through, his vest snagged on the wire. Setco reached under and cut off the fabric. When they pulled him free, he cut away the rest of the vest.

"Makes him a lot lighter," said Setco, as if an explanation was necessary. "He doesn't need it anyway."

They started across the field, angling to the right in the direction of the plane. Park limped heavily, but was able to walk with only a little help from Kam. After a few yards, a beam of a searchlight began sweeping in their direction. They went down to the ground, waiting as it passed.

"OK," hissed Setco, staggering to his feet with the dead man on his back.

They got about ten yards before the light returned and everyone ducked again. It didn't seem aimed, at least not at them, but they couldn't take a chance.

"This is going to take forever," said Kam. "And we still have to get past those military trucks."

"Yeah, let's think about this." Setco raised his head, observing the field.

"Why don't we grab one of the trucks?" Zeus suggested. "They'd let an army truck go right through."

"Yeah, but there's bound to be sentries on it, or at least a driver with a gun," said Setco. "Besides, there are too many people nearby. What do you think about one of the fire trucks?"

Zeus looked to the left. There were two fire trucks parked along the runway, one on each side, not quite parallel to each other at the end of the runway.

"That might work."

"All right."

Setco started to get up. Zeus grabbed his arm and pushed him back down.

"Just a couple of us go," suggested Zeus. "Then we swing the truck over to the road. The others catch up. It'll be quicker."

Setco thought about it for a moment. "I don't want to split up."

"We're already split up," said Zeus. "Half the team's back at the plane."

"All right. Kam, when you see us at the truck, start moving up the roadway there. Squirt and Zeus, come with me."

"Three is too few. I can come," volunteered Solt.

"No, three's fine. Stay."

Crouching as he ran, Setco led the small group back toward the fence, moving into the shadows before looping back toward the fire truck. They stayed near the fence until they were roughly even with the truck, then began crawling toward it on their hands and knees.

When they were about thirty yards away, Setco stopped and studied it more closely. It was a large pumper with a double cab and a long, flat body. Two firemen sat in the front.

They couldn't see much of the second truck from where they were. But whoever was in it would have an unobstructed view across the runway.

"Squirt, how's your Chinese feeling?" asked Setco.

The Korean said something. Setco frowned.

"That's going to have to do. Go up to the driver's window and distract them. Tell them you're looking for infiltrators or something. Here, tuck in your uniform." Setco pushed the Korean's shirt down, straightening it a little. "Zeus and I will get into the cab behind them. If we shoot, get ready to take out the guys in the other truck. Understand?"

"*Shì de.*"

"Right."

Zeus checked his rifle, then began crawling toward the rear quarter of the truck. There was a compartment there for the pump controls. He froze, thinking he saw something move across it.

It was only a play of light, shadows crisscrossing wildly from the far end of the field.

Relax, he told himself. They were almost home.

Zeus had just gotten up to move again when someone inside the truck began shouting. Squirt stood and waved his hand.

"Shit," muttered Setco, starting to run.

Zeus began running as well. Squirt began saying something in Chinese to the effect that they were looking for infiltrators—had the firemen seen any?

The fireman was shouting. He appeared angry, though it wasn't clear why.

Setco cursed again. Zeus looked toward Squirt and saw that he was raising his rifle.

Zeus began running. Setco dropped to a knee and fired at the cab, taking down the man who'd been on the passenger side.

Zeus changed direction, sprinting behind the vehicle, aiming to get around to the driver's side in case the driver made a break for it.

There was a man on the running board of the other fire truck, on Zeus's left. He was holding a pistol, looking in the direction of the truck that had just been attacked. Bringing his arm and the butt end of his gun against the side of his chest as he ran, Zeus pressed the trigger of the AR-15.

The shots went wide, wild and poorly aimed. The fireman started to turn. Zeus stopped, shouldered and squared properly, and put three bullets into the fireman.

The truck on the left started to move.

Zeus threw himself back into motion, racing to catch the vehicle before it got away. He pulled even with the cab before it gained momentum, but as he reached for it its steady momentum started to tell. It was accelerating faster than he could run.

Zeus lunged at the side, but there was nothing to grab onto. He kept running, and saw the control bay at the rear coming toward him. As it drew parallel, he leapt up, grabbing the fairing on the back opening. But his feet had nothing to step onto, and they slipped back to the pavement.

The truck was moving so fast his legs couldn't keep up. He swung them up and in desperation managed to get his right foot into the opposite end of the galley. He was all crossed up, twisted, hanging off the end of the truck. He willed his other leg in alongside the other, then pulled himself up and managed to grab onto the rail at the top of the truck.

From there, it was almost easy: He did a pull-up, rising up and over to the roof of the vehicle.

The driver, meanwhile, thought he had lost him and started to slow down. He reached for his radio, flipping the switch when Zeus swung his fist down and pounded on the driver's side window.

The driver, terrified and surprised, veered hard to the right, nearly knocking Zeus off the top.

Having lost his rifle somewhere along the way, Zeus struggled to grab for the pistol in his drop holster while still remaining on top of the slaloming fire truck. He managed to get the gun and smack the front of the windscreen.

The driver ducked down below the dash, pulling the wheel as he went and jamming his foot on the gas. Zeus felt the truck starting to tip under him. He flattened himself on the roof, holding on as best he could.

Panicking, the driver turned the wheel back the other way. The rear of the vehicle swung back. Momentum pushed it over to the other side.

Zeus lost his grip and flew off the cab as it bounced back the other way. The truck flipped off the runway, skidding on its side.

Zeus stayed on his knees a moment, stunned, his brain momentarily floating in a void away from his body. Then he heard Setco shouting at him.

"Let's go, let's go," yelled Setco. He was in the cab of the other fire truck, a few feet away.

Zeus got up and went to the truck, climbing in the back of the cab as it started down toward the others.

"What happened?"

"Squirt thought the guy was going to shoot him. The firemen are military. They're soldiers. Something about the uniform or the way Squirt started talking to him made him suspicious. It doesn't matter now."

Squirt was sitting in front of him, hunkered over in the front, gun pointing out the window.

Solt rose from the shadows ahead. Zeus squeezed across to the opposite side of the cab. She came in next to him, her body soft and warm against his. Welcome.

"All sorts of vehicles coming to find out what's going on," said Kam, getting in. He had the dead man on his lap.

"Yeah," muttered Setco.

He floored it toward the airplane, hitting his siren for good measure. The radio was squawking, but they ignored it.

Longjohn and one of the Vietnamese soldiers ran out to the truck as they came up. When everyone but Zeus and Setco had piled out, Setco threw the vehicle into reverse to get it out of the way.

"Let's go, Major," said Setco.

Several vehicles were headed in their direction. As far as Zeus could tell, no one fired at them, though in truth the aircraft engines were so loud, he might not have heard any bullets anyway.

The plane was already moving when they reached the rear door. Kneeling in the doorway, Longjohn pulled them up, one by one, Zeus first, as the plane gained speed.

"Brace for a crash!" yelled someone in the cockpit.

Zeus, already lying on the floor, covered his head with his arms and closed his eyes.

In the next moment, he was weightless, his brain flying again, far away from his body.

The rest of him caught up a second or two later. They were airborne, having cleared an APC by a few feet.

55

North of Malipo

The Vietnamese had worked feverishly, digging a mine-field into the entrance of the town. General Li Sun had not expected this, and when the first company of tanks he sent into battle stalled badly, he lost the entire momentum of his attack before it had really gotten underway. The advance bogged down at the northern entrance to the city.

From an overall tactical point of view, this was not the worst development, as it limited the Vietnamese as well. The geography that funneled Sun into an attack along the highway trapped the Vietnamese there as well. As long as his forces remained in contact with the enemy, the Chinese general would be able to sweep around and trap them with the vanguard of his infantry units, now due to arrive in the morning.

But he didn't intend on waiting that long. He had more people than the Vietnamese had, and he didn't need any fancy tactics to defeat them. More importantly, the late-evening satellite image showed that Li Sun had literally a clear road south to Hanoi. If he could punch through Malipo, his tanks would be at the outskirts of Hanoi within forty-eight hours, perhaps even less.

Li Sun began recalibrating his attack even as his tanks started to withdraw. He had a good view of the battle from the high ground at the north side of the city; there was a decent amount of moon and starlight, though he still needed the night binoculars to get a good view of the city.

The Vietnamese had set themselves up well, mining the entrance to the town and arranging their handful of tanks and large guns. But even taking maximum advantage of the geography, their forces were small and impotent compared to Li Sun's. Once the minefield was breached, the Vietnamese tank rounds would be ineffective against the Type 96s.

He radioed Zhi, and gave him advice on how to move the tanks.

"Your best company in the lead," Li Sun told him. "Take the Vietnamese armor from the edge of the minefield, where the Vietnamese infantry won't attack. Concentrate your firepower on each tank and gun. Once that's done, proceed through the minefield."

The next problem was the Vietnamese infantry in the buildings. Militarily, the best solution was to flatten the structures, but that was dicey politically—he would be destroying Chinese property to save it.

But there seemed no other way. He had infantry, but he didn't want to risk them in a slow house-to-house fight.

He was just reconciling himself to destroying the buildings when his communications aide came running over.

"General?"

Li Sun looked over at the young man who was charged with working the mobile radio. He had the pack with him.

"There has been a disaster at the headquarters," said the soldier. "We are not in contact with them."

"What do you mean?" said Li Sun.

"I have the missile battery commander. There was an attack. The building has been blown up."

56

"We're in. They have the connection. We're inside the Chinese defense network."

Peter Lucas sat upright in his seat. The special projects manager of the NSA Asian desk was on the secure line.

"We're completely there?"

"You want to reprogram their missiles to hit Beijing? I can do that. Your boy Setco did a hell of a job. He deserves a medal."

"I'll see that he gets one. If he gets out alive."

Ten minutes later, Lucas was ushered into Peter Frost's office on the top floor of the CIA headquarters building. Though the CIA director used the office for long hours every day, it looked as if it was simply for show or reserved for ceremonies. The books on the shelves were in perfect order, and the top of his desk was bare, except for his computer monitor. The phone bank behind the desk sparkled as the lights on it blinked.

"How are Vietnam and China?" Frost asked.

"We're inside the Chinese defense network. It should be a few hours before they detect us, and a bit longer than that for them to shut us down. By that time, we'll have our code in everything. We can cut them off at the legs."

"The president will be very happy. Stay," added Frost, swiveling around for the phone.

57

The South China Sea

In many ways, Commander Dirk Silas was a throwback to an earlier era when sea captains were a law unto themselves, and there was no such thing as a ship's captain being too aggressive.

But Silas was also a man of the twenty-first century, and he couldn't have become a ship's captain without being aware of how Navy politics worked. As soon as his conversation with the admiral ended, Silas began a procedure known in the modern military as CYA. He ordered the tapes of the encounter copied and prepared for immediate transmission. He had his key officers and enlisted personnel record their memories of the encounter—with special emphasis on who had fired the first shot. And he monitored the transmissions from the Chinese vessel, just in case they decided to present their own view of what had happened.

They didn't, though perhaps they wished to. Both ships had very limited ability to transmit by radio. Silas had his radioman ask if they needed help, though he got exactly the answer he expected—nothing.

Unsure of their exact status, he launched a small UAV to fly over the ships and beam video back. Someone aboard the frigate apparently saw the small aircraft even though it was night time, because one of the anti-aircraft guns aboard began firing as it came overhead. The gunfire was wildly inaccurate—clearly it must have been optically aimed—but Silas decided that was enough information for now.

The cruiser went alongside the frigate and began taking on its crew; clearly the Chinese had realized the smaller ship wasn't going to be saved.

In the meanwhile, *McCampbell* pulled close to the Korean vessel. The ship's bow and a good portion of the forward deck area had been mangled by the Chinese blast. Even so, the master of the ship insisted that the vessel was seaworthy and that he did not require assistance.

Naturally, this convinced Silas that the ship was in fact carrying contraband. But there was no way he was going to inspect it now—that would only convince some people that the Chinese vessel was justified in opening fire on it.

Not legally, perhaps, but legalities were always of secondary importance. The Korean changed to a more southerly course, heading toward the Philippines. As that was further from the Chinese fleet, he let her go.

58

Washington, D.C.

President Greene and his chief of staff, Dickson Theodore, had closeted themselves in the White House study with the president's spokesman Daniel Priest to discuss how to deal with the pending *L.A. Times* news story when word came that the Chinese had opened fire on *McCampbell*.

Greene bolted from his chair as soon as he heard it. Without saying a word, he headed downstairs toward the national security situation room. Theodore and Priest followed.

Walter Jackson, the national security advisor, met Greene in the hall and started briefing him along the way. Greene felt invigorated—not happy, certainly, but crisis mode was something he felt comfortable in.

Not to mention the fact that this would surely overshadow the *L.A. Times* story.

"Apparently the Chinese were firing at a freighter," said Jackson. "Our guy got in the way, and they fired at him. He shot back four missiles, damaging the cruiser and coming damn close to sinking the other ship. It may sink soon. It's smaller—a corvette or something."

"A frigate. It was a frigate," said Greene, remembering an earlier briefing.

"I'm sorry, you're right. His command ordered him to stop firing and move off—"

"What the hell did they do that for! He should have sunk the damn thing!"

"His initial orders were to use restraint, and I think he was just trying to be prudent," said Jackson.

"His ship is OK?"

"Not a scratch."

"You know what the problem is with these admirals and generals, Walter? They're afraid of war. Afraid."

"I don't know if that's fair, Mr. President."

"He was defending himself is my point," explained Greene. "All right?"

"Yes, sir."

Priest caught up to Greene at the entrance to the situation room. While he had a top secret clearance, ordinarily he didn't come in for briefings. He worried that he might inadvertently give out information he shouldn't. But tonight was a special case.

"I want you to be able to give a statement as soon as we're done," said Greene.

"What about the *L.A. Times* story?"

"That'll take care of itself."

"No it won't, Mr. President."

"This is more important, Danny."

"Sir, Congress—"

"Don't worry about Congress."

"That story, this clash . . . it's not going to go well."

"Sure it will. We came close to sinking two of their ships. We were not harmed." Greene took his spokesman by the arm. "Americans want to win, Danny. They don't necessarily care how, or where even. They just want to win."

"Well—"

"You and I know there's more involved. A lot more. But let's just take these things one at a time. *McCampbell* first, then we'll deal with the *Times* story."

"Maybe we should preempt them," said Priest. "Say we have advisors in the region."

"I don't think that's a good idea at all," said Jackson. "That will put everyone in the embassy at risk."

"I agree. We'll play it by ear. Come on, Danny. Don't be such a worrywart."

59

Beijing

Everywhere Cho Lai looked, he saw blue—tanks, ships, small men representing divisions. The situation board in the People's Liberation Army military command center looked extremely impressive, depicting the extent of China's campaign into Vietnam. The red units—the traditional color of the enemy, even though historically it was linked to China's own forces—looked paltry by comparison.

But if one had been studying the map carefully over the past several days, the picture would appear far less positive. The red units had made nearly all of their advances within the first twenty-four hours of the war. More ominously, the premier was beginning to wonder exactly how much of the table he could trust. Rumors were reaching the capital that not all of the units are the front line were moving as quickly as claimed.

In the west, where the army had recently restarted its campaign after being stopped by flooding in the valleys, there were hints that all was not going as expected. Rather than sweeping down to Ho Chi Minh City as originally planned, the generals had revised their objectives and were now aiming at capturing Hue before going further south. Whatever strategic sense that might make—there were various arguments—it constrained the mobile force tactically, as it had to slug through rough terrain and meet the enemy head on.

Cho Lai was not a military man and often felt unsure of his generals' explanations, but he had a good sense when people were lying to him. He realized he had been given only a small part of the story tonight. The Army chief of staff, General Libo, had concentrated on the difficulties the western army faced, so that by the end of his brief, Cho Lai was left to wonder what army he was facing.

"Do not we outnumber the enemy by a factor of ten?" he asked, looking up from the board.

"That is a slight exaggeration, Your Excellency. And an army on the move, so far away from its own lines, is always at a disadvantage."

Cho Lai controlled his rising anger, looking again at the board. He hadn't even heard from his nephew, Li Sun, whose forces should be starting their own campaign directly above Hanoi. He would call him later; he needed some optimism.

The premier turned to his admirals—Wu, the head of the navy, and Tan Jin Mu, his personal advisor.

"And what does the navy say tonight?" he asked.

Wu launched into a dissertation on the American carrier to the southwest, claiming that it was being kept at bay by the prospect of conflict with their own carriers and the antiship ballistic missiles, the DF-21Ds based in Hunan Province. The American carrier task group, he noted, was skirting the arc that represented the missile's range.

"Why are our carriers so close to the coast?" asked Cho Lai, bluntly interrupting the admiral.

Wu began a long explanation of their needs. Cho Lai glanced at Tan Jin Mu, who was clearly bored by the explanation. The older admiral shared Cho Lai's feelings that the navy was being far too passive and defensive, just as the army was.

The problem was how to change that.

Cho Lai was just about to interrupt Admiral Wu when an aide rushed into the room and walked up to him. The aide's face was ashen.

Ordinarily, Admiral Wu would not have stopped for him or anyone—there was not a man in the navy who better liked the sound of his voice—but as soon as he saw the aide's face, he stopped speaking.

"Excuse me, Your Excellency," said the admiral. He took two steps backward, away from the situation table, and listened as the aide whispered in his ear.

The aide was a commodore—not a mere messenger. Cho Lai glanced at Tan Jin Mu; the old admiral appeared apprehensive.

"What?" demanded the premier. "What is the problem?"

"No problem, Your Excellency," said the admiral.

"I see my admirals are stricken with the same disease as my generals!" Cho Lai's anger began to unwind from the coil he had set it in. "They fear to tell me bad news. If this continues, my solution with both forces will be the same—I will find new leaders! I will fire generals and admirals until I find one willing to tell me the truth!"

There was now complete silence in the room. The army general staff stared at Admiral Wu with what Cho Lai was sure was a combination of nervousness and anticipation—to this point the navy had escaped much criticism, and they were no doubt eager to see that change.

"There has been a conflict," said Admiral Wu. "Two of our ships have been struck very seriously. One may sink."

Cho Lai felt a pain in his chest so severe that for a moment he thought he must be having a heart attack. He knew instantly what had happened, even before Wu said anything else. He glanced over at Tan Jin Mu. The older man had turned his face to stone; there was no more emotion there than on a doll.

It was General Libo who spoke. "The Vietnamese were able to hit one of our ships?"

Cho Lai regretted having forced Wu to tell him what had happened in front of the others. But there was nothing to do about it now.

"It was an American," said the admiral.

"How were the Americans involved?" asked Libo. "Their carrier is far off."

"It was their destroyer, near the coast of Vietnam," said the commodore who had brought the news. "Our cruiser and frigate—one of them fired as it attempted to stop a smuggler, and a weapon was launched at the American ship."

The admiral made a face, trying to warn the aide to be quiet, but it was too late. He turned to Cho Lai.

"The cruiser, Your Excellency. You directed that he be more aggressive," said the admiral.

"I did not direct that it be sunk," said Cho Lai. He glared at Tan Jin Mu. "I was told that it was more powerful than the American ship. We had two ships there. How could they both be sunk?"

"They . . . they have not sunk yet," said the commodore.

"What happened to the American destroyer?"

"It was seen steaming away," said the aide, this time glancing at the admiral before speaking.

Cho Lai listened to the details of the engagement, scant as they were. The cruiser *Wen Jiabo* had attempted to exercise its rights to inspect suspect shipping in the Chinese interest area. The American *Arleigh*

Burke destroyer had attempted to interfere, sailing close to the cruiser in what her captain interpreted as an aggressive act.

An overzealous officer aboard the cruiser's escort, a frigate, had opened fire. The Americans had responded with a deadly salvo that had killed or wounded half the men aboard the frigate. The damage to the cruiser was less but more strategic—the ship's captain and the admiral in charge of the squadron had both been killed.

"Both of our ships are crippled," said the admiral's aide. "The cruiser is seaworthy. It is not clear that the frigate will survive."

Cho Lai turned to the aide. "The Americans—what are they doing?"

"They ended their attack and broke off. They went to help the merchant vessel. It was damaged."

"Was the merchant ship sunk?"

"I don't know."

They had to sink the destroyer, Cho Lai knew. If they didn't, the Americans would simply push their navy aside.

And they had to do it quickly. There were political ramifications, complications—those would have to be dealt with, but the most important thing that they had to do was to sink the destroyer. Otherwise the Chinese public would grow even more restless.

He also had to show the army generals that poor performance wouldn't be tolerated. That was even more critical, Cho Lai realized—he needed this war to end quickly, and aggressively. Before the military fell back into a shell.

"You must sink the destroyer." Cho Lai reached down and took the yellow plastic toy that represented the American ship. "It must be crushed."

"I regret to say . . ." The admiral's voice trailed into nothing.

"What?" demanded Cho Lai.

"The cruiser is in no shape to fight. Its radio transmissions are limited. All of its weapons systems are . . . damaged. Its captain, and the fleet admiral are dead."

"Then some other way must be found to sink it." Cho Lai glanced at Tan Jin Mu—more dead wood to be removed at the first opportunity. "The ship must be sunk. What about the carriers?"

"They could move west and be ready to attack within a day, perhaps two," said Tan Jin Mu, finally finding his voice.

"That's too long. Send aircraft from Hainan. Find a way. Attack with the ballistic missiles if necessary. But attack promptly. No more time should pass than is absolutely necessary. I'm sure the Americans will be broadcasting the outcome of this as soon as they can."

"There are political considerations," said General Libo. "With our own people and with the Americans. If the Americans were to fight—"

"You don't understand, General," snapped Cho Lai. "They are already fighting this war. We must act quickly precisely because of the politics. That ship must be sunk. Vietnam must be subdued. We have only a short time to act. If America declares war on us, all of this is over. We must present the world with a fait accompli. Do I make myself clear?"

Cho Lai's last words were a loud rasp, his voice straining to the point of becoming hoarse. He looked around the room, daring the others to speak. It was an outrage that men who couldn't even prosecute a war against a third-rate enemy were daring to talk to him about *politics*.

The bastards, they had placed his position in great jeopardy.

"I will expect an update in two hours," Cho Lai told Admiral Wu, pointing his finger in case there was any question about who he expected to brief him. "At that time, you will tell me that the American ship has been sunk. And we will discuss how we will tell the public what has happened."

60

Over Kunming

A few seconds after the Antonov An-24 left the runway with the CIA-organized assassination team, the plane took a hard turn to the east and dipped sharply, attempting to disappear temporarily from the Chinese control radar. The pilot pushed the plane's nose down, hunkering into the narrow valley between the nearby mountains, hoping to get lost in ground clutter and confuse anyone who might be interested in following.

Zeus, still on the floor at the rear, rolled against the rear bulkhead. Setco landed next to him, crushing against Longjohn. Their dead companion rolled at their feet, his body flopping like a ragdoll's.

The aircraft straightened and began a steep climb to avoid the next mountain. Clawing at the wall, Zeus managed to get to his feet just as the plane pushed down again, this time on its right wing. It seemed to *chutter* in the air. The engines made a grating sound, straining as if gasping for air.

The plane bucked, close to a stall. The nose pushed down and Zeus once more lost his balance and flew against the last row of seats, vainly trying to catch himself. The lights blinked out. Then the aircraft's wings straightened out, and after a brief flutter left and right, the craft steadied and began a very modest climb.

"What the hell is going on?" said Longjohn.

Setco stumbled forward to the cockpit. Zeus found a seat in the back, and put his seatbelt on. After cinching it, he looked up and saw that he was sitting across the aisle from Solt. She was staring straight ahead. Her hands were clenched together, a two-handed fist so tight that the tips and knuckles were red.

The cabin smelled of vomit and spent gunpowder. Someone in front of him was muttering in Korean. Zeus guessed it was a prayer.

Setco emerged from the cockpit a few minutes later.

"We're on one engine," he said. "Something shot at us when we took off. We're maybe thirty minutes out of Malipo. We'll land there."

No one said anything. Setco walked back to Zeus's aisle.

"Could you move over one for a second?" he asked Solt.

She stared at him, not seeming to understand, then finally undid her belt and moved next to the window. Setco sat across the seat and faced Zeus.

"You figure Trung is still in Malipo?" he asked Zeus.

"I wish I could say he wasn't. There's no way he can hold it."

"The radios are knocked out," said Setco. "I tried using the sat phone to call Trung's headquarters but I can't get through to anyone who could make the connection for me."

"How bad is the plane?" asked Zeus.

"Bad."

"We'd be better off if we could fly to Hanoi," said Zeus. "Or somewhere on the southern coast."

"Yeah." Setco glanced at Solt, then looked back at Zeus. "They shot up the wings and I guess got the fuel tanks or lines, too. Between the rate of fuel we're losing and the one engine, we're going to be lucky to make it to Malipo."

"Oh."

"I was going to make a joke about the pilots always losing an engine but it didn't look like it would go over." Setco frowned. "You did a good job."

"I'm sorry about your guys."

"Yeah. That's the way it goes."

"Let me see the picture," said Zeus.

"What picture?"

"The general. It's not Li Sun, is it?"

"What difference does it make? We went in and blew up their command center. The Chinese will stop now. They've been kicked in the balls."

"And you planted the device. Was that the real reason the agency sent you in the first place?"

"I think they sent me to get rid of me," said Setco. "Surprised them again."

"Who was the general? Was he definitely a general?"

Setco reached into his pocket for the camera. He handed it to Zeus.

"I uploaded it in the car while we were looking for you," said Setco. "He was some sort of logistics commander earlier. They think he was just made chief of staff or second in command or something. They're still trying to figure it out from signal intelligence. His name was Chan, if that means anything to you."

"You knew it wasn't Li Sun."

"Yeah. I also knew we weren't going to be hanging around to look for anybody else. We accomplished our goal, Major. The Chinks'll freak. We whacked them good."

Zeus flipped through the images. They'd taken a shot of everyone in the building.

"Where the hell Li Sun was, I have no idea," continued Setco. "Maybe we'll get him next time."

Zeus handed the camera back and went up front. Solt changed seats so she was next to Zeus across the aisle.

"He's right," she told him. "The Chinese will be very cautious. Just like your plan against Hainan."

"I hope you're right."

"I know I'm right." She put her hand on his knee. "You have done much for the Vietnamese people. We are very in your debt."

Zeus smiled, but her hand on his knee made him feel wary. He didn't trust his emotions. He didn't trust anything.

"You're tired," said Solt.

"That's true."

Solt slid her hand up his leg, then raised it toward his face.

He caught it gently.

"Thanks," he said. "But . . ."

He couldn't think of what else to say. She pulled her hand back.

"I'm sorry," she told him.

"There's nothing to be sorry about."

Zeus sank back into his seat. He let his eyes close.

The next thing he knew, Solt was shaking him awake.

"Look out the window," she told him. "The city is under attack."

"What?"

"Malipo is under attack."

Zeus followed her back across the aisle. There were fires burning below; he saw shadows moving near the buildings at the top of the ridge, and little pinpricks of white light—gunfire. Much of the city was in blackness, obscured by heavy smoke.

"Looks like Trung's got his hands full," said Setco, coming back from the cockpit.

"Can we get down to Hanoi?" Solt asked.

"We have five minutes worth of fuel, if that. We're going to have to land at the airport, assuming it hasn't been overrun. It's south at least."

"What do we do then?" asked Zeus.

"Either we try and take off with the other plane, or we go out by land," said Setco. "We'll see what we can do with the other plane first. If the Viets keep fighting, we should have a half hour. Maybe a little more."

"If they're attacking the city, they're bound to start shelling the airport," said Zeus.

"Not if they want to use it," said Setco. "Frankly, Major, we don't really have an alternative. We don't have parachutes. We either land at the airport, or we crash somewhere. Take your pick. Nice to see you back awake, by the way. Get your seatbelts on!" he added in a bellow.

The airplane was already shuddering, the wings wobbling as it descended toward the landing strip.

Zeus checked his seatbelt, then put his hand forward against the seat in front of him, bracing himself.

As the good engine surged, the plane dipped on its wing to the right. It felt like it dropped a few hundred feet before leveling off and steadying itself above the end of the runway. It came in fast, bouncing and jerking but remaining straight and most importantly intact.

Setco leapt to his feet and walked swiftly to the cockpit as the plane rolled. Zeus pulled himself upright, undid his seatbelt and grabbed his gear.

"All right, listen up," yelled Setco. "Here's what we're going to do. We're taxiing over to the other plane. We should be able to get south with it, hopefully to Hanoi. Farther than that's out of the question—

depends on how much fuel we can load and still take off."

"I want to go into the city," said Zeus, interrupting. "I want to get Trung out."

"You're welcome to do what you want," Setco said. "But we're not going to wait for you."

"That's fine."

Setco frowned. No one else said anything.

The CIA officer came down to the back and leaned into Zeus's face.

"It'll take us a half hour to get the plane fueled and ready, assuming we're not under fire," said Setco. "You come back, you can get aboard. Assuming we got the weight."

"Trung's important," said Zeus.

"No shit. That's why I'm giving you a half hour."

"Fair enough."

"It's more than fair, Murph. More than fuckin' fair."

The only vehicle at the terminal building was a Chinese Hummer-knockoff used as a utility vehicle around the base. While its ignition system ostensibly required a key, one of the Vietnamese soldiers who had come up when the airport was first taken had jammed in a pocketknife and rewired the ignition so the knife now functioned as a switch; it was an admirable piece of piracy, the sort of thing Zeus would expect from American GIs. Ingenuity was apparently a staple of grunts around the world.

There was something wrong with the steering, and Zeus had to manhandle the truck just to get it to turn onto the road. Making turns was a strain, but once he was pointed in the right direction the vehicle moved easily enough.

About a half mile below the city, Zeus found the

way ahead blocked by vehicles, many of them wrecked. He pulled off the road as best he could, then got out and started running toward the building where he had last seen Trung. By now it was well past midnight, and the waning moon cast a hazy light across the center of the small city. The buildings stacked up around the center street. One story houses dotted the hills, petering out quickly as the elevation changed. This would be a small town in the U.S., barely a village even in West Virginia, which seemed the closest parallel to the darkened landscape.

There were several fires, red and orange flares that cast the nearby structures deep black by contrast. Soldiers were crouched near mortars and a few sand-bagged positions. The firefight had reached a temporary lull, with only sporadic machine-gun and rifle fire and the occasional blast from a Chinese tank on the north side of the town.

Zeus stayed close to the buildings as he ran up the main street. The north end of town was littered with vehicles, the uneven and worn mouth of a gaping jaw in the darkness.

About halfway up the first block, Zeus came up on a gun emplacement—a ZSU-57 pressed into service as an antitank weapon. It was parked up against a building and nestled into a low wall of sandbags. A handful of infantrymen were standing near the tank. He found an officer and told him that he needed to speak to General Trung with hand signs, English, and a smattering of Vietnamese. The officer picked a sergeant to serve as his guide, and Zeus began following him up the street and then into an alley that came off on a perpendicular from the main road.

The police station and municipal buildings on the east side of the street had been shelled by the Chinese, but Trung had expected that. Alerted to the advance by his scouts, Trung had moved his command post to the basement of a building on the side of the hill just behind the main street. His security detail was small—only two soldiers guarded the entrance to the building—but they wore blue bands, making it obvious that Zeus had reached his destination.

His guide saluted Zeus as he retreated on a full run back to his post. The security detail eyed Zeus warily, playing a flashlight's beam on his face. While they must have realized who he was, they nonetheless insisted that he hand over his weapon before being shown in. Zeus decided it was quicker and easier not to argue, and after a perfunctory search, they led him into the basement.

General Trung was hunched over a map, checking the enemy positions with the aid of a battery lantern. Two of his subcommanders—colonels—looked on intently.

Trung stopped in the middle of what he was saying and turned to Zeus. "You have returned from a successful mission."

"We killed one of the generals on the staff." Zeus felt his voice quivering. "But not Li Sun, not the head general."

Trung stared at him. Zeus wasn't sure that he understood.

"You attacked their headquarters." Trung nodded his head. "That will be enough. We have taken their city. The Chinese will halt their attack into our country."

"You have to leave the city," Zeus told him. "We have a plane ready."

"The Chinese have only one armored division here," said Trung. "They can only move a few companies of tanks against us at a time."

What he said was undoubtedly true, thought Zeus, but it was also wildly optimistic—the Chinese were surely a match for the Vietnamese, even if they had to go through a meat grinder to get to them.

"Eventually they'll get through," said Zeus. "You weren't supposed to hold the city. If you wait too long, you'll be surrounded."

Trung said nothing.

"General, you have to retreat," insisted Zeus. "There's nothing to be gained by staying here. You can leave a small rear guard and get down the highway. Have your force move south in the dark. The Chinese will have to consolidate in the city. If they're afraid of being ambushed again, they won't move their armor down the highway after you until their infantry catches up. Your men can escape and fight another day."

Trung didn't answer.

"You have to retreat yourself," added Zeus. "Your job is to lead the entire army, not just these men here."

Zeus knew Trung understood what he was saying, yet his stare belied that. Zeus went to the map and swept his finger south of the city.

"They'll swarm here and here—you have the advantage now because the tanks have to stick to this narrow plane. But that won't last. Once they reach this point, they'll cut off any retreat. Your men can't get up the hills with their equipment. You'll be completely cut off."

"We will fight before that happens."

"There's a plane at the airport. We'll take you out."

Trung shook his head.

"General—"

Trung turned to the others and dismissed them. They moved quickly, nervously it seemed to Zeus.

"I did tell Major Chaū to delay you," said Trung when they were alone. "I am sorry for it. It was only a delay. You needed an excuse. You wanted to stay, and

I wanted your help. It was the right decision for my country. A bad decision for you."

"What do you mean, I needed an excuse?"

"You wanted to stay for love; you wanted to be noble. But the reason you stayed was war. You wanted to fight. I saw it in your eyes, and heard it in your voice. She was just something you told yourself."

"That's bullshit," said Zeus. "Come on, stop wasting time—we have to get out of here."

"We always lie to ourselves. Easy lies. You stayed not because you loved Vietnam, or even the girl. You needed to think that. You loved war."

"Come on, damn it."

Zeus reached to grab the general's arm, thinking he would drag him from the building. But as he did, there was a loud explosion nearby. The ground shook. There was another and another—the Chinese had resumed their assault.

61

North of Malipo

General Li Sun watched the tanks launch their salvos. The big vehicles shuddered as the muzzles of their 125 mm smoothbore guns flashed. A white halo rose around the tanks, a bright burst of energy as his forces renewed their attack with a barrage of shells.

In the next moment, large flashes appeared on the Vietnamese side, the massive shells hitting home. At the moment, the tanks were firing armor-piercing shells, obliterating the Vietnamese's thin force of tanks and APCs one by one. When that was accomplished, they would switch over to high-explosive frag rounds, clearing the barriers near the north end of the town of men before proceeding.

It was an impressive show, one so bright that it was better appreciated with standard binoculars, rather than the night glasses Li Sun had favored earlier.

Li Sun shifted his weight on the hill. He was standing with his communications aide and Captain Niu. Lt. Colonel Zhi, the tank commander and new general of the division, stood a few feet away, a radio pressed to his ear.

The strike on his headquarters had been bold and

daring—far beyond anything Li Sun imagined the Vietnamese capable of. For that reason alone, he suspected that the Americans were behind it. He might in fact be fighting them now; he would have to proceed with caution.

Some caution. In order to live—in order to survive what he knew would be his uncle's wrath and backstabbing from other generals—he would have to take Hanoi. He fully intended to.

Or die. There were no other options. Beijing was already trying to contact him to find out what was going on.

The smell of burnt metal and flesh drifted in his direction.

An idea occurred to him: He would find the commander of this unit and kill him personally to avenge Chan's death.

"General, the tanks are ready to proceed," said Zhi. "The Vietnamese positions have all been silenced."

"Proceed colonel." Li Sun motioned over his radio man and spoke to the commander of the lone infantry battalion accompanying the 12th Armor's attack.

"Move ahead," he told him. He picked up his night glasses to follow the progress.

A few minutes later, infantrymen began swarming down from the western hill. Li Sun had sent the infantrymen there to surprise the Vietnamese, attacking their flank as the tanks came in on the main front. In that way, he hoped to spare a few of the buildings—but he was prepared to demolish them all if necessary. He would blame it on the Vietnamese.

At the center of town, the tanks moved slowly—a little too slowly for his liking—but steadily. They made it past the burned-out hulls where the mines had been laid. One tank nosed into the dead hulk of a Vietnamese Type 54 and began pushing it aside. An RPG flew out from one of the buildings and exploded against the reactive plates at the side; the tank kept moving. Meanwhile, the tank behind it leveled its gun at the building the RPG had been fired from. The building disintegrated even as Li Sun heard the clap of the shot.

This was more like it.

Vietnamese soldiers began running from the buildings and yards on the west side of the town, chased out by Sun's infantry. They were cut down by the Type 96s' machine guns. The armor began sallying down the middle of the town, machine guns blazing.

It was the start of a rout. Finally.

He would tell Beijing that he was alive and proceeding. He would tell them that the Americans had launched a sneak attack and helped the Vietnamese. He would claim he had evidence—by the time they began asking questions, he would be in Hanoi.

Two days. Less if he could manage it. He must get the infantry moving.

"Colonel, what is our progress?" asked Li Sun.

"Moving forward, General."

"Shouldn't you be leading them?"

Zhi stiffened. "I am about to go down."

"We'll go together," said Li Sun. He wanted to savor the victory.

"Send a message to all units," he told his radioman as he strode to the command car. "Tell them that I prefer the Vietnamese officers captured alive if possible. I want the commander of this force brought to me."

"For intelligence, General?"

"I want to shoot him with my own gun," replied Sun. "I will watch him die slowly, and as painfully as possible."

62

Malipo

Zeus stayed by Trung's side as the general moved up the hill to get a better vantage of the battle. They were dangerously exposed, with heavy machine-gun fire tearing through the street less than fifty yards away, and shells from a second wave of tanks falling on the buildings nearby.

"It's time to retreat, General," Zeus told him. "You have to order a withdrawal while there are still people who can follow it."

Trung didn't answer. Two radiomen and two other aides, both majors, had come down from another room inside the building and joined him; they formed a loose circle around Zeus and Trung as the general picked his way through a backyard to a wide ledge that had an unobstructed view of the street. The two soldiers who had been guarding the entrance to his headquarters trudged up the hill behind them.

The flashes from the tanks painted the center of the town the way a set of strobe lights would, illuminating the battle in ferocious installments. The Vietnamese had by now fired all of their major antitank weapons; there was little they could do to stop the Chinese armor. The tanks fit roughly two abreast on the wide street; as they pushed past the obstructions at the north end of the city and moved south, they came in a staggered but tight formation. They appeared to have a minimal infantry screen with them, but that was immaterial now, because the Vietnamese were too thin and poorly armed to mount a defense, let alone a counterattack.

Trung watched stoically as his forces on the west side of the street tried to retreat from an infantry attack there, but got cut down by the tanks. The Vietnamese were in chaos. The battle was clearly lost.

There was an explosion on the hull of one of the lead tanks—a hand grenade or some improvised device had blown up. The tank behind it turned its gun and fired point blank into a building. When it fired again, the flash was nearly obscured by the thick brown and black dust in the air.

The first tank never stopped. The explosion hadn't even slowed it.

Trung was speaking with his radiomen, relaying orders. Zeus saw a wedge of men coming up from the south. They were met with heavy gunfire from the tanks.

The Chinese Type 96s now began widening their killing field. One rammed into a building on the west side of the street, backing up under an avalanche of bricks. A flare shot up from the Vietnamese side, illuminating the sky. But it did nothing except make it easier for the Chinese to see their victims. The Vietnamese fire was drowned out by waves of fire from the tanks. There were now a dozen crowding onto the main street, and more behind them.

An artillery shell whistled overhead and exploded in the middle of the tank advance. The shell didn't hit any of the tanks, but the explosion stopped them nonetheless. Another shell came over, and this one hit a tank on the far right side of the street. The tank's turret popped up; smoke flew from the vehicle.

If the Vietnamese had had more ammunition, an artillery barrage at this point might have stopped or at least slowed the onslaught. A dozen shells expertly placed, and the Chinese once more would have had their noses bloodied badly enough to convince them to regroup. But only two more shells fell in the next minute and a half; neither one did any good. By then, Chinese artillery had started to answer, lobbing charges back at the howitzers, which were parked about a mile south along the road. The Vietnamese fired twice more. One shell hit the front of one of the gutted tanks; the other landed in one of the buildings. Then the Vietnamese heavy guns fell silent, either destroyed or out of ammunition.

More Chinese appeared on the street. Vietnamese soldiers came out to meet them, but were cut down quickly.

"General," said Zeus. "It is time to escape."

"Your woman has been freed," Trung told him. "Chaū will take her to the embassy in Hanoi."

"We have to go."

It was already too late. The two soldiers down the hill dropped into firing positions.

Trung's aides began yelling at him to join them. Trung started toward them, then turned back and walked to the soldiers crouching at the edge of the small plateau where he'd been observing the battle. Zeus and one of the majors followed.

"You, give me your weapons. Save yourself," Trung told his guards in Vietnamese. "Both of you—go. Save yourselves."

Zeus tried to intervene. "General."

"You go, too, American," said Trung sharply. "You

have done much for us. Too much. Save yourself now. If you can."

The last words were nearly drowned out by the sound of machine-gun fire on the street. Zeus ducked as bullets whizzed up the hill. One of the soldiers began returning fire. The other fell nearby. As Zeus picked up his rifle, a shell or a grenade flew nearby. Zeus started to duck but slipped and fell facedown, spilling across the hill and then sliding away from the explosion when the grenade skipped into a small culvert.

He tried to get up. A fusillade of bullets rioted around him, chewing up pieces of rock from the nearby ledge. Zeus scrambled blindly for cover. He saw a wall on his right. He pushed toward it, rising but quickly diving back down, practically swimming in the dirt, moving to the house.

Another grenade landed, this one further away but still close enough for the air-shock to slam him against the wall, knocking him out.

63

Forthright, Ohio

"Heading into town," Josh yelled to his cousin's sister. "See ya later."

He was almost to the car when she opened the front door and shouted to him.

"Can you swing by the supermarket and get that ice cream for Chrissie's birthday party?"

"Sure. What flavor?"

"Vanilla's fine. Nothing fancy."

"You got it."

Josh started up the car. As the price of gas had begun to increase dramatically, his cousin had looked into alternative fuels. Ethanol mixes were popular with farmers here, as were hybrids. This car had an all-electric engine, built by a car mechanic who moonlighted as a tinkerer and inventor. It was a fine vehicle as long as you didn't want to go fast or very far, but you had to be very careful about checking the gauge at the bottom of the dash that showed the battery charge. You needed at least three bars to get into town and back.

He had five. Good to go.

* * *

Sitting in his perch in the trees behind the house, Jing Yo saw the vehicle starting out of the driveway. Unable to see who was in the vehicle, he debated what to do.

By his count, there had only been two people in the house. One was Josh MacArthur; the other a female relative. He'd only seen the woman driving before.

If Josh was in the house, why not take him there now? It would be quickly accomplished, a knife across the throat.

Jing Yo strapped the gun to the tree and shimmied down, angling to the far left of the woods to decrease the likelihood that he would be seen from the back of the house. He hadn't spotted the scientist in the woods or even the back of the house since his first day, when he wasn't ready to shoot. It was a disappointment. He was tiring of the assignment, starting to think about what else he would do, what he would do next.

That was dangerous, for it divided his attention.

He wouldn't go back to China. Even if he made it there, he would surely be seen as a liability.

He would sneak out of the States, to Mexico maybe, and then from there, to a place where China's reach didn't extend.

Difficult to find.

Jing Yo focused his thoughts as he left the woods, sprinting in the direction of the barn.

He'd examined the house the previous night without going in. Now he retraced his steps, moving to the back kitchen door. He guessed from what he had seen that this was never locked during the day, and he was right: he put his hand on the small brass knob, turned it quickly and quietly, and he was inside the house.

There was a small vestibule between the kitchen and the outside where people hung their coats and left their boots. The interior door had a large glass window. Jing Yo leaned toward it, saw that the kitchen was empty.

In an instant he was inside.

This was a very different room than the American kitchens he'd been in before. It was several times the size, with a large table filling a long section of the space in front of the windows. There were a dozen seats with plenty of room for people to sit without crowding.

Jing Yo stood near the large white refrigerator. Next to him was a stove with six large burners, the sort of appliance he thought was used only in restaurants. There was a sink next to it with two very deep basins, and another sink, only slightly smaller, opposite it on an island counter. Pots hung from a board over the stove, and from a bar in the middle of the room. The place smelled of coffee and chopped onions.

Jing Yo stepped toward the hallway door opposite the table. He couldn't quite picture the layout of the house in his mind; it was as if he had entered a dark jungle where any shape or configuration was possible.

The hall was dim, without its own light. There were small rooms on either side, doors closed. A little farther down, Jing Yo saw larger openings, square archways into other parts of the house. There was a set of stairs perpendicular to the hall; he could see only the landing and a small part of the first tread.

Jing Yo took a quiet step, then another. He was almost at the stairway when he heard footsteps above, coming in his direction.

He reached his hand to the knife at his belt. It was a large Bowie knife, purchased at the gun shop where he'd bought the rifle.

"Damn, I forgot," said a woman's voice. "Josh, did you leave yet?"

Jing Yo hesitated, then stepped backward. He

thought of going into the kitchen, but then realized the woman was most likely heading there, in search of Josh. He continued down the hall to the door on the left, opened it, and stepped in.

"Josh?" said the woman, coming down into the hallway.

Jing Yo controlled his breathing so that it was nearly silent. He stood against the inside of the door, waiting and listening. The woman walked down the hall and into the kitchen as he had guessed, calling after her cousin.

Then she came back into the hall and started in Jing Yo's direction.

Jing Yo pressed his fingers against the hilt of the knife. He exhaled slowly.

The woman walked past the room, stopping at a closet at the end of the hall. She got something out, then turned around and went upstairs, whispering softly to herself.

Jing Yo turned around after she had gone up the stairs. He was in a child's room, a girl's—the walls were a shade of pink, and there were dolls lined up along the dresser.

He thought of Hyuen Bo, his dead lover. She had kept one doll from childhood, an American Barbie, slightly battered, procured from God knew where.

Jing Yo went to the dresser and stared at the dolls. This child had four different Barbies, all in far better shape than Hyuen Bo's.

He could wait inside the house for the scientist to return. He would catch him by the door, take him then.

No. There was no reason to rush. He could set the assassination at the time and place of his choosing.

Not here. Not inside the house. He would take his prey, discharge his duty, but kill no one else.

It was not within *the way* to kill an innocent person. *Leave*.

Jing Yo glanced at the window, noticing it was unlocked, then decided it was smarter to go back out the way he came.

64

The South China Sea

As the initial excitement of the clash with the Chinese vessels dissipated, Silas felt his body begin to sag. He hadn't had more than two hours of sleep in row for a few days, and he couldn't remember having had more than four in a row for at least two weeks.

If he was tired, his crew must be even more exhausted. As the situation stabilized—the Chinese kept to themselves, the freighter moved off, no other civilian vessels came within radar range—Silas decided to make a tour of his ship.

Nearly every young naval officer who fanaticizes about being a ship's captain sees himself in his dreams walking across the deck to the great admiration, and even the occasional applause, of his crew. Reality, or perhaps cynicism, soon sets in, and by the time that officer in fact reaches command rank, he knows that even a commander such as Nimitz would be hard-pressed to attract more than a sustained shrug from his people most days.

Silas was as idealistic as any commander in the navy, but his experiences before joining the military had always tempered his expectations. He had watched his father struggle to run a small mechanical construction business, and he knew full well that having your underlings like you was often the starting point for failure. So Silas had set out not to be liked but respected, focusing on results rather than people. He'd never gone out of his way to antagonize the crew, but he'd certainly come down on the side of discipline at every turn. It was to this, he felt, that he owed the success they had just achieved.

Walking through the ship now he fought against two impulses. One was an I-told-you-so smugness, a sense that their victory had been due to his being a hard-ass from the moment he took the bridge. The other was an impulse to bask in the victory's glory, to raise his hands—figuratively, not literally—in a champion's arm pump.

The victory, he realized as he moved down through the ship's various compartments, was not about him, or the way he had treated and trained the crew. The exchange had come as the culmination of millions of separate actions, not just by *McCampbell* but the Navy and Department of Defense, the manufacturers and the designers.

His crew was good, true, but his ship was also much better than her opponents, and the combination had been unbeatable. Such a notion could be taken too far, but keeping it in mind added a note of humility to Silas's stride that hadn't been there before the conflict.

It was a heady thing, being captain of a ship. Even with the entanglements of modern communications and the constant and irritating interference of supervisors whose own experiences and intelligence were sorely lacking, commanding *McCampbell* was the nearest thing to being a god any mortal man, especially Silas, could experience.

Yet somehow today he felt not his power but his

limitations. He was dependent, utterly, on his machinery, his technology, and his crew. And it made him admire them—even wretched Greg in the galley with his pimple-torn face, who couldn't even brew a decent cup of coffee if his life depended on it.

The CIC broke into applause when the ship's captain entered, and for the first time since he had come aboard *McCampbell*, Silas felt embarrassed. His first reaction was to scold them.

"Now, now, we've got a lot of work to do yet," he said gruffly. "Pipe down, pipe down."

There were some smirks. No U.S. vessel had sunk an enemy warship of note since the Second World War. It was natural to bask in the glory.

Silas took a step toward the consoles, intending to simply continue around the compartment silently as he normally would. But he felt the urge to say something.

"I want to say job well done," he told them loudly. "You are the ones who deserve the applause."

Clapping his own hands, he turned toward Li and nodded in her direction, then went around the space. The others quickly joined in, and for a few seconds it was a love fest out of character with anything that had gone on aboard *McCampbell* under Silas's command.

"All right now, get your asses back to work," he growled. "Damn Chinese are still loaded for bear, and they may be looking for a little taste of revenge. Go to work all of you."

Silas continued his tour of the ship, moving through the mechanical departments and lingering briefly in the engine room, where he knew from experience as a young officer that sailors occasionally felt neglected.

He was on his way back topside when Li alerted

him that they'd just gotten word from a radar plane that a Chinese aircraft was moving in their general direction.

"I'll be right there," he told her, heading for the command center.

B y the time Silas reached the CIC, the plane had been identified. The label appeared on the Aegis's main display. It was a Russian-designed Tu-16 Badger, known to the Chinese as the H-6. While originally designed as a bomber, the Chinese used the Badgers as long-range reconnaissance aircraft, and this particular plane appeared to be tasked with keeping an eye on *McCampbell*—it began orbiting some eighty-five nautical miles away, just outside of the range of *McCampbell*'s SM2s.

"He's watching for something," Silas told Li. "Or someone."

Silas mentally reviewed the possible threats. The most logical possibility was from the air.

"A pop-up attack," he warned Li. "That's my first guess."

"We'll be ready, Captain."

"Backfires at eighty miles. With Sizzlers." That would give him a true workout—very possibly the sixteen Sizzler or 3M-54E antiship missiles he calculated the large bombers could carry would come close to overwhelming his defenses. "Dozens of other possibilities."

"We're prepared," answered Li.

As the minutes passed and nothing happened, Silas began to wonder if he had guessed wrongly. Maybe the Chinese simply wanted to keep better tabs on the cruiser, and were afraid of getting too close to him.

Or maybe not.

"Contacts! Four aircraft," said the radar operator. They were climbing rapidly from very low altitude some thirty miles from *McCampbell*.

Only one reason for that.

"Contacts. Missiles in the air," declared the radar operator.

65

North of Chùa Cao, Buddhist shrine, Vietnam

Not only did the driver Kerfer had hired like the idea of taking him to Chùa Cao, he told Kerfer a long story in Vietnamese and fractured English detailing how the spirits of the temple were working to protect Vietnam from her traditional enemy. Kerfer wasn't sure exactly how that worked—he thought Buddhists believed the world really wasn't important—but he let the driver prattle away.

He checked their progress every so often against the GPS to make sure they were on the right course, but otherwise let the driver make his own way. The roads were almost completely deserted, without even military or police checkpoints.

The temple was not what Kerfer expected, even after looking at the satellite image. There were ruins visible from the road, and what looked like a miniature palace, but it was clear even in the dim light the place was little more than a narrow façade.

Funny what people chose to venerate.

According to the coordinates, he had to go another two miles to the west. They found a narrow dirt road in that direction, but there was a cement barrier across it less than fifty feet from the turnoff.

"I'm going to walk," said Kerfer, grabbing his ruck and rifle. "Can you wait?"

All of a sudden, the man's English disappeared, and Kerfer's pigeon Vietnamese—admittedly not the best—somehow failed to communicate what he wanted the man to do.

Fortunately, Kerfer had come equipped with the ultimate communication device. He took five one-hundred-dollar bills from the fanny pack concealed under his shirt, held them out, then ripped them carefully in half.

He handed the bottom halves to the man, waving their missing partners.

"When I return, you get the other halves," Kerfer told him. "And gasoline back in Hanoi."

"Ten. To return."

More money than the man would earn in a year, or maybe five. Kerfer resisted the impulse to bargain.

"When we reach Hanoi, then everything," he told the driver. "But only if you are here, waiting."

This seemed to satisfy the driver. "Wait," he said.

"You wait?"

"Wait. Car here."

I have a fifty-fifty chance, Kerfer thought to himself. Better than nothing, though.

He got out and started to walk.

66

Malipo

Dazed, Zeus fell into a gray-lit consciousness, aware of what was going on around him and yet not aware, as if he were lying on the ground watching a movie through the partially opened doorway of a theater. Bullets buzzed overhead, then voices; he stayed facedown as boots ran past, then managed to squirrel himself around and peek his head up.

Chinese soldiers had come up the ridge. Trung, wounded but not dead, had been captured.

They pulled and half carried Trung toward the road. Zeus struggled to get up, but there was something on him, weighing him down.

The ground nearby was littered with dead and dying. Zeus started to crawl, pulling himself out from under a beam that had fallen.

All of Trung's aides had been shot or hit by one of the grenades.

Trung will tell the Chinese that you helped them and ran the mission to Kunming.

Taking a deep breath, Zeus struggled to clear his head. The rifle he'd taken was on the ground nearby, an AK-47, old and battle-scarred.

Zeus managed to shake off the last bricks from his legs. He crawled up to his knees, then picked up the AK-47. A wave of blackness hit him, and once again he had to struggle to clear his head.

As the fog lifted, he started scuttling along the side of the building. The night glowed red with the fires burning up and down the street.

He had to escape. But first he had to shoot Trung—otherwise the general would tell the Chinese that the Americans had been helping them.

He had to shoot Trung.

The general was below, in the middle of six men, who took turns pushing him enthusiastically. They turned right, walking northward along the street.

There was no more gunfire. The battle was over. The only Vietnamese left were either dead or hiding.

Zeus scrambled through the backyards to parallel the men below. In the second yard, he saw a lean-to with a roof maybe four feet below the main building's roof. He went to it, slid the rifle up, then jumped and pulled himself onto the lean-to. From there he climbed onto the main roof, only to find that it was just the first story—the building itself was three stories high, and there was no way up to the top except to climb the wall.

The structure next to it, however, had a metal fire escape. Leaning across to the ladder, Zeus was just able to grab the rungs. He swung up and climbed through the gridwork, then ran from the landing to the next set of steps, ascending to the top floor. There he found a steel ladder that went to the roof. He climbed through the shadow and emerged in an orange halo of light and heavy dust.

Zeus had climbed onto the roof of the tallest building still intact on the east side of the street. He ran toward the edge, unsure of his bearings or where Trung had gone.

A car had pulled up near the top of the road, just past the area where the first attack had floundered in the minefield. It was clearly a command vehicle, a Chinese-made Mercedes knockoff.

Zeus spotted the group with Trung on his left. They'd stopped. Someone got out of the car.

It was an officer. A flash of white light caught the stars on his shoulder—a general.

In the distance it was difficult exactly to see, but Zeus thought it was Li Sun, the man they'd meant to kill.

Zeus went down to his knee, suddenly aware of how exposed he was here.

Should he take the Chinese officer?

No. Trung was the person he had to kill. Trung. He had to kill Trung. That was where the danger was.

Then escape.

But there'd be no escape, would there? He'd been foolish and reckless—and in the end it was him, not Setco, not any of the others who had been self-destructive.

What had Kerfer told him?

Nothing here worth dying for, Major.

Zeus turned back toward Trung. The Vietnamese general was walking stoically, head high, moving toward the car. There were two officers approaching him.

Shoot now.

Zeus brought the rifle to his shoulder. He was a good two hundred yards from the street—not out of range for the AK, certainly, but far enough away to make the shot less than guaranteed, given the iron sights and the age of the rifle.

Shoot now! Now!

Zeus closed his left eye, steadied the front of the gun with his left hand. His finger slid against the slick curve of the trigger.

A shot rang out nearby, thin and metallic. Another and then another.

They weren't aimed at him. Zeus looked to the right, saw the Chinese officers starting to fall. Then there was a blur, Trung moving. He led with his rifle and fired. Just as he squeezed the trigger, Trung exploded.

A grenade!

"Motherfucker blew himself up. Good for him."

Zeus turned. Setco was standing right behind him. He had a modified Russian SVD marksman rifle with a large scope in his hands.

"Let's get the hell out of here," said Setco.

"I thought you left."

"I figured I owed you something. Come on. Before we have to shoot our way out of this fuckhole."

67

The South China Sea

There were eight missiles coming at them, and even as the radar operator reported that he saw them, the Aegis system had started firing.

The missiles were air-launched versions of the YJ-83, the weapons used by the frigate earlier to sink the Vietnamese ship. They were subsonic, but at thirty nautical miles, *McCampbell* didn't have a lot of time to defend itself.

"Take them down," said Silas.

A salvo of six SM2s left the launchers. The Aegis system immediately queued and dished out a second and then a third wave of Evolved Sea Sparrow missiles, a shorter-range anti-air weapon.

"Nulka, countermeasures," ordered the captain with his next breath. The Nulka—officially, the Mk-53—was a rocket-launched radar target, a decoy that tried to seduce the incoming missiles with a more attractive radar and infrared target. As *McCampbell* ducked away, the Nulka flew upward and hovered over the sea, flaunting its vulnerability to the greedy attackers.

They never reached it. The first volley of SM2s took

three of the incoming missiles down. The next wave took two. The final three missiles were struck by the Sea Sparrows just as the Phalanx readied to take out the leakers.

"Those planes. Shoot them down," barked Silas, even as the debris from the last missile hit the water.

"Sorry, Captain," reported Li. "We have no targets. They popped up and popped down. They knew we'd be mad."

"The Badger?"

"Out of range."

"Son of a bitch," grumbled Silas. He considered sending an SM2 in its direction, just to see it run.

"Watch for more," warned Silas. "This may not be over."

But it was. The four JH-7As reappeared on radar, briefly, well beyond the Badger. The reconnaissance aircraft took one more turn around its surveillance track, then pushed north. Silas spent five anxious minutes wondering if this was a trick of some sort. Finally he concluded the Chinese had gone home.

McCampbell had escaped any damage from the missiles, and the only human casualty seemed to be a broken leg suffered by a seaman scrambling to his post. The poor man would probably suffer more from the bruise to his ego than the broken bone; he was due for quite a lot of good-natured ribbing.

Fleet, meanwhile, wanted to know what was going on. Silas held them off until he was sure there were no more airplanes or missiles inbound.

"Go ahead," he growled, switching into the Fleet channel. He expected he was talking to some ensign or perhaps a lieutenant tasked to get an update. Instead he found himself talking to his boss, Admiral Meeve.

"What the hell is going on out there, Silas?" demanded the admiral.

"Sorry to keep you waiting, sir. Four Chinese aircraft tried to sink us. We took down their missiles. Unfortunately, the little bastards were too far away to shoot down. They put their tails between their legs and ran away."

"You're just a one-man navy out there, aren't you, Silas?"

"One ship navy, sir," said the commander, looking around at his crewmen. He started to ask permission to sink the cruiser, but he was cut off by Lt. Commander Li, waving a hand in his face.

"The Chinese have launched DF-21s!" Ordinarily calm to a fault, Li's voice was high-pitched and strained.

"At us?" said Silas.

"What the hell is going on?" asked Meeve.

Silas pulled his headset off so he could concentrate. The executive officer had strode across the compartment and was crouched over a console.

"At us? The missile?" asked Silas.

Li put up her left hand and held her right to her ear, listening to her own radio. The DF-21 antiship ballistic missile had been launched from a base in northern Guangdong Province, a considerable distance from *McCampbell*. The area was well north of Hong Kong, and the initial climb of the missile would not give its target away. There were American carriers to the southwest of Taiwan, and while in theory they were outside the range of the DF-21, there was no way to tell immediately where the weapons were going.

American satellites as well as spy planes and a radar ship were watching the launch. Li spoke directly to an Air Force specialist tasked with coordinating real-time intelligence on the launch. She also had a Fleet intelligence officer on another channel, who was seeing the same data.

"Is it coming for us?" asked Silas again.

"Four missiles, moving in our direction!" snapped Li. "Engage!"

"Amen to that," said Silas.

68

Washington, D.C.

President Greene had barely digested the news of the sea battle when Jeremy French looked over from the communications desk.

"The Chinese have launched four DF-21s at *Mc-Campbell*," said the officer.

Greene looked up at the Pentagon screen, where the chairman of the joint chiefs of staff and the Air Force chairman were just receiving the same news.

"Nail them," said Greene. "Get the B-2s in. Turn that missile base into a gravel pit."

69

Near Chùa Cao, northeastern Vietnam

Kerfer still had close to a mile to walk when he heard the trucks. They were coming from the southwest, taking another road up into the area of the mines, but the sound echoed loudly through the hills.

Until he heard the trucks, Kerfer had nearly convinced himself that the whole mission was a wild goose chase—from what he had seen of the Vietnamese, he had doubted that they had the wherewithal to hide missiles, let alone obtain them or arm them in the way Lucas had said. The CIA was always seeing ghosts in cemeteries. But now he realized they were right—just from the sound he knew these were military vehicles, and their only possible destination must be the mines.

He started to trot along the dirt road in the direction of the sounds. The satellite images had shown a network of narrow work roads scratched through the low scrub of the humpbacked hill before him. If the vehicles were coming, all he would have to do was find the high ground and wait.

Kerfer took out his paper map, orienting himself and trying to see how he might get to the high ground without taking too much time. But the dull colors of the features were difficult to decipher in the starlight, and he decided it was easier simply to keep going in the direction of the sound. He cut up a hill, moving through the scrub into a copse of larger trees. He was through it in three strides, passing onto a bald rise, his boots scraping the stone.

The summit had a perfect view of the nearby mine shafts, all closed off by boards and in one case what appeared to be a stone and cement wall. They were arranged in an elongated W, each shaft opening at the side of a small mound and ringing an area that had been bulldozed flat. Kerfer pulled out the radiation detector and pressed the sides. The LED letters jumped.

The indicator light at the side of the screen was yellow, not red. That made sense, though—this far up, he was only gathering small traces.

Kerfer pulled out the designator and laid it on the ground in front of him. Then he took the satcom and dialed into the bomber frequency. Fifty miles east, an Air Force pilot in a Strike Eagle, answered his hail.

"Striker One on."

"Striker, this is Flashlight. How do you read?"

"Strong coms. What's your favorite baseball team?"

"I'm a soccer fan." Kerfer cringed at the CIA imposed authentication. Like anything the agency touched, it was goofy.

"They call it football in the rest of the world," said the pilot, giving the proper response before adding on his own, "but I think it's a sport for chickenshits."

"Damn straight on that, Striker. I'm at the location."

"Roger. We have a preliminary ballpark—that where you are?"

"Almost to the dot." Kerfer counted the shafts. "I have seven target portals. Give me the high sign and I'll beam the bitches."

"Seven?"

"Affirmative."

"Seven?"

"I say again, seven."

"Stand by, Flashlight."

"Problem?"

"Stand by."

Freakin' air farce, thought Kerfer.

"Flashlight, this is Striker."

"Go ahead, Striker."

"We can take them. We will be on station in zero-five minutes. I'll call when we're roughly one minute out."

"Affirmative. Striker, how far should I be from these suckers when you hit them?"

"Two countries away would be optimum."

Just what I need, thought Kerfer, a freakin' comedian.

"Was a serious question, Striker."

"Yeah, sorry, roger that. Listen Striker, you want to be as far away as you comfortably can be."

"Distance?"

"Fifteen hundred yards, for starters."

"Can't get that far away."

The pilot didn't answer.

"Striker?"

"Uh, Flashlight, just get yourself as far away as you can. The way these work, first bomb comes in—"

"Yeah, roger, I understand," replied Kerfer. He didn't need the actual details—he wasn't going to like them anyway. "Call me when you're a minute out."

Kerfer was only two hundred yards from the nearest mine site—way too close for comfort from what the pilot was telling him. He took a few steps back, looking around and trying to figure out a solution.

Then he realized that the trucks had stopped moving. Which didn't make sense if he had the right spot.

Damn.

He pulled the satcom back out to call the pilot and tell him to hold off. As he did, he saw something moving on his right. He dropped to his haunches, then rolled as a shot rang out. There was no place to go but down—he scrambled and slid forward, diving and falling down the hill as a spray of bullets flew overhead.

Kerfer caught himself on a rock, slamming against it to stop his fall. He pushed up and leapt to the side, ducking away from the gunman, who fortunately was still a distance from the edge of the slope.

Pulling out his pistol, Kerfer circled to the left, pausing to catch his breath behind a large pile of dirt and stone.

He could hear whoever had shot at him coming down the hill. Kerfer flattened himself on the ground, then peeked out from behind the pile. It took him a few seconds to locate the descending shadow; when he did, he saw the man raising his rifle. Kerfer fired central mass, aiming for the biggest possible target.

He missed. The shadow slid back against the hill.

Kerfer fired again, this time with better aim. He heard an almost girlish grunt. But that was quickly followed by a burst of automatic rifle fire, tinny and metallic—Kerfer threw himself back.

Rocks and dirt fell as the other man slid down to the bottom of the hill. Kerfer moved to his left, looking to possibly circle around the pile, but there was no space between it and the hillside. He thought of climbing up but decided that would leave him too exposed. Instead, he moved toward a cluster of large rocks off to his right, deciding he could use them for cover. He hunched forward, held his breath, and dove behind them the way a baseball player might go head-first into second base on a delayed steal.

Kerfer scrambled upright. There was enough space

behind the rock for him to peek out from the other side, and to end up with a good view of the side of the hill. He pushed through and waited.

His enemy didn't appear. Meanwhile, the sound of the trucks had grown louder. They must be on the other side of the hill with the mine shafts he'd seen earlier.

So his target must be must be one set of hills over. Not that he was in a position to do much about that now.

Kerfer glanced up the hill where he'd left his gear. It was dark, but not so dark that he couldn't be seen from the ground and become an easy target.

He edged out from the rock, not sure which option he was taking. Leaning back toward the hill, he took a step, then another—he was going after the shooter who'd ambushed him.

He crouched down, ready.

Nothing moved. He skirted past the pile of stones, then moved slowly to his right, hunkered low to the ground. He had his gun in his right hand, his left out for balance.

Bad way to fire.

Something was lying at the bottom of the hill. He stared, moved his head slightly to make sure it was a body, not just a shadow.

He looked up at the ridge top. Nothing. No one.

The gunman had been alone.

Kerfer rose and sprinted to the body. It was moving.

A rifle lay nearby. Kerfer picked it up. It was an M16, a relatively new one, a Marine rifle. That's why it had sounded different than the AK earlier.

The body writhed. He went and pushed it over with his boot.

American consul, Juliet Greig.

Greig?

"What the fuck?" he said.

She groaned, blinking her eyes at him.

"What the hell?" said Kerfer. "What are you doing here?"

She groaned again, then went to reach for something. Kerfer, unsure what she was doing, took no chances and kicked her hard in the chest. She struggled, and so he kicked her again, this time in the face. He dropped to his knee and found her pistol. He took it.

"What are you doing?" he asked. "I got a bomber on the way."

"Let them go," said the consul, struggling to talk between wheezes. Kerfer's first blow had knocked the wind out of her. "Let the Vietnamese kill the bastards."

"China?"

"They're our enemy, too. They'll attack us next."

"You're nuts."

"You don't see it."

"You were the spy?"

"Ric—we have to stop the Chinese. The Chinese."

"You crazy bitch," said Kerfer. He kicked her in the head, knocking her unconscious, then started scrambling up the hill for his gear.

70

West of Malipo

Setco led Zeus through the backyards to a narrow trail in the ravine, then across a field that paralleled the main road. He had managed to commandeer a vehicle after leaving the airport, but it was lost now at the end of main street, undoubtedly too shot up to be of use.

The few Vietnamese left as an organized force were attempting to withdraw under fire from the vanguard of the tank battalion. The gun battle was a mishmash of confusion, the perfect example of the infamous fog of war.

"There's a truck up there," said Zeus, spotting a pickup near the side of the road.

Setco changed direction, running toward it. Exhaust curled from the tailpipe, forming a thin cloud in the cold air. As they got closer, Zeus saw that the windows had been shot out.

The driver was slumped over the wheel.

"One of the civilians picked a bad time to try to get away," said Setco, pulling the man from the cab.

Zeus ran to the other side. Setco got it into gear and jerked it back onto the road. It bounced wildly, but except for the shattered windows it appeared to have escaped real damage. And it was certainly better than walking.

They drove onto the south side of the airport across the empty infield, heading directly for the terminal building. The damaged An-24 was exactly where he had last seen it, wing practically touching the corner of the building.

The other plane, the Chinese Xian Y-7-100 that Setco had arrived in, was gone.

"Shit," said Zeus.

"I told them to get the hell out," said Setco, driving toward the hangars. "There's a Cessna in the hangar."

"That old plane?"

"It's about all I can handle."

"You're a pilot?"

"No. But I can fly that."

"You sure?"

"The hard part is landing. That I just aim and cut the engine way back. I've flown these before," Setco added.

It didn't sound reassuring.

"I'm taking it," said the CIA para. "You can walk if you want."

Still covered with thick dirt and crud, the Cessna had been moved out in front of the hangar.

"Jesus," said Zeus. "You sure that thing can still fly?"

"We fueled it, and I started the engine," said Setco. "Otherwise we'd be on the road south by now."

Zeus remained doubtful, but there was no sense arguing or even questioning him. He jumped from the truck and ran for the plane.

Setco went over to the engine compartment. He put his hands out, and for a second Zeus thought he was going to spin the prop as if it were attached to an old-fashioned jump-start engine. But he was doing a preflight inspection, starting with the propeller and moving around the aircraft, checking control surfaces and rivets in the wing, moving his hands along the fuselage.

At least he's had *some* training, thought Zeus. He climbed in the passenger side and waited.

A paper checklist was taped to the windscreen. The writing was all in Chinese characters.

Zeus saw speckles of light beyond the runway.

Muzzle flashes and tracers.

"Roth! Come on!"

"Yeah," said Setco, climbing in. He started hitting switches. "I'm pretty sure this says flaps at twenty percent."

Zeus of course had no idea.

"Magnetos, off. Master on." Setco was reading off the checklist, following the instructions as he went. "Come on fuel." He thumped the gauge. "I know it's full. Needle, up."

Zeus looked over at the indicator. It was on empty.

"Shit. Screw it." Setco set the throttle, then spun the engine. The plane coughed but didn't start.

Meanwhile, the gunfire at the end of the runway had become intense. This amazed Zeus—as far as he knew, there was no one there: the small Vietnamese contingent had fled by the time they arrived.

The engine finally came to life. The aircraft rocked unsteadily.

"Seatbelt," said Setco.

"You sure we're going to make it?"

"Close your eyes, Major."

The airplane bucked forward. Zeus scrunched his body down. The sparkles from the guns were now coming in their direction.

"I gotta get the mixture rich," said Setco, talking to himself. "Whoever wrote the damn checklist doesn't know shit."

They were moving. The engine revved.

"We aren't going to make the runway," said Zeus.

"We don't need it. Hold on."

An APC climbed up the hill at the right. The gun on the turret began to blink. Something ripped into the back of the plane, and they moved sideways.

In the next moment, Zeus felt himself weightless, moving upward.

To die like this, in an unknown moment, distant from home—to die for my country, for someone else's country, for love . . .

To die for love sounds romantic, to die for your country patriotic, yet in the end death is death, the meaning exists for other people, not you, not me . . .

To die is only to die, to be crushed back into the endless wave of nonexistence, to return to the ashes you were made, not even to see God . . .

I wanted her. Trung was right about war—I was addicted to the adrenaline, to the rush.

But it was her I came back for. She's the reason I'm here.

I died for love, not war.

Zeus's head bounced against the window. He fell back, falling into an endless pit.

"We're OK," Setco said. "We're away from them. We're good. We're good."

Gradually, Zeus came back to himself, regaining his senses.

They were still flying. The Cessna had been hit in the fuselage, but was still airworthy. Setco had her at roughly a thousand feet, threading his way through the hills toward the border.

"I think I can get us to Hanoi," he told Zeus. "Not too much farther than that, though. We're going to have to find another way south to Thailand."

"Thailand," said Zeus.

"Thailand is not Eden," added Setco. "But it's a hell of a lot safer than 'Nam."

Zeus realized belatedly that he had failed to put on his seatbelt. He buckled it now. He looked down at his pant leg. It was crusted with brown mud—not mud but blood. He'd been grazed by a gunshot at some point and not realized it.

Anna will fix it. Anna will make everything right.

No. Love couldn't do that. Love couldn't change much, certainly not death, certainly not war.

Zeus looked at Setco. He was leaning forward, staring out the windscreen. There were still a few hours left before dawn, and it was difficult to see where the ground was. Without radar, they were in constant danger of running into a hill or mountain. Yet it was far from the worst danger they'd faced.

"I'm not going to hit anything," said Setco, seemingly reading his thoughts. "I flew this way once before."

"You did?"

"A while back. They didn't just throw me up here because they were trying to kill me, Zeus. Well, maybe that was an ulterior motive."

"That black box—"

"I don't know nothin' about it," Setco said, shaking his head, "and you don't, either."

"I was wrong about you."

Setco looked away from the window, but only for a moment. "How's that?"

"I thought you wanted to die up there."

"You weren't necessarily wrong." Setco leaned closer to the windscreen.

"What changed your mind?"

"Who says I did?"

Setco's face was a range of different emotions—bemusement and anger, and maybe a little fear.

"I don't know," he added after a while. "Maybe you're right, though. Maybe you changed my mind."

"How?"

"You were so goddamned gung-ho. Like you were a frickin' innocent virgin." He stared out the windscreen. "I hope she was worth it."

They flew on in silence for a few minutes.

"It's all right," said Setco, speaking again. His voice was almost dreamy. "We all need reasons to do things."

"What was yours?" asked Zeus.

"Orders."

"That's all?"

"I had to remember what it feels like to be alive."

71

Forthright, Ohio

Josh had called and gone straight to voice mail so many times that he was surprised when Mara answered—so surprised his first thought was that he had dialed the wrong number.

And then he didn't know what to say.

"Josh?"

"Mara."

"Hey. How are you? Are you OK?"

"Yeah, yeah, I'm fine."

One of the kids yelled in the other room, and ran screeching down the hall.

"What's going on?" Mara asked.

"Oh, just my cousin's kids. They're having a birthday party. The little one is a piece of work."

"Is that the one with leukemia?"

"Yeah. You'd never know it from the way she acts. She's a pisser."

"I hope she's OK."

Josh didn't answer. She wasn't OK, and wouldn't be, unless someone came up with a miracle cure very soon. But there was no use dwelling on the subject.

"I miss you," he told her. "You oughta come out here. The farm's beautiful right now."

"Is it?"

"Yeah. It's real pretty. Nice place for walks. Real quiet."

"Squeals not included?" Mara laughed.

"It's quiet during the day. They're all at school. It'd be great to see you."

"I was thinking I might come out."

"You were?" Josh's heart leapt. "Would you . . . could you?"

"I've been given a vacation. Forced to take it."

"Forced?"

"It's all right. It's something—I have to adapt to changes. My job. Now that my cover's blown."

"Right."

"I can't really go into it right now. But if I can get a flight first thing in the morning, would you be able—"

"I'll drive all the way to D.C. and bring you here myself if I have to," said Josh.

"You won't have to do that. Give me the address."

72

South China Sea

For nearly all of man's existence, war was a personal endeavor, conducted at very close range, near enough for the antagonists to smell each other's fear. Technology had gradually changed that. Now it was commonplace to be threatened by an enemy a thousand kilometers away—roughly the distance the DF-21Ds had to travel to hit *McCampbell*.

The flight of the missile could be broken into three phases: ascent, travel through exoatmospheric space, and final descent. The ascent or launch phase was the most vulnerable for the DF-21, but the location of *Mc-Campbell* and the timing of the warning made it impossible to strike the missiles at that point. Instead, the four SM3s that Silas's ship launched were aimed at catching the warheads during their long arc in *Mc-Campbell*'s direction.

To Silas, standing at the side of the ship's CIC, the roar of the interceptor missiles as they left their square cocoons was less than comforting. The SM3s thundered upward, but in his mind's eye they moved at a painfully slow pace. They built speed slowly as they went up, their engines burning through their fuel like hungry horses devouring sugar.

The SM3s were designed specifically to deal with ballistic missiles, including the DF-21D. They were unfortunately in short supply; *McCampbell* had just fired half her stock.

The command center, a cacophony of voices on its calmest day, was now a beehive of chatter, with the operators and supervisors conferring back and forth. Silas strove to keep his head clear; he had already cut the line to the admiral, deciding it was only a distraction.

"One Chinese missile off radar," reported the radarman.

"Gone, or have we lost it to countermeasures?" asked Li.

"Unclear."

As soon as the launch was detected, Silas had the helm come hard around. He aimed to turn exactly into the missile's path and proceed at flank speed. The missiles were being directed by a series of satellites as well as their own sensors and a preprogrammed target profile, but Silas hoped that by moving from the expected position he could fool them.

Like all ballistic missiles, even when absolutely on-target the DF-21 could "miss" its bull's-eye by a few meters and still be considered on target. This was inconsequential when launched against a large target like a city or military base, and even against an aircraft carrier a few meters was generally not critically important. But *McCampbell* was smaller than an aircraft carrier, shorter and nowhere near as wide abeam. Throwing the weapon off a few meters could easily be the difference between a close call and death.

The engine room reported that the turbines were delivering 110 percent of spec'd power.

"Great," barked Silas. "Keep this ship *moving!*"

Two more SM3s left the deck—the computer had decided that they were going to miss two of the missiles.

Seconds later, one of the DF-21Ds was destroyed, leaving *McCampbell* to deal with only two.

"More launches, Captain," reported Li. "Four more missiles."

Silas targeted them immediately, and fired his last two SM3s.

One of the Chinese missiles failed right off the launch pad. The SM3 automatically reprogrammed itself for a new target. But even if all their missiles now hit, a single missile would have to be intercepted by an SM2. They were out of the more advanced long-range weapons.

The overall flight time from launch to strike was roughly five minutes, and nearly four minutes had passed from the launch of the first volley. The destroyer began deploying chaff and using other countermeasures in an attempt to blind the satellite that was guiding the five remaining missiles.

"Strike! Strike! We have another," said one of the operators.

"Shit, there are sixteen missiles now," he added a few seconds later. "What the hell?"

"Steady," said Silas. "It's their countermeasures."

A few seconds later, the Phalanx close-in system began rattling furiously. Silas felt as if he were plummeting down an elevator shaft . . . How had they had missed the missile so completely?

He braced himself for the impact. Then the gun stopped. The system had picked up some of *McCampbell*'s own chaff and temporarily confused it with a missile; programmed to be safe rather than sorry, it had highlighted the threat and then responded until the correct data identified the actual source of the contact. It had all happened in milliseconds.

The threat screen cleared. They had one missile left in the first volley, and three still in the second.

"Get our second wave of missiles up," said Silas. "The Standard 2s."

"Launching," said Li.

The warhead of the lead DF-21D was only a few miles away, hurtling toward *McCampbell*. One SM2, confused by the countermeasures, sailed by it without igniting. The second exploded in its path, knocking it slightly off course.

The Phalanx lit again, this time with a legitimate target. There was an immense splash in the water a hundred yards off the fantail.

The Chinese missile had missed.

"Three more incoming," warned Li.

73

Near Chùa Cao, northeastern Vietnam

"Striker, you gotta hold off. Repeat, Striker, you gotta hold off."

"Flashlight, where the hell have you been?"

"I ran into some trouble," explained Kerfer, huffing into the satcom. "You gotta wait."

"Yeah, roger that. My whole flight's been pulling their puds up here for the last ten minutes, waiting for you to get your act together."

Glad to see you put the time to good use, thought Kerfer.

He grabbed the ruck and the designator, and then with his rifle ready he ran down the hill. He jumped over Greig's body and kept running.

The truth was, he couldn't argue with Greig about the Chinese. But it wasn't his call.

Kerfer heard more truck engines as he reached the flat ground. He angled left, running through a small pass in the low hills, then went up a much longer, more gradual incline than the one he'd started from. After about sixty yards, huge boulders blocked his path. He went right, hoping to get around them, but the ground dropped off sharply after ten feet.

At that point he decided his only choice was to climb the rocks. Finding one he could get his right hand on, he boosted himself by kicking his toes into the side and working his feet desperately. The loose dirt at the top of the boulders made it difficult to climb; he scrambled on all four limbs through pebbles and sand, swimming as much as crawling until finally he came to the top of the hill.

The complex lay before him, about three hundred yards due west, down in an almost geometrically perfect circle. There were three large mine shafts, all with steel doors recessed two meters into the cave where they could not be seen from overhead.

In front of them sat three pickup trucks and an SUV. One of the pickups had a large generator in the back, and it was on, supplying power to something at the door. The generator was loud; Kerfer realized he'd have a hard time hearing the radio over it, even with an earphone.

The other pickups had obviously carried soldiers. A dozen were now posted around the area. The rest of the men were gathered near one of the bunkers, working on the door.

Kerfer pulled out the satcom.

"Striker, this is Flashlight. I'm at the location."

"Copy that, Striker. You're a little hard to hear, but I got you."

"There are three mine shafts that I can see. Separated by about maybe fifty yards, maybe a little less. They're in a semicircle."

"That's more like it. Stand by."

Going back to pulling your pud, thought Kerfer.

He looked more closely at the security detail. There were eight soldiers; the others were technicians of some sort.

Not great odds, even so, no matter what the movies claimed about SEAL prowess.

424 | Larry Bond and Jim DeFelice

The bombs would take them out.

Him, too, maybe.

"Flashlight, you still there?"

"Shit yeah."

"We want you to beam the middle bunker. Can you do that?"

Kerfer's frustration got the better of him. "You think I'm retarded?"

"Come again?"

"Affirmative, Striker, I can beam the middle bunker. I can get the door. Listen, I got twenty guys down there. They look like they're working on the shaft to the immediate south. I think they'll be opening it."

"Copy."

"You don't want to hit that one first?"

"Flashlight, we're going to do it this way. We hit the middle one and we may get secondaries to take out the other two shafts. I have another two waves of aircraft coming in that will take out anything that manages to get out of a bunker. After the first missile hits, you hold steady for a second shot. Then beam the one on the north. You copy?"

"If I'm still here, sure."

"Repeat?"

"Yeah, I read you loud and clear."

"We're zero one from launch point. Start beaming it." The pilot continued talking on the circuit, apparently to the rest of his flight, saying they were cleared hot and giving some other directions. Kerfer put down the radio-phone, leaving the earpiece in his ear, and picked up the designator. It was bulky; he felt like he was holding a movie projector in front of his face.

He had a clear line of sight to the shaft, maybe a quarter mile away.

He turned the beam on and waited.

There was movement on the ground near the shafts. He resisted the sudden urge to drop the designator and see.

Someone firing at me?

There was a very shrill whistle above him, a thick shout from a teakettle that turned into a freight train, then a loud crack as the point in front of the laser target flashed.

Nothing happened for a moment.

Damn. A dud?

Stinkin' air farce shitheads.

The ground rumbled beneath him. There was another whistle, but no loud crack this time, no explosion.

Then the ground buckled. Kerfer felt as if he was falling into the earth. He pushed his upper body around, aiming for the other shaft.

He held the light there. A cloud began spewing from the tunnel that had just been hit.

Son of a bitch. I bet that's radioactive.

The missiles hit the second shaft in quick succession.

"Three's a charm," said Kerfer out loud. He held the designator as the ground rumbled. The last missile seemed to take forever to arrive, and then struck high on the hill over the door, perhaps because the laser beam had been diffused by the smoke and debris.

"Keep beaming it," squawked one of the pilots.

Kerfer shifted the designator to the spot where the first GBU-28 had gone in. A few moments later, the second missile popped into his viewer, then disappeared into the hillside.

Kerfer scooped up his rifle, hooked his arm into the ruck and ran down the hill. He had taken only two or three steps when the rumble of the ground threw him off his feet.

The SEAL officer landed on his side. As he started to get up, he lost his balance and then his footing, and flopped all the way to the bottom of the hill.

By the time he stopped, he had a mouthful of dirt. He got to his feet and began running in what he thought was the direction he had taken earlier. Instead, he reached a hard-packed road. Struggling to get his bearings, he began trotting eastward. When the road swung south, he stayed with it. After ten minutes alternating running and walking as fast as he could, he came out on a paved road.

Deciding he must be on the road that led past the Buddhist shrine, Kerfer debated which way to go. He figured that the driver would be gone by now, but turned north anyway, calculating that he was less likely to see any of the Vietnamese soldiers this way.

Kerfer was surprised some ten minutes later to see the car exactly where he had left it.

The driver was sleeping behind the wheel. He'd locked all the doors; Kerfer had to pound on the window to wake him up. The man reached across slowly to the door and unlocked it.

"Thanks." The SEAL threw his gear in the front, then practically fell into the seat, exhausted.

Had he been radiated?

He took out the radiation meter and pressed the sides. It clicked and blinked.

The dial spit up zeroes. There was a one at the very end, but the light remained yellow.

"Hmmmph."

"Money, now," said the driver.

"When we get to Hanoi."

"Money," insisted the man.

"We gotta get the hell out of here." Kerfer switched to Vietnamese, casting considerable doubt on the man's parentage. The man continued to insist that he be paid, launching into a long sob story about how he needed money to send his young daughter to school for a better life.

"Yeah, yeah, yeah," said Kerfer, finally tiring of the harangue. He dug into his pocket and retrieved the set of torn hundred-dollar bills. "Here."

The driver grabbed them greedily, counted and matched them up. Then he asked for the rest of his payment.

"Not until we get to Hanoi," said Kerfer in Vietnamese.

"Now," insisted the man.

"No."

This time, Kerfer didn't give in. When the man started telling him about his daughter again, Kerfer replied that he was tempted to shoot him through the head, and might just do so if he didn't shut his mouth and start the car.

The driver's face clouded, and he began to cry.

"Oh for Christ's sake." Kerfer slapped his hand on the dashboard, exasperated. As he pulled it back, trying to get control of himself, the air cracked above. He heard the whine of a jet engine, and then a distant explosion.

The F-15Es were making their runs.

He sat there for a moment, absorbed in the sound of the bombing. Then he realized what that meant.

"Out of the car! Out of the car!" he yelled, grabbing his ruck and gun as he threw open the door.

The driver didn't move. Kerfer ran to his door, but it was still locked. The man was paralyzed inside. Kerfer took his rifle butt and broke the glass. Putting his arm around the driver's neck to keep him from moving, he unlocked the door and dragged the driver out of the car.

"Run, damn you," he said, pulling the driver with him up the road.

They were a good two hundred yards away when the first bomb hit the vehicle, far enough away that the shrapnel didn't quite reach them. Kerfer and the driver didn't stop running until they reached the shrine. They hunkered beneath it, listening as a jet made two low-level passes. By the third, Kerfer had regained his breath enough to get the satellite radio/phone out.

"Knock it off, knock it off!" he yelled on Striker's frequency. "I'm at the shrine. Don't fire! Blue on blue! Blue on blue, motherfucker!"

Striker came back a second later, asking for authentication.

Kerfer replied with a stream of curses.

"Sorry, Flashlight, we assumed you had exited south, per your plan," replied the pilot.

"What plan?" said Kerfer.

"Uh, we're sorry."

"Sorry ain't getting me back to Hanoi, asshole."

74

South China Sea

It was a battle of nanoseconds and eternity, a conflict fought in instants and pauses. The SM2s rose toward the last three warheads; the warheads employed their electronic camouflage and digital mind games.

Silas felt as if he should be on the bridge. Even though he was in the literal heart of the ship's battle systems, there was something off-balance in the captain being anywhere but near the ship's wheel when the bullets flew.

One last vestige of incurable romance, a last speck of swashbuckling nostalgia, cried out within him: the fight is personal. You need to see it to win.

The ship rocked—another salvo of SM2s headed skyward.

"We have a hit," reported Li. "Two contacts. Sixty seconds out."

Silas put his hands on his hips. The sway of the ship had long ago become second nature. Now he felt as if he were an ensign again, feeling his way aboard a vessel for the first time.

What had his first sea daddy told him?

She'll talk to you. If you listen.

The old man had laughed. He was a chief, who for some strange reason had taken Silas under his wing. The best chiefs were like that, eager to show the new kids, even the officers, the way.

He had gray hair, a lot of it, and he chewed tobacco so much that his lips and clothes were constantly stained. You could smell him coming from a mile away—a sweet tobacco smell that mixed with salt water and maybe something else.

But he knew that ship.

"She'll speak to you," he told Silas, practically every day when he came on watch. "Remember to listen."

"Their guidance is jammed!" said Li. "We have a hit on missile two. Missile two down. One is still inbound."

The ship lurched in the water.

She was speaking—but what did she say?

Silas pushed his microphone to his mouth.

"Helm, hard right rudder," Silas told the helmsman calmly. "As hard as you can."

The vessel lurched as the sailor followed Silas's direction.

The Phalanx gun began rotating. Firing.

"Harder," Silas told his helm.

The missile hit with a tremendous impact, exploding instantly. The shock lifted *McCampbell* sideways into the air, slamming her down on the side of her hull. She plunged down beneath the sea, her decks covered with saltwater. The waves rolled up over the missile launchers and across the gun mount, angry Neptune grasping for his due.

Then she righted herself and came to, bobbing ferociously in the water. The missile had struck just ahead of the bow as *McCampbell* turned away; the last second maneuver ordered by her captain had saved her.

The violent maneuvers had thrown Silas against the bulkhead. He fell to the deck, dazed.

Pain rushed over his body. His head and chest felt as if they had imploded.

Voices buzzed. Silas strained to open his eyes.

People stood over him. The whole world it seemed.

Someone bent down to ask how he was. Silas managed to blink open one eye.

It was the old chief, stinking of his chew. He said nothing.

"Tell them that I listened," said Silas. Then he fell back into the ocean, warm and deep, surrendering to Neptune his prize.

75

Beijing

Cho Lai remained silent for nearly five minutes. The aide who had brought him the news—a young lieutenant, clearly selected because he was of low rank and couldn't push off the job—waited at the other end of the office.

"General Libo sent this message?" asked Cho Lai finally. He could think of nothing else to say. "Personally? He sent it?"

"Yes." The young lieutenant barely opened his mouth to speak, but even then his voice cracked.

The Vietnamese had attacked far into China. Malipo had been taken, albeit briefly. They had even launched a raid on Kunming, where Li Sun's headquarters were. The reports there said it had been turned back with light casualties—including Li Sun's chief of staff.

Li Sun himself had been killed retaking Malipo.

According to the report, General Li Sun had counterattacked after his predecessors had allowed the Vietnamese to come across the border. The Vietnamese general in charge of the assault had blown himself up with a grenade rather than be taken alive.

Further details were lacking. Cho Lai wondered how much of the report was accurate.

Ultimately, it wouldn't matter.

"We have the city back?" asked Cho Lai.

"Yes, sir. I'm told we do. I was to mention that. There are no more Vietnamese forces on our land."

There was a knock on the door. The lieutenant glanced in its direction.

"Come," said Cho Lai.

Lo Gong, the defense minister, came into the room. He moved in fits and starts. He appeared distraught, barely able to contain some unspeakable emotion.

"Lieutenant, you are dismissed," Cho Lai told the poor man who had been detailed as the messenger of doom. "Go back to your post."

The man bowed his head and left.

"Minister, sit down," Cho Lai told Lo Gong. "You are making me . . . agitated."

"I am . . . I have to report horrible news."

"I know it." Cho Lai held up the paper the captain had brought.

"You've heard?"

Lo Gong began rubbing his hands together. Annoyed, Cho Lai rose himself.

"Please sit down, Defense Minister. I insist."

Lo Gong collapsed into his seat. Cho Lai walked out from behind his desk, trying to control some of his own energy. The matter could be controlled. It would have to be.

"I am not sure when we will get it back," said the defense minister.

"What are you saying? We have the town back," snapped Cho Lai. "The lieutenant just told me. Is that a lie?"

Lo Gong stared at him. Cho Lai stopped moving.

Cho Lai had been through many difficult and trying

moments in his climb to the top of China. He had learned long ago that it was critical to master his emotions at times of stress, as this certainly was.

He glanced down at the floor to gather himself, but it was only for the briefest moment.

"Tell me the entire story," he said, making his voice as gentle as possible.

"Our control system for the ICBM missiles is completely off-line," said Lo Gong. "We cannot even launch manually if we wish."

"What?"

The minister shook his head.

"American B-2s attacked the DF-21D launch site about a half hour ago. They destroyed four missiles and their launchers on the ground. The entire site has been wiped out."

"I don't care about those missiles," said Cho Lai. "What has happened to our missile force? Are you telling me we have no defense against an American attack?"

"None," said Lo Gong. "It's a cyber-attack."

"Retaliate!"

"We've tried. We can't get past their firewalls. We've had some minor successes."

Cho Lai realized that his hands were trembling. He went to his seat and sat down.

"Get out," he told the defense minister. "Out."

Lo Gong rose to go. He almost looked relieved.

"Prepare a withdrawal from Vietnam," said Cho Lai. "Prepare—reinforce all of the home guard units in the cities. There will be a reaction to this. We must head it off with an extreme show of force."

"Premier, I—"

"Out!"

Cho Lai's voice was so loud the window behind him shook. He waited until Lo Gong had left, then buried his face in his hands.

76

Washington, D.C.

The president's national security advisor was ecstatic as he barged into the Oval Office.

"They're withdrawing their forces from Vietnam unilaterally," said Jackson. A child at Christmas couldn't have sounded happier. "They've given up. They're defeated."

Greene frowned. He pushed back in his seat, then looked up at the ceiling.

"They're not defeated, Walter. They're pushed back. For now."

"That's all we can ask for."

"Mmmm."

William Jablonski, freshly arrived from New York, rose and shook Jackson's hand. They were old drinking buddies, their sharp contrasts notwithstanding. Priest, the president's spokesman, remained crouched in his corner of the couch, deep in thought.

"Congress will stop this impeachment business," Jackson told Greene. "You've won, Mr. President. You've won."

Somehow, Greene didn't feel as if he had. As he stared at the ceiling, he remembered staring at another ceiling, one made of concrete and pockmarked with mold and rot: the ceiling of the prison he'd been kept in while a POW in Vietnam.

The day he'd been released, he felt the same sort of odd mixture—relief, and yet not relief. He'd won there by surviving, and yet he knew he faced a struggle nearly as intense to readapt himself to the world, and reconcile the fact that he had survived.

It had taken a long time. In some ways, the process was continuing, though anyone who looked at him would say, would assume, that he had not only survived but triumphed.

In the prison he learned many truths, most especially about himself. He learned that there was never really such a thing as a final victory. He learned that there was never really such a thing as a triumph that didn't contain the seeds of another downfall. He learned to move in small steps, with small victories—the late rising from the floor, the ability to withstand one more punch before giving in.

He had won a great victory here, one that many Americans would not really know about. They would see the news stories and assume it had more to do with China and Vietnam than Greene or the men and women who had risked their lives in Asia. Which was fine by him.

But the next time—and there would be a next time—things would be even more difficult. He was sure Cho Lai already had his people studying the victory, planning on how they might have overturned it. His generals and advisors were doing the same.

"This will take some of the immediate pressure off," said Priest. "But we still have the *L.A. Times* to deal with. That story is going to kill us."

"Deny it," said Jackson. "Just stonewall."

Priest looked at Jablonski, then at Greene.

"I could, I suppose," said Greene.

But was that what he wanted? His time in captivity had taught him much.

"The American people deserve the truth," said Greene. "I have no problem admitting it."

"Congress will impeach you," said Jablonski. "There's no doubt about that. You don't have the votes."

"Let them."

"Do you think that's wise?" Jablonski folded his arms. "Chet . . . if you're impeached and kicked out, who wins? Doesn't China?"

"China?" asked Jackson. "How do you see that?"

"This is a long conflict. You can't stand on principle," said Jablonski. "You have to do what's right for the country."

"Lying?" shot Greene.

"If that's what it takes."

Greene frowned. He wasn't sure what he would do.

"You have a way of being the skunk at the party, Billy. You know that?"

"It's the first line in my job description."

77

Forthright, Ohio

Mara found the driveway and pulled in, following the curve down to the house.

She suddenly felt extremely nervous. Her hands trembled as she put the car into park and turned off the ignition.

"Am I ready to do this?" she said aloud, though she was the only one in the car. "Do what? I'm just seeing Josh. A friend. Oh, more than a friend . . . am I ready to see him? Why not? Who cares what it all means, if it means anything. God, I am *so* overthinking this and talking to myself in the car."

She reached over for her pocketbook. When she straightened, she saw a trio of children coming out from the house, followed by a middle-aged woman.

And, a few feet behind everyone else, Josh MacArthur.

His face was framed in the doorway for just an instant, but the image burned itself into her brain. He was handsome in a slightly nerdy way—if he'd worn glasses it would have been too much. He didn't look particularly athletic, though as she had seen in Vietnam he was deceptively strong and tough, extremely resilient.

And protective. Not embarrassingly so, not inappropriately, but he had saved the little girl's life, and even though it was Mara's job to watch after him, he had done his share of watching after her as well.

And that was the endearing factor, the thing that made her love him. Or rather, told her that she loved him.

She wasn't the type of person who let others take care of her. A man who looked after her had to do it in a subtle, careful way, without fuss. And Josh was completely without fuss.

The children arrived at the driver's side window and began banging on it.

"Hey, hey," said their mother, helping Mara open the door. "Settle down, all of you."

"Hello," said Mara, stepping out.

"Hello. I'm Debra," said Josh's cousin's wife. "I'm their mom."

"I'm Mara."

"Yes." Debra folded Mara in a bear hug. "Josh has told us so much about you. You're our hero."

"Oh, I didn't do—"

"Thank you for saving him," said Debra, her arms still clamped around Mara's back.

"I think you're smothering her," said Josh. "Leave some for me."

Jing Yo couldn't quite see what was going on in the front yard. All he knew was that a car had pulled into the driveway and some people had come out of the house.

He would sit high in the tree with the rifle and wait them out. Eventually, the scientist would come to him.

After he shot him, Jing Yo would descend the tree and run across the field behind these woods, coming out on the road near where he had left his car in the little turnaround off the road. He would walk quickly but with determination to the vehicle. He would drive to the bus station three towns away, where buses left every hour for Dayton. From Dayton, he would take another bus to Indianapolis. There he would check into a motel with another alias, and arrange for a flight to San Antonio. From there, Mexico and beyond.

Jing Yo wasn't sure where "beyond" was. He had come to like America, but he couldn't stay after murdering one of its citizens. And of course he couldn't go home to China. He would never be able to go home to China.

Anywhere he went would be empty without Hyuen Bo, in any event. It didn't much matter where he ended up.

He couldn't help think about her. She was a constant ache in his chest.

The former monk turned soldier scolded himself. He should be beyond petty feelings. One of the firmest principles Shaolin preached was that this world was an illusion. Human emotions were the biggest part of that illusion, and were to be contemplated only at distance.

Yet the loss he felt was not an illusion. It was an emptiness and ache that had a physical place inside his body, at his rib cage, where her head had rested so often.

It had changed. First, it was despair, and it was in the pit of his stomach. Then it was anger and lust for revenge. That was deep in his muscles, in his shoulders and his back and his thighs.

Now, just loss.

The people were moving into the house. Jing Yo got the rifle ready.

* * *

Josh hadn't felt this giddy since he was fifteen or sixteen. He did his best to clamp down on his excitement. Debra had found an empty bedroom for Mara—the big old farmhouse was full of them—and Josh helped her bring her bag upstairs. As soon as they were alone, he took her hand, then pulled her toward him and kissed her.

She didn't resist. In fact, she reciprocated.

"I missed you," he said.

"I missed *you*."

They stood together for a few moments, holding hands.

"Are you coming down to see my painting?" called Chrissie.

"Coming," said Josh. He let go of Mara's hands. He still wasn't sure exactly how intimate they were, or should be. And in front of others, even his family, he felt awkward.

They went downstairs. Each child had to show the guest something special as they vied for attention. Josh watched Mara as she *ooo'd* and *ahh'd* over each.

After they met in the jungle, he had watched her and thought to himself that she wasn't particularly pretty. But now, she seemed more beautiful than any woman he had ever met.

Objectively, her hips and shoulders, while certainly not fat, were a bit broad compared to her breasts, and her face was rather plain. Her blond hair shaded toward brown and was not well cut. She didn't wear makeup.

And yet the whole was so much more than the parts. And her voice was music.

She listened to each child in turn. Debra finally cut them off when they started the third round of their show-and-tells, with Chrissie bringing out her Barbies.

"Ms. Duncan needs a little time to herself," said Debra. "Shoo now. Get your homework done."

"Want a beer?" asked Josh.

"I'd love one."

He fetched one from the refrigerator. Debra fussed around the kitchen for a few minutes more, then excused herself to check on the children. Josh listened to Mara talk about how she was looking forward to getting a few days off, and how open the country had looked on her way out.

"You forget that about America, being away," she said. "I've been away so long."

"Are you going to stay for a while?"

"For a long while," she said. She smiled at him, then took a sip of the beer. "You know, I don't think I've had an American beer in a couple of years."

"We had some in New York."

"Oh yeah, that's right."

They sat in silence for a moment. Josh felt the awkwardness growing, but wasn't sure what to do about it. Finally, he got up.

"Want to go for a walk? I'll show you those woods. And that mushroom in the e-mail."

"You sent me a mushroom?"

"A picture."

"I didn't get a picture."

"I must have screwed something up when I did the attachment. Come on."

Peering through the tree branches, Jing Yo saw the door to the back of the house open. Instantly, his breathing changed, becoming more controlled. He relaxed his muscles. He remembered the advice of his mentors: ease into the weapon, absorb it, make it an extension of yourself.

The scientist was walking toward him. He was with a woman.

The CIA officer?

Jing Yo couldn't be sure. It would make sense, however.

So he would kill her, too. He wouldn't feel bad about that.

They came across the field, striding onto a path that led into the woods. They would come practically beneath him.

Jing Yo watched through the scope. Perhaps ten feet from the trees, they took each other's hand, then twined them, stopped, and kissed.

There was such tenderness in that moment, such understated emotion.

His ribs ached. He thought of Hyuen Bo.

They kissed for a long time. Jing Yo stared at them, thinking not of them, but of himself, of the love that he had lost.

A precept he had been taught sprang to his mind:

Nothing is completely lost. No energy is destroyed. It remains within the universe where it was given birth.

They began walking again, now hand in hand, arms swinging. In love.

He was seeing himself, just before Hyuen Bo was killed. It was the happiest moment of his life.

Jing Yo stared, watching as they walked into the woods, watching as they fussed over the trees, as they laughed. There was nothing special in the way they treated each other, and yet everything was special. You could see the bond growing between them.

Jing Yo stared, and continued to stare as they passed through and out the woods.

Jing Yo stared, and continued to stare, well after they were gone.

At night, when it was dark, he left the gun in its

strap and climbed down from the tree. He walked across the back field and found his car.

There was no need to go back to the hotel. He still had plenty of cash. He would find a new identity, and he would establish himself somewhere.

Where exactly, he didn't know. America was a big place, full of possibilities.

78

South China Sea

The ship's company stood at attention as the pipe sounded its plaintive cry. The sun was just setting, the ocean calm. There could not have been a more perfect evening.

Lt. Commander Li struggled to hold back the tears as the litter lifted and the sack holding Commander Silas's body slipped into the sea.

A freak accident, the ship's chief medical officer called it. A combination of the blow and an undetected aneurysm. Officially, death by traumatic injury to the head, with natural complications.

But Lt. Commander Li thought it must be something else, some deeper bargain that Silas had struck: my life for my people, me for my ship.

It was a romantic notion, impossible. And yet so full of truth that she was certain of it.

She stared at the waves for several minutes, tears streaming down her face. Had she looked at any of the ship's crew, she knew their faces would mirror hers. Silas had been the perfect commander, a strict but caring father who knew them better than they knew themselves. A difficult man to get close to, yet full of warmth and insight once you did.

A ship's captain, in the finest sense. A throwback. A leader.

"All right," she said finally, turning to the crew. "Let's get to work. We're going home."

79

Hanoi

The man at the end of the bar was wearing a sweatshirt with the hood pulled up over his head as he hunched over his drink. He looked like a monk contemplating the afternoon benediction.

"Hey," said Zeus, pulling the stool out. "How you doing, Roth?"

"Same," said Setco.

"Always Mr. Sunshine."

"I smiled when I landed the plane, right?"

Zeus laughed. Setco had not only smiled, he had roared with laughter. He confessed that he had been exaggerating about his flying abilities, and had only landed twice before, both times with a flight instructor next to him.

Cringing the entire time, he claimed.

"Ready to go?" Setco asked.

"I'll have a drink first."

The bartender came over, refilled Setco's glass, then got a beer for Zeus. They drank in silence.

"You hear from Kerfer?" asked Setco.

"Ric? Nah. We're not exactly close."

"No?"

"There's nobody close to me, Murph."

Funny, thought Zeus. "Murph" didn't bother him anymore. Something about the way he said it had changed.

"I kinda thought *we* were friends," Zeus told him.

Setco smirked at him, then extended his hand. They shook.

"I'm ready to go," said Zeus.

Setco led him outside to the car he'd secured. The agency had assigned him to stay in the capital for a few days to "tie up loose ends." What those loose ends were, Zeus could only imagine.

The city was relatively quiet, perhaps still not believing the war was truly over. Traffic moved slowly on the battered streets.

The closer they came to the embassy, the more nervous Zeus became. It had taken him the better part of two days to get in contact with Major Chaū. Anna was safe, the major assured him, and free. They had arranged to meet at the embassy this afternoon.

It had only been a few days since he saw her, but so much had happened—it was enough danger for several lifetimes. And now suddenly he couldn't remember her face. He couldn't remember anything about her, the way she looked or walked, her voice, her perfume.

What if she wasn't as beautiful as he remembered? What if her touch didn't heal?

The more he thought about it, the more overwhelmed he became—the more he didn't want to face anything, or anyone, let alone her.

He folded his arms and lowered his head, exhausted, wanting to fall into a cocoon.

Setco stopped at the gate. Zeus's heart jumped. The guards checked the IDs quickly and they were waved past.

Zeus lowered his head again. He couldn't face her. He couldn't. It was just too much.

They stopped. "I'll see you around, Zeus," Setco told him. "I gotta go use the phone."

"Thanks for the ride," said Zeus.

He slipped out of the car.

She was there when he turned around.

"Zeus?"

She was every bit as beautiful as he remembered, every bit as inviting. And when their lips met, it was as blissful and energizing beyond anything he could have hoped.

And though there were no equations that took war and death and love, and put them into balance, and though there was no way to justify any number of chances he'd taken or things he'd done, and though there was no romance in risking your life for love, any more than there really was in war, her kiss reached deep into him, and for that moment, he felt peace.

It would be a moment that guided him for the rest of his life.

Authors' Note

What's in a name?

Some sharp-eyed readers have pointed out that the name of the destroyer in the South China Sea off Vietnam inexplicably changed from book two of the series to (some editions of) book three. They've wondered if it was indeed a different ship, some sort of action to confuse the Chinese, or a deliberate ploy to see how many readers are paying attention.

None of the above—it was a mistake on our part.

We'd started with one name and then, very late in the process, decided to change to another name for reasons that are now obscure. And for reasons that are even more obscure—no heavy drinking was involved, we promise—the original name apparently remained in book two. We should have checked when it was published and made everything conform, but alas . . .

We apologize for the confusion, but thank all the readers who have pointed it out (including those who have had a bit of fun at our expense). We've returned in this edition to the original name, hoping that it will create less overall confusion. We appreciate your help and support.